DEDICATION

Sincere thanks:

To Gloria Clover, Ellen List, Sherry Walters, Carol Hamilton, Linda Turner, Audrey Stallsmith, Laura Hervey, and Barbara Sutryn, the great writers and wonderful friends who cheered me on and helped me revise and edit along the way;

And to Earl McDaniel, mentor and long-time friend, who was one of the first to encourage me in the direction of writing and who also helped to revise and edit this project;

And to Rachelle Emmett and the rest of the Emmett Orchard family for their tour and the ideas that sprang from it. You were an inspiration;

And to Dorie at Sunny G. Acres for her invaluable insight about miniature donkeys. I enjoyed writing about them;

And to the two talented artists who created the visual expressions for the outside covers of the Pennsylvania Series and helped to reveal the stories within:

Andy Heckathorne of Andy Heckathorne Illustration + Design for *Lion's Awakening* and Adam Suscheck of Solo Bird Design for *Perfect Timing*;

And to my dear husband Mark, who joined me in my leap of faith from full-time teacher to full-time writer and marketer of writing. You are the best.

TABLE OF CONTENTS

Perfect Timing

Pennsylvania Series

by

Cindy Bingham

First Edition

Debbie
May the Lord
bless you,
Cindy Bingham

INTRODUCTION

Welcome to the Pennsylvania Series by Cindy Bingham.

Lion's Awakening
Perfect Timing
The third, to complete the series, will be published in 2015.

Each is available in both print form and as an e-book (in both Kindle and EPub formats). Look for them at www.cindybinghamwrites.com or through amazon.com or other book sellers.

CHAPTER 1

Pepper Staley clutched the envelope, shouldered the post office door, and flung herself outside. The brisk April air squeezed her tension-filled chest. She gasped but raced ahead into the darkening evening.

Halfway down the block, she halted under a street lamp. Flipping the envelope, she dashed her finger under the flap and slid her gaze past the preliminaries.

"Dear Ms. Staley:
We regret to inform you . . ."

Hot tears and hotter blood rushed to her face. "No! Not again." Heedless of anything or anyone around her, she stomped into the night. "Stupid football program. Selfish, moronic ego maniacs." Expletives she seldom uttered flew from her in frustrated spurts. "Worried only about themselves. Taking everyone else down with them." Her long-handled purse slipped from her shoulder. Jerking to a stop, she plopped onto a nearby bench and dug into the bag's recesses, retrieving five other rumpled envelopes.

Six letters from medical schools. Six rejections.

Four years of pre-med classes, countless hours of study, more than a year of the application process, a GPA of 3.81, and now her dream of being accepted to a prestigious medical school was disintegrating in the blaze of campus scandal.

One degenerate coach, dozens of innocent victims, years of cover-up, and Penn State was blacklisted. Sanctioned by the NCAA. Put on five years' probation. Hit with significant scholarship cuts. Threatened by the accreditation board.

How could medical schools punish her?

She couldn't prove they were, but she'd heard rumors. Rumors of more than one qualified PSU grad being snubbed. Rumors of graduate school openings being given to others with lower GPAs and fewer qualifications. Rumors weren't always true, but she'd bet on these. Her grades were more than adequate, and she'd done summer internships at

Geisinger Medical Center in Danville and received glowing recommendations. Her MCAT score spoke well of her preparation.

Pepper slammed her fist into the wooden bench. "This is so not fair." Tears still threatened, but she squelched them and jumped up.

Her phone rang. She ignored the first strain of the familiar ring tone. On the second, she grasped the phone before letting it fall away.

Dad would ask. She couldn't answer.

* * *

Late Saturday morning Pepper slogged from her bed, questioning which part of her felt the worst. Her brain had developed its own heartbeat, pounding against her skull in perfect but excruciating rhythm. Her stomach roiled, intermittently coinciding with the pulse in her head. The rest of her simply yearned for bed and solitude.

Why had she drowned her sorrows in alcohol?

She could count on the fingers of one hand the times she'd gotten drunk. Inebriation was a quick fix with a slow recovery—and it never changed anything. Pepper knew from her own experience and from that of others.

But last night she'd succumbed. And today she'd pay.

At least Sophie wasn't here to make fun of her hangover. Sophie hadn't been at PSU since Christmas. Not long after the November scandal hit the news, Pepper had returned from a late afternoon class to find her roommate's luggage covering both of their beds.

Pepper had blurted, "Where you going with all this stuff?"

Sophie had barely looked up. "Home."

"For how long?" Even a fashionista like Sophie could survive a few days without taking everything.

"Until September." She'd unceremoniously dumped an armful of expensive lingerie into one suitcase. "I've already been accepted at Michigan. Daddy pulled some strings. I'll take the fall semester there, add a class or two, if necessary, in the spring term, and graduate the following May."

"From Michigan? The following May? Have you lost your mind?" Pepper had slammed her books onto the nearest desk. "Michigan!" Only a few other universities rivaled Penn State like Michigan did. "You're trading a Lion for a Wolverine?"

Sophie had ignored Pepper's sarcasm—but only until Pepper had marched over and ensconced herself directly in front of her tall, blonde roommate. "You'll be wasting a whole year."

7

Finally, Sophie had leveled an intense gaze on Pepper. "No, I'll be saving three."

"What are you talking about?"

"Don't you get it? This football thing's huge."

"Yeah, it is. To the players, the recruiters, the entire football program."

"To all programs." Sophie dropped the sweater she'd been folding. "It's got more arms than I have credit cards."

No chance of that.

Months later Pepper knew better. Her friend's last words on the subject still rang in Pepper's ears.

"My education may be largely a product of Penn State, but my diploma's going to be from Michigan."

Over the past two weeks, with rejection after rejection, Pepper had been forced to admit the cold, hard truth. Sophie's GPA might be a point lower than Pepper's, but Sophie was one smart coed.

Pepper was the box of ignorant rocks.

Her plight increased the throbbing in her head. Could she stomach a Tylenol? She grabbed her purse. Seeing her phone brought daggers of guilt. Dad's call. Had he tried later?

Pepper retrieved her cell and glanced at the display. Only one missed call but four texts. Dad wouldn't have sent a text. Who had?

Two were from Marcy, probably wanting to set up a study group time. Out of the question. She'd text Marcy later.

The second was from Ranie Phelps Staley, the run-away mother, who'd deserted her husband and her infant child. Why would this woman, whose texts were always signed in her maiden name, think that Pepper Staley wanted anything to do with her now? Why had her dad ever given Pepper's cell number to Ranie? She punched the delete button.

The last read, "How are you?" and was signed, "Zeke."

Who was Zeke? Pepper's heart raced. How did he have her number?

Despite the shifting floor and her rising nausea, Pepper grabbed the pill bottle and hurried to her mini fridge for a bottle of water. Then she lay back on the bed, trying to recall the events of the previous night.

She remembered the post office, the contents of the letter, and her trek into the darkness. Vaguely, she recalled entering one of Sophie's favorite watering holes and settling onto a bar stool. Her coherent thoughts ended with her saying "I'll have a whiskey sour."

A whiskey sour? Where had that come from? On the rare occasions that she imbibed, beer was her drink of choice. Sophie was the whiskey sour girl. How much had Pepper consumed? Since she rarely drank more than one, alcohol hit her hard and fast. She racked her brain for faces—especially unfamiliar ones that might belong to the name "Zeke." Nothing materialized.

Bolting upright, Pepper groaned loudly, her head doing imaginary pirouettes as she tried to steady herself. She stumbled to the trail of discarded clothing, stifling a gag when her nose encountered the reek of alcohol vomit. Her clothes divulged the answer of how much she'd drunk—far more than she could handle.

What else could they tell her? Pepper lifted each piece. Her Penn State hoodie had taken the brunt of the onslaught. It was crusty and noisome, but not torn or bloody. Her T-shirt and jeans also bore liquor and vomit but nothing worse. She still wore the same underclothes. Nothing indicated a struggle. Was that a good sign?

Drawing on her training as an Emergency Medical Technician, she examined her face, arms, and legs for bruises or any other evidence of her being coerced. She didn't see any. It appeared that whoever Zeke was, he hadn't harmed her.

Had anything consensual occurred? Had the alcohol compromised her?

As soon as the question entered her mind, Pepper felt heat creep up her face. She prided herself on keeping her love life on hold. She rarely dated and never allowed herself to be set up by a friend. Becoming a doctor was her goal. Medical school was the next step. How stupid of her to let down her guard, for even one night. One night was sometimes all it took to ruin a lifetime of dreams.

If only she could remember.

What should she do now? Pillowing her head between her palms, she eased herself back onto her bed and pondered.

Could she retrace her steps from last night and somehow reconstruct the evening? Would her cell phone company tell her Zeke's full name? Could she recall any friends who might have seen her with a guy? Each question increased the thundering drumbeats in Pepper's head until, exhausted and miserable, she succumbed to sleep.

When Pepper resurfaced, the room was growing dark, but her head felt lighter, and the tomtoms in her brain had ceased. Once she had rinsed the ghastly taste from her mouth, she might feel almost human.

On her way to the bathroom for a drink and some mouthwash, she noticed her phone and headed toward it. "Don't!" Forcing herself back to her original plan, she brushed her teeth, guzzled water from the tap, gargled, and headed back to the bedroom.

The phone waited. This time Pepper couldn't resist.

Three texts. Marcy, again. Ranie, again. And Zeke.

Pepper paced. To Marcy's question about biochemistry study group, she texted back, "Can't tonight." To Ranie's request that Pepper meet her for Sunday lunch, she stuck out her tongue before sending the message, "Not interested."

Her heart thudded as she opened the third text. "Are you OK?"

"No, I'm not OK!" she bellowed.

Her thumbs flew across the keypad. "Who R U?"

* * *

Backing toward the next fence post, Zeke Davies unrolled the fencing wire as he went, erecting a barrier to protect the newest addition to his family's apple orchard. This two-acre plot had recently become the home of nearly two hundred dwarf apple trees. It would be the feeding ground of every white-tailed deer in the county if he didn't finish the barricade.

Normally, fencing was one of his favorite tasks around the orchard. But today hadn't been easy. He'd encountered a section of wire that, although brand new, was damaged. He could have returned the bundle and gotten another, but the trip to town and back would've been more trouble than the repair. So he'd fixed the fencing, only to discover two other breaks later on.

The splitting maul he'd used for years to pound the fence posts had suddenly decided to separate itself from its handle and fly off the post—crashing into the John Deere Gator and adding another dent to the numerous ones in the utility vehicle. Thankfully, the head had missed Lady, the family's border collie. A cut hand and two trips back to the shed for supplies had put him so far behind that he'd missed supper.

His stomach growled at the thought of Mom's lasagna. Hopefully she'd saved him some. If she hadn't, he couldn't expect his brothers to leave any. Zeke had his own home but almost always ate his evening meal with his family. The refrigerator at his place didn't have much to offer if the lasagna fell through.

Ten minutes later, he loaded the Gator, whistled to Lady, and headed for food. He was walking up the path from the shed to the house when he thought to check his phone for messages. Ike, one of Zeke's younger brothers, was a texting junkie. He usually sent Zeke three or four messages a day. Zeke flipped the cover.

"Who R U?"

Another of Ike's ideas of a joke. Zeke grinned. Typing as quickly as he could while he walked, he quipped "As if you don't know."

The next half hour ticked by. Physically, Pepper was better. Mentally she resembled confetti, her thoughts tossed in the air and scattered. She couldn't study. She couldn't eat. She really couldn't call her dad, even though she knew she should. Her text message jingle sent her scurrying for her phone. The one right beside her.

"As if you don't know."

"I don't know. You moron," Pepper yelled into the screen. Her heart racing and her blood boiling, she zipped off, "I'm serious. WHO ARE YOU?"

"Did you save me anything?" Zeke crossed to the kitchen table.

"Would I forget my firstborn?" Mom handed him a plate with a tossed salad and a roll.

"Start on those while I heat the lasagna."

He grinned. "You're the best mom ever."

"Remember that the next time I volunteer you to escort someone to the Apple Harvest Gala." She set a glass of iced water in front of him and smiled back.

Zeke would have demurred, but his mouth was full. Then he heard the text tone. He gulped before saying, "Ike is sending crazy texts again."

"I don't think so."

"Mom, you know he does."

She held up a cell phone. Bold yellow letters declared it to be Ike's. "He does, but he isn't."

"Then who is?" Zeke snagged the cell phone. "It's her. She finally answered." Why hadn't he looked at the sender's number earlier? He set down the roll he'd been buttering.

"It's who?" Mom retrieved the steaming lasagna from the microwave, placing the hot plate in front of him.

"The girl Anna and I helped last night," Zeke replied without looking up. The faster he tried to type, the larger and slower his thumbs became. Finally he accomplished, "Sorry. Thought you were my brother. I'm Zeke Davies."

"He thought I was his brother?" Pepper couldn't believe her own voice. "He's Zeke Davies. Who in the world is that?"

Quickly she typed, "How did you get this number?"

* * *

"You gave it to me. Last night."

After he and Anna had left Pepper, Zeke wondered whether she would remember them. Apparently she hadn't. Not their names or the fact that she'd divulged hers. She also seemed not to recall that she'd told them where she lived and had given them her cell phone number. She'd been plastered. The kind of girl that made a perfect victim. Cute. Alone. Drunk. Zeke could recall horror stories. Thankfully, Anna had noticed Pepper before anyone else.

Texting this account would take all night. "Could I call?" he added to the message before sending it.

* * *

Staring at the screen, Pepper gulped. She'd tortured herself for hours with scenes of what might have happened last night. She had to find out, if she could. Zeke was her best chance. She pushed the keypads four times before hitting "send."

* * *

"Call."

Zeke stood. He lifted the still-warm plate from the table. "I'd better call her. Thanks for supper, Mom. See you tomorrow." He bolted from the kitchen before his mom, who gaped at him, had time to probe.

Reaching his house, he switched on a light and set his food on the coffee table. He punched in the numbers and waited.

* * *

"Hi, it's Pepper. Is this Zeke?"

"Yeah, it's me."

"How'd you get my number." *No sense wasting words.*

"We found you—on the grass—outside a bar."

He wasn't laughing. He seemed—sympathetic. "We?"

"My sister Anna and I. She lives in South Halls. We were coming from there."

He has a sister he hangs out with. Maybe, just maybe, things weren't as bad as Pepper had thought. "Was I sleeping on the grass?" Pepper solemnly vowed never again to put herself in that type of situation.

Seconds passed.

"You were being sick."

He was being kind. "You mean puking?"

"Yeah. A lot. Anna rescued your purse."

She had nearly vomited into her purse. How disgusting. "Is that how you found my phone and my number?"

"No."

Pepper heard the bristles in his voice.

"Anna asked where you lived." His words were calm but frank. "You told her."

That still didn't explain the phone number. She nearly asked again.

"By the time we'd reached your dorm, you were telling Anna all sorts of things."

"And you were writing them down?"

"No!"

She'd offended him. Again. Why was she being so rude? "I'm sorry, really. It's just that I don't know—"

"You don't remember any of this, do you?"

He was perceptive. "No, none of it."

"So when you saw a strange guy's name on a text—"

"I wondered—what—how— Well, I wondered."

The pause dragged on.

"Nothing happened after we found you. Really."

She knew what he was saying. And somehow, she believed him. Tears stung her eyes. "Thank you."

"I was stupid. I should have had Anna check on you."

That would have been better, but she didn't say so. "I shouldn't have gotten drunk."

After a long pause, he asked, "Are you okay?"

With her future in limbo, Pepper knew that "okay" was a stretch. "I'm not drunk," she replied. "And I'm not going to be again."

"Good." His sigh was audible and long.

"Someone was looking out for me."

"Yes, He was."

"Maybe a guardian angel."

"Maybe."

13

This pause was shorter but still pronounced.

"Maybe God who sends the angels," he said.

"I doubt that. God and I aren't on speaking terms."

* * *

Zeke gasped. Pepper was blunt to a fault. And bordering on irreverent. Did she realize Who God was? "Mind telling me why?"

"You going to tell me I'm wrong about God?"

He would have wanted to. "Not tonight."

She hesitated. "I'm qualified for med school, but I've been turned down by six of the best schools. The last rejection letter came yesterday."

The reason for her drinking. Things were beginning to make a little sense.

"If God had held off that Grand Jury ruling for six months, I would have graduated and been safely at Harvard, Duke, Stanford or any of the others. Now, because of the scandal, PSU grads are marked."

"How do you know?" Zeke had graduated with a degree in agricultural science five years earlier. With no desire for a Master's Degree and having a ready-made job at the orchard, he'd left Penn State without any regrets, except for a hefty school loan. Was Pepper right in what she believed about the cause of her rejection letters?

"I know it. I can't prove it."

He heard a deep sigh.

"Sometimes life stinks."

Her words were serious, but Zeke smiled. Pepper's "tell-it-like-it-is" philosophy stood out in a world of "tell them what they want to hear." Still, she needed to know that God wasn't her problem. But she'd already stated her resistance to hearing more. Maybe Anna could check up on Pepper early next week.

* * *

Shortly after breakfast Monday morning, Zeke headed for his mom and dad's. Anna would return to campus today, and he needed to talk to her before Mom drove her back.

"I can't meet her today, Zeke. I'll call and talk to her, but today is out."

Pepper's defiance toward God replayed in Zeke's mind. "I'm not asking you to spend an hour in a heart-to-heart, just a few minutes to get acquainted."

14

Across the breakfast table, Anna stared at her brother. "Not today."

Zeke opened his mouth to argue. Then he caught the hard stare from his mom who sat next to Anna. He grabbed his coffee cup, mindlessly slurping the scalding liquid. The result was a burned mouth and a coffee-splattered shirt.

Sometimes life did stink.

CHAPTER 2

Pepper plopped her backpack onto the library table with a thud. Miffed looks met her noisy interruption. Ignoring them, she sank onto a chair and tried to focus on the notes she'd taken in her last class. Fifteen minutes later, not recalling anything she'd read, she glanced again at the wall clock across the room. Five minutes until the rendezvous. She still had time to make a run for it. If she left now, she'd avoid both Anna and the guilty thoughts of last Friday. She clicked the cap of her retractable pen in rapid succession while staring at the sweep of the ticking seconds.

Flee.

Coward. What's gotten into you?

Pepper couldn't answer. She could make a dash for it. She jammed the pen closed and unceremoniously shoved books and notes into her pack. Sizing up her escape route, she slipped from her chair, hefting the heavy mass behind her.

Bad idea.

Instead of settling on her shoulder, the flying bag clipped the high back of the chair, toppling it with a crash. When Pepper bent to right the chair, the contents of her pack spewed forth. With a huff, she flung the backpack to the floor, scrabbling for the errant books and papers. Groans and snickers erupted around her. Then Pepper noticed a pair of light blue Nikes next to her bag. Glancing up, she saw a pair of blue-jeaned knees and a printed T-shirt. Shortly, two brown eyes stared into Pepper's green ones.

The girl in front of her said, "Hi, Pepper. I'm Anna."

Pepper blinked. "Hi—hi, Anna—I—I'm." With the bag's contents restored, Pepper stopped stammering and stood up. When they were both on their feet, she managed a coherent, "Thanks."

"Glad to help."

Sincerity tinged Anna's words. Lingering stares and giggles caught Pepper's attention. "Meeting at the library wasn't such a good idea. Let's get out of here." She resumed her previous plan and bolted toward the exit, half hoping to lose Anna in the maze of people and furniture.

In turbo speed, she scurried out the door and down the sidewalk. A hand on her shoulder eventually halted her.

"Something wrong?"

Pepper exhaled before turning. "Yes—no—I don't know."

Strands of Anna's shoulder-length auburn hair whipped across her face in the cold April breeze. Pepper wasn't sure why she'd expected her rescuer to be a petite blonde, but somehow, that mental picture had formulated. The girl in front of her had to be at least 5 feet, 8 inches tall, with long arms and longer legs. Her pale skin was tinged pink at the cheeks. She personified the phrase "natural and healthy." Pepper craned her neck toward Anna. "You're taller than I imagined."

Anna grinned slightly. "You're standing taller than you were last Friday."

Pepper coughed away her embarrassment. "Worst night of my life."

"You remember it?"

An uncharacteristic flush lit Pepper's face. She started down the sidewalk. "No, but I remember the morning after. I'm assuming the rest."

"I'm glad we found you."

The seriousness of the girl's words, coupled with the gravity of her gaze, halted any of Pepper's usual flippant replies.

Anna kept pace with Pepper. "I've never seen Zeke so white. I thought it was because you were being sick."

Pepper remembered Zeke's use of that same phrase. "He can't handle someone barfing?"

Once again Anna's demure smile appeared. "Never has been able to. Mom steers him outside if anyone's about to throw up."

Pepper halted. "No way! What is he? Some kind of . . ." She glanced up at Anna just in time to choke back the word *wimp*. And to see that Anna had read her thoughts.

"I've seen Zeke hoist one-hundred-pound bags of fertilizer and cart them wherever he wants them. And in arm-wrestling matches with my brothers, he always wins."

Daggers of guilt stabbed Pepper. "Sorry. I should shut my big mouth. You and Zeke—"

"He wasn't pale because of vomit," Anna interrupted. "He was scared. For you."

Pepper shivered at the thought of what could have happened that night. She hated to admit it, but fear stalked her dreams. "I was stupid." Anna's lips never moved, but Pepper knew she concurred. "I told your brother I won't do it again."

17

"He was relieved." Anna's eyes misted slightly. "Zeke's a protector. It's another of his 'always been that way' characteristics. He's the oldest of five children."

"Five kids in your family?"

"Yep. All boys except me."

Pepper's jaw dropped. "I've always wanted a brother." It was true.

"I'd loan you any of mine." Anna's eyes lit mischievously. "Some days I'd give them away."

Pepper laughed. She kept laughing. She couldn't have said what spawned her giggles. Maybe the thought of Anna handing over brothers to whoever would take them. Maybe relief over last Friday's rescue. Maybe the knowledge that she hadn't needed to dread this meeting. Whatever the cause, she continued to laugh. Anna joined her. There the two stood, people passing on both sides, shaking their heads as they went.

Finally Anna said, "My next class isn't until after lunch. Want to get something to eat?"

Pepper squelched her erratic laugher. "Do you like Girl Scout cookies?"

"Thin Mints?"

"Is there any other kind? I have a stash in my mini freezer." Pepper darted off toward her dorm. "I've been saving them for a 'Med School Acceptance' party," she said when Anna had caught up, "but let's celebrate my safety."

The soft, thoughtful look returned to Anna's eyes. "Great idea."

Pepper hooked her arm through the taller girl's, compelling both of them in the direction of chocolate and peppermint.

* * *

Even before they'd finished the sleeve of Thin Mints, Pepper liked Anna Davies. Underneath Anna's quiet, serious shell lurked a kind heart and a ready smile. Pepper quickly discovered that, contrary to her earlier offer to loan out her brothers, Anna was close to all of them.

Twenty minutes after they'd reached Pepper's room, Anna's text jingle sounded. She snatched the phone, read the message, and said, "It's Ike, brother number three."

In response to Ike's message, Anna giggled and zipped a speedy reply. Mere seconds passed before the sound returned.

"Ike's a texting maniac." Anna sighed, reaching for the phone. She glanced at the screen. "It's Joe." Her eyes registered surprise. "He hardly ever texts." Her fingers scrambled over the keypad, and seconds later, she sent the message into cyberspace. Looking up then, she added, "Joe is number two. Reserved and sober-minded—with a serious crush on a girl from our church."

"And he's asking your advice?"

"I'm his only sister."

"I'm so jealous. No one ever asks my opinion." At Anna's slightly raised eyebrows, she remonstrated, "Last Friday night was not indicative of my level of insight." Pepper rolled her eyes.

Anna grinned and reached for another cookie.

* * *

"How'd it go today?" Zeke had meant to call his sister earlier, but the orchard kept him busy all day.

"With Pepper?"

"Yeah."

"A few rough spots, at first. But after half a box of Thin Mints, everything was fine—until we calculated the calories. We met at the gym this evening to run laps. Just got back. That girl can move."

Anna was no slowpoke. If she called someone else fast, Zeke believed her. "Did she beat you?"

She giggled. "Not these long legs."

"Good job." Zeke laughed with her. "Did you find out why she's mad at God?"

"No, I didn't ask."

"But I—"

"I realize that's my mission, Zeke, but I need to get to know her first. I don't want to offend her." The airwaves quieted. "I prayed for guidance. I never felt comfortable asking her." Without warning, Anna switched her attack. "Why haven't you asked?"

"She doesn't know me."

"She didn't remember knowing me either."

"I'm a guy. I thought it would be easier—"

"Easier for whom?"

Zeke flinched at his sister's stark analysis. He was still formulating his answer when she said, "She mentioned it to you."

"But she told me not to talk to her about God."

"Forever?"

"No, but—"

"Pray about this, Zeke."

19

One of Anna's most convicting traits. She prayed, often and earnestly, and expected others to do the same.

His sister continued her analysis. "Pepper has walls. I have to find a crack in one of them before I talk to her about God."

Zeke didn't reply. Anna read people well, usually better than he did.

"Either give me time to build this friendship or ask her yourself."

"I'm not on campus. I don't see her."

"But you're in luck. Pepper's coming home with me next weekend—my last visit before the term ends. I just got off the phone with her. I cleared it with Mom first."

Zeke clutched his cell phone. This wasn't what he'd planned. Things would have been so much easier if Anna had done as he asked.

Easier for whom? Her words echoed in his brain.

* * *

Pepper entered the room and slipped off her shoes. Dad's ringtone chirped. She plopped her backpack onto the floor and snatched the phone. He usually called after her last class on Friday. He was later than normal.

"Hey, Pops." For about a year she'd been searching for a special name to call her dad. Recently, she'd tried this moniker, and she liked it. Every time she used it, he chuckled. "How was your week?"

He obliged her with a quick laugh. "I talked to you on Tuesday, remember? The rest of my week's gone fine. How about yours? Thought any more about accepting Pitt? Better hurry or you'll miss the deadline."

"My heart's not in it."

"Is your heart still set on being a doctor?"

"Since I was eight."

"Then the next thing is med school."

He was right.

"Go to Pittsburgh. It's a fine program. It might not have the prestige of the University of Pennsylvania, but it's one of the best in this state."

From the beginning, Dad had prompted her to consider a school within the Keystone State. The University of Pennsylvania, in Philadelphia, was one of the highest ranked in the country. Pepper had demanded quality but had stubbornly resisted applying to anything in her home state. "I want to broaden my horizons."

Only at the last minute had she included both the University of Pennsylvania and the University of Pittsburgh in her considerations. Last Friday night's debacle had been set off by the rejection from the University of Pennsylvania. Pitt's acceptance was her only positive response. It had arrived earlier in the week.

"I wrote my acceptance last night." She couldn't keep the hollowness out of the words. Dad must not have noticed.

"That's my girl. How much is the first semester deposit?"

"I'll take care of it."

"How?"

"My plans for robbing First National of State College are right here next to my blueprints of the vault."

"That's not funny."

"Not even a little bit?" Pepper suppressed a snicker.

"I want to visit you at a hospital, not in a penitentiary." He paused briefly. "Let me send you the money. I'll deposit it into your account. You write a check and get that acceptance in the mail tomorrow. You need to be in med school."

"Okay, Poppy." She giggled. "How's that one strike you?"

He cleared his throat. "I'll have to think about it."

"Too bad. It might be my latest number one."

"As long as I'm still your number one, any name will do."

"No one else but you, Pops." She could almost hear him smile.

Empty space filled the seconds before he continued. "Have you answered any of your mom's messages?" His tone had sobered.

Why did he have to bring her into this? "We're not on speaking terms."

"So you've said." He didn't mask his disapproval of her sarcasm.

"Ranie left us, remember?"

Dad's loud gulp crossed the air waves. "Only too well."

Pepper clunked herself in the head with her hand. What an idiot she was. "Sorry."

"You have most of your life to live. That's a long time to be bitter."

"How can I not be?" Pepper flopped onto her bed. "She abandoned me. Left me all al—"

Pepper gasped and plunged her face into the comforter. Dad's silence screamed at her. She cleared her throat. "I'm sorry, Pops. I wasn't alone. I always had you."

"But I couldn't make her stay. And she—"

"She must have hated me even while she carried me."

Her mother's abandoning her while she was still an infant troubled Pepper more than anything else. What could a newborn have done to make her mother leave?

"She didn't hate you. She had—"

"But she didn't love me."

"She was young and scared. And she—"

"Neither of which was my fault. She's the one who got pregnant at seventeen."

"That wasn't all her fault either."

Through the years, during all the conversations about her mom, Pepper had never understood why her dad defended the woman who had left him. He should be bitter, too. Only eighteen himself and in college a few hours away from his own family, he'd had to trade university classes for night school, delay his dream of starting a business, and provide for an infant daughter. He deserved to blame Ranie. Although he never completely acquitted her, he always accused himself as well.

Pepper loved her dad. She felt no warmth for her mother.

"You know only my side. Maybe it's time you heard hers. From her."

"Not interested, Pop."

Dad sighed and waited. "You've always been stubborn, even when I tried to explain—"

Pepper didn't even blink. "Whose side are you on?"

"Didn't know I had to choose one."

Pepper punched the pillow next to her.

"She hurt you. She knows that. She wants your forgiveness," he said.

"She doesn't deserve it."

Pepper missed the alarm bells she'd just set off.

"Did you deserve forgiveness when you took my car without asking, drove too fast, and crashed it into a tree?" He took a deep breath. "Or when you told me that you and your friends were going to the movies and you left the state on an excursion that could have landed the four of you in jail or worse. All bad choices that you made deliberately when you were seventeen."

"Okay. I get it." Pepper knew his list could go on. And he wasn't even aware of last Friday night, or a few other things. "I didn't deserve your forgiveness."

"But I forgave you because I love you and—"

"I don't love her."

"*And* because you're human, and humans make bad decisions. Sometimes for no good reason." He stopped talking.

"Pops, you still there?"

"I'm here." The silence returned. Finally he said, "Sometimes because we don't know what else to do. We need to be forgiven." Another paternal sigh reached Pepper's ears. "You've forgiven me."

A memory bombarded Pepper. She cringed. She could hear herself as a teenager, whining to her dad, pitying herself about some injustice in her life, and vilifying her mother as the cause. Dad had explained how he'd pushed his girlfriend, a high school senior, into intimacy. When Ranie got pregnant and had wanted to abort their child, he'd been adamant about her not doing so, but had also been blind to her fears and had minimized her feelings of being trapped. After their hurried marriage, he'd assumed that everything would be fine, that his love for her—he really had loved her—and the love of their child would hold their tattered lives together. His dreams hadn't transpired, and he'd had to admit his own part in vaporizing them.

"I didn't deserve forgiveness, but you forgave me. Maybe you shouldn't ha—"

"Of course I should have." How could he think that? "Don't say that, Pops."

"You do know that I've loved you from the moment your mom told me she was pregnant?"

Dad's emotion-choked voice halted Pepper's search for the perfect comeback. Around the warm lump clogging her throat, she finally gulped, "I know."

"My love for you helped to keep me from hating her."

Pepper searched for a sarcastic retort, a verbal barb, a witty remark targeted at her mom. Nothing materialized.

"Don't make her wait any longer to see why I love you so much."

CHAPTER 3

"You have a Mustang."

Anna hadn't wasted any time in commenting on Pepper's car. "I do." Pepper giggled and then unlocked the driver-side door. "Dad picked it out. This 1975 model was his dream car." She unlocked her door and leaned inside to unlock Anna's. She stood, looking across the roof at her friend. "But I'm seriously smitten now." She pushed the back of the seat forward and tossed her bag inside. Anna did the same.

"Spoiler alert. My brothers will drool over this baby."

Pepper laughed. "As long as they wipe up the mess and don't get any other ideas about my ride."

"How about test drives? Toby will flip when he sees it."

"Toby's your youngest brother, right?"

"Yep, the baby. A typical last child: life of the family party, always ready for an audience. And from the womb, a lover of cars."

Pepper laughed before pressing on. "And he's the only one younger than you."

"Right."

"Give me their names, in order, one more time."

Anna turned toward Pepper, who had entered the traffic on Beaver Avenue. "There won't be a quiz."

"Good thing." Pepper's gaze never left the road. "But I want to be able to match a name with a face."

"You're controlling."

Anna had quickly recognized Pepper's need to know everything, about everyone, all the time. "Humor me."

"Toby's the youngest. He's eighteen and a senior in high school. I'm twenty. Ike, the compulsive texter, is twenty-three. Joe—"

"The one with the serious crush." Pepper remembered Anna's description from the first day they talked.

"That's the one. Also the best looking, according to most girls I know."

"They chase him?"

"Always have."

Anna's muted chuckle temporarily pulled Pepper's attention from the road.

"He's gotten so good at warding off advances, that when Bethany came along—her family moved here from Virginia last November—she took him by surprise."

"She's not interested?"

"She is, but she's shy. Even quieter than Joe. He's had to work hard to gain her attention."

"Think he'll win her over?"

"I hope so. If she's the one God has for him."

Anna often said things like that, things that reminded Pepper of how important God was to Anna and her family. Every comment sent a prickle down Pepper's spine. God rarely entered any equation in her life. What was she getting herself into by agreeing to spend an entire weekend with the Davies family? Would these two days bring the end of a new friendship?

Anna continued with the roster of brothers. "Joe's twenty-five. And then there's Zeke. The firstborn. My father's right-hand man, and the protector of all of us younger ones. He's twenty-seven."

Pepper changed the focus slightly. "Are they tall like you? Do they have red hair?"

"Yes. No."

"Very funny."

"Yes, they're all tall. Our dad's six feet, four inches. Zeke's only six feet, two inches—the runt of the boys. They got taller as they went. Toby's a couple inches taller than Dad."

"Why can't I ever meet someone who's on the shrimpy side like me?"

"There must be advantages to being short."

It wasn't something Pepper dwelt on. She pondered briefly. "You mean like never bumping your head on door frames."

"That's it." Anna's rich laugh filled the car. "Or being able to shop in the Petites department."

"Or having things land on your head when you need something from the top shelf."

"Ouch." Anna rubbed her crown. "Maybe that's not one for the list."

"Yeah, maybe."

The friends chatted and laughed for nearly an hour and a half on their way to Lewisburg.

"We're not going all the way into town." Anna resumed her role as navigator. "Our turn is coming right up."

"We're passing a cow pasture." Pepper couldn't keep the smirk off her face. "You can't mean there's a town anywhere near here."

"Yes, Miss Philadelphia Suburb Native, that's exactly what I'm saying. Lewisburg, population 6000, which swells to almost double that during the school year because of Bucknell University, is about two miles beyond our road."

Before leaving home, Pepper had pictured Pennsylvania as Philadelphia and its many suburbs. Of course, she knew of Pittsburgh, the second largest city in the state. From geography class, she'd also learned of Erie, the city that shared a name with one of the Great Lakes. But during her nearly four years at Penn State, she'd actually experienced some of the variety of Pennsylvania. State College itself seemed plopped into the middle of nowhere. A few minutes off Atherton Street, which teemed with people and traffic, a motorist could see sheep grazing or view trees and streams, untouched by multi-level buildings and parking lots. She'd come to grips with towns appearing unexpectedly along the route. But Lewisburg in two miles? No way.

"If you weren't so jaded by the hype of the big city, you'd appreciate real living."

Pepper rolled her eyes. "Oh, sure."

"Next road to the left. The one where that tractor's pulling out."

Tractor pulling out? Pepper riveted her gaze toward where Anna pointed. Surely enough, two front tires and a green hood protruded beyond the tree-lined entrance to a small road. Pepper signaled and began to slow down.

"It's Joe."

Anna lowered the window and waved furiously, yelling her brother's name. Pepper's heartbeat quickened. Introduction number one was coming up.

Four-way caution lights began blinking from the machine a second before the driver drew his long leg over the steering wheel and jumped to the ground. Pepper negotiated the turn and stopped. Reminiscent of a Hollywood heroine greeting her returning hero, Anna flew from the car, engulfing her brother in a hug. Joe returned her squeeze and then backed away, glancing toward Pepper who was opening the driver's side door.

Anna readjusted her coat and hat, unsettled during the hug. She scurried toward the car, clutching her brother's hand and urging him forward. "Pepper, this is my brother, Joe." She grinned up at him. "Joe, this is Pepper."

The man in the brown overalls and jacket lifted his right hand and lowered his gaze to Pepper. Neither the bulky clothing nor the oddly perched knit cap could detract from Joe's lean, angular limbs and his curly auburn hair. His green eyes sparkled, and his smile, though not large, was quick and warm.

"Glad to meet you." Then he glanced beyond Pepper. "Nice wheels." Turning to Anna, he added, "Better hide the keys from Toby."

"I already warned her, about all of you."

Mentally agreeing with Anna's assessment of her brother's handsome appearance, Pepper asked. "You have a safe at your house?"

"Yes." Joe grinned. "Not much help to you, though. We all know the combination."

Backing toward the tractor, he said, "Gotta run. Dad's waiting for me. Nice to meet you, Pepper." He climbed aboard and then yelled. "Glad you're back, Sis."

"I am so jealous." Pepper clutched Anna's upper arm. "You have four brothers." Pepper didn't have even one. Life wasn't fair.

"They are great—most of the time." She glanced in the direction Joe had driven. "Don't be fooled, though. My brothers like a good joke, especially on the unsuspecting." She stared at Pepper.

"I can take care of myself."

* * *

The sign bearing the name "Davies' Orchard," with smaller letters adding "Cider Press and Gift Shop," proclaimed the entrance to Anna's home. Pepper turned in, then blinked twice at the long driveway and the buildings beyond.

"That's the house, up there. Park in the nearest spot in the gravel area."

If Anna noticed Pepper's amazement, she didn't comment. "That's your house?" Aside from historical homes in Philadelphia, this was one of the largest single-family dwellings Pepper had ever seen.

"Yeah, Dad built it himself. He and Mom wanted a large family."

Pepper flinched. Her mom hadn't wanted the one child she did have. "Your dad built this?" She couldn't keep the skepticism from her voice.

"With some help from family and a few things hired out, yes, he did."

Once again, Anna had taken Pepper's retort without the sting it carried and had simply accepted it with grace.

"Not many people do that today, I know. It was a different time. Dad was nearly thirty when he and Mom married. He'd lived with his mom and dad and had saved his money."

Couldn't just listen, could you? Always have to say whatever enters your brain. Pepper guided the Mustang into the space Anna had indicated. The two had stepped from the car and were reaching into the back for their bags when Anna shrieked and slammed her head into the roof.

"Ouch!" Whirling quickly, she cuffed the arm of the young man standing behind her. "Don't scare me like that, Ike." She rubbed her head.

"Sorry. I didn't mean . . ."

Pepper shut her door.

"Are you Pepper?" He draped an arm around his sister and ignored her attempt to introduce them. Stretching his other arm over the car, he leaned forward to shake Pepper's hand.

"Yes. And you're Ike." Extending her free hand, Pepper strained to reach his. "Brother number three."

"Only in birth order. In her heart, I'm number one." He clutched Anna to himself and grinned.

"Right now, you're not. I'll probably have a headache, and it will be your fault."

"Aaahhh. Poor baby." He donned a sad clown face and pooched out his lower lip. "You were tougher as a kid."

"I had to be to survive."

Pepper stood gaping at the exchange between the two. Ike seemed as extroverted as Joe had been reserved. Taller and thinner, with hair more red than auburn, Ike lacked the heartthrob qualities of his brother, but he probably had no trouble getting a date, especially with his apparent love of fun.

"You poor thing." The mocking tone earned him a scowl from Anna. He withdrew his arm from around her shoulders and pointed to the house. "Mom's waiting for you. She's excited to have you home." He started toward a large nearby building before calling back, "She's probably the only one." Walking backward, he winked at Pepper. "Great car. I'll take you for a spin in it later."

"*He'll* take *me* for a spin in it," Pepper said, joining Anna. "He's kidding, right?"

Hurrying toward the door, Anna laughed. Loudly. Pepper scurried along, shaking her head.

* * *

"Mom. Mom." Anna called several times while she and Pepper searched for Mrs. Davies in the lower level of the massive home. "Let's take our things upstairs and get settled. Then we'll look outside. She's here somewhere."

Pepper's chest tightened. She remembered thinking the same thoughts as a young girl. If she searched through the house each day after school, one lucky day she would find that her mother had realized her mistake and returned home, just in time for supper that evening.

Ranie had never materialized. Pepper clutched the handles on her bag and shuffled onward.

"Here's the guest room."

Anna showed her into a large bedroom with light gray walls and wood trim. The furnishings weren't fancy, but they looked well-made, inviting, and practical. "This is really nice."

"Thanks." Anna hefted her backpack higher onto her shoulder. "You asked about the bathroom. It's just down the hall on the left. I'll drop my things in my room, which you'll pass on your way. Stop and get me when you come back."

Pepper emerged from the bathroom a couple minutes later. Thundering footsteps rattled up the stairs. A bellow accompanied them. "Anna, you home? There's a Mustang parked outside. Is it your friend's? Can I drive it?" Instantly, Anna hurried from the room and into the grasp of a gangly giant who swooped her into his arms and whirled her around in circles. His strawberry blond hair flopped in the breeze he created.

None other than Toby, to be sure.

"Put me down, Tobe." Anna's giggles hindered her attempts to stop him.

"I have to drive that car. It's hers, isn't it?" He set his sister back on her feet. "You said you were coming in her car." Then he spotted Pepper. His words halted momentarily, and his feet dashed toward her. "Hi, you're Anna's new friend. I can't remember your name. It's something weird." Out of breath, he gulped, "Please, let me drive your car."

"My name's Pepper." She offered her hand as a gesture to forestall any ideas he might have about greeting her as he had Anna. "Odd, huh?"

Toby gawked as if he hadn't a clue what she was talking about. Then her words seemed to hit him. "Mine's Toby. Some people think it's odd, too. Can I drive your Mustang?"

The whirlwind that was Toby finally subsided a bit when Pepper promised him a test drive after supper—as long as she was in the car. He charged off to change into his work clothes, whooping and hollering as he went. Anna and Pepper headed to find Mrs. Davies.

"I told you that car would raise some testosterone."

Anna held the kitchen door open and waited for Pepper to go outside.

"You said it would create drool, not a cyclone."

"You said you wished you had brothers."

"A brother." Pepper reiterated her earlier words. "Just one." Now wasn't the time to admit her desire for more. They were nearing the door of the building closest to the house.

"You could have one of mine."

"Your mom might object."

"Usually, yes. But you might be able to make a deal with her once in a while."

Anna was kidding. Still, Pepper's having been deserted made her condemn any mom for even jesting about giving a child away.

"You okay?"

Pepper hadn't realized that her feet no longer moved. Stashing her memories away, she caught up to Anna. "Yeah, sure."

Anna opened the door. She breathed deeply. "It's pie day. I forgot Mom baked on Fridays during the winter. It doesn't smell like apple. Wonder what she's up to."

Pepper couldn't have said whether it was pie of any type, but she did appreciate the enticing aroma, whatever it was.

Anna's long legs gobbled up the distance through the expansive room that looked to be both a storage area for baking supplies and other ingredients and a large cooler for the finished products. Pepper had no time to inspect further. Anna was entering another room.

"You're here just in time." Mrs. Davies engulfed her daughter in a long hug. Then she turned to Pepper. "I'm Sue Davies." In lieu of a handshake, she held up a floury hand and grinned. "We're so glad to have you. Thanks for bringing Anna with you."

Such a welcoming, disarming greeting. Pepper swallowed hard. "Th—thanks for having me." She searched her usually ample repertoire for something witty. What had happened to her brain? Finally she mumbled, "Whatever you're baking sure smells good."

"I'm ready for taste testers."

Pepper plunged forward. "I'm in."

Anna and Sue Davies both laughed.

* * *

Having worked at Emma Porter's chocolate shop, Pepper appreciated fine desserts. She'd sampled many of Emma's cocoa-based creations. She had listened to people gush over their quality and flavor. And she was woefully ignorant of pastries. But if there was anything wrong with the hold-in-your-hand creation that Pepper now enjoyed, she couldn't detect it.

Mrs. Davies called it a turnover. Its flaky crust, she explained, was a cream cheese and flour base that she had modified from several others. The triple-berry filling, also an original, oozed with blueberries, blackberries, and raspberries, additions that Zeke had planted and begun nurturing in the orchard four years ago.

"Do you want to make one?"

Sue's question dragged Pepper's attention from the turnover she had nearly devoured.

Pepper popped the last bit into her mouth and then swallowed around the words, "I'd love to." She rolled up her sleeves.

Mrs. Davies handed her a small amount of chilled dough and a rolling pin. "Roll this out right here." She moved aside and pointed to a floury area in front of where she had been. "You need it big enough to cover this section." She gestured to the circular portion of a small hand-cranked machine near Pepper. "Then you lay it on top of the turnover maker."

Pepper rolled, not too carefully or with much skill, until Mrs. Davies declared the odd-shaped concoction big enough to cover the turnover press. Picking it up too hastily, Pepper tore the dough. She started over.

"This one has a much better shape than the last." Anna said.

Mrs. Davies coached. "Now slide those tiny fingers—I wish mine were so small—carefully underneath the dough as far as you can so that you can lift it without tearing it."

After Pepper glided the dough into place, added the berry filling, and turned the handle of the machine to fold and seal the dough around the filling, all three cheered.

"Great job. You're a quick study."

Pepper basked in the praise of Mrs. Davies. Without warning, resentment reared its ugly head. She could feel the anger toward her own mother rising, quashing the filial emotion she should have, threatening to ruin the camaraderie she already felt for Anna's mom.

Her friend's voice rescued her. "Mom. Pepper. Come quick." She motioned the two of them to the window where she stood. "I told Pepper that car of hers would cause a stir."

Grinning behind her hand, Sue Davies watched the scene in the driveway.

Two men circled Pepper's car. Each one paused, intermittently, to admire some part of the machine or to send a brief comment to his companion. Pepper recognized Anna's father immediately. He was a picture of Ike thirty years from now.

She also knew the younger man—the dark brown curls protruding from the seemingly obligatory knit cap, the straight nose and angular frame, and the penetrating gaze emanating from deep-set eyes. The man she desperately wanted to thank but seriously dreaded to meet. The second admirer—she would bet her Mustang on it—was Zeke Davies.

CHAPTER 4

Pepper's recognition of Zeke coincided with the end of Anna's patience. Her new friend hurried out the door, yakking as she strode. "Dad, what is it about a nicely put together piece of metal that makes men crazy?"

Good question. Pepper awaited the answer.

"Don't get high-handed with me, daughter." He wagged his finger at her, smiling as he did so. "I've seen you women gawp and grin over some silly cloth creation that looks ridiculous to me."

He had avoided the question but had shown both humor and spunk. Pepper grinned. Spreading his arms wide, Anna's dad welcomed his only daughter, planting a kiss on her cheek. He nodded toward Pepper. "I'm Harold Davies. Good to meet you."

Zeke turned toward Anna. "And how many pairs of shoes do you own?"

He evidently shared his dad's opinion of clothes and cars—and his unwillingness to divulge any secrets about men and metal. After delivering his two cents' worth, Zeke hugged his sister. He turned toward his mom and Pepper, who stood side by side.

"Hi. Has Mom been giving you the tour?" He pointed toward Pepper's sleeve. "Or putting you to work?" He stared toward her elbow.

Pepper glanced at her arm. Powdery flour smudges intermittently lightened the Penn State navy blue from her wrist to her elbow.

Mrs. Davies grinned warmly at Pepper. "On her second try she created a masterpiece."

"So she did put you to work." Zeke smiled at his dad.

Pepper patted the flour from her sleeve. "She paid me. I had to do something to earn it."

He glanced first at his mom and then at Pepper. "What's the going work load for a free apple turnover?"

"I wouldn't know." Pepper cast a conspiratorial look in Mrs. Davies's direction.

"She didn't give you a turnover?"

"Not an apple one."

Confusion clouded his features. "Then what . . ." His eyes dilated, and a slight grin lit his face. "You used my raspberries?"

"And your blueberries, and your blackberries. Triple Berry Turnovers. Davies Orchard's newest original." Zeke's mom gushed.

Pepper stared into space, searching for Sue's earlier words about the berries. Evidently a new product at Davies Orchard made the headlines.

"Did you like it?" Zeke asked, looking directly at Pepper for the first time.

"Loved it." Pepper hugged her cold arms with her hands. Why hadn't she brought her jacket? "I might not be the one to ask, though."

Zeke furrowed his brow. "Why's that?"

"I'd take berries over an apple any day."

He cleared his throat. "You've never had a really good apple."

"What?" Had Zeke missed Pepper's praise of the delicious turnover those berries were a part of?

"Nothing better than a crunchy Honey Crisp straight from the tree." He gestured to the nearby orchard. His gaze followed.

"I'll have to take your word for it, right?"

Zeke surveyed the orchard more closely before turning his eyes back to Pepper. "You will until August."

"And in August?" This guy was fun and even a little shy. Why had she worried about meeting him?

"In August, I'll hand pick one for you and watch you enjoy it." He pantomimed handing her the imaginary apple.

"But you planted the berries."

Zeke glanced at his mom. "Not in preference to apples. In addition to them." As though his answer explained everything, he squeezed Sue's arm and began walking away.

"But what—" Pepper called in his direction, stretching forward on her tiptoes to help her words reach him.

"Catch you later."

He quickened his pace. Had he suddenly remembered he was late for something? A long-haired dog joined him on his way.

A few steps farther, he turned and yelled, "Count on me for supper, Mom."

"I guess Zeke's plans have changed," Sue said.

Her words dragged Pepper's thoughts away from Zeke and his puzzling response.

"What plans?"

"Dinner plans, at least."

34

* * *

All right, so the girl was cute. Zeke had already known that. Even plastered she hadn't been repulsive. Cleaned up and sober, she looked— what was the word? Attractive? Eye catching? Perfect? No. Definitely not perfect. No one was perfect.

Nor should he have been surprised at her chattiness. She'd talked constantly to Anna that night, divulging so many details that Zeke had wondered how much the alcohol had loosened her tongue. Evidently not that much.

Anna had found a new friend. Mom seemed favorably inclined. Dad, well, Dad didn't pass judgment on anyone very quickly. He'd need six months for sure to make up his mind. And the guys? It would be hard to beat a Mustang for making a good first impression on Toby and Ike. Joe would have a clearer head, but Zeke hadn't seen Joe.

The crucial question to Zeke wasn't what everyone else thought about Pepper, but what he thought. After all, he'd been the one to suggest helping her when Anna saw her lying on the grass a few weeks ago. He'd also been the one to encourage Anna to get to know her and to speak to Pepper about God. What if Pepper wanted nothing to do with the Davies' "religion," as most people called it? Had he unguardedly welcomed a person who could negatively influence his sister? Had he made a decision without weighing the consequences?

And what about supper? He'd told Mom earlier of his plans to go into town, do his banking, get a haircut, grab a burger somewhere, and then go home to spend the evening with the latest edition of the *Good Fruit Grower*. The magazine was, perhaps, a stall tactic while he figured out how to broach the subject of God to Pepper, but it was the best one he had. Now he'd tossed it away under the influence of a perky smile, a quick wit, and a choice between apples and berries. His sweatshirt collar suddenly seemed a size too small.

* * *

Seldom part of a large family gathering, Pepper floundered and bumbled to help. Sue and Anna coached her along. She dropped some lettuce on the floor and nearly broke a glass.

At 5:55, Anna whispered, "Here come the hordes."

Right on cue, footsteps thumped across the porch. Ike appeared seconds later.

"Hey, there, Pepper."

35

He carried thick black rubber boots in one hand.

"Ready for me to take you for that drive? I'll show you all of the Davies' property that can be seen from the road." Amber speckles glistened in his eyes.

"I promised to go along while Toby drives right after supper. Maybe you could ride with us."

"Toby called dibs, did he? Not surprised. I'll wait." He lifted his boots higher in a sort of salute as he passed. "Smells great, Mom. I'll be right down."

Within ten minutes, everyone was inside, cleaned up, and settled at the dining room table in a time of family togetherness, not grab-and-go chaos. The meal began with Mr. Davies asking a blessing on the food and thanking God for providing it. The prayer flowed easily from his lips. Pepper peeked to see if God stood next to Harold. She'd have to ask Anna what made her father's prayer so real.

She had never experienced such an evening meal. Seated between Anna and Zeke, she found herself warmed by everything from the unexpected white tablecloth and napkins, silver flatware, and china plates to the cliché brotherly squabbles and good-natured teasing.

Mr. Davies' voice rose from one end of the table when everyone was nearly finished eating. "So you got that mini donkey home, did you, Zeke?"

Zeke swallowed quickly. "Yep. Just before I saw you walking toward the house."

"A baby donkey?" Pepper's heart warmed toward animals of any kind.

"Not a baby, a mini." Zeke offered clarification. "He's full grown, but he stands only about three feet tall." He gestured beside Pepper.

"Another addition to your petting zoo?" Anna raised an eyebrow at her brother.

Pepper's face lit. "You have a petting zoo?"

Zeke coughed. "For the kids."

"What kids?"

He wiped his mouth and cleared his throat. "The kids who come to the orchard."

"They come with their parents to buy apples?"

"Or with their grandparents, aunts, or uncles," Anna said.

Toby joined the conversation. "Lots of teachers bring their classes here for a field trip." His glance darted around the room. "Kids everywhere you look."

Pepper's thoughts had lingered on the petting zoo. "What animals do you have?"

Before Zeke could answer, Toby piped up. He marked each animal on his fingers as he listed. "Two goats, a mule, a scattering of chickens, two sheep, one mini donkey, and three rabbits—with more expected any day." He rolled his eyes at Zeke.

Pepper laughed and then cleared her throat. "What's wrong with baby bunnies?"

Laughter rang out again, and everyone stared at Zeke.

He avoided Pepper's eyes. "The guy who sold me the rabbits told me they were all males."

"And the guy with the petting zoo doesn't know the difference?" Pepper blinked twice. This was more fun than the "Zeke-can't-be-around-puke" info that Anna had told Pepper earlier.

"It's hard to tell."

"Maybe you'd better figure it out." Pepper grinned at his discomfort.

"Just call him 'Old MacDonald.'" Toby's eyes glistened as he teased his oldest brother.

When the laughter subsided, Pepper said, "It must be lots of fun."

"And lots of headaches." Zeke ran his hand through his short hair. "But it has increased the number of both visitors and sales."

"And brought lots of smiles." Sue's eyes glowed softly. "And some sweet pictures for us to post on the website."

"I'd better go check on Axle." Zeke slid his chair away from the table. "He seemed okay with his new place, but—"

"But you never know with animals." Mr. Davies finished Zeke's sentence.

Pepper's words tumbled out. "Can I come, too?"

Zeke swallowed hard. "Sure." He stood and then helped Pepper with her chair. "Sis, you coming?"

"I'll meet Axle later. Mom could use extra hands cleaning up."

Zeke was leaving the dining room when Toby called, "Hey, Pepper, what about my turn with the Mustang?"

Pepper turned to Toby. Then she glanced up at Zeke, who shrugged and said, "It'll be here when we get back." He motioned Pepper ahead of him.

Toby's words followed them. "Don't take forever."

* * *

Anna's refusal to accompany them shouldn't have surprised Zeke. She'd been slower than Zeke wanted her to be in talking with Pepper about God. He had an open door, Anna said. If he felt the time was right, he could go through it. Couldn't his sister at least have walked him to the entrance? Pepper was her friend.

"Did you hear me?" Pepper asked.

Her question interrupted his complaints. "No. Sorry." They were halfway to the barn.

"Can you do anything with a mini donkey except pet him?"

"Feed him. Water him."

"Very funny." Pepper started to laugh.

Zeke hadn't been kidding. He searched for another answer. "Some people hitch them up to a mini cart and drive them around."

Pepper bounced up and down, clutching his elbow. "Oh, I want to try that. Can I drive?"

"Whoa. Whoa, there." He stopped and faced her. "Some people have carts. We don't."

Instantly she frowned.

"Didn't want to 'get the cart before the donkey,' if you know what I mean." He smiled at his almost funny comment.

She rewarded him with a grin. "When you do get one, I want to learn to drive it. I'm perfect for the part."

What made her think so?

"A mini cart, for a mini donkey." She pointed both hands toward herself. "And a mini person for both."

She had Zeke on that one. Once again the word *perfect* trotted through his mind. He shook his head slightly and continued toward the barn. Pepper followed along, hurrying her short steps to keep pace with his longer ones.

"How did you ever find a miniature donkey?" Pepper waited while Zeke slid the cumbersome door open. "I wouldn't know where to begin to look for one."

"It wasn't hard." He stepped around Pepper and led her down an aisle on one side of the row of wagons, stacked hay, and numerous oddities stored in the center of the enormous building, "I looked in the . . ." His words and his feet halted simultaneously.

Pepper's shoulder slammed into his back. "In the . . . what?"

"Axle's gone."

"What?" She sidestepped him and gaped between the slats of the empty pen.

Zeke gazed over the top rail. His mind raced to some words of advice he'd been given earlier in the day when he picked up the donkey.

"Axle likes kids, and he'll be good with a cart. But I'm warning you. He's kind of a magician when he wants to be somewhere other than where he is."

"That magician." Zeke rapped the top rail with his hand. "Wait till I find that sneaky—"

"Excuse me." Pepper tapped Zeke's bicep forcefully. "He might be gone, but he's no—magician."

Zeke turned toward her.

"Did you say he's about this tall?" She motioned just above her waist.

"Yeah, about that."

"The bars on this pen are too far apart." While Zeke stood dumbfounded, Pepper wriggled herself between two slats and ended up inside the pen. Then, oblivious of the dirt and straw, she lay on the floor and squirmed underneath the lowest plank. Outside the enclosure once again, she stood up. "If I can do it, Axle can, too." She brushed the debris from her clothes. "We know how he did it. We still need to know where he is."

"You—you crawled on the floor." Anna had told Zeke that Pepper was a city girl.

"I did. I like animals. And I had to make a point."

Zeke stared at her. What would she have done if her point were really important? He shook his head. "Let's find that beast."

"Okay, boss." She rubbed her hands together rapidly. "Where do we look first?"

He paused and then blinked. "You head down this row." He gestured along the path where they were standing. "I'll take the row on the other side. If you find him, yell."

With one quick head bob, Pepper was off. For a few seconds, Zeke gawked in her direction. Then he shook himself. "Axle, where are you?"

* * *

The pen beside the one Axle should have occupied was empty. In the next, Pepper found two black-faced sheep. Oblivious of the hubbub over the newest addition to the petting zoo, they quietly munched their hay. She paused long enough to rub each head before hurrying on. The next enclosure housed a mule, a long-eared white creature with dark eyes that dismissed her as she scurried by.

The outer wall of the barn lay a short distance beyond the mule's pen. The space between was a storage cubbyhole. Rakes and shovels, along with several other tools that Pepper couldn't name, hung on or leaned against the wall. Buckets and baskets covered part of the floor.

Pepper peered into the corner. She gasped. Two spindly gray legs stood above two dark round hooves and beneath a short-haired gray tail. Looking more closely, she discerned, partially hidden behind large plastic buckets, Axle's shoulders pressed against the mule's pen. Reaching his head between two slats, the greedy little donkey was helping himself to the mule's supper. Pepper stepped among the tools. "There you are."

The donkey started. He brayed. He banged his neck against the slats. He kicked his back legs. He bellowed again.

Pepper opened her mouth. Zeke grabbed her arm. "Get back."

Taking a shovel from the wall, Zeke approached the ruckus maker. "Easy, Axle. Easy there." Using the shovel as a shield against the donkey's flailing back legs, Zeke edged nearer. "Calm down." He set the shovel aside and began stroking the donkey's back. "You got your head in there. You can get it out."

Pepper blinked. Axle's head was stuck? Riveted to the spot, she watched. While continuing to pet Axle with his one hand, Zeke grasped some hay with the other. Gradually, Axle stopped braying and kicking.

"Turn your head, and you can have this."

Spotting the hay, Axle cocked his head slightly, wedged his skull and ears between the slats, and munched from Zeke's outstretched hand.

Pepper exhaled loudly and whispered, "You did it."

Zeke barely turned as he continued stroking Axle. "He did it."

Pepper smiled. Zeke was the perfect Davies to run the petting zoo.

CHAPTER 5

Pepper's Mustang and the test driving of it consumed much of Friday evening. Every Davies male took a turn at the wheel. Toby rambled non-stop about engine power, special options, and body detailing. Ike became Pepper's tour guide, naming the various trees of the fields they passed and explaining future plans. Joe said little but ended his drive with, "Sweet ride."

Mr. Davies and Zeke traveled together, one driving and the other riding shotgun. Anna joined Pepper in the back seat. Harold drove first.

"What do you think, Dad?" Anna asked after only a short distance. She raised her eyebrows at Pepper.

"Well, you know I'm partial to trucks, but I guess I wouldn't turn down one of these if someone wanted to give me one."

"That's exactly what Pepper's dad did. He gave her one." Anna reached forward and nudged his shoulder. "Hint. Hint." She pressed on. "And I'm your favorite, Dad."

"No, daughter, you're my 'only.' I don't have a favorite."

Pepper smiled when she heard a chuckle from the front seat. Zeke approved of his dad's answer.

Driving past the field that Ike had named as the outer limit of the orchard, Harold stopped the car, and Zeke walked around to take the wheel.

Zeke had barely picked up speed when Harold asked Pepper, "How much upkeep is involved?"

"My dad's friend, the mechanic that found Priscilla for me, looks—"

"Priscilla?" Male voices sounded in stereo.

"You named this blue hotrod 'Priscilla'?" Zeke groaned. "Sissy name."

"Excuse me!" Pepper scooched forward in her seat right behind him. "It's not a sissy name. It's a princess name." Speaking directly into his right ear, she added. "My car is a girl. I share lots of things with Priscilla."

Zeke shook his head. "If you say so." He cast a glance toward Harold. "Wait till Toby hears this." Harold grinned back at Pepper.

"Toby will just have to get over it because this car's name is Priscilla, and that's final." Pepper slid back and flopped herself against the leather. Crossing her arms in front of her, she looked toward Anna who giggled and squeezed Pepper's arm.

Pepper was still plotting her defense before Toby, when Zeke turned into the drive.

He glanced back at her through the rear-view mirror. "Whatever you call this machine, it's a classic." He waited until she glanced up and then looked away.

"That it is, little lady." Harold had turned to address Pepper. "And we're mighty glad you shared it."

At his heartfelt words, Pepper leaned forward. "My pleasure." Could he sense her sincerity. A few seconds passed. "I'm glad you liked—" She grinned widely. "Priscilla."

Laughter filled the car.

Zeke parked, edged his long legs from under the steering wheel, and flipped the seat forward so that Pepper could climb out. He extended his hand to her, but turned his stare down the driveway. "Someone's coming."

Pepper briefly touched his rough fingers while she expertly removed her petite frame from the back seat. Being short did have some advantages. Maneuvering around Zeke, she followed his gaze.

"It's Gramps." Zeke automatically shut the car door.

On the other side of the Mustang, both Anna and Harold had emerged and stood watching the approaching pickup. It had the age of a classic, but the not the appearance of one. It sounded worse than it looked.

The driver pulled up next to Zeke and Pepper, opened the dented white door, and hopped to the ground, all in rapid succession.

"Ezekiel, where'd you get those fancy wheels?"

Ezekiel. Pepper blinked and gulped. Zeke's name was Ezekiel. By the time she digested this food for thought, Zeke had elbowed her. She jerked herself back to the moment and to the man who stood only a few inches taller than she did. The realization that the Davies clan were not all giants brought a smile to her lips.

"So this American-made beauty is yours, huh?" The man reached forward to shake Pepper's hand. "I'm Fred Hanna. Gramps to all this crew." He gestured broadly. Then he stepped closer to Priscilla and whistled. "Can't believe Tobias isn't camping out right here in the driveway." He ran one hand along the hood. "That's one beautiful piece of engineering."

Pepper pushed aside the oddity of Toby's real name. She discarded the questions about Joe's and Ike's full monikers. But she couldn't dismiss

42

the mystery of the gait of Fred Hanna. The man's obvious limp displayed itself with each step he made around the Mustang. His right shoe, with its built-up sole, clearly indicated the man's shorter right leg. The pre-med student in Pepper longed to know the cause of his hobble. She turned toward Anna.

But Anna was on a fast-paced jaunt toward the house. She jogged the last few steps and bounded onto the porch, disappearing inside the door. Pepper considered following her friend.

Then she felt someone's gaze on her. She looked up. Zeke's expression combined an accusation of her curiosity with a defense of his grandfather. He'd caught her stares, seen her questions. Still, she had to ask. She mouthed one word. "How?"

Zeke lowered his gaze. He dragged the toe of one boot across the stones. He shifted his weight. Then, without looking at her, he whispered, "Polio."

That one word cleared Pepper's muddle. Facts scrambled through her brain. The last major polio outbreak in the United States had occurred in the early 1950s. Each year 25,000 to 50,000 people, most of them children, had contracted the dreaded disease of the central nervous system. Some had died. Most had suffered some form of paralysis.

Fred Hanna's illness had obviously curtailed the growth of his right leg. But he'd survived. And apparently he'd gone on to live a normal life: grown up, landed a job, found a wife, and had a family. How had he achieved all of that? Pepper's curiosity bubbled up like the fizz on root beer. She had so many questions for Anna's grandfather. Would Zeke let her ask them?

The commotion of approaching family halted Pepper's musing.

"Well, it's about time the rest of you joined us." Fred's loud pronouncement greeted Sue, Ike, Joe, Toby, and Anna as they walked across the yard.

"Whadda ya think of Pepper's car, Gramps? Is it sweet or what?"

"Guess I'd have to say 'what,' Tobias. 'Sweet' sounds too much like candy." Fred whacked Toby's arm, and then looked toward his other grandsons. "Isaac, Josiah. What do you two think?"

The other mystery was solved. Pepper rehearsed the brothers' names. Ezekiel, Josiah, Isaac, and Tobias. Odd names. But they sounded vaguely familiar, as though she might have heard them somewhere. Where?

Again she sensed someone watching her. She looked up. Again she met Zeke's gaze. This time his eyes concealed a secret of their own, and his lips bore a slight smile. He couldn't know what she was thinking, could he? She challenged him with an open stare.

Without looking away, he grinned broadly, "The Bible."

The Bible. Pepper's jaw dropped. *Who gave their children Bible names? Stupid question. Harold and Sue, obviously. At least they had for their sons.* Anna wasn't a Bible name, was it?

Looking across at her friend, Pepper watched Anna nod, not at Pepper, but at someone beside her. Zeke. Again. Pepper sighed and waved in Anna's direction. This time Anna waved back, nodded, and smiled.

"You girls having a waving party?" Fred signaled to both of them.

Sue stepped close to the older man. "Good to see you, Dad." She hugged him. "How did Mom's appointment go today?"

"That's what I came to tell you. Guess this fancy vehicle made me lose my train of thought."

Sue linked arms with her dad. "You, along with a few others I could name."

* * *

"Doc says Maggie's coming along real well."

The entire family had settled in the living room. Sue sat next to her dad.

"Says she's his star patient." Fred beamed.

"Star patient for what?" Pepper couldn't resist asking.

"Double knee replacement."

Pepper nearly choked on her cookie. "Double knee replacement."

"Yep. Two weeks ago. Both were badly arthritic. She was in so much pain. Doc agreed that both should be done at the same time."

His eyes suddenly clouded over.

"Wasn't sure we'd survive the first few days at home. Maggie's pain was even worse."

Sue squeezed his hand. "But you did." Tears glistened in her eyes, too.

"Praise God." Fred looked heavenward. "He is faithful. And He's blessed me with a gem of a wife. 'Far above rubies.'"

Tenderness swelled in Pepper's heart. Then resentment stole into her mind. Why did some people have so much and others so little?

So much? What was she thinking? Fred Hanna had survived polio. His wife had endured double knee replacement. Maybe there was more to it than simply what a person encountered in life.

"She's taking a few more steps each day with the walker. She's weaning herself from the pain pills. Her spirits are still good." Never letting go of Sue's hand, Fred rose from the couch, and she got up with him. "I'd best be getting back. She'll be wondering what's taking so long."

"I have some more meals for you." Sue headed for the kitchen. "I'll get them from the freezer."

Fred snapped his fingers. "I brought some of your dishes back. They're still in the truck. I'll—"

"I'll get them." Both Zeke and Joe had spoken.

"I'll walk you to your truck, Mr. Hanna. And bring the dishes back when I come." Pepper wanted to know more about Fred and his beloved Maggie.

If Pepper's suggestion surprised him, Fred never let it show. "I guess you boys can stay where you are. I haven't had a nicer offer all day."

Pepper ignored the brothers' banter and Zeke's obvious stare. She and Mr. Hanna started down the driveway a minute later. Fred didn't walk fast, but he kept a steady pace. Part way down the driveway, he tripped and pitched forward.

"Mr. Hanna." Pepper reached to stabilize him. "Are you okay?"

He righted himself quickly, but stopped where he was. "I'm fine. I trip a lot. These stones are tricky." He nodded toward the offenders. "But I'm not Mr. Hanna. Makes me feel old." He winked at her.

How many birthdays had he celebrated?

"I'm Fred or Gramps to anybody who cares about me."

Fred Hanna had spunk. Pepper kept her hand on his upper arm as he took up the pace again.

"Usually Maggie steadies me. Now I have to try to help her. We're a pair, all right."

"I bet you are." Pepper had no doubt. "I wish I could meet her. I'd love to hear all about her surgery. And your experience with polio."

He halted suddenly.

If only Pepper were physically able to kick herself.

"What's this?"

"I'm sorry," she blurted and rushed on. "I'm a pre-med student. Your gait caught my attention. I stared. Zeke let me know about it. I asked him." She gulped. "Then you mentioned your wife's double knee replacement. I—"

"Hold your horses, there, girl." He raised both palms toward her. "Slow down. My ears can't hear that fast."

Pepper sighed. Twice. She took a deep breath. "I don't mean to be rude. But all this fascinates me."

Fred's loud laugh filled the yard. "Little lady, you need some excitement in your life if you find Maggie and me fascinating." He patted her arm. "You and Anna going back on Sunday?"

Pepper nodded.

"I'll tell you what. You get her or one of those brothers of hers, the whole bunch if you can, to bring you over on Sunday afternoon, and Maggie and I'll give you all the details. She'll love the company. Us old folks get a kick out of retelling our war stories."

He reached for the handle on the beat-up white door.

"I gotta scoot before Maggie gets worried." He leaned in and snatched a plastic Wal-Mart bag from the seat. "Here are Sue's dishes. Thanks for delivering them." He climbed aboard, rolled down the window, and stuck his head out. "Hope to see you Sunday."

* * *

What were she and Gramps talking about? Not that Zeke worried about his grandfather. Fred Hanna could talk to anyone about anything. And Pepper wanted to be a doctor. No wonder Gram and Gramps were interesting to her as medical cases. To tell the truth, Gramps probably welcomed the opportunity to share his experience. Only Zeke, it seemed, had taut prickles in the pit of his stomach.

When Pepper re-entered the living room, his nerves stood more on end. She handed a bag, of dishes, presumably, to his mom, before taking a seat next to Anna. The two were engrossed in conversation immediately. It was definitely time to go home and find his copy of the *Good Fruit Grower*. It never made him nervous.

* * *

"Do you think we could stop by your grandparents' house before we go back?" Pepper had waited until they were heading upstairs for bed before she broached the idea to Anna.

"I can't think why not. Mom usually has lunch ready soon after we get home from church. We could leave here by 2:00, at least. Gram and Gramps' place isn't much out of the way. As long as I'm ready for my 10:00 class on Monday, I'm fine." Anna paused at the top of the stairs. "When's your first class?"

"Ugghh! Eight o'clock." Pepper tipped her head back and looked at the ceiling. "Whatever possessed me to take an early-morning class, especially on Monday?"

"Always seems like a good idea, doesn't it? Until Monday morning."
Anna hugged Pepper briefly. "I'm glad you came."

"I am, too."

* * *

An hour later Zeke faced the truth. The *Good Fruit Grower* was not enough to divert his attention from his troubles. Were they troubles, exactly? No. But they were distractions. Not distractions, plural. Only one distraction. Definitely. What was so distracting about Pepper Staley?

Her car was definitely a distraction. Toby would be yammering on about it for weeks.

Her bubbly personality provided another. Everything intrigued her. A mule. Some sheep. A miniature donkey. She did first and thought later. His first encounter with her was the primary proof. But she'd provided more recent ones. Her climbing into and out of Axle's pen. Her staring openly at Gramps because of his limp. Zeke had been angry at first. But he'd watched her after he'd said the word *polio*. He'd almost seen the cogs in her brain processing the concept.

Her tender heart was another. He'd heard the emotion she felt for her Priscilla—the Mustang that was more than a car. He'd read the concern she registered for Axle when the donkey disappeared. He'd also observed the softness in her eyes when Gramps spoke about Gram.

Maybe the biggest distraction was the way he felt, when, only once, he'd been able to catch her off her guard. Their Bible names had given him that opportunity. Her green eyes had clouded over, deep in thought, and somehow, Zeke had known what was puzzling her. Even better than that, he had known the answer. He wished he had captured the look on her face when he'd whispered those words to her.

He kept searching for a way to see that look again. No wonder he was distracted.

CHAPTER 6

Pepper opened her eyes. Where was she? The colors were different. She rubbed her hands across her face and then blinked. What day was it? She licked her dry lips. Her muddled thoughts began to clear. The guest room at Anna's house.

Clutching the thick blanket and hand-made quilt close to her chest, Pepper smiled. She replayed the highlights of Friday night and savored the thought of a Saturday in the Davies' home.

What time was it? She rolled to her side and glanced at the clock. Nine o'clock. How had she slept so late? Where was everyone else? She hadn't heard anything. Time to go find out.

Sliding to the edge of the double bed, she draped her legs over the side and slipped her feet into the fuzzy pink slippers she'd set there last night. Wondering whether to change her clothes before going downstairs, she smiled at her Hello Kitty sleep pants and matching T-shirt. They weren't the most stylish, but they were her favorites.

She grabbed a comb and did her best to untangle the web of curls that had overcome her hair while she slept. After making her bed, she opened the door and stepped into the hall.

Breakfast scents, coffee and bacon, met her as she descended the stairs. She loved the smell of both but rarely partook of either. She followed the aromas to the kitchen. Three boxes of cereal and a note waited on the table for her.

Good morning, Pepper.

We're early risers, more out of habit than necessity, but I'm glad you were able to sleep in. Help yourself to anything you'd like for breakfast. Milk and juice are in the refrigerator, eggs and bacon, too, if you'd rather cook. I'm making more pies. The boys and Anna are pruning. Make yourself at home.

Sue

Pepper surveyed the cereal choices. Fiber-filled bran flakes with nuts, seeds, and exotic fruits. Might as well throw out the cereal and eat the box. Small squares of shredded wheat, without frosting. Better, but still not appetizing. Wheat puffs coated with honey. Bingo. Someone else indulged his sweet tooth at breakfast. Pepper reached for the bowl beside the boxes and poured the sugary treat. Within minutes she had downed the cereal, chugged a glass of orange juice, and returned the milk to the fridge.

She was preparing to sprint up the stairs when she heard the front door open. She paused on the first tread and waited. Anna walked around the corner a few seconds later.

"You're up."

"I am, and I'm fed." Pepper patted her lean abs. "Sorry I slept so late. I couldn't believe the time."

"Glad you could rest. Everyone here gets up with the chickens." She joined Pepper at the foot of the stairs. "That was true even before we had any."

Pepper's eyes gleamed. "I'll blame Zeke for it anyway, the next time I see him."

"Blame me for what?" Zeke had rounded the corner and now stood, beanie cap in hand, a few feet from Pepper and Anna.

Sly glances passed between the girls. Pepper spoke first.

"Blame you and those chickens for making everyone get up so early. You're robbing everybody of one of the joys of youth. Sleeping in."

Zeke's demeanor sagged. "Sorry." He pulled the hat back onto his head. "The rooster's the problem. Can't stop his crowing." He turned toward the kitchen.

Pepper closed the distance between Anna's brother and herself. "I'm teasing, Zeke." She laid her hand on his forearm. "I've been up for all of about fifteen minutes. I never heard a rooster."

"You're sure?" His questioning gaze searched her face.

"I had to harass you a little." She grinned up at him. "You and those chickens are too easy a mark."

He breathed deeply before starting toward the kitchen.

"You'll have to learn not to take me so seriously."

Zeke turned back, his glance moving first to her legs and then to her face. "It shouldn't be too hard."

Pepper glanced at her kitten pants. She looked back at Zeke. "See how easy that was?" Even though he was headed toward the kitchen again, she thought she caught a glimpse of his smile.

* * *

49

While Pepper dressed, Anna put away breakfast things. Within minutes they were back outside, and Pepper had become a member of the cleanup crew.

"These branches fell from the trees?"

Still reaching for a branch at her feet, Anna looked up. "They had help. Dad, Zeke, and Joe—and some pruning shears."

"They cut all these branches?" Pepper couldn't fathom it. "On purpose?"

"Yep. Apple trees like to reach for the sky. But the best bearing branches grow outward, not upward." Her arms filled with branches, twigs, and leaves, Anna walked toward a wagon a short distance away. "We have to cut back the extra stuff so that the tree has more food and sunlight for the fruit."

"How often do you do this?"

"Every year. It's a huge part of late winter and spring." Anna smiled at Pepper. "With several hundred trees to do, we take all the help we can get."

"Can't say how much help I'll be, but I'll do what I can." Pepper reached for the limb nearest to her.

"That one's almost as big as you are." Anna strode toward Pepper.

"It's not that big." Ignoring Anna's approach, Pepper gathered the gangly branch into her arms and began hauling it to the wagon. It wasn't heavy, but the twigs blocked her view and grabbed at her clothes. "So much for you, you troublemaker." She hoisted the limb onto the wagon and headed back for another load. Something stung her neck. "Ouch." She grabbed her nape and rubbed the spot.

Farther up the row, Anna yelped in pain. Pepper watched her stand up and scan the horizon.

"Did you get stung, too, Anna?" Pepper hurried down the path.

Rather than answer Pepper's question, Anna continued to stare off to her right. Another pain struck, this time in Pepper's right arm. She rubbed the spot. "Oooh, that hurt." She stopped next to Anna. "Is it bugs or bees?"

"It's brothers."

"What?"

Her arms akimbo, Anna called loudly to no one Pepper could see. "I know you're out there. And I know where every one of you sleeps. And I know how to get even. Quit throwing things at us."

A tumult of tiny pieces of wood pelted them from various directions. Pepper and Anna squealed and covered their faces, but the barrage continued for several rounds. Finally, the attack ceased, and both girls looked up.

"I mean it. You guys are in trouble."

The words had hardly left Anna's mouth, when Toby ran from behind a nearby tree and scooped up his sister, flinging her over his shoulder.

"Not as much trouble as you're in right now."

"Watch out, Pepper." Anna pummeled Toby's back.

"For what?"

"For me." Ike followed Toby's lead and slung Pepper over his shoulder.

Both girls pounded and maligned, but the brothers carted them off in the direction of the wagon.

"You should have seen your face, Anna, when that first piece hit you."

Anna rewarded Toby's taunt with a sharp pound to the middle of his back.

"And Pepper thought something stung her. That was great." Both boys chortled.

"What are you two doing?"

Four heads turned towards Zeke's voice. Even from her upside down position, Pepper perceived the exasperation in his eyes.

"Put them down and get back to work."

"Ah, c'mon, Zeke. We're just having some fun." Toby must not have comprehended the look on Zeke's face. "You should've seen how surprised—"

"We still have over half the orchard to prune, and we're about two weeks behind schedule. We don't have time for this."

Zeke now stood toe to toe with his youngest brother. Without another word, Toby restored Anna to her feet. Ike followed his lead. As soon as Pepper had righted herself, Zeke said. "I apologize for the behavior of—" He gestured toward both offenders. "These two clowns." He cast a meaningful look at both brothers. "It won't happen again."

Without another word, Toby and Ike headed toward a nearby pile of branches.

"They didn't hurt us." Could Pepper smooth things over? "Don't be too hard on them."

"They know what has to be done around here."

"Thanks for rescuing us." Anna patted Zeke's arm and gave him a gentle shove. "Get back to Dad and Joe. We'll see you at lunchtime."

"Guess I'd better." He paused as though wanting to say more. Then he walked off in a different direction from Toby and Ike.

* * *

51

By Saturday night at supper, Pepper's arms hurt, and her feet ached. She couldn't remember ever having done so much manual labor in one day. She groaned as she reached for the meat platter filled with roast beef.

Harold's grin was one of empathy. "Did those branches get the better of you?"

"I think they grew as the day went along."

Everyone laughed. Pepper managed the platter and the rest of the meal. No one mentioned the twig bullets or the confrontation between the brothers. Before Pepper realized what had happened, Saturday evening completely disappeared, and she hadn't asked about Sunday morning. Was she expected to go to church? Whatever happened, she would cope.

* * *

Pepper had worked hard. Zeke smiled to himself when he thought about how tired she'd been at supper. She'd carried nearly as many prunings as Anna had. Together, the six of them had accomplished about a week's work, even with Ike and Toby's foolishness. She'd been a good sport about that, too.

When he'd seen Pepper draped over his brother's shoulder, part of Zeke had wanted to punch Ike. Another part of him had wanted to switch places with his brother. Would she have pounded his back and tried to get away from him? He'd spent the day wondering. With each chop of the pruners, he'd asked himself questions only she could answer. Among the many that ran through his mind, two dominated his thoughts. Did she enjoy being near him as much as he enjoyed being around her? Was she willing to hear more about God?

* * *

Once again Pepper slept late. It was nearly 9:30 by the time she had showered, dressed, and gone downstairs to eat. Another note greeted her.

Pepper,

We'll be back from church around 12:30 and have our Sunday dinner then. Save room. Make yourself at home.

Sue

Pepper poured herself another bowl of sugary puffs and decided to stroll out to see Axle. Somehow, Zeke had found time in his busy Saturday to modify the donkey's pen. So far the changes had deterred Axle from making any other unauthorized jaunts around the barn. He might enjoy a little company.

Carrying her cereal with her, she headed outside. She was finishing the milk in the bowl as she approached the heavy sliding door. Knowing she would need both hands free, she set her bowl on the ground beside her and tugged on the massive portal. The movement of the door was negligible. The pain in Pepper's arms, substantial. She gritted her teeth and yanked again. The door careened down the track, dragging her along with it. When it stopped, she was clinging to the handle. Her bowl rested several feet away. How had she—

The answer materialized in the form of Zeke who stood inside the barn. He'd obviously pulled on the door from the inside at the same time she had from the outside.

"What are you doing here?" She collected herself and hurried to pick up dish and spoon.

"I could ask you the same question," he countered.

He certainly didn't seem as though he were headed to church. His blue jeans looked like the ones he'd worn yesterday, and she couldn't imagine his going off to worship God in the hole-ridden coat he had on.

"Did you know I was trying to get in, or do you simply have perfect timing?"

Removing his knit cap from his head, he whisked the sawdust from his coat before looking at Pepper.

* * *

"My timing's not perfect." *But God's is.* All morning Zeke had wondered when to search Pepper out so that he could talk to her. He hadn't wanted to wake her, but he knew the time would be gone faster than he wanted it to be. He'd stayed home with the sole plan to broach the subject of God. Now, here she stood, on his most familiar turf, in a setting she had sought out.

"Sure seems perfect. My first effort was pitiful." She rubbed one arm.

"Feeling muscles you haven't used much?" He avoided her eyes but looked at her arm.

"Am I ever. After working here for one day, I don't wonder that Ike hefted me onto his shoulder as if I were a sack of feathers." She tapped the spoon on the edge of the bowl until he looked at her. "I bet you could have done the same."

He could have. And he'd wanted to. "Probably." He watched her fingers as she held the spoon.

"Probably?" Her tone dared him to look at her.

He complied. "If Ike did, I could have."

She smiled. "Is that the boast of an older brother?"

"It's not boasting if it's true." A narrow smile curled his lips. He looked away.

"Sounds like a debate for another day." She raised the spoon and pointed it at him. "Why aren't you with the rest of your family?"

"I—I need—we need to talk."

Her eyes narrowed. "About what?"

"Remember our first conversation?"

"After that horrible night?"

Zeke nodded. "You said you were angry with God."

"I am."

"You told me I wasn't allowed to say that you're wrong about Him. I let it drop."

"And now you want to pick it back up?"

"I'd like to." Zeke saw the struggle in her face.

"God isn't fair," Pepper said, marking each word with a gesture of the spoon.

This was one of the arguments Zeke had prepared himself for. He breathed a sigh. Then he glanced again at Pepper. Her rigid stance and the glint in her eyes gave him second thoughts. "What makes you say so?"

She opened her mouth. She shut it. Then she tried to drill the spoon through the Pyrex bowl. Opening her mouth again, she blurted, "Your family is great. And they've been wonderful to me. Taken me in. Treated me like I belong. But . . ."

"But?"

"But why do you have them, and I don't? I've always wanted a family like this."

Her outburst backed Zeke up a step. Then he remembered that he had heard Pepper talk of her father. "You have a dad."

Again the spoon became a pointer. "He's all I have. No brothers. No sisters. Not even a mom. She left Dad and me as soon as she could get me home from the hospital and pack her bags."

Zeke reached for the spoon and the hand that held it. "I'm sorry— for all the—pain that's caused." Could Pepper read his pain? He gently squeezed her hand.

54

She looked away. "Everyone's sorry." Then she drew herself up and challenged him. "No one can help."

Zeke lowered his hand, drawing her enclosed hand with his. Her eyes followed his movement. "That's where you're wrong."

"I'm not wrong." She lifted her gaze toward him. "All those lonely years without a mom, without anyone to share things with. No one can bring them back."

He swallowed hard. "But that's not what you said. You said, 'No one can help.'"

Pulling her hand from his grasp, she lifted the spoon to within a few inches from his nose. "But that's what I meant."

"That's not the only kind of help." He glanced at the spoon before meeting her intense stare.

"Now you're playing word games."

"I'm not playing any game."

The spoon drooped slightly. "What other kind of help is there?"

One part of Zeke wanted to praise to God for this impromptu meeting. Another part desired to engulf her and that crazy spoon into his arms. A split second later, he formulated a third plan.

"Let's you and me—and this spoon—go inside." He lifted the spoon from her hand, grasped her shoulder, and turned her toward the house.

CHAPTER 7

Pepper plopped onto the sofa in the living room. Zeke paused beside her, moving a small pillow in order to clear a seat. Then he avoided that space and walked a few steps to a nearby stuffed chair. How serious did Zeke plan to be in assessing the help Pepper needed?

He stretched his long legs out in front of him but looked toward her. "I can't undo your past. Can't make your mom come back."

Pepper pinched her lips together. "I don't want her back." It was too late. She couldn't "forgive and forget" being abandoned. "Ranie had her chance. I'm not giving her another. I don't care how many text messages she sends or phone calls she makes." Ranie had better brace herself. This war was on.

"Your mom is back?" Zeke drew his legs toward the chair and leaned in Pepper's direction.

"She wants to be." Pepper snagged the pillow Zeke had moved a moment earlier and clutched it to her chest. "I finally got over her being gone. No way am I letting her in." She squeezed the pillow more tightly.

"You said you wanted help. Said you'd always wanted a family. Now your mom—"

"I needed her to sing me to sleep. To kiss away my hurts. To help me with my homework. To be all the things—the things—the things your mom is." Pepper pulled her bare feet onto the couch and angled her body closer to Zeke. "Not to waltz in twenty-one years too late and expect me to forget about everything she's missed."

Zeke shifted his gaze from her and stared at the wall behind the couch. He sighed heavily. "I guess you really don't want help then, do you?"

"What?"

He looked directly at her. "You said, 'No one can help.' I'd say that your mom can."

"Could have, Zeke. If she'd cared." Wasn't he listening? "But Ranie didn't care." Pepper challenged Zeke's intense gaze. "You care more about Axle than she did about me."

* * *

Pepper's words hit Zeke harder than a mule's kick. She couldn't really mean them, could she? Yes, she could. Both conviction and resentment glinted in Pepper's green eyes.

She's not ready. The message dashed through Zeke's head. *She's not ready.* Did the words come from God or from some reluctance on his part to confront Pepper's spiritual need? He was still searching for an answer when he remembered Anna's admonition from a few weeks earlier. "She has walls." If only he'd known the cause and extent of Pepper's strongholds. In most areas of her life, Pepper's spirit roamed free. Concerning her mom and God, it pawed and snorted like a penned wild stallion. Zeke blinked away the mental picture.

Pepper's stare confronted him.

"I like to talk. But not about Ranie or God. Both have let me down." Her features softened. "Can you live with that?"

The two most crucial topics in Pepper's life. Could he live with it? Did he have a choice? "When you change your mind, will you tell me?"

"If I ever change my mind . . ." She rose quickly, releasing the death grip on the pillow but retaining the cushion long enough to slam it down on Zeke's arm. "I'll tell you."

* * *

Pepper paced away the hour before the family's return. Then she fidgeted during the noon meal. But Zeke was politeness itself, and the others chatted with Pepper as amiably as they had on Friday and Saturday. By meal's end, Pepper's fingers and feet had finally quieted, and she breathed freely. Zeke wasn't easily offended, and he didn't blab.

Shortly before two o'clock, Anna and Pepper stood at the passenger side of Priscilla. Their stuffed bags rested in the back seat.

Both Mr. and Mrs. Davies had walked them to the car. Harold spoke first. "Thanks for bringing this girl of mine home." He clapped an arm around Anna's shoulders. Then he extended his other hand toward Pepper. "This will help to pay for the gas."

Pepper shook her head at the twenty-dollar bill. "No, Mr. Davies." She pushed the money away. "You've put up with me for a day and a half." She grinned toward Sue. "And it'll take lots of laps to run off all your wife's great meals. I should be paying you."

"You worked for those meals. And you were a good sport about everything." He released Anna and took Pepper's hand in his. Turning her

57

palm upward, he set the money in her hand. "Come and see us again. Soon." He glanced back at Anna. "Bring this one with you, if you can drag her away."

Sue stepped up and engulfed Pepper in a hug. "We've enjoyed you so much." After releasing Pepper, she said, "Drop by on your way to Philadelphia. Or take a weekend in June or July and come to see us when we're busy."

Pepper back stepped and then swallowed hard. "You mean that?"

"Sure do." Ike's voice drifted up from behind them.

When had he joined the group?

Pepper turned. Ike stood across the car from her. His elbows rested on the roof above the driver's seat, and he grinned broadly at Pepper.

"Just be sure to bring this beauty with you." He stroked the blue metal. "Think of the money we'd make by taking people for rides in this thing."

Pepper's jaw dropped. "The money *you'd* make?"

"We'll give you a cut of the profits." He winked at her before turning to Anna. "Zeke and I will meet you at Gram and Gramps'." He headed for a pickup parked nearby.

The phone inside the house rang. Sue yelled to them as she hurried through the yard. "Drive carefully, Pepper. Love you, Anna."

Mr. Davies grabbed the handle that Anna was reaching for and swung the car door wide. "Let your mother know when you get back to school." He waited while Anna climbed in. Pepper walked around the car and settled herself behind the wheel. After Anna put her window down, Harold rested his arms on the door and bowed his head. "Lord, please keep these young ones safe during their travels. Bring them back to us soon. Amen."

Pepper had barely had time to shut her eyes. Opening them quickly, she saw Sue hurry outside. Tears streamed down Mrs. Davies' reddened face. "Mom's in the hospital." With a tissue, Sue dabbed at her eyes. "She has a high fever. The doctors think it might be . . ."

Infection. Pepper anticipated Sue's next word. A rare but formidable foe of those undergoing joint replacement surgery.

"Dad took her in about ten this morning."

Anna sprang from the Mustang and ran up the sidewalk. "I want to see Gram."

Pepper waited while Anna spoke with her mom and then walked back to the car.

"I can't ask you to wait. You have an early class."

Anna needed time with her family. Pepper needed to get out of everyone's way.

* * *

Zeke flung the grain from the scoop into the sheep's trough. He hadn't told Pepper goodbye—hadn't had the chance. He and Ike had been on the way to Gram and Gramp's when Mom called Ike's cell. In all the pandemonium of getting Gram to the hospital, Gramps had forgotten about his grandchildren and their bringing Pepper for a visit. By the time Zeke and Ike had returned, Pepper was gone. By now she should have reached Penn State.

The sliding door opened, and Ike joined Zeke in the barn.

"Any more news from the hospital?" With another scoop of feed ready to go, Zeke moved toward the mule's pen.

Ike followed him. "Not yet."

A text message rang. Both brothers reached for their phones. Zeke's had the message. "It's from Pepper." At least she was still talking to him.

"What's she say?"

Zeke translated the mobile phone shorthand. "She made it back. She wonders about Gram. She wants me to thank Mom for letting her come." He chuckled. "She says Priscilla enjoyed being the center of attention."

"The name sure doesn't fit the car." Ike strewed some hay in the mule's pen and reached for some more from the opened bale in front of Zeke.

"Don't tell Pepper that."

Ike halted in front of Axle's stall. "Why?"

Zeke imitated Pepper. "It's a princess name."

"A princess!" Ike rolled his eyes.

"My thoughts, exactly." Zeke nudged Ike's arm and pointed toward the pen. "You're going too slow."

"What?"

Axle's muzzle protruded through the much-narrowed space between the slats. He strained to reach the hay. "Sorry, buddy." Ike lifted the hay over the top rail, placing it in front of the voracious donkey. Then he rubbed Axle's head.

Another text sounded.

"This one's mine." Ike read the screen. "It's from Pepper, too."

When had Ike given her his number? Why did Zeke care that he had? Ike read aloud. "Don't get any ideas."

Ideas? Zeke clenched, unclenched, and reclenched his left hand.

"About my Priscilla."

Ike laughed aloud. Zeke must have missed the joke.

"You can quit making a fist now."

59

"I wasn't—" Zeke stared at his hand.

"You were, big brother." Ike snatched the feed scoop from Zeke. "I told Pepper we could make money by charging people for a ride in her car. She's reiterating her opinion of my plan."

Had Zeke considered punching his brother? The two of them had been close for most of Ike's twenty-three years. Pepper had appeared only a few weeks earlier.

"Breathe, Zeke."

Zeke sighed, and the breath he actually had been holding, rushed out. "Sorry. I don't know why—"

"You like her. That's why." Headed toward the end wall, Ike stepped in front of Zeke. He took a pitchfork and handed another to his brother. "Forget about her for a bit, though, and let's get this finished."

"It's that obvious?"

"Yes."

Great. If Ike knew, Mom surely suspected. Joe, too. And probably Anna. Had Pepper said anything? He could text his sister and find out what she knew.

"Zeke." Ike had prodded him with the handle of the pitchfork. "She's cute. And funny."

Zeke smiled.

"But you told me she's not saved."

Zeke's shoulders sagged. "I know."

"Be careful."

Would Ike understand Zeke's dilemma? "When Anna and I found her, she needed help."

"So you helped."

"Yeah, and when she told me she's mad at God, I knew she needed more help."

"So you tried to help there, too."

Opting for cleanup over soul searching, Zeke headed for Axle's stall. Ike's words followed him.

"Then those green eyes sparkled at you."

So Ike had noticed.

"And that feisty attitude challenged you."

Ike's words continued to prod him. Zeke looked up.

"And her love for animals snagged you."

"Now I need help."

* * *

60

"Infection has set in." Shortly before five, Mom and Anna had returned from the hospital. Gathering the family together, Mom relayed the information to Zeke and everyone else. "At least it's in only one knee. And it appears to be in the skin and tissue, not in the artificial joint itself." A bit of good news. "They're concerned about the other knee, but they hope the antibiotics will stop this infection and prevent another."

"How's Gramps?" Toby gulped the words.

"He's worried. He thinks it's his fault."

"How could she have had such a good report on Friday and be so bad today?" Joe voiced Zeke's own question.

"Infection works fast on the inside." Mom clutched Dad's hand. "The symptoms often arise quickly."

"But it can be cured, right?" Toby's optimistic words contradicted the worry in his tone.

"Almost always." Mom's voice cracked. Dad drew her to his shoulder.

Anna spoke. "It depends on the case. But it's rarely quick or easy."

* * *

Pepper had broken her own speed record on the way back to campus. Good thing no police were monitoring her route. As soon as she'd entered the dorm, she began texting. Hospital regulations prohibited cell phone use, but Pepper tried Anna anyway. No reply.

She had numbers for both Zeke and Ike. Their quick responses helped, but neither relayed any solid information. She'd reached text number seven, when Anna finally called, relaying the serious prognosis and pouring out her concern for both Gram and Gramps.

"What can I do?" There had to be some way to help Anna.

"You could check on my goldfish."

"Didn't you ask Kendra to?" Anna's roommate never went anywhere on the weekend.

"Yeah, but I told her that two days ago. Who knows how long she remembered?"

It wasn't much, but Pepper jumped up. "I'm putting on my shoes right now."

"Gram will get better, won't she, Pepper?"

Being a pre-med student and EMT had its drawbacks. "The doctors have seen this before. New antibiotics are approved every day. Try not to worry."

"Everyone's praying."

61

Pepper imagined the family gathered around the table, asking God to help Mrs. Hanna. Would He? Perhaps this was the test case that Pepper needed. If Mrs. Hanna recovered, Pepper might be willing to trust God— a little. Another thought rushed through Pepper's brain. Maybe her bitterness that He hadn't kept Ranie in Pepper's life would be even more pronounced if He healed Mrs. Hanna. God was in a tough spot with Pepper, no matter how Mrs. Hanna fared.

* * *

Zeke paced the hallway of his house. Each step brought back a portion of the conversation with Ike. Even though he'd done his best to hide his feelings for Pepper, several people knew or guessed. *You let her tease you about apples.* Mistake number one. *You sat next to her at supper.* His second mistake. If only he'd stuck to his original plan. *Then you allowed her to come with you to see Axle.* The clincher.

His steps halted. A smile crossed his face. He shook his head, again, when he replayed the picture of her climbing into and out of Axle's pen. Had he ever known a girl who'd do something like that? Never.

Rapping himself on the skull with his knuckles, Zeke halted the memories. This was getting him nowhere. He had to look forward. Anna was the logical first step. He would volunteer to drive her back to campus first thing in the morning. He needed answers and the time to get them.

* * *

"Zeke, stop tapping the steering wheel."

He stilled his fingers and turned to Anna. "Sorry." He negotiated a curve. "Did Mom say Gram was any better?"

"You asked me that five minutes ago. I told you, yes."

"Guess I forgot."

Anna turned her attention back to the textbook she was reading. Zeke concentrated on the road.

"You're tapping." Anna's tone was sharper. "What is wrong with you?"

"Guess I'm nervous—about Gram." It was partly true.

"You're making me nervous. Calm down, and let me study."

He tried. He really did. The clutch of Anna's hand on his wrist indicated his lack of success.

She slapped her book closed. "What's up?" She stared at the side of his face. "And don't tell me it's 'nothing.'"

62

Anna would know if he lied. And she'd tell him so. He checked his rear view mirror. He adjusted the temperature knob. He sat forward in his seat. He coughed. "It's Pepper."

"Uh-huh."

"Uh-huh, what?" Zeke sneaked a quick glance at his sister. "What's that mean?"

"It means I was wondering." Anna turned slightly toward him.

That made two of them. "Has she said anything?"

"About you?"

Of course, about him. Why else would he ask?

Anna rested her back against the passenger door. "She's been uncharacteristically quiet."

He cleared his throat. Of all the times for Pepper not to volunteer her opinion.

"What do you want her to say?"

Zeke struggled for words that wouldn't make him sound like a desperate teenager. "That she likes me." Exactly the phrase he had hoped to avoid.

"Because you like her?"

Could the conversation be any more juvenile? "I do." The crack of his voice completed the junior high scene. "But she doesn't know the Lord. She has no desire to." His driving gave him an excuse not to look at Anna. "It's bad enough I've gotten myself involved. I mixed you up in it, too."

"She's my friend." Anna reached for Zeke's forearm. "We may have met her when she was drunk, but Pepper's not usually that way. She's never encouraged me to drink. Or asked me to do anything else I wouldn't want to do." Anna squeezed his arm. "I can be a testimony to her. I've already told her about our church and some of my beliefs."

"And she listened?"

"And politely told me that she disagreed with much of what I said."

Zeke spun his head in her direction and gaped.

Anna pointed her index finger at him. "Politely told me." Conviction coated each word. "And she didn't ask me not to talk about God again."

Why had she stopped Zeke in his tracks when he mentioned God? "I guess I was right. You should have talked to her about her need."

"I will."

Zeke shook his head. "She doesn't want to hear."

"She doesn't want to hear now. Or from you." Anna's scowl resembled the one his mother wore when she chided him. "You rushed her."

First the words from God. Now a reprimand from his sister. Zeke bristled. "It's not something she should put off." He set his jaw and gazed out the windshield. "She rushes headlong into everything else."

"And you deliberate on everything. Except her."

"Wait a minute—"

"Think about it, Zeke."

He clamped his mouth shut.

"You groused at me because I wouldn't talk to her on the Monday after we met her."

He flinched.

"Almost every time since then, you've asked me if I've spoken about God." Anna stopped until he glanced in her direction. "You had marked this weekend as THE time. You even skipped church."

"I wanted to be alone with her."

Anna tilted her head and glanced sideways at him.

Too late, Zeke recognized his admission. "So that I could talk to her about God and not be interrupted."

"Did you talk to God about it first?"

An imaginary knife stabbed his heart. He hadn't prayed. Not specifically about Sunday morning.

"Until you barged in yesterday morning at breakfast and announced your intention to stay home and talk with Pepper, I'd planned to ask her to come along with us."

"She wouldn't have."

"Maybe not. But she really wants to see Bethany." Anna assumed Pepper's voice and inflection. "'The girl who has captivated the much-sought-after Joe is worth meeting.'"

Zeke resisted the urge to bang his head on the steering wheel. No sense in causing an accident. He'd done enough damage already.

CHAPTER 8

Before the deluge of rejection letters, Pepper had looked forward to the last few weeks of her senior year. She'd imagined her return home, the victorious undergrad ready to tackle the rigors of a prestigious, out-of-state medical school. Now she dreaded the explanations she'd have to make. Chafing over her rejection letters, she hated to set foot anywhere near Philadelphia.

Wednesday night she sat munching microwave popcorn and contemplating. Snagging a piece from the bag next to her on the bed, she tossed it into the air and positioned her mouth under it. It landed accurately. Her phone went off. She smiled at the screen. Anna should have news about Mrs. Hanna.

Pepper hit the button and leaned back against the wall. "I'm so glad you called."

Anna's quick laugh preceded her cheery voice. "Why?"

"I need a distraction."

"From what?"

"A pity party served up with popcorn."

Anna's voice sobered. "What has you down?"

"I'll tell you after you tell me why you called."

"I needed to share some good news about Gram."

"I love good news."

"Her fever is down. She's responding well to the antibiotics."

Relief rushed from Pepper in a huge sigh. "Great. Any idea about when she'll be released?"

"Not yet, but Gramps is already making plans. Mom is worried."

"Why?"

"Maybe caring for Gram will be too much for him, especially when the orchard gets really busy."

"Do you need him at the orchard?"

A sigh reached Pepper. Time elapsed. Finally Anna spoke. "He needs to be there."

65

Pepper's popcorn-filled hand halted in its path toward her mouth. "It means that much to him."

"He spends the cold winter counting the days until summer." She exhaled. "Mom wondered before Gram's surgery how the two of them would cope. Now she's really concerned."

"Could you hire a visiting nurse to come?"

"We could, but Gramps isn't keen on that idea. Says he doesn't want a stranger 'checking up' on him every day."

Pepper could imagine the words coming from his lips. "Maybe you or one of your brothers could do it."

"The best choice would be me. But Mom needs my help. Every day and early."

Soft rhythmic thumps met Pepper's ears. "What's that sound?'

Anna giggled. "Sorry. I'm tapping my phone against my head. Hoping I can pound an idea into my brain."

"Don't hurt yourself. I don't want to have to rush out and administer CPR. I . . ." She gasped, choked, and then coughed hard to remove popcorn from her windpipe.

"You okay?"

"Yeah." She cleared her throat. "Anna, I've got it."

"Got what?"

Pepper bounced up and down on the bed, scattering fluffy kernels everywhere. She dropped the phone on the bed and clapped her hands together. "Yes!" she exclaimed before reclaiming her phone. "Your solution. Me. I'm it." She clambered over the bed, gathering up popcorn with her free hand. "I'm an EMT and a soon-to-be pre-med graduate who needs a summer job. Gramps knows me, sort of, and after a day or two, we would be fast friends." Pepper flopped backward. "I'm the answer."

* * *

At Anna's suggestion, Pepper had called Sue and explained her idea. Sue had talked with Harold and with her parents. Mr. Hanna had discussed the plan with his wife.

A few days later, Sue Davies had called Pepper. "We've all prayed about it, and everyone agrees. We need you for the summer. Does your offer still stand?"

"Yessss!" Pepper's happy dance had nearly made her drop her phone. She'd recovered quickly and listened carefully as Sue outlined the plan.

Pepper would go through Mrs. Hanna's morning routine with her each day and then would go to the orchard to work. She'd have lunch with the Hannas, help Maggie through a round of physical therapy, and return to the orchard. At suppertime, armed with a meal Sue had promised to supply for the three of them, Pepper would go back to the Hanna's home. Her evenings would be hers to spend as she liked.

Pepper had assented readily. Pops had been more reluctant.

"You haven't been home since Christmas. I miss you."

"But we talk a lot. And I promise I'll call more often."

"It's not the same."

"I know, Pops, but the Hannas need my help. Besides, you're coming to graduation, aren't you?"

"Of course, I am."

"Plan to stay a few days. We'll take a road trip."

"And go where?"

"Your choice. Just tell me where I need to be and when."

Within a few minutes, the plans were set. Pepper would graduate on Saturday. She and her dad would set out from State College on a short vacation and would return to settle Pepper in at the Hannas' on Wednesday.

Anna's brothers agreed to get all Pepper's things, including Priscilla, to their grandparents' home after graduation. Pepper had saved the text from Ike.

"We'll cart your stuff. And wrestle over who gets to drive your Mustang. Cost = one more turn at the wheel for each of us when you get back."

Pepper had grinned. Pretty cheap, and very predictable, wages.

* * *

Pepper's last few days of undergrad studies flew by. Her dad arrived on Friday afternoon.

"You look great, Pops." She raced down the sidewalk and flung herself into his outstretched arms.

He squeezed her hard before releasing her and holding her at arm's length. "You do, too." Pulling her forward again, he hugged her. "You'll be a college graduate tomorrow. I don't know where the years have gone."

Pepper untangled herself from her dad's embrace and began, "I don't know where they went, either."

"Are you ready for supper?"

"Seafood?"

He laughed and nodded. "I figured that's what you'd want. How about Harrisons'?"

Pepper clapped her hands in front of her. "You're the best, Pops." She dashed toward the car. "I'm starving."

* * *

Pepper set her fork on her plate, wiped her mouth with her napkin, and slid her chair slightly back from the table. "I may not need to eat at all tomorrow." She smiled across the table at her dad.

His eyes were focused on her face, but his gaze lacked any comprehension of her words.

"Pops." She waved her hand in front of him. "Did you hear me?"

"Wha—what?" He shook his head and blinked. "I'm sorry. Guess I wasn't listening."

"You haven't been."

He sighed and leaned forward in his chair. Setting his fork and knife beside the half-finished shrimp scampi on his plate, he focused his gaze securely on his daughter. "We need to talk."

"If you're still concerned about my living with the Hannas, you can relax. You'll meet Anna and her—"

"It's not about summer."

His intent stare raised goose bumps on Pepper's arms.

"It's about tomorrow."

Pepper exhaled. Her dad was so silly and sentimental. "C'mon, Pops." She nudged his shoulder with her hand. "I promise you. I'm going to graduate." She grinned impishly.

"Ranie's coming. To your graduation."

Pepper tasted his words, digested their meaning, and spat her answer back. "She's *not* welcome."

Dad's stare bore a determination Pepper seldom saw in it. "She's your mother. She has a right to see you graduate."

Leaning closer to her dad, Pepper hissed, "She gave up that right when she deserted me."

"She didn't desert you."

Had her dad lost all sense? "She walked out. No, not walked. Ran." Pepper kept an unrelenting stare riveted on her father's face. "I call that desertion."

"I call it fear—and protection."

"Protection?" Dad really had lost his mind. Pepper couldn't sit in Harrisons' and listen to any more. She jumped up. "I'm going back to the dorm."

"Pepper, wait." Dad rose, too. He threw cash onto the table.

68

"I'll see you after commencement tomorrow." She bolted toward the door.

But her dad wasn't ready to end the conversation. And he was still quick. By the time she had reached the door, he was shoving it open for her. He snatched her upper arm, halting her immediately.

"You're going to hear me out."

Pepper flexed her arm, trying to release it from her dad's grasp. His grip held firm, and his eyes narrowed in their intensity.

"You owe me that much." His face pleaded with her to agree.

"This isn't about you," Pepper snarled. "It's about her."

Dad released her arm, turned away from her, and exhaled with a loud huff. Running a hand through his hair, he looked back at her. "It's about both of us. It always has been."

* * *

Dad opened the door to his hotel room and flipped on the light. Pepper entered the room, crossed to the large bed, and plopped onto the end of it. How had a great night out with her dad taken this turn?

Her father hung his coat in the closet before coming to meet her. Drawing something from his shirt pocket, he placed it in front of her. After she had taken it from him, he walked a few steps and sat in the chair in front of the desk.

Pepper stared at the crumpled, yellowed envelope in her hands. *Ken Staley* and the street and city of a home Pepper vaguely remembered stared back at her. She searched for a return address. There was none.

Pepper glanced at her dad. At his slight nod, she lifted the flap and slid a single sheet from the envelope. The blue ink had faded, but the message was clear.

You hate me. I know you do. I don't blame you. I hate myself. So much that I think about ending my life. I've been thinking about it for a while. What if, one day, I finally give in? What if Pepper is with me when I do? What if I harm her, too?

I won't hurt you anymore. I won't risk injuring her. Take care of my little girl.

Ranie

Pepper read the words twice. A third time. Then she glanced at her dad. Redness rimmed his eyes.

"How long have you had this?" Pepper looked for a postmark. There wasn't one. "Did she leave this the day she took off?" All this time her dad had known. Why hadn't he told her?

He shook his head. "She didn't leave it with me. It showed up in the mailbox about a year later. She must have driven by and put it there herself or had someone else do it."

"About a year later? That's over twenty years ago. You never said . . . You let me think . . ."

"You never wanted to hear. Every time I tried to explain, you blamed her and got angry. You stormed out or you vented with a verbal tirade." He braced both hands on the arms of his chair. "I didn't want your anger to be turned on me. Maybe I'm a coward. Maybe I was irresponsible. I still don't know." His head drooped. He studied his shoes. Finally he looked up. "I do know this. You needed a parent who loved you and was there for you. I couldn't risk your throwing me aside, too."

"I wouldn't have done that." How could her dad think she would?

"What did you, an adult about ready to graduate from college, do at the restaurant tonight when I mentioned your mom?"

Pepper's outburst replayed in her mind.

"How would you have reacted when you were a teenager?" His gaze remained after his words faded.

Daggers of guilt stabbed Pepper's heart.

"How was I to know you'd treat me any differently?"

Pepper gaped at her dad. Then she switched tactics. "You believe this?" She waved the letter at him. "How do you know it's not a lousy mom's attempt to make herself feel better?"

Dad stared at the floor. "I loved her." He raised his head but wouldn't look at Pepper. "Even before we found out about you, I saw her pain. I didn't understand it. I should have tried to."

On her dad's face, Pepper read the guilt of two decades. Her heart constricted. Her defiance wilted. She dragged a chair in front of his and faced him. "You were a kid."

"So was she." His gaze searched Pepper's face. "A troubled kid."

Waves of compassion instantly turned to prickles of resentment. "Maybe you can believe her, but—" Pepper released herself from his stare and looked past his shoulder.

"But you can't." He slapped both hands onto his knees. "You don't know what she was going through. You don't know what she has experienced since or what her life is like now." Intensity gleamed in her dad's eyes. "But you're sure she was lying. You're positive she's unworthy."

70

"I don't trust her. Why should I?" She held up the letter. "According to this, I'm right not to."

"Do you trust me?" The earnestness in his words chilled Pepper's spine.

"I always have." Foreign thoughts invaded her mind. *He had the letter. He should have told you. You deserved to know.* She stared at the paper she held.

"Do you still?"

She forced her gaze back to his.

He didn't wait for her answer. "Ranie wants to see you."

"Why, now?"

"It's a long story. It's her story."

Pepper inhaled, ready to dissent.

"She wants to tell you. She's been trying to for weeks." His tone rebuked her. "How many texts and calls have you ignored?"

"I've never had a mom."

"Are you willing for that to change?"

She glanced at the letter she held.

His gaze lowered.

She studied the man who had concealed information from her for years. She examined his slumped shoulders and dejected stance.

Then she saw Pops—her number one fan, her shoulder to cry on, her protector, her counselor. She leaned forward. His strong, warm arms engulfed her.

* * *

Pepper paced and fretted Saturday morning. Repeatedly she punched in a text to her dad telling him that she had changed her mind. She had decided not to meet Ranie after commencement. Each time, just before sending it, she would delete the message and drop the phone into her purse.

Despite her warring thoughts, graduation activities went off without a hitch. Before Pepper knew it, she had a diploma in her hand and groups of new grads crowding around for pictures. Coming across the lawn, her dad beamed at her. He held out a bouquet of flowers and reached in for a hug.

"I'm so proud of you." Out of character tears streaked his cheeks.

She squeezed his neck. "Pops, don't make me cry."

Releasing him, she scanned the people nearest her. Anna rushed toward her. Pepper squealed, and Dad stepped aside.

"You did it. Hooray for you." Anna snagged Pepper's diploma and looked inside. "You're official."

"Kinda hard to believe, huh?" Happy tears persisted. Pepper wiped them away with her flowing sleeves. "Anna, this is my dad, Ken Staley."

Anna offered her hand. "Nice to meet you, Mr. Staley." Mr. and Mrs. Davies caught up with Anna just then. She motioned toward them and spoke to Pepper's dad. "These are my parents, Harold and Sue Davies."

"Glad to meet all of you. I'm Pepper's dad." Releasing Sue's hand, he strode down the sidewalk to his right. "And this is Pepper's mom."

Ranie Phelps—Pepper's mother—had indeed come. Pepper studied the person next to her dad, mentally comparing the woman's face with the one in a faded photo she had seen. Her mental image was a younger version of the person standing at Dad's side. She was short, like Pepper. But today she wore high heels that Pepper never would have been able to manage without falling on her face. Ranie's navy blue dress had classic lines and was a perfect fit. Her tight, dark curls, so like the ones that Pepper battled each morning, framed her face in an attractive way. In appearance, Ranie Phelps was a woman any girl would have been proud to claim. Too bad that appearance wasn't everything.

While Anna's parents greeted Ranie, Zeke stepped toward Pepper. He held out a small teddy bear which wore a blue mortar board and gown and carried a diploma. "It's corny but traditional."

Pepper grinned and took the bear from him. "Thanks, Zeke." She stood on her tiptoes to hug him quickly. Then she turned to the other well wishers. "Dad, this is Anna's oldest brother, Zeke."

Pops looked up. "Another tall person." He clenched Zeke's hand.

"Zeke, this is my dad, Ken Staley." Pepper caught Ranie's glance. What was the look on Ranie's face? Apprehension? Regret? "And this is Ranie Phelps."

Ranie offered her hand. "I'm Pepper's mother."

* * *

Pepper's mom.

Zeke managed not to gulp. After shaking hands, he moved next to Anna who handed him her phone. "Take a picture of Pepper and me."

He did. Then he took one of Pepper, Anna, and Kendra, who had suddenly appeared. Then Anna pulled Mom and Dad into the group and the three of them posed with Pepper. He had just snapped the last shot when Mr. Staley slid a camera into his free hand.

"Take a few for me, will you?"

He draped his arm around Pepper. Both of them gleamed. Zeke pressed the button. Great picture.

Then Mr. Staley left Pepper and stepped to the fringe of the group. Taking the arm of Pepper's mom, he urged her forward until mother and daughter stood next to each other. He positioned himself on Pepper's other side. Zeke counted to three and took the picture. Tension creased the faces of both women, but their posed smiles nearly matched. Mr. Staley turned to talk to Zeke's dad. Pepper and Ranie looked at each other. Zeke snapped one last photo.

* * *

"You're sure you have everything?" Pops asked as he and Pepper stood beside his car in the Hanna's driveway.

Leaving State College after commencement, the two of them had traveled together for the better part of five days, and he'd asked several times about things that she might need. He'd bought several items and had wanted to purchase more, but she'd curtailed him.

"I'm staying in someone's home. I have access to kitchen, laundry, food, couch, beds—everything. I can't take over their house." She grinned at his chagrined face. "I have only one room."

"You'll buy it if you need it?"

"I will."

He slipped a piece of paper from his wallet. "Walt says this mechanic is very good. If you have any trouble with Priscilla—" He paused as Zeke paced down the sidewalk toward them. "Do you know of this place?" He handed the paper to Zeke.

"Sure. About ten miles from here. He takes care of all our vehicles."

"If Priscilla needs anything—"

"We'll take her to Red Kauffman."

Dad turned back to Pepper. "Did you write down the addresses of both the orchard and the Hannas?"

"No, I forgot. You could look them up online. Or put them into your phone."

Dad pulled a small tablet and a pen from his shirt pocket. Handing them to her, he said, "I'm old school. Humor me."

Zeke spoke. "Gramps is inside. Have him get you a business card for the orchard and then write his name and address on the back."

Thrusting the paper and pen toward Zeke, Pepper said, "Write them in here, will you?"

Pops intercepted the items before Zeke took them. "I like the business card idea." He nodded up the sidewalk.

Pepper huffed a sigh. "Come on, Pops."

Angling his head toward her, he raised his eyebrows and pointed in the direction of the house. "Have him add his phone number in case I can't reach your cell."

Pepper lifted one hand in his direction. "Not necessary."

"Humor me. I'm—"

"Yeah, I know, you're old school."

* * *

After watching Pepper until she reached the door, Mr. Staley pulled his own business card from his shirt pocket. "Give this to your grandfather, please. Tell him to call me if anything comes up that he thinks I should know about."

"Everything will be fine."

"Probably. But I'll feel better if he has this."

"We'll take good care of her."

"We?"

Zeke coughed. "We. All of us." He forced himself to look Mr. Staley in the eyes. "She'll be like part of the family."

"Make sure she's like a sister. Not like someone's wife."

Zeke's face blanched. "That won't happen."

"Four boys—young men—in your family." His gaze continued to peg Zeke where he stood. "You understand my concern."

Zeke nodded.

"I've been hearing a lot about your family these last few days." He glanced in the direction that Pepper had gone. "I think I can trust you. If I didn't, she wouldn't be staying, at least not with my blessing."

"She has your blessing?"

"She does. And your family—" The wording included everyone, but Mr. Staley had cornered only Zeke. "Your family does, too. Don't do anything to change that."

Ken Staley turned to the car and reached into the glove box. Looking back, he held out a photo to Zeke.

"Thanks for catching this shot of Pepper and Ranie. It's special. From what Pepper says, you're encouraging her to reconnect with her mom."

Mr. Staley shifted his weight.

"I appreciate your help," he said. "Thought you might want your own copy."

* * *

She has my blessing. Don't do anything to change that. Hours later Zeke still wondered why Mr. Staley had manufactured the opportunity to deliver his admonition to Zeke alone. Could he sense Zeke's attraction to Pepper? What all had she told her dad about him over the past few days? And what about the photo? Zeke had been staring at it when Pepper reached the car.

"Whatcha got Zeke?" She'd leaned toward the picture.

"Me?" he'd sputtered. "Oh, nothing." He'd dashed the picture into his back pocket.

After shaking hands with Pepper's dad, Zeke had gone into the house to say hello to Gramps and get the latest report on Gram. Gramps had been in the kitchen when Zeke walked into the living room. Zeke pulled the picture from his pocket and then glanced out the window. Pepper hugged her dad tightly before releasing him and stepping back from the car. She blew him a kiss and waved as he drove down the driveway. She never turned away until the car had pulled onto the road.

"Ezekiel. Are you in there?"

"What— what?" Zeke shook his head and blinked.

Gramps stood a few feet from him. "Thought you were a thousand miles away."

"Not quite that far."

CHAPTER 9

Pepper unpacked the essentials for her first night, followed Fred on a tour of the ranch-style home, and then rode along with him to the hospital.

Her heart knit immediately with Maggie Hanna's. Pepper had no trouble seeing why Fred loved his wife so much. Even with the pain of bilateral knee replacement and the added complication of infection, Maggie was sweet to the core.

"I'm grateful that you were able to come this summer. Fred's days will be so busy. And I wouldn't want him to miss any of it."

"They could get along without me just fine."

Maggie reached an IV-bearing hand toward him. "I don't want them to have to because of me."

Fred had timed their visit with what he hoped would be the doctor's rounds. Dr. Girardi didn't disappoint.

"Good afternoon, Maggie. How are you today?"

"You tell me."

The young surgeon, wearing a blue dress shirt and coordinating tie but devoid of a lab coat, leaned toward her. "Looks like you're making progress." He turned to Fred. "How are things with you today, Mr. Hanna?"

"Looking up." He nodded in Pepper's direction. "I brought my summer helper with me. Graduated in pre-med from Penn State last week."

Raising his eyebrows, the doctor reached over to shake her hand. "Congratulations. Been accepted to med school yet?"

Her heart flip-flopped at the first time to have to publicly proclaim her way-down-the-list choice. "I'm going to Pitt this fall."

His broad smile revealed beautiful white teeth. "That's my alma mater."

"Really?"

"Yep. Their med school doesn't get the credit it deserves. Great program."

"What made you choose orthopedics?"

"Transformers toys. Sci-fi movies."

While they talked, he examined the skin around Maggie's right knee. "Infection appears to be lessening. I think we caught it in time." He flipped the bed covers over the right knee and lifted them from the left. "I don't see any signs of infection here."

"Do I get to go home?"

"Sorry. Fred and—what's your name?"

"Pepper."

He titled his head and smiled. "Fred and Pepper will have to survive without you for a few more days." He slapped Fred's shoulder. "Can you do it?"

"We don't like it, but we can take it."

The younger man laughed. "We'll send her home as soon as we can." Walking toward the door, he motioned to Pepper.

"I'll be right back, Mr. Hanna."

"My name's Fred," he called without even looking toward her.

Once in the hall, Pepper found Dr. Girardi.

"She has several points in her favor." He'd started talking as soon as she approached. "No diabetes, no immune disorders, no chemo or steroids, good circulation, no extra weight." He leaned back against the wall. "Knowing how it happened could be important now so that we can prevent it from happening again or in the other knee."

"Contamination during surgery?" It was rare, but it occurred.

"You don't mince words, do you?"

"Trying to analyze the possibilities."

"One knee and not the other makes me doubt that." He closed his electronic tablet. "That and my perfect record."

"Impressive."

"Crucial in today's society."

Pepper nodded. Surgeons paid dearly for malpractice insurance. "I'll guard her from cuts that could introduce bacteria."

"Keep her away from dental procedures. And moisturize her skin daily so that it doesn't crack open." He shoved away from the wall. "They're great people. I'm glad you're staying with them."

"Me, too."

"See you around." He reopened his tablet as he continued down the hall.

Still pondering his advice, Pepper re-entered Maggie's room.

"Did he ask you on a date?" Fred grinned widely at her.

She couldn't help but smile back. "What?"

"A date. You know. A man and a woman going out somewhere together."

Pepper laughed aloud. "I know what a date is." She hadn't been on one in a while, but she wasn't going to make any such admission to Fred. "What I don't know is why you'd think he would ask me on one."

"A doctor, a pre-med student. You have things in common."

"I have things in common with other guys, too." She pulled a chair closer to where Fred sat. "That doesn't automatically lead to dates."

"Anything in common with any of my grandsons?"

"Fred, you're meddling." Maggie's admonition earned her a quick scowl and a wave of dismissal from her husband.

Pepper pulled her feet up onto her chair. "All of them seem to like my Mustang."

Fred cackled and leaned toward Maggie. "You shoulda seen those boys and that car."

"I can imagine."

"Probably that's not quite enough in common to initiate dates." Pepper directed her comment to Fred. "Especially with all four of them."

"Let's hope not."

* * *

Thursday promised to be filled with not much except unpacking and making another visit to the hospital. Maggie didn't need at-home care yet. Fred was headed to the orchard. Pepper puttered around, stowing some clothes in a dresser and hanging others in a roomy closet. She carried a few things to the kitchen and then sat down to enjoy a mug of hot chocolate. The night had been clear and crisp. Hopefully, the forecast of a sunny day proved true.

She was sipping contentedly when she heard her phone. Too bad she hadn't remembered to bring it with her to the sofa. Plopping the cup onto an end table, she scurried to her bedroom.

"Can you come over?" Anna blurted the words.

"Is something wrong?"

"Gramps fell and bumped his head. We're wondering whether he should go to the ER."

"Is he bleeding?" Pepper heard voices in the background.

Anna relayed the answer. "A little. He has a small cut."

"Is he alert?"

"Alert enough to be complaining that we're calling you."

"Is there a bump?"

78

"Yes. It's big."

"Is it discolored?"

"No."

"Have you applied ice?"

"Yes."

"Good. Keep it on. I'll be right there. Bye."

Pepper scurried back down the hall. Fred's injury didn't sound serious, but he would need observation for a while. She dressed quickly, washed her face, ran her fingers through her mass of curls, and then snagged her coat and keys. Slipping her phone into a pocket, she headed for the door. Then she remembered.

She didn't know how to get to the orchard. She'd have to call for directions. She plunged her hand into the pocket and pulled out her ringing phone.

"Do you know the way?" Zeke's voice was much more controlled than Anna's had been.

"I was just reaching to call you."

"Turn right out of the driveway."

"Wait." She scanned the desk for a paper and pen. "I have to write this down."

Zeke completed the simple directions and finished with, "Watch for the orchard sign at the end of the road."

The obtrusive sign was much more obvious than the entrance to the tree-lined road.

"Be careful."

Pepper smiled. That was Zeke. Always the protector.

* * *

"Those stones got the better of you this time, didn't they?" Fred was settled in a kitchen chair when Pepper arrived. She'd examined the cut and the swollen bump and had heard his story of what had happened.

"Shifty, tricky things."

"Were you hurrying?"

"You sound like Sue and Anna."

Pepper cleaned and dressed the wound as they talked. "Were you?"

"People were waiting."

"Your hurrying made them wait longer." She bent slightly and looked squarely at him. "And worry about you."

"They worry too much."

"Because they care." Pepper applied the small Band-Aid and stepped back. "I think Maggie would have called me if she'd been here."

"I'm glad she wasn't. And don't you tell her." His eyes gleamed. "I'll be the one to do that. She knows I fall."

Pepper rested her hand on Fred's shoulder. "I bet she hurts with you when you do."

Fred nodded his bruised head. "I think she hurts more."

* * *

Headed back outside with the cell phone his dad almost always forgot in the house, Zeke left the living room where he'd retrieved Dad's phone from the coffee table. Nearing the kitchen, he heard Pepper's voice. "Were you hurrying?"

Zeke froze where he was. Several seconds later he raised his head and looked toward the ceiling. God's voice hadn't been audible, but Zeke had heard His reassurance in the words Pepper spoke to his grandfather. Having her here for the summer was by God's design. Zeke knew his next step.

* * *

"I want to show you something." Zeke handed the catalog toward his father who sat in his easy chair after supper Thursday night.

Dad closed the newspaper he'd been reading. "What's on your shopping list?"

Zeke coughed as he lowered himself to the nearby sofa. "A cart for Axle."

"A what?" Dad ignored the pictured items and stared at his oldest son.

"A miniature cart for Axle. So that kids can take rides in it."

Dad finally looked at the catalog in his hand. "Whew!" A low whistle accented his opinion. "Steep."

"I know, but I found a guy who has one used. It needs repairs and some paint, but I could fix it up. And we could charge a little for each ride."

Zeke's dad studied the page more carefully. "This thing is small. Perfect for Axle, but terrible for the rest of us. We'd be eating our knees while we tried to drive it." He leveled a skeptical glance toward Zeke. "And I'd worry that any of us would be a heavy load, especially with an extra passenger." He let the catalog drop into his lap. "I don't see how—"

"Pepper could do it." Placing his hand on the arm of the sofa, Zeke leaned over the end and toward his father. "She suggested it. The first night she was here."

"She suggested driving a cart we don't have?" Dad placed both hands behind his head, resting them against the cushion and his head on top of them. Then he waited.

"That's exactly what she did." Zeke gulped and plunged ahead. "She asked what you could do with a mini donkey besides pet him. I said some people hitch donkeys up to a mini cart and drive it around. She started jumping up and down, saying, 'Can I drive?'"

"But we don't have a cart."

"That's what I told her." Zeke nodded emphatically.

"What did she say then?"

"That when, not if, we got a cart, she wanted to learn to drive it because she'd be perfect for the part."

Zeke's dad began to laugh. "I like her spirit." He set the recliner forward, bringing himself nearer to his son. "I think she may be right." He deliberated a moment and then patted the arm of his chair. "Besides, if she can bring in the money we spend on food for that mangy mule, I may have to give her a raise."

Just like that, the decision was made. Zeke left the room muttering to himself. Dad never made his mind up so quickly. God was at work.

* * *

Pepper moved her checker into an adjacent black square. A discreet cough met her ears. She glanced toward Fred, who was shaking his head.

"Why is that not a good move?"

"Because if you move there," he said, pointing to the square her piece now occupied, "I'll move like this." He jumped two of her red checkers and landed in a square where his piece was completely safe.

She gaped at her stupidity. "I'm looking at the same board you are. I never saw that move. I stink at checkers."

Fred laughed. "You do need some practice." The sound of a car engine caught their attention. Fred shuffled to the window. "Sounds like we're getting company."

Pepper joined him. "Were you expecting anyone?"

"Nope." He elbowed her. "Thought you might have a hot date with Maggie's doctor."

Pepper nudged him in return. "I don't." But it might be fun if she did.

Fred narrowed his gaze as a black vehicle neared the house. "Guess Zeke will have to do. That's his Jeep."

"I'll take care of the checkers." Pepper headed toward the table, but Fred's words halted her.

"No need for that. I might be able to convince my grandson to challenge me in a game."

Pepper pulled herself to her fullest height and faced him, her arms akimbo. "I thought I was challenging you."

Fred's guffaw was loud and long. "You were pushing the pieces around while I challenged you." He headed toward the kitchen. "Get the door, will you? I need a drink of water."

She hurried to comply. The phrase "hot date" raced through her mind and back. Dr. Girardi definitely fit that description. Young, good looking, professional. What about Zeke? Could he be considered "hot"? She tripped on a small throw rug near the door and pitched forward, nearly falling. Clutching the knob, she righted herself. The doorbell rang. She gave the knob a quick twist. Better to think about Zeke's temperature later.

"Hi, Gramps—uh—Pepper," Zeke stammered. He opened the storm door and stepped inside.

"Hi, Zeke." He wasn't wearing the brown insulated jacket. And, uncharacteristically, no knit cap covered his wavy brown hair. "You surprised us."

He held some rolled up papers in his hands and tapped the pages against his palm several times before he spoke. "I need to ask you something."

Hot date. Pepper gulped.

"Evening, Ezekiel."

Zeke and Pepper turned toward Fred.

"Hi, Gramps. How's your head?"

"Good as ever." Fred leveled his gaze toward Pepper. "Some folks worry too much."

She angled her head in his direction. "Some folks hurry too much."

"Hummph." Fred looked toward Zeke. "Got time for a game of checkers?'

"Not tonight." Zeke slid his fingers back and forth under his shirt collar. "Mind if I borrow Pepper for a bit?"

"Borrow me?" She grasped his wrist. "Is someone else hurt?"

"No." He finally looked directly at Pepper. "Everyone's fine."

Pepper exhaled.

Fred answered. "I can spare her for the rest of the evening. I was about to head in and read any way. Haven't got to my Bible today." He turned toward his room. "See you kids in the morning."

* * *

Zeke needed to focus. He tried. But the small fingers that still held his wrist overshadowed ideas of Axle and a miniature cart.

"What did you need to know?"

Her glinting, green eyes befuddled him further. He looked away. Then he remembered the pages in his hand. He unrolled the catalog and pointed to a picture. "Will you . . ."

She grabbed the papers from him, stared hard at the page, and then stomped the floor quickly while turning in circles. "Yes! Yes! A hundred times, yes!"

Zeke clutched her elbow as it spun by. The storm calmed. "The cart I'm getting isn't as fancy as that. It's a used one that will have to be fixed up."

"Who cares?" She waved the paper in front of him. "We're getting a cart."

How had she figured the "we"?

Rescuing the crumpled catalog from her grasp, he stuck it into his coat pocket. Then he removed the coat and hung it on a peg near the door. "We have to discuss some things, but first I need something to drink." He stepped toward the kitchen.

"Several choices in the fridge." She followed him.

When he stopped and turned abruptly, she bumped into him. He reached to steady her. "I can get my own drink." A half-smile crossed his lips. "I've been here before."

"Who says I'm waiting on you?" She freed herself and plunged ahead, looking back to wiggle her eyebrows at him. "If we're discussing business, I need fortification."

So did he. But it had nothing to do with something to drink.

* * *

Pepper rolled over, blinked her eyes into focus, and stared at the clock. The red letters declared 5:30. She groaned and pulled the pillow over her head. Why had she agreed to start training at 6:30?

Images from last night reappeared.

"If Davies' Orchard is going to offer donkey cart rides, we have to advertise." Zeke's soft voice cracked with conviction. "If we advertise, we have follow through." He'd reached across the short space between them on the couch to clasp her shoulder. "We can't do that without you."

Pepper had had to look away under his intense earnestness.

She'd seen sincerity of purpose in numerous doctors whose lives were devoted to healing others. She'd seldom noticed it elsewhere. Maybe she hadn't been looking.

Zeke certainly had an ardor for what he did. She'd seen it during his long hours in the orchard each day and in his constant efforts to keep improving the family business. She'd read it in his eyes when she accepted the challenge of training Axle. His quiet demeanor had tricked her into underestimating the emotion that lay beneath Zeke's calm exterior, but the man was passionate.

Passion. The word had startled her. It had also ignited a blazing truth. Zeke Davies could definitely be considered hot.

* * *

"You're up with the birds this morning."

Pepper jumped. Her hand flew to her chest. She peered into the darkness. "Fred?"

"Over here, in the rocking chair."

"You scared me."

A soft chuckle rose from his direction. "I didn't mean to." The rocker creaked. "I could see you. Never thought that you might not see me."

Her eyes located the chair and his shadowy form. "How long have you been sitting here?" She stepped closer.

"Since about five o'clock."

"Ugh. Do the people in this family have some type of early-riser gene in their blood?"

His arm motioned to her in the darkness. "Do you have time to sit a minute?"

"Remind me how long it takes to get to the orchard, assuming I can find the road through bleary eyes."

Another quiet laugh. "About five minutes. Watch for the patriotic mailbox on your left. The sign is about one hundred yards beyond that. The road is on the other side of the sign."

"Thanks for the tip." She sat down on the couch. "I have a few minutes. What's up?"

"You ever sit and watch the sunrise?"

"Not very often." She giggled. "It's beautiful but beyond reach for those of us who like to sleep in."

"You have to make a choice."

"Yeah, I guess so." Why was a sunrise so important?

"Seeing a sunrise is sort of like recognizing God in your life."

Stop. From seeing a sunrise to recognizing God. All in one second. Pepper couldn't keep up, especially at this hour.

"It happens every day if you take the time to notice."

In the murkiness of the early morning, Fred Hanna's steady gaze made Pepper squirm.

"I hope you'll take time to notice."

"Yeah. Okay." She jumped from the couch. "Gotta run."

* * *

Confusion reigned during the five-minute drive to the orchard. Pepper had felt a bond with Fred Hanna from the day they'd met. He had grit. He liked to laugh. He was kind to everybody.

But he might be a religious fanatic. Could she field his questions and stomach his comments during the course of this summer? And if she couldn't, what about Anna? And Axle? And Zeke?

The appearance of the patriotic mailbox halted her thoughts. The sun hadn't yet peaked over the horizon.

CHAPTER 10

Zeke had told her to park in his driveway and ring the doorbell when she arrived. Lights at one end of his home showed a glimpse of his kitchen. She mounted the porch steps and pushed the button.

"Be right there."

Heavy footsteps clomped in Pepper's direction. The door opened.

Zeke's hair was still wet. He hadn't buttoned his shirt. He was threading a belt through the loops of his pants. Avoiding her gaze, he muttered, "I overslept." He backed up. "Have a seat." He shoved some paperwork aside and motioned to a chair. "Happens about once a year. Had to be today."

Pepper tried not to stare. Thick brown waves of hair. Enough beard stubble to be fashionably scruffy. Tight lean abs. She might have swooned.

Then she saw his heavy work boots. "Your shirt isn't buttoned, but your boots are on. And tied."

Turning his back to her, he mumbled. "Pants first so you're decent." He paused. Once he'd buttoned his shirt, he faced her again. "Boots next, so you're ready to run."

"Out into the cold with no shirt and wet hair."

"Throw a shirt on as you go and jam a hat on your head when you get there."

How could anyone argue with that logic? But how was she going to forget the results of his reasoning? Seeing him without shoes would have left a much less indelible impression.

"Come on." He grabbed the brown jacket, snagged a knit cap, and ushered her out the door. Before they were halfway to the barn, he had the coat on and zipped. The hat covered the top of his wet head. Reaching the door before Pepper did, he tugged on the handle. "Should've put in a man door."

"A what?"

"A man door. Like the ones you find in a house. Wouldn't have to fight with this heavy thing every time." He leaned inside the barn and extended his arm. A light came on. Back outside, he shook his head. "City girl."

"And proud of it." She crossed in front of him. "Morning, Axle." Reaching the donkey's pen she extended her hand. Axle lifted his head. He didn't move from his spot. Zeke joined her. Now Axle did, too.

Slack jawed, she stared at Zeke. "I like him, but he prefers you."

Zeke's too rare smile curled the edges of his lips. "I feed him." He strode a few paces and grasped part of an open bale of hay.

Pepper beamed. "I knew there had to be a reason."

"Huh." Lifting the hay over the top rail, he deposited most of it next to Axle. One handful he tossed at Pepper.

"Hey." She glared in his direction before brushing the pieces from her jacket.

"You figured it out."

"What?"

He retrieved the clump from the floor and held it in front of her. "It's hay." He flung it at her again and strode toward a large wagon nearby.

"Very funny."

His voice floated from behind the equipment. "I thought so."

"Two can play this game," Pepper muttered to herself. She retrieved the hay, tucked both hands behind her back, and advanced in search of sweet revenge.

She didn't locate her target anywhere near the first wagon. She'd circled it once when Zeke came up behind her—from some undisclosed location—deftly snatching the hay from her hands and tugging her by the coat sleeve.

"I had plans for that hay."

"I figured." He nodded but kept moving. On the other side of a flatbed wagon, he stopped, halting her progress, too.

What was she looking at? This couldn't be the cart. There were two wheels attached to a metal frame, but everything screamed disrepair. The boards of the wooden seat were warped, and the poles that extended from the front of the cart were a dingy gray color, dotted with the bronze of corrosion. The cushion that had been on the back rest was now only partially there. She gulped.

"The basics are sound." Zeke stared at her staring at it.

"It's not what I expected."

"Not quite like the catalog picture, is it?"

His understatement didn't go far enough.

"Give me a few days." He headed toward the far wall of the building.

Pepper gawked a few seconds longer. Could she spend several hours a day in that? Would anyone want to ride along with her?

When she caught up with him, Zeke was stepping from the cubbyhole where she'd first met Axle. In his hands, he held shiny black leather straps with silver medallions sprinkled around.

"Not quite sure how all of that works, but I like the look of it."

"Come and find out." He headed toward Axle's pen, draping the conglomeration over the slats when he reached it. Grabbing a soft rope, he stepped inside the pen. Axle came to him.

"Today's the day you start earning your keep, my friend."

Pepper smiled. A different side of Zeke emerged when he worked with the animals. He talked freely and grinned often. She watched and listened.

"Hold him, will you?" He handed the lead rope to Pepper. She stepped inside and to the other side of Axle.

Lifting the leather mass from the slats, Zeke untangled two strands that Pepper soon recognized as reins. The rest formed a harness, which he held under Axle's nose. The little donkey sniffed it thoroughly and then tried to take a bite.

Zeke pulled his hands back. "No. It's not food." He petted Axle's head and waited before giving the donkey another chance to acquaint himself with the harness.

Several minutes passed. Zeke laid the reins across Axle's back. The donkey continued to breathe in the scent of the leather under his nose. Zeke opened the harness. Axle began to snuffle the inner surface.

"Here comes the test. Hold on."

Zeke slid the gear over the donkey's head and toward his back.

Axle stepped away.

"It's okay, Axle." Zeke looked at Pepper. "Pet him."

Pepper stroked the donkey's fur. With steady movements and constant verbal reinforcement, Zeke slowly navigated the harness onto Axle's back. Once everything was in place, a few buckles and snaps brought the whole process to completion.

One shiny medallion adorned Axle's forehead. Two decorated the sides of his head. The clasps and loops added other silver accents. Bending over the donkey, Pepper hugged him around his middle. "You look fabulous. You're the best miniature donkey ever." She released her four-footed friend and stared at the man across from her. "You are amazing with animals." Zeke busied himself with removing the lead rope, but Pepper didn't look away. Finally, she drew his attention. "Thanks for letting me be a part."

"The harness is only the beginning," Zeke said. "Axle still has lots to learn."

Pepper took quick steps to keep up with Zeke as he headed for his mom and dad's for coffee. His persistent yawns confirmed his need of it.

"What kind of things?"

"*Gee, haw, whoa,* and *back.*"

She halted and grabbed his arm. "*Whoa* and *back* I get. But what in the world are *gee* and *haw?*"

"Such a city girl." He started off again.

"Will you quit saying that?" She brought her hands to her hips and challenged him with a glare.

His bloodshot eyes almost smiled. "Thought you were proud of it." He clutched one elbow and propelled her along.

"Not the way you say it." She cocked her head and squinted at him. "But I bet I can navigate circles around you in city traffic."

"Maybe."

"No argument?"

"I need coffee."

"Will Anna be up?"

Zeke looked at his watch. "Two hours ago."

"I'll talk to her while you drink."

"In the bake shop helping Mom."

Pepper should have known. She turned toward the other building. "Pick me up there when you're finished with your coffee."

"Okay."

She started off and then heard him call.

"Come and get me in half an hour."

"What?"

"The house. Half an hour."

* * *

Still laughing from her conversation with Anna and Mrs. Davies, Pepper entered the kitchen. Zeke's coat and hat hung over the back of one chair. His sturdy shoes sat beside it. He was still here. She'd half expected him to come and get her. She was ten minutes late.

She crossed through the empty dining room. "Zeke?" The living room seemed empty too, until she noticed the couch. Stretched across it, with his feet dangling off one end, Zeke lay sound asleep. The ring of flattened hair indicated where his hat had been. Soft snores interrupted the stillness. Waking him would disturb what appeared to be a peaceful rest. But he'd told her to come and find him.

She called softly. "Zeke. Wake up, Zeke." No response. Stepping closer, she spoke again, more loudly. "Zeke. Hey, Zeke, wake up." Standing beside him now, she bent over slightly and directed her voice into his right ear. "Zeke."

He bolted upright. His arms flailed. His right elbow caught Pepper across the bridge of her nose and sent her reeling backward. Now fully awake, Zeke jumped from the sofa. "Did I hit you?" He erased the distance between them.

Tears threatened. Pepper blinked them back. Her eyes and nose stung from the blow. "I shouldn't have startled you."

"Are you hurt?"

Zeke's face looked as though he'd received the blow.

"My nose. I'll be all right." She pulled her hand away from her face. "I'll go take a look at it." She scurried from the room—toward a mirror and away from Zeke's compassionate gaze.

* * *

Having assured him that her nose and face would survive, she tugged him up from the kitchen chair where he sat lacing his boots. "Don't forget these." She handed him his hat and coat and headed out the door.

They returned to Axle to explore the world of donkey training.

"I still don't understand why I can't say *right* and *left* instead of *gee* and *haw*."

The one-sided conversation had begun during the return jaunt to the barn, during which Zeke showed Pepper the paths he had mapped out for Axle and the cart.

"Because *gee* and *haw* are the standard for horses and donkeys." Once inside the pen, he had given a gentle tug on Axle's reins to start the animal's progress toward the door.

"But if Axle learned *left* and *right*, he'd be smarter than the average donkey." For effect, she added big eyes and several quick head bobs.

"He'd know commands no one else uses." Zeke's response to her theatrics included a glare, a sigh, and a shake of his head. He turned to the donkey that trailed along behind. "Whoa, Axle." The animal stopped immediately.

"Way to go, Axle." Pepper patted his furry back. The donkey knew more than either of them had given him credit for.

90

"Do you want to do this?"

Zeke wasn't talking to Axle. Pepper ignored his question.

"Do you?"

She finally succumbed to his probing gaze. "You know I do."

"Can you do it the way I ask you to?"

He hadn't raised his voice, but his challenge blasted through her brain like screaming sirens. Weighty seconds elapsed before Zeke looked at the ground. With the toe of his work boot, he skimmed the surface of the dirt. And waited.

"Okay, you win. I'll do *gee* and *haw*." The words galloped from her lips. "I don't see the—"

"It's not about winning." The restless foot paused momentarily. "C'mon, Axle." Zeke pulled the reins. Four dark hooves and two brown boots started out of the barn.

Realization and guilt hit Pepper simultaneously. Realization that she was being left behind and guilt that what Zeke had asked wasn't unreasonable. The medical field had its protocol. Probably every profession did. Why shouldn't donkey trainers have theirs? "Zeke, wait."

One step later, the long legs halted as if Zeke's shoes had suddenly been set in concrete. He stood still, but he didn't look back.

He wasn't making her next move any easier. She hurried to him. "Sorry."

His jaw muscles relaxed.

"I'll do what needs to be done. And try not to argue."

"Okay." With Axle in tow, he headed down the path.

Pepper burst ahead. "Okay?" Once past him, she turned to walk backwards while he strode on. "This big confrontation, followed by my sincere apology, and all I get is 'Okay'"?

"Apology accepted."

What made him think this response was better? "You don't have anything to say?"

She stationed herself directly in front of him, crossing her arms and looking up to stare him down.

Zeke found something. "You were being childish."

The lack of malice in his tone kept Pepper from flinging out retaliatory insults and maybe a right jab.

"You apologized. I accepted." He nodded to Axle who had crept up beside him. "We have work to do." He clutched her elbow. Taking off again, he spun her around and propelled her along with him.

A few feet away from their destination, Pepper glanced up at him. His gaze quickly darted away. Maybe if she were a sheep, a rabbit, or even a donkey, he might have tried to put his thoughts into words. Maybe.

She shuddered away her disappointment. They did have work to do.

* * *

"Can I get my burger to go?" Zeke stood at Anna's shoulder as she placed large patties on the stovetop grill in front of her.

"I'm not a short-order cook." She arranged the last one into the remaining space and stepped to the sink to wash her hands. "And you know Dad's rule."

"I know. 'If you eat food from this kitchen, you eat it with the family.'" Zeke leaned his side on the counter and watched as Anna pulled lettuce, tomatoes, and an onion from the fridge. "But you know he makes an occasional exception. Especially for the orchard. Especially when we're busy."

"We're not busy. We're not even open." She brandished a kitchen knife in his direction.

"You're not busy. I'm always busy."

"You mean like right now?" She waved at the vegetables in front of her and then at him as he stood watching.

"I'm taking a short break." He shoved away from the counter "So how about it? Ten minutes?"

She contorted her face and rolled her eyes. "Anything else you need?"

"Lettuce, tomato, and ketchup." He rested a hand on her shoulder. "You've always been my favorite sister."

"Pffft." She shook her head and shoved him. "I'll see you in ten minutes."

"You're the best."

"Yeah, yeah, yeah."

Zeke headed to the barn. He could gather a few supplies while his burger cooked. His phone rang. "Zeke Davies," he said.

"Hello, Zeke."

The voice sounded familiar, but Zeke couldn't place it exactly.

"It's Harvey Milton. You bought a mini donkey from me a few weeks back."

"Yes, Mr. Milton." Zeke recalled the man's white hair and dark eyes.

"Everything okay with Axle?"

"He's fine." Zeke didn't elaborate on Axle's first night at the orchard. "We were working with him today."

"Doing what?"

"Getting him ready to pull a cart. Rides for the kids who visit the orchard."

"Sounds like a plan. I'm glad I called."

"Why's that?"

"A good friend passed away suddenly, and . . ." Harvey's voice broke.

"I'm sorry to hear that." Zeke stopped walking and waited for the voice to continue.

"Thanks." Another pause. "Walt had three mini donkeys and a cart. Took the grandkids for rides when they came to visit." Mr. Milton halted again. Swallowing hard a few seconds later, he continued. "Walt's son wants a pair of them and the cart, but they need a home for the other donkey. I thought of you."

Another donkey. Zeke shoved the knit hat around on his head as he pondered.

"This one's already trained to pull a cart."

A definite plus. Axle seemed willing enough to learn, but June would arrive soon and with it the first wave of visitors coming to pick strawberries. The donkey rides had already been advertised as part of opening day.

"Can you tell me where I can see him or who I can talk to?"

"Right now he's at my place. His name is Buster."

Zeke nudged the gravel around under the point of one shoe. Axle and Buster. "Will you be home this evening?"

"Sure." Mr. Milton's voice had regained some cheer.

"Give me a few minutes. I'll call you back." He would snag his sandwich and then hop into the truck and go to meet his dad who was working in one of the orchard's farthest fields.

* * *

"How long before you're ready to leave for the hospital?" Her bedroom door open, Pepper heard Mr. Hanna's voice as he called to her from the hallway.

She stuck her head out and yelled, "Just long enough to brush my teeth and grab a coat."

"I'll meet you in the truck."

Fred Hanna might have a limp, but Pepper struggled to keep up with him. If he told her they were leaving in ten minutes, he was putting on his coat in five. If he said to be ready at noon, he was waiting at 11:50.

In the bathroom a minute later, she coaxed toothpaste from the nearly empty tube. "Can't you see I'm in a hurry?" She dashed the small dab onto her brush and swished both under the running tap.

"Thought you had the night off."

Pepper shut off the spigot. Had Mr. Hanna called?

Toothbrush in hand, she walked back to her adjoining bedroom. Fred Hanna stood right outside her door. "Did you call me?" she asked him.

"I thought you were finished for the day."

"I am."

"Your boss is waiting for you in the living room."

"Mr. Davies?" Why would Harold need to see her?

"Yep."

"Is someone hurt?"

"I don't think so." Fred shrugged his shoulders.

Pepper started past him.

"You probably won't need that," he said, pointing to the toothbrush.

"Hope he doesn't mind if I take a minute to finish brushing." She pivoted and hurried to the sink. Her hand was poised above the faucet handle when Fred's voice drifted in from the other room.

"You don't care if she brushes her teeth, do you, Ezekiel?"

Zeke. She'd been expecting Harold. Technically Zeke was Mr. Davies, but now wasn't the time to be reminded of that fact. Fred Hanna liked a good joke. Too bad this one was on her. She brushed and spit with vigor. Wiping her mouth on a towel, she glanced at her damp curls. Why was Zeke here?

* * *

"Want to meet a donkey?"

"What?"

"A donkey. Do you want to go look at a mini?"

"Another one?" Her eyes widened. "A friend for Axle."

Zeke suppressed a grin. She had a heart for animals. "Someone to share the load."

"We'll train him, too?"

She didn't shy away from the thought of extra work. "Mr. Milton says he—"

Both of her fists shot into the air. "Yea! Two donkeys for cart rides." She gasped, and then her arms dropped to her sides. "I'm going with your grandpa to the hospital. He's waiting for me." She scurried toward the door.

"Gramps left as soon as he told you I was here."

She turned back toward Zeke. Her shoulders slumped. "I feel like I let him down."

"Don't worry. He said you could go tomorrow night."

"Was he disappointed?"

Less disappointed than I'll be if you don't go with me. The thought came easily, but Zeke couldn't muster the words. He gulped. "He was in a hurry to see Gram."

"I know. They're so cute together." She sighed through a smile. "I want that someday."

Zeke avoided her eyes. "Me, too." He stuck both hands into his pockets. "Are you going with me?"

"I'll race you to the truck." She scooted toward the door. "Don't forget to lock up."

A minute later, Zeke opened the driver's side door and climbed in. "You know you cheated."

She giggled and nodded. "And you know that those long legs give you an unfair advantage." She twisted toward him as far as the seat belt would allow. "I was evening out the odds."

"Is that what you call it?" Scanning her face quickly, he put the key into the ignition.

Her laughter filled the truck cab. "How long 'til we get there?"

At Pepper's child-like question, Zeke smiled into the darkening night. Once again he was glad that he and Anna had helped her.

* * *

"You have to buy him, Zeke."

After showing them to Buster's stall and answering Zeke's questions, Mr. Milton had returned to the house to let Zeke think it over.

"Look at those doleful brown eyes. He lost his master, his home, and his friends." Pepper stood beside the stoic donkey, patting his head and stroking his mane. "He needs Axle."

Zeke couldn't disagree. Buster seemed downcast. Did donkeys cheer up if their circumstances improved?

Overall, Buster looked healthy. Slightly taller than Axle, he wouldn't be likely to escape from the stall. He was nine years old. Axle was five. But since minis often lived to be about twenty-five or older, the two could be at the orchard for many years. Would they be compatible?

"Please, Zeke." Pepper clasped both hands around his elbow. "We have to take him home."

Her combination of *we* and *home* pulled hard at his heart. Ten minutes later, with Buster fastened securely in the bed of the pickup, the three of them headed off to meet Axle.

CHAPTER 11

Ten days with the Hannas. Where had the time gone? Just over a week until Memorial Day. With Maggie back home for the last four days, Pepper's life was as packed as that of an overworked surgeon. Up at 5:30. Who was this early riser? And what had she done with Pepper Staley? At the orchard by 6:30. Training Axle until Maggie called her, usually around 8:00. Assisting Maggie for an hour or two. Back to the orchard until lunch around 1:00. A small meal. Therapy. Then whatever light housekeeping Maggie needed help with. More training with Axle until around 3:00. Three trips back and forth by the afternoon.

The work day always ended with Pepper stopping by the Davies kitchen and asking Sue a crucial question. "What's on the menu tonight?" Whatever Sue handed her, Pepper took home and enjoyed with Fred and Maggie.

Mr. Hanna had insisted that he and Maggie could cope in the evenings.

"You need some time to yourself. If we need help, we have others we can call on."

So far, they were managing well. The most Pepper could handle, however, was a quick game of checkers (Fred always won) and a much appreciated soak in the tub. Bedtime never arrived soon enough. Had she always been so soft?

This, her second Saturday, had been busier than her first. Even though she'd crossed a few things off, her "to do" list kept growing. One item at the bottom snagged her attention each time she glanced at the page. *Decide about Sunday.*

Neither Mr. Hannah nor Zeke had pressed her about going to church last Sunday. Anna had extended an open invitation to Pepper weeks earlier. "When you want to meet Bethany, I'm sure Joe will be happy to introduce you." Pepper had slept late and then driven into Lewisburg to look around.

This week she had toyed with the idea of accepting Anna's offer. Anna would lend moral support, but she wouldn't press. True to his word, Zeke hadn't said anything more since her first visit to the orchard. And Fred?

He read the Bible every day. And he talked about God. A lot. God was real to Fred Hanna. And he wanted the same for Pepper, but he didn't nag her about it.

Overall, Anna's family were some of the nicest, most giving people she'd ever met. Could there be a link between that and their being religious? Maybe. Was she brave enough to attend church as the next step to finding out?

Brave enough? Of course she was. She picked up a pen. Next to the last item, she wrote, *Call Anna about the time.*

* * *

Zeke stepped away from the donkey cart, bent his spine backward, and stretched his knotted muscles. He circled the cart, testing the finish on the wood at the front of the cart and on the floor boards. His hands glided across the polyurethane like they would over a freshly polished apple.

The shiny black seat, brand new from its wooden base to its vinyl-covered cushion gave padded comfort to the driver and rider. Smaller, but matching in style and color was the backrest that would relieve the strain of sitting for extended periods of time. The wheel rims, rusty and grimy before, now gleamed in metallic silver.

The most painstaking transformation had involved the metal shafts which extended from the cart to the donkey's harness. Made of aluminum so that their weight could be manageable, they had been covered in a pock-marked corrosion. The first step of their reclamation had involved a combination of several pieces of steel wool and a muscle-aching amount of hard scrubbing. Once the pieces were smooth again, Zeke applied a primer coat. The last step, an overcoat of, appropriately enough, Apple Red paint, completed the transformation. It wasn't brand new, but in appearance, it would rival those in the catalog. And the padded seat and back were extras.

With the object of secrecy, Zeke had undertaken the whole process in the utility shed with its poor lighting and non-existent heat source. A transported stand light aided his vision, and a portable heater expedited the drying times of sealers and paint.

Pepper's disappointment when she first viewed the cart had sent daggers to his heart. He should have expected it, should have realized that the catalog picture would overshadow anything that wasn't brand new. He hadn't. Her reaction had sent him scurrying to redeem himself. Axle's training and Gram's care had kept Pepper so busy this week that she'd asked him only once about the cart.

Each cut of wood, push of steel wool, and stroke of paint reminded him of Axle's harness. He hadn't told Pepper how it had looked when he'd purchased it from Mr. Milton. She didn't need to know he'd spent hours that night conditioning the leather straps and rubbing boot polish into them. He hoped she'd remain clueless about the amount of elbow grease it had taken to make the silver clasps and buckles shine. And he didn't plan to divulge that it had been the cause of his sleeping through the alarm. Going to bed at three and getting up at six hadn't been the best idea.

But he'd do it all over again if it meant seeing her beaming smile and the enormous hug she'd given Axle. Maybe he'd get the hug this time. The unveiling was close.

* * *

What was the matter with Zeke? He was fidgeting. He'd barely touched his meal. He responded with "huh?" to several questions from those at the table. It was the first family dinner that Maggie had shared with the Davies family since her operation. Pepper had been invited too. Everyone except Zeke seemed to be having a wonderful time.

"What's wrong with you?" Pepper had finally whispered to him when he picked up his knife to eat his pie.

"Nothing."

She pointed to the knife. "Try your fork."

He gawked at it and then at her. "Dad, I'm going to check on the animals," he blurted, before shoving away from the table and leaving the dining room.

Pepper gave thought to running after him, but Harold's words interrupted her.

"How's that new donkey, Pepper?"

"Great." She craned her neck to watch Zeke as long as possible.

"Has he perked up?"

"Yes, sir." Hadn't anyone else noticed Zeke's odd behavior? "He's eating a little better. He seems to enjoy Axle's company."

"Good to hear." Harold polished off his pie before continuing. "Is Axle catching on?"

"I think so. He takes directions better."

"He'll have to. We can't have him running off with you and your passengers."

Pepper chuckled. "I guess not." She reached for her water glass.

"You suppose he's far enough along for a little demonstration?" Harold wiped his face. "I'd like to see his progress."

"Sure." Nothing like being put on the spot. "Name the time."

"How about right now? Zeke's out in the barn. He can help you harness Axle." Voices of agreement echoed around the table. "We'll come out and meet you directly."

Pepper quelled the nervous butterflies and stood. "See you in a few minutes."

Her heart thudded as she navigated the gravel at break-neck speed. Hopefully the normal Zeke had returned and would be willing to help her. She sighed deeply when the heavy door was already slightly ajar, and she could scoot in without having to wrestle it open.

Lights greeted her. He must be here somewhere. "Zeke. Where are you?" She headed toward the stalls.

At the corner of animal alley, she screamed to a halt. A donkey cart, gleaming in polished wood and shiny paint blocked her way. She jumped. She squealed. She clapped her hands together and ran forward to touch the seats. "It's beautiful."

* * *

Crouching behind Axle, Zeke heard Pepper's footsteps on the concrete, recognized his own name, and watched her abrupt halt. Her green eyes sparkled. Her hands flailed in numerous directions. All thoughts of long hours and aching arms faded from Zeke's memory.

He unbent his long body. Axle brayed. Pepper turned toward him. Her hands still stroked the cart, but her eyes looked only at him. "It's amazing. You're amazing!"

Zeke stared. Then he coughed. "It's just paint and wood."

"It's a masterpiece."

Zeke reached for the latch on the gate. Pepper closed the distance separating them. Voices intruded.

"Did we give you enough time, son?" Dad's face beamed. The entire family, minus Mom and Gram, flocked along with him.

Not quite. Zeke squelched the words. "Yeah, I guess so." He left the pen and closed the gate behind him. Anna caught his attention. A sympathetic grin lit her face.

Pepper cuffed Anna's arm. "You knew?"

Anna rubbed her arm and nodded. "For about three days."

Pepper scanned Zeke's family's smiling faces. "You all knew about this?"

"Zeke was so nervous he couldn't even eat." Toby elbowed Joe and chortled.

"I finished off his pie after he left." Ike patted his stomach.

Zeke shook his head. Why couldn't he hide anything from them? Joe, Toby, and Ike had spent suppertime silently chuckling at his discomfort. Anna had read his thoughts a few seconds earlier. Did the rest suspect, as she did, the deeper reason behind Zeke's agitation? What about Pepper? Did she know?

"I say it's time to see this thing in action." Dad patted the seat. "You got that donkey harnessed up?"

"Yep."

Pepper glanced in the pen. "Axle's not—"

"Not Axle." Zeke laid a hand on her arm and pointed. "Buster."

Pepper squinted in the direction of Zeke's outstretched arm "But he's not—"

"He is." Her jaw dropped, and Zeke grinned. "I tried to tell you that night, but you kept talking about a friend for Axle and how sad Buster looked and couldn't we take him home."

Hands on her hips, she tapped her foot and stared up at Zeke. "He's been here a week. You might have been able to tell me sometime."

Her eyes really gleamed when she wanted to make a point. "If I'd said something, you would have been in more of a hurry to have a cart. Probably would have tried to convince me to buy the one in the magazine."

"I would not."

Her pouty face urged him on. He mimicked her voice. "C'mon, Zeke. We can earn back the money."

She wrinkled her nose at him.

Snickers from the onlookers nearby encouraged his antics. "It'll only take us two years if we give cart rides day and night all year around, even in the snow."

"I wouldn't say that." She swatted his arm. "Besides, we would pay off your investment much faster than that."

"I wouldn't bet against her on that, Zeke." Dad patted his arm and laughed.

* * *

Pepper darted away from the others. She reached the furry donkey and petted his soft, gray muzzle. Buster inched toward her.

"You get sweeter and happier every day." She stroked the shiny harness that she had become familiar with. "Make me look good, will you?" she whispered in his ear. Walking behind him, she gathered the reins. "Giddyup." Buster started down the lane. Pepper blessed Zeke for making

101

her learn the strange-sounding command. When they reached the front end of the cart, Pepper called, "Whoa." Buster obliged. She sighed loudly before patting his rump. "Good job."

Zeke stepped up. A few minutes and several buckles later, he had Buster hooked up to the cart. "Lead him outside," Zeke said.

Pepper glanced up at him.

He nodded encouragement. "You can take Buster up and down the driveway. The path is lit."

Evidently everyone else already knew the plan, because they were walking toward the door. "What if Buster doesn't— What if your dad—"

"Don't worry."

She felt the pressure of Zeke's hand on hers. She looked up. His eyes exuded confidence.

"Okay." Walking in front of Buster, she headed toward the door.

Reaching the opening ahead of them, Zeke widened the gap in the doorway. Pepper, the donkey, and the glistening cart stepped out for their inaugural run.

* * *

"He did it, Zeke. That sweet little donkey did everything I asked."

Pepper had babbled nonstop for the past five minutes. He hadn't replied. She hadn't seemed to mind. Now she stopped and looked at him.

"Say something."

"Like what?" He carried the harness to the back of the barn and hung it on a hook.

"Like anything that will let me know you've heard anything I said."

His pulse quickened. "I heard everything you said."

"Name one thing." She stopped at the mule's pen and reached through the slats to pet her newest friend at the orchard.

"How did it feel to be driving a donkey cart?" He set a pitchfork into the storage area.

"That is not something I said."

She was right. "But how was it?"

"Fun. Challenging. I love challenges."

No doubt about that.

"You've managed to get me completely off track."

"Didn't know you were on one."

"Of course I'm on one." She plunked herself onto a bale of straw outside the mule's pen. "Your dad. What did he think?"

Reaching Axle and Buster's pen, Zeke halted in front of Pepper. "You're sitting on Buster's bed."

"What?"

"The straw. It's bedding for Buster."

"I thought you said this was hay." She patted the bale.

"City girl." He walked a few steps and picked up a handful from the trough where the sheep were feeding. "This—dried grass with a greenish color—is hay. It's food." He kicked the bale on which she still sat. "This—yellow, inedible stalks of oats—is straw. It's bedding." He fed the hay to Buster. When he looked back, she was still sitting.

"I'm not moving until you answer my question." She leaned her back against the pen and bent her knees, pulling her feet onto the bale.

Standing at the opposite end of the bale, Zeke bent and grasped the twine that held it together. Lifting enough that the bale began to tilt, he said, "You like sitting on the floor?"

Pepper yelped. Leaning toward him, she put both arms around his neck. "Don't do it, Zeke." Emerald sparks glimmered from her eyes. Each one touched and held his gaze. She giggled. He tilted the bale more. She squealed. "I'll pull you over before I'll let go."

Did she really mean it? Standing to his full height, he simultaneously tugged the bale out from under her and tossed it aside. The end result was Pepper clinging desperately to his neck, her feet resting lightly against the floor.

Having both hands free, Zeke placed them at her waist. She stopped laughing. Tightening his grasp slightly, he cleared his throat and asked, "What was the question?"

She peered at his face. "I can't remember."

He couldn't have either.

* * *

"Why didn't he kiss me or tell me he likes me or—or—at least give me a good strong handshake?" Pepper muttered to herself on the way to the house. "Our faces were this close." She raised her nearly-touching thumb and forefinger. "He had every opportunity." She kicked some loose gravel. "Men." She clenched her teeth and balled up her hands. "Give you a job to do. Let you feel needed. Help you do your best. Encourage you when you do well." Her feet suddenly halted as if in quicksand. "Make over a rickety cart so you can drive it." Tears stung her face. "There is something between us."

The moment before the family arrived replayed in her memory. Her joy over the beautiful cart. His pleasure over her joy. Even now her heart thudded. "He feels it, too."

Going up the steps to the porch, Pepper flopped onto the top stair. Unshed tears still lingered. She couldn't go inside.

* * *

Zeke added straw to each pen. He fluffed the straw with a pitchfork. He gave fresh water and more food. Then he retreated to his office, a ten-foot by ten-foot storeroom that had, crowded among feed bags and galvanized buckets, an old desk, a rickety chair and the necessary office supplies for him to keep up with the paperwork involving the petting zoo. Setting his elbows on his legs, he folded his hands in front of him.

Disaster. That's what the bale of straw had led to. Pepper had dashed out of barn. He hadn't watched her go, but he'd heard her rapid footsteps.

Despite the intensity in her eyes and the inviting smile on her face as she stood there in his arms, he hadn't kissed her. She had wanted him to. He had wanted to. But he hadn't. And he hadn't told her his reason for not kissing her. Why hadn't he told her? Why had he confused her?

"Your reasons involve God. She doesn't want to hear about God." Voicing his rationalizations soothed his conscience, for a moment.

He leaned back in his chair and stared up at the rafters. *What are you going to do now?* "I'll tell her."

* * *

As soon as Pepper regained some semblance of composure while sitting on the porch, she went in and found Anna. "I'm going back to your grandparents' house."

"Is everything okay?" It was a polite question. But Anna's compassionate heart had already guessed the answer and telegraphed it to her face.

Pepper bit her lower lip. "Yeah, sure."

"Call me if you need to talk. Anytime. Day or night." Anna had then given Pepper a Herculean hug. "I mean it."

Pepper nodded. "Tell your mom thanks. And let Fred and Maggie know that I've gone."

The Hannas had returned about forty-five minutes later. Lying in bed wide awake, Pepper listened as Fred went through the nightly routine with his wife. After everything quieted, she flung back the covers and grabbed her fleece throw. Might as well watch an old movie from Maggie's collection. Sleep wasn't coming anytime soon. Wrapping the soft warmth around her, she ventured into the darkness.

"Can't sleep?"

Fred's voice again caught her off guard. She jumped, gasped, and then, after scolding him for scaring her, sat on the couch next to him.

"Has my grandson asked you out?"

Prickles ran up her spine. Zeke was the last person she wanted to talk about right now. "No. He hasn't." She couldn't keep the crispness from her tone.

"Good."

Pepper bristled. "Why is that good?"

A brief silence ensued. "You two aren't headed in the same direction." She felt, more than saw, him angle toward her. "The Bible asks, 'Can two walk together, unless they are agreed?'"

Where did he think they were going? An idea formed. "Do you mean because I want to be a doctor, and his life is here at the orchard?"

"That's the easy part."

Pepper sighed. "What's the hard part?"

"Ezekiel has dedicated his life to serving God." Fred's thin, bony hand clasped hers. "You never mention God."

God again. "He's never been important to me."

"He is to Zeke."

* * *

Pepper wrestled with herself well into the night. Why would God care whom Zeke loved? Did Zeke love her? Could he? Maybe she should go to church. She didn't have to listen. She could smile and nod as well as the next person. If she looked interested, would that be enough?

Fred would be up early. Pepper hadn't heard what Maggie's plans were for Sunday. If she was going with her husband, Fred had a lot to take care of. Pepper could help, and then she could tag along.

Was Zeke worth all this? Envisioning his dark eyes and shy grin as he pulled up on the hay bale, Pepper felt warmth pool around her heart. She set her alarm for 6:00.

* * *

"You are a grump this morning." Anna slapped the cereal box in front of her oldest brother. "Maybe you should eat breakfast at your own home."

105

Reaching for the milk, Zeke stared at her. "Maybe you should let Mom and Dad worry about that."

"You're not bossing them around. 'Get the milk, Anna. Where's the sugar? Who ate all the raisin bran?'"

"I need the milk and sugar." It wasn't rocket science.

"And you know where they are." She plopped down across from him at the kitchen table.

Zeke studied the cereal in his bowl. Anna quietly crunched the granola from hers. He ignored her stares. Snatching up the bowl, he rose and mumbled, "Guess I will eat at home."

Anna tilted her face upward. "Talk to me." Her eyes pleaded with him.

"Maybe later."

* * *

An hour and a half later, Zeke drove toward church. He hadn't spoken to Anna again. And he'd groused at Toby who'd been on his way toward the house as Zeke left.

"Just in time for opening day." Toby's face had beamed as he held a handful of ripe strawberries in Zeke's direction.

"For paying customers."

Toby's smile had vanished. "I'm taking them to Mom," he'd mumbled and hurried on.

And he would. He'd sample some. She'd try one. The two of them would marvel at the wonder of plants and fruit. It was that way with every crop. Toby was always the first to notice when something really began to "come on." Others would find a berry or two when they looked. Toby would come in with half a pint cradled gently in his large palms. Usually Zeke would have clapped him on the back. Not today.

Zeke's apology list was growing.

And neither Anna nor Toby was at the top. When could he see Pepper and explain that he had, this one time, to amend his pledge not to talk to her about God until she asked him to?

He should have explained last night. She was right in front of him, arms around his neck, and staring into his eyes. He'd been one heartbeat from kissing her. But he hadn't. Both then and now, he knew he'd made the painful but right decision.

But she had no idea. And he'd left her clueless. Clueless as to why he couldn't pursue or allow an attachment with someone who didn't share the same personal relationship he had with God.

He'd opened his mouth to say something. "Uh" was what came out. Trying to regain his equilibrium, he'd placed his hands on her arms and removed them from his neck.

And she had turned and bolted from the barn, leaving him with his head hanging and his heart hurting.

In his present state of mind, offering praise to God seemed impossible, but he pulled into the church parking lot, mustering as much hope as he could. He grinned and raised a hand when he recognized Gramps waving at him from up the row. Heading his Jeep in that direction, he found a spot nearby and parked.

The trunk of Gram and Gramps' Buick popped open, and Gramps headed around to pull out the wheelchair. Gram was obviously with him.

So was Pepper. She stepped from the backseat and helped Gram stand up. Zeke gulped. The outlook seemed brighter, but the way ahead promised speed bumps.

He sighed and climbed from his car. Crossing the asphalt, he waited until Gram was seated. Then he stepped behind her. "Mind if I push?" He nodded to Gramps and Pepper before grasping the handles of Gram's wheelchair.

She turned and reached for his arm. "Not at all." She settled her purse in her lap. "Ready."

Zeke forged ahead, grateful for a reason to be helpful and an excuse not to look at Pepper. Church folk greeted them along the way and thronged them just inside the doors. Making himself as inconspicuous as possible, Zeke entered the chapel and found a seat.

As the pastor made his way to the platform, the Davies crew entered en masse, descending upon the row in which Zeke sat. A discussion, not a quiet one, ensued as to who should sit where. Anna must have lost the argument, for she was elected to go first and sit next to Zeke. She smiled at him. Hers was a generous heart.

Pepper followed Anna. Mom and Dad came next. Gramps occupied the last seat in the pew, and Gram, in her wheelchair, sat at the end in the aisle. Zeke's brothers dispersed to places elsewhere.

With Pepper ensconced between Anna and Mom, Zeke could relax— a little. They familiarized her with the hymnbook and explained other things along the way. She nodded and smiled.

The song service seemed to puzzle her. She stared at the words, but didn't move her lips. But when the congregation began "Amazing Grace," Pepper looked up at Anna and whispered, "I've heard this one." Should Zeke be encouraged?

In the middle of a series on the parables of Jesus, pastor's sermon today addressed the Parable of the Soils, often referred to as the Parable of the Sower. He asked everyone to turn to Matthew, chapter 13, verse 3.

* * *

Anna turned pages in her Bible and then held it out for Pepper to share. The pastor began reading: "And He spoke many things to them in parables, saying, 'Behold, the sower went out to sow; and as he sowed, some seeds fell beside the road, and the birds came and ate them up.'"

Pepper nodded as he read. These words would appeal to Zeke and his family. They were all about what the Davieses lived every day. She listened again.

"'Others fell on the rocky places, where they did not have much soil; and immediately they sprang up, because they had no depth of soil. But when the sun had risen, they were scorched; and because they had no root, they withered away. Others fell among the thorns, and the thorns came up and choked them out. And others fell on the good soil and yielded a crop, some a hundredfold, some sixty, and some thirty. He who has ears, let him hear.'"

So far, the Bible made some sense, except maybe the last line. Pepper relinquished her grasp on Anna's Bible and looked at the man up front.

"If we focus on the one who sowed the seed, or if we stop at the parable itself, we've missed most of the point."

He referred the people to verse 18. Anna held out her Bible.

"'Hear then the parable of the sower. When anyone hears the Word of the Kingdom and does not understand it, the evil one comes and snatches away what has been sown in his heart. This is the one on whom seed was sown beside the road. The one on whom seed was sown on the rocky places, this is the man who hears the word and immediately receives it with joy; yet he has no firm root in himself, but is only temporary, and when affliction or persecution arises because of the word, immediately he falls away. And the one on whom seed was sown among the thorns, this is the man who hears the word, and the worry of the world and the deceitfulness of wealth choke the word, and it becomes unfruitful. And the one on whom seed was sown on the good soil, this is the man who hears the word and understands it; who indeed bears fruit and brings forth, some a hundredfold, some sixty, and some thirty.'"

These verses didn't seem to be as much about planting and reaping as Pepper had first thought. What was the "word of the kingdom?" Was she supposed to be one of those hearers?

Without noticing, she sat forward.

* * *

Zeke cast sidelong glances at Pepper while the pastor read. Her eyes seemingly followed the words, and she looked up when he paused to explain. Zeke prayed that she would have understanding. Anna glanced toward him. She was praying, too.

When the service ended, Gramps pushed Gram's wheelchair, making sure to stop beside Pastor White. "This little lady is Pepper." He placed a hand on her shoulder. "My right-hand girl who's helping my right-hand lady get back onto her feet."

Pepper laughed. "Right-hand girl?" She reached for the pastor's outstretched hand. "He makes me sound like a kid."

The elderly pastor smiled. "When you're as old as Fred and I are, people your age are kids—or grandkids."

"Ready for strawberries, Zeke?" Pastor White asked.

"Almost. Toby carried in a handful this morning. When he does that, they're coming."

Gramps hadn't moved on yet. "Weather report is calling for sunny days, today, tomorrow, and Tuesday.

"We'll be out to get some Tuesday morning."

Pepper and Anna were waiting outside when Zeke and Gramps left the building. Anna stepped up and grabbed her brother's elbow. "Take Pepper and me out for fast food."

"Uh, yeah, I guess." Her eyes seemed to suggest more than a need for calories and grease.

"I'll tell Mom and Dad. They'll tell Gramps." She headed off.

Was Anna sure about this? How much cash did he have? He reached for his wallet.

"I'll buy my own." Pepper's direct tone stopped him.

"Zeke can buy, can't you, big brother?" Anna had returned. "He rarely buys his own food. And he's not happy when we eat our favorite cereal if it happens to be his favorite, too."

Anna had put him in his place, smoothed over a difficulty that would arise at the restaurant, and given Pepper a reason to relax. She'd also let him know that this morning was history as far as she was concerned.

Without looking into his wallet, Zeke said, "I can handle it." He elbowed Anna. "As long as you two don't super-size everything."

"We might." She raised her eyebrows and grabbed Pepper's arm. "C'mon. We'll sit in the back. Zeke can be our chauffeur."

How could Anna make him feel good one minute and old the next? He shook his head all the way to his Jeep.

* * *

"What is 'the word of the kingdom'"?

It was only one of the thought-provoking questions that Pepper had asked during their meal. The three had decided to eat outdoors, and when Anna asked about the church service, Pepper's inquiries had begun.

Had Zeke ever had a more important conversation or answered a more crucial question? He rolled his paper cup around in his fingers. "*Kingdom* refers to the kingdom of heaven." He tried to gauge her response. "*Word* means message." Her brows wrinkled. "The whole parable speaks of how people respond when they hear about the things of God."

"So which one of those soils am I?"

She had been listening.

Anna clasped her hand. "Only you know the answer to that. But you might not know right now."

"I don't know." Pepper looked hard at both Zeke and Anna. "I'm not sure when or if I will know."

Anna spoke quickly. "How can we help?"

Pepper looked at her hands. Then she looked up. "I don't have a Bible. I can't check into any of it."

"Gramps has several Bibles. And lots of study materials." A smile lit Anna's face. "He would love to help you however he can."

"I'll ask him." She tapped her fingers on the table. Then she turned toward Zeke. "You can help by answering some questions about other things."

Anna rose from the table. She placed one hand on Zeke's shoulder and one on Pepper's. "Take your time."

CHAPTER 12

"I like you, Zeke." There. She'd said it. He hadn't fallen off his seat or clutched his chest. He wasn't totally surprised. But he hadn't looked closely at her either. "I thought the feelings were mutual. Was I wrong?"

His gaze finally met hers. "No."

"Then why? Last night."

He set both elbows on the table and stared straight ahead before glancing sideways at her. "What do you know about animals and plowing?"

"Animals? Plowing?" He'd lost his mind.

"Do you know what a yoke is?"

"It holds two animals together."

"So they can plow as a team. No good farmer would put a cow with a horse, or a mule with an ox."

Pepper shook her head. Of course not.

"Why?"

"Because they're not the same size or the same strength."

"And they wouldn't be pulling together." He placed his fists next to each other on the table. "One would be dragging the other." His hands illustrated his words. "Or the other would be slowing the first down."

"Okay." Where was the connection?

"The Bible warns those who follow Christ against being in an 'unequal yoke' with those who don't follow Him."

Fred's words resounded in her ears. "You two aren't headed in the same direction." They made more sense now.

"But if I were to follow Christ?"

"The yoke would be equal."

* * *

On Sunday night Pepper lounged on her bed with her favorite flavor of Orville Redenbacher's straight from the microwave. All afternoon she'd pondered the church service and Zeke's words about unequal yokes. Tomorrow was the Monday before opening day. Everyone in the Davies family would be gearing up for the yearly event, which, this year fell on June 9. Pepper would be making a few practice runs with Buster, receiving last-minute instructions about her duties, and probably still trying to decide her next step.

She could postpone making a decision about God. "This is new to me" would become her mantra. It would be true, and it would buy her some time to think. Would it change the standstill between her and Zeke? Probably not. He would want to wait and see.

She could be like the "good ground" in the parable and soak everything in. She'd say whatever words they wanted her to say, do whatever the pastor said to do. And willingly follow Zeke off into the sunset, enjoying those deep brown eyes and that wavy hair. She'd act the part, and God wouldn't have to play a real role in her life at all.

Could she trick Zeke? Did she want to? What about Anna? Could she purposefully dupe a true friend? Goose bumps rose on her arms. If only Zeke and Anna weren't so nice.

She grabbed her phone and punched in a familiar number. "Hey, Pops."

"Hello, honey. What a nice surprise."

Music in the background suddenly became softer.

"I'm in my car," he explained.

"Singing with the radio?"

"You know me."

He always sang along with anything that had words he could remember.

"I did some singing today, too."

"Anything I know?"

"'Amazing Grace' and other songs that I'd never heard but Anna knew all the words to." Pops started to say something, but, with the delay over the wireless phone, she was already rushing on. "Did you know 'Amazing Grace' has about six verses? How do I even know that song?" She stopped to let him catch up.

"Commercials. The Salvation Army folks. Country music or rock stars when they speak about their roots. It seems that many began singing in church." The pause was brief. "But back up. You went to church?"

"Yeah. With Fred and Maggie." Pepper curled the top of the popcorn bag down to reach to kernels at the bottom. "The whole Davies family goes to the same one. We filled a row, and not everyone could sit with us."

"Were there lots of people?"

"Fifty or more. Pops, how come we never went to church?"

He cleared his throat. "I guess because I never had. And I've not always been favorably impressed by church people."

Should Pepper ask why? He continued before the words formed.

"I did send you to Sunday School for a while, though, when you were a kid. Don't you remember?"

Pepper deliberated a moment. "I remember a group of boys and girls sitting around a table, and a man and woman showing us large pictures of—Jesus—I think."

"You went for about six months. And then you came home one Sunday and told me you weren't going back."

"Why not?"

"Your words were, 'I'm just not.' Your teacher called the next day. You'd asked her, 'If God can do anything, why doesn't He bring back my mom?'"

Pepper smiled. "Even then I asked good questions."

"But you didn't like her answer."

"What was it?"

"She said, 'I don't know, honey.'"

A car door closed.

"You told her 'If He can bring her back, but He won't, I don't like Him.' That was the end of Sunday School."

"You never went with me?"

"No. I never had as a child. Never met anyone who made me think I should start as an adult."

"Did you ever pray?" Pepper rolled onto her stomach. "Fred Hanna prays every day. Gets up early to do it."

"I know I've talked to God, at least tried to, a few times when I needed help."

"Me, too." She kicked her feet up and down on the mattress. "Maybe I'll try it more now."

"Why?"

She heard the jingle of keys and the opening of the front door of the Staley home.

"Because of animals and yokes," she explained.

"You've lost me."

"Zeke says—"

"So this whole church thing concerns Zeke?"

Dad's tone had changed. "Not only him."

"But mostly?"

"Fred and Anna talk to me about God."

"And Zeke? What's he do?"

113

"He makes me wonder if I might be wrong about God."

"Why's that?"

"If Zeke loves Him, God can't be all bad."

Dad coughed. "That's a change. Are you sure there's nothing extracurricular going on between you and Zeke Davies?"

By *extracurricular*, he meant *physical*. If he only knew. "Nothing, Pops. And I mean nothing."

"Good. I thought I liked him."

Pepper heard the clink of ice cubes in a glass and the pop of an opening soda can. Dad was pouring his Sprite.

"I was afraid I might have to change my mind."

"No. But I have to make up mine."

* * *

The second Monday in June arrived in a whirl. It started with an earlier-than- usual morning routine for both Maggie and Pepper, followed by Pepper's turbo-charged trip to the orchard because she was late in spite of getting up ahead of schedule.

Maggie had struggled during therapy as she usually did on Monday. Sunday afternoons were spent with family, and often Maggie did more than usual, and sometimes, more than she should. Today's session had been slow even for a Monday.

Zeke met Pepper as soon as she put her Mustang into *Park*. He opened the car door, stepped out of her way, and said, "I needed you at the barn five minutes ago."

"Good morning to you, too, Zeke." Didn't she at least deserve a chance to explain? She scowled at him and handed him a paper bag. "Those go to your mom." She gathered her small purse, stepped out beside him, and then closed and locked the door. Zeke hadn't moved. "I'll be out as soon as I deliver these." Snatching the bag from him, she hurried up the walkway.

She turned back when she heard, "I'll be waiting."

In another context, those words would have made heart race and flutter. Under these circumstances, they raised her hackles. She toyed with the idea of having a cup of coffee in the house before making her way to the barn. Opening the door, she called, "Morning, Sue. I brought your containers." Silence. The table was free of any breakfast fixings. The coffee pot was empty and turned off. Pepper set the bag on the table and glanced at the clock. By 8:00 everyone had been at work for at least an hour.

114

Sighing, she set the dishes and her purse on the table and slumped off to find Zeke.

Brays, shouts, and general commotion greeted Pepper as she neared the barn. She quickened her pace. What she saw when she arrived was Buster, drenched and soapy, standing placidly while Toby rinsed him off with the hose. The noisemakers stood a few feet beyond. Zeke clutched Axle's neck in one arm and sprayed water from another hose onto the scruffy donkey. With each squirt of water, Axle jumped, brayed, and bumped Zeke's hand. Water droplets flew everywhere. Toby laughed. Zeke yelled. Buster seemed oblivious.

Pepper grinned. Axle was being as uncooperative with Zeke as Zeke had been with her.

"Where is Pepper?" Zeke's bellow drowned the donkey's protests and erased Pepper's smugness. She raced toward him.

"I'm right here."

Without looking up, Zeke flung the handle at her and barked, "About time." He clamped his free arm around Axle's middle. "I'll hold. You spray. But watch out."

Pepper grasped the handle and squeezed firmly. Water shot from the nozzle, pelting the donkey's side. Axle reared. Pepper squealed, jumped, and dropped the hose. The handle hit the ground first, sending a spray of water cascading onto the three contenders.

Zeke snapped, "Pick that up and try again."

"It's too hard."

"It's not too hard." He growled before looking at her. "Just squeeze the handle and hold on."

"The force is too hard. It's hurting him."

"Hurting him?"

Zeke released Axle and stood up. Snatching the nozzle, Pepper clasped the trigger and sent a stream into Zeke's midsection.

He gasped and flinched. "What are you—"

"Showing you how it feels."

His shirt soaked and dripping, Zeke stepped around Axle and grabbed the hose from Pepper's hand. She turned away, bracing herself for an onslaught of water.

Seconds later, she looked back. Zeke had kinked the hose and was unscrewing the nozzle from it. He tossed the handle to the ground and extended the hose toward Pepper. "Let's try this again."

"Okay, Axle. This won't hurt." Pepper held the hose above the donkey's back. Axle docilely allowed the soft stream to soak his coat. Zeke lathered the donkey, starting at his hind feet. As Zeke moved forward, Pepper rinsed what he had washed.

A few minutes later, Zeke inspected the now-clean Axle. Resting his hands on the donkey's back, he nodded his approval to Pepper who stood facing him. "I'm sorry about Axle and for snapping at you earlier."

"I know." Pepper stepped forward, holding the still bubbling hose just beyond Axle's back legs.

Reaching toward Pepper, Zeke clasped the hose right where she held it. His cold, wet fingers surged heat into Pepper's hand. She smiled.

"Look at that car coming up the driveway." Toby's excited voice cracked as he stepped from the barn.

When had he taken Buster inside?

"Probably some tourist thinking that today starts our season." Zeke's voice lacked Toby's enthusiasm.

"Tourist or not, that's a Porsche."

"Porsche or not, we're not ready today." Zeke handed Axle's lead rope to Toby. "Dry Axle off and put him into the pen." Zeke strode toward the parking spaces.

"C'mon, Zeke. A Porsche."

Zeke halted and turned. "Which you can drool over as soon as you take care of Axle."

"He's your donkey." Toby's glare matched his challenge.

"But right now, he's your responsibility." Zeke stared and waited. When Toby reached for a nearby towel, Zeke resumed his trek down the stone-lined path.

Pepper turned to Toby. He shook his head and began rubbing Axle's back with quick, hard strokes. Would Axle survive this bath? Not waiting around to find out, Pepper scurried after Zeke.

* * *

As he strode toward the visitor, Zeke's thoughts ran as quickly as his feet. Why was opening-week Monday always like this? Today had gone wrong from the start. Why had he been so impatient with Pepper? Why hadn't he noticed the water pressure? His soaked shirt reminded him of the consequences.

A man stepped from the white Porsche. Zeke opened his mouth, but before he could call out, Gramps emerged from the bake shop and hurried toward the guy. Then Pepper flew past Zeke, reaching the visitor and Gramps at the same time.

116

Nearing the cluster, Zeke heard three voices ask the same question simultaneously. "Is anything wrong?"

The visitor spoke. "Nothing with me or with Maggie. I just came from your house." He shook hands with Gramps. "But you'll be my next patient if you're not more careful on these stones."

Pepper nodded and raised her eyebrows at Gramps. "That's what I've been telling him."

Zeke joined the group, and Gramps spoke up.

"Doctor Girardi, this is my grandson, Ezekiel. Ezekiel, this is Maggie's young surgeon, Dr. Girardi."

Zeke recognized the name but had never met the doctor. He extended his right hand. "Glad to meet you. Call me Zeke."

"You, too. I'm Marco."

"How'd you come to see Maggie?" Gramps interrupted the introductions. "Didn't know you made house calls."

The doctor laughed. "Usually I don't. But today—" His gaze turned toward Pepper. "I'm doing some research."

"What kind of research?"

Gramps may have needed to ask the question, but Zeke already knew the answer. The subject of Marco Girardi's research was Pepper. She knew it, too. Her smile was warm and inviting.

Disregarding both Zeke and Gramps, Marco eased closer to Pepper. "I'm wondering what evening you have free this week and if you'd like to go out to dinner with me."

Zeke didn't wait to hear either answer. With a wave and a mumbled goodbye, he turned toward the barn.

* * *

A surgeon who drove a Porsche and had enough confidence to ask a girl out while other people looked on. Zeke couldn't complete with that. And he doubted that Pepper could resist. More than that, Dr. Girardi probably wouldn't have the "spiritual incompatibility" concerns that Zeke did with Pepper. Marco would simply appreciate her spontaneity, her zest for life, and her sparkling green eyes.

"I like you, Zeke." Was it only yesterday that she had spoken those words to him? Had she meant them? Did she still? Why had he let the pressures of tomorrow's opening turn him into such a grump?

This day had become a train wreck. And there were still several hours in which to accumulate residual damage.

* * *

Focus. Stay focused on your job. Buster needs you to be alert and prepared. Heading back toward the barn, Pepper skimmed the driveway on feet almost ready to dance. Marco Girardi. The name suited him. His deep brown eyes, dark hair, and olive-toned skin attested to his Italian heritage. Maybe it was advantageous that orthopedic surgeons who replaced knees and hips often dealt with an elderly client base. Dr. Girardi's winning smile might be enough to make younger women faint.

Why hadn't Pepper been impressed by all of this before? She'd seen him four or five times. They'd discussed Maggie's care and talked about his training and his practice. She'd noticed his good looks but had never been so appreciative of them. Today her vision was 20/20.

Apparently Fred Hanna had seen something she hadn't. He'd wondered several times if Maggie's doctor had asked Pepper out. Today he'd nodded slyly to Pepper before turning back to Marco.

"I guess you don't need me around for this kind of research." With that, he and Zeke had begun walking away.

No. An image flashed through Pepper's mind. Fred had walked away by himself.

Marco had called to him, "Go slow." Without looking back, Fred had waved one arm behind him and kept walking.

When had Zeke gone? Where was he now? Would he care how she'd answered Marco Girardi? Should she volunteer the information?

She slipped through the narrow opening and into the dimly lit barn. Whoever was inside hadn't moved the heavy door more than necessary. Silence and the dusty odors of hay and grain greeted her.

"Zeke." More silence. "You in here?" Pepper recognized the squeak of the rickety desk chair Zeke had reclaimed from a neighbor's dumpster. She turned toward the creaking. He appeared in the office doorway.

"What's next for today, boss?" She clicked her heels and saluted. Zeke's smile didn't materialize.

"We need new posters for the animals. There's a printout of the different kinds of animals along with the name of each one." He pointed at his desk. "Take the marker and write one name on each of the laminated sheets." His gaze had included the desk, the marker, and the pages. Not once had he looked directly at Pepper. "Then use this staple gun to attach the correct names to the animals' pens." Still avoiding her eyes, Zeke placed the stapler in her hand. "Let me know when you're done." The thud of his heavy boots on the cement floor punctuated his exit. He never looked back.

118

Entering the cluttered room, Pepper flopped into the decrepit chair. She gasped when it tilted sideways, nearly dumping her onto the floor. *Watch out. You know this thing narrowly escaped the scrap yard.* She centered herself on the chair, located the posters, and reached for the marker.

Zeke's avoidance had screamed that he knew she'd accepted Marco's offer. Explanation wasn't necessary. Removing the marker cap, Pepper formed the first name from the list. Maybe this way was best. Because of the whole "God thing" Fred hadn't wanted Zeke to ask Pepper out anyway. Now someone else had.

And Zeke? Well, maybe this would make his life easier too. Pepper set the marker down, massaged her forehead with her fingertips, and sighed heavily. *Easier* wasn't the first word his expression had brought to her mind.

* * *

Over and over, Zeke paced four steps toward his living room window and four steps back. When pacing didn't help, he resorted to bouncing a tennis ball off the walls. But each splat of the ball dredged up a memory of Pepper. He flung it one last time. The ball clipped an empty plate on the coffee table and sent it crashing to the floor. The thud roused him from his stupor. He picked up the plate and collapsed onto the couch.

She was going on a date with someone else. Nothing he could do about it. Maybe this was God's way of showing him that all of his misgivings had been warranted. Zeke argued internally to justify his jealousy and anger. She led him on. *You flirted with her.* She told him she was interested. *You shared that interest.*

She'd be at the orchard all summer, working with Zeke each day but going out with Marco at night. If only Gram didn't need her. If only she hadn't proved herself to be an excellent worker.

She'd been stapling two signs onto the sheep pen when Zeke and his mom entered the barn looking for Ike. Mom had examined them and exclaimed, "These are lovely. The nicest ones we've ever had." She had hugged Pepper. "Your calligraphy is impeccable, and the swirls add such a nice touch."

Every job he'd given her—always as far removed from him as possible—she had accomplished quickly and well. Her crowning moment had been Buster's final tests runs. The donkey and his driver had completed all three circuits without any glitches. Stepping down from her seat, Pepper had embraced the donkey with gusto. "You little sweetie. You've earned this." She'd reached into the cart and pulled a flat package

119

from the floor. Removing the tissue paper, she had held up a small metal plate with the word *BUSTER* on it. Then she'd turned to Zeke. "The man who made it said that you could attach it to Buster's harness. It goes across his forehead."

Zeke had swallowed hard. Such generosity and thoughtfulness. "It should be—perfect." Why was that always the word he thought of?

"I got one for Axle, too, when he's ready."

Zeke had had to avert his gaze from those earnest green eyes. In a scratchy voice through clenched teeth, he'd croaked, "I'll get to it as soon as I can." Grabbing Buster's bridle, he'd hurried himself and the donkey back to the barn.

CHAPTER 13

At 8:45 Tuesday morning, Pepper joined all the Davies family, including Fred Hanna, at the entrance to Davies Orchard. Harold gathered everyone into a circle.

"Any problems I should know about before we open?" He scanned the group. "Bathrooms all in order?"

Anna signaled two thumbs up.

"Those critters ready for lots of attention?"

Zeke shrugged. "They were five minutes ago."

"No glitches with the oven?"

Sue took her husband's hand. "Everything's good in the kitchen."

"Just what I wanted to hear," Harold said. "Let's pray." Each man removed his cap. "Lord, You've blessed us with another year and another crop. Help us to remember that all things come from You. Give us helpful hands and kind words as we serve the public today."

"Amen" echoed around the circle.

Harold continued. "Pepper, as soon as we greet the first few customers, you'll go with Toby to the berry patch to pick."

"I get help picking this morning?" Toby raised a high five toward Pepper and then lowered his hand so that she could reach it.

"For about forty-five minutes. Then she needs to come back to give cart rides." He turned toward his eldest son. "Zeke, you have Buster all ready to go before ten."

"I will."

Harold examined the faces around him. "Everyone set?" When no negatives reached him, he removed the heavy chain that was stretched across the bottom of the driveway as a barrier. Engines started, and cars that were already parked along the road moved forward.

Anna tugged on Pepper's arm and propelled both of them to one side of the drive along with Harold and Sue. The opposite edge was flanked by Anna's brothers and Fred. As cars entered the orchard in two rows, the earliest visitors were personally greeted by the Davies family. Once several had passed through, family members moved toward the buildings, each headed to his or her assigned responsibility.

Toby motioned to Pepper to follow him. "You ever pick strawberries before?"

"Nope."

"You're about to learn how." They climbed aboard a green vehicle everyone called a Gator. Toby started the engine. "Hold on." He zoomed down a grassy path, stopping as abruptly as he had begun. "We're here."

He emerged from the Gator, snatched a stack of small, green cardboard containers, and strode on. A few feet beyond lay a field of neat, straw-lined rows of short, dense plants. Pepper followed him into the field. Bending over one of the rows Toby pushed back the foliage. Strawberries—some red, many green—lay waiting. "Pick the ripe ones. Like this one." The berry he held was an even-toned red on all sides. Pepper's mouth began to water. "Make sure they're ripe, but pick them all. Look carefully. Smaller berries like to hide under the leaves." He dropped the berry into a basket and handed both to Pepper. "You take this row. I'll work next to you. When you fill a basket, set it in the row, pick up another, and start where you left off."

"Okay." Pepper stepped next to the plants, set down her basket, and started in. Collecting the berries from the low-growing plants was backbreaking work. Sometimes she bent over the plants. Sometimes she knelt beside them.

She was working on her sixth basket when Toby called, "It's a quarter to ten. I'd better get you back to the barn. Zeke'll have my hide if you're late." Toby was already using a large metal tray to gather the baskets he'd filled. He added Pepper's stash to the tray and deposited them into the Gator. "Anna will be glad to add these to her supply."

"Her supply?"

"The fifty quarts we picked early this morning."

Pepper's eyes bulged. "Fifty quarts!"

Toby grinned. "Yeah. Usually we sell that many before noon."

"Will you keep picking?"

"Yep, that's my job." He and Pepper climbed in, and within a few seconds, were on the way.

"Will it take all day?" Pepper yelled above the noise.

He rolled his eyes and nodded. "Ike's picking a few black raspberries that are ripe. He'll join me later." Toby elbowed Pepper's arm. "He's not as fast as you are."

"I'll be sure to tell him that."

Toby dropped Pepper off right outside the barn. She hurried inside.

Zeke had done his job. Pepper's apple-red coach awaited. Metal gleamed. Leather shone. Buckles sparkled. Buster inched toward her.

Tears welled in Pepper's eyes. Then a hand touched her shoulder. She gasped.

Zeke held out a box. "Take these into my office and change. Anna says they'll fit."

Pepper stared upward. His half smile momentarily met her eyes. She took the box in one hand and squeezed his outstretched arm with the other.

Inside his office she opened the package and lifted out a pair of western-cut blue jeans. They matched the ones that each of the Davies family members wore during orchard hours. Underneath the jeans was a bright red polo shirt bearing on the upper left the insignia for Davies Orchard along with the name *Pepper*. With slightly blurry eyes, she hurriedly donned her new outfit.

Raking her fingers through her hair, she ran from Zeke's office a minute later. "They fit great." She twirled once before racing on.

Zeke looked up from checking one of Buster's hooves. "There's one more thing on the seat." He nodded toward it. "Hurry. There's already a line."

Pepper grabbed the gift bag, pulled out its contents, and found two engineer-styled caps. Each was blue and white striped. One had the name Buster stitched in red letters across the front. Axle's name had been monogrammed onto the other.

Pepper hugged Buster's neck. "We're official, Buster. Let's get going." She donned the cap and climbed into the cart. "Giddyup."

* * *

The inaugural hour of cart rides sped by. Riding alone or sometimes with a friend, each child dropped a dollar into the metal box that Zeke had attached to the front of the cart. Before starting out, Pepper would make sure each passenger was buckled in. Then she'd ask, "What's your name?" Billy, Micah, Allison, and Ayden were some that she remembered. The most common answer to "How old are you?" was "I'm five."

Pepper couldn't remember an hour of work that had ever been more fun. Buster seemed to be enjoying himself, too, especially when Pepper occasionally slipped him a chunk of carrot while the next rider climbed aboard.

During one of the circuits around the orchard, Pepper noticed a tall, brown-haired young woman standing next to two small girls. She bent to speak to one them, and the child grinned and waved to Pepper. On the next trip, one that took a different route, Pepper saw the same young woman. This time her companions were two small boys, who were dressed alike and had the same blond hair. She spoke to them as Pepper and Buster approached. The boys' faces lit up, and they waved. As she had previously, Pepper waved back.

Shortly after eleven o'clock, Pepper drove Buster into the barn. Joe met her inside and helped her unhook the cart and unharness her little friend.

"It went well?"

Using few words was one of Joe's trademarks. "It went great." Pepper jumped from the cart and unhooked the cash box. She'd carry it to Zeke's office before she left the barn. "Not everyone got a ride, but Zeke doesn't want to tire Buster, especially when Axle's not ready yet to take the next shift."

"Sounds smart."

"I'll rub him down once he's in the stall so that—"

"I'll do that." Joe cut Pepper's explanation off short. He led Buster into the donkey pen. "Zeke wants you back outside to answer questions." Tipping the cart onto its wheels so that the shafts pointed upward, he added a bit brusquely, "Seems like you have a fan club."

Today, apparently, Joe wasn't a member of it. Must be the news about Marco Girardi was getting around. What would strawberry picking be like tomorrow if Toby had found out?

* * *

"How much does Buster eat?"

"Is the cart hard for him to pull?"

"Do his feet hurt?"

As accurately as she could, Pepper fielded each question from her pint-sized fan base. At one point she looked back to see the tall, young woman watching her. When the crowd began to disperse, Pepper approached the visitor.

"Hi, I'm Pepper. Where are your little friends?"

The girl smiled. "They all rode back in the van."

"What van?"

"The Son-Light Preschool van. We brought some of the kids here for a few hours this morning." Her blue-green eyes sparkled. "This is one of their favorite places, especially the petting zoo." She glanced toward the rabbit hutch a few feet away. "They wanted to ride, but we have so many, and when we arrived, there was already a line." She shifted a large purse more securely onto her shoulder. "After lunch another group will come. I'll ride back with them." Smiling slightly, she said. "We'll bring them another day so that they can ride."

"You work there?"

"I'm helping out for a few weeks. I'll be a senior in high school this fall."

"At a nearby school?"

"No, I'm from California."

"Why are you working at a day care in Pennsylvania if you're from California?"

The girl giggled behind her upraised hand. "I went on a spring mission trip to a Romanian orphanage" Our team repaired the camp the orphanage owns so that campers could use it during the summer."

Pepper squinched her eyebrows. "You live in California. You traveled to Romania. You're working in Pennsylvania. I'm confused." Pepper glanced at her watch. "But it's noon, and I have a half hour for lunch. Want to share a sandwich with me? Mrs. Davies makes a fabulous turkey on wheat."

"I have my own lunch, but I'd be glad to tell you the rest."

Pepper nodded her pleasure. "I'll be right back."

She scurried into the house and gathered her sandwich, some fresh strawberries and a bottle of water from the fridge. Then she scooted back outside. Her new friend waited at the end of the sidewalk. "Come on."

The two found a nearby empty bench and sat down. Pepper thumped herself on the head. "I'm eating with you, and I never even asked you your name."

The girl looked up from the large handbag she'd been searching through. "It's Tayzia. Tayzia Santiago."

"Tayzia Santiago." The rhythmic syllables rolled from Pepper's mouth. "What a lovely name. Is Tayzia short for something? Like Anastasia?"

"No, but people do ask me that." She smiled. "It's something my mom loved."

"I can see why." Pepper unscrewed the cap from her water bottle. "So, what brings you to a day care in Pennsylvania?"

Tayzia swallowed. "Mom and Dad have dear friends who moved here from California years ago. Their daughter and I had been best friends before they moved. We're still close even though we seldom see each other. As a present to both of us, her family flew me here so that we could spend a few weeks together. They know the lady who runs the day care and asked her if I could work there for a short time."

"So you're on a working vacation?"

Tayzia nodded. "And trying to decide if maybe I should work with children someday. I never used to enjoy little kids, even though my mom has taught them for years." She retrieved an apple from her bag but didn't bite into it. "I think I was afraid of them."

Pepper placed both palms onto her knees and leaned forward. "You sure didn't seem scared today." Pepper reached for her bottle of water. "Those little ones love you."

Tayzia swallowed a bite of apple. "I changed because of a previous mission trip to Guatemala with my church's youth group." She pushed a strand of hair from her face. "Those children were so needy I couldn't be afraid of them."

Needy kids. Pepper recalled the admiration in the eyes of the children she'd seen with Tayzia earlier. No wonder they loved her. Pepper glanced at her watch. "I'm going back into the house for a minute." She studied Tayzia's over-sized bag. "Want me to put that inside so you don't have to carry the heavy thing?"

Tayzia clutched the bag to herself. "I'll keep it." She sighed. "That must sound silly. It's because of my journal."

"Your journal?"

Tayzia once again searched the recesses of the flowered bag. She pulled out a brown book. "It's my moleskin thought keeper. It goes everywhere I do."

"What's in it?"

"Quotations I hear or read. Ideas that impress me or make me wonder. Scenes that I don't want to forget. Questions I want answered."

"You write in there every day?"

"Sometimes more than once." She caressed the book with her long fingers. "Do you write?"

"I text. I update Facebook. Does that count?"

Tayzia giggled but didn't answer.

"Must be not." Pepper wiggled her eyebrows at her new friend. "I'd rather talk than write." She cast a puzzled look in Tayzia's direction. "But as often as my mouth gets me into trouble, maybe I should write more and talk less." She jumped up. "I'll be right back."

Tayzia grinned and nodded. "I'm going to wander around and take some pictures. Maybe I can write an article about this place and have it published in my local paper when I get back to California. Having pictures to go with it will help."

Tayzia really did love to write. What would that be like? Pepper dismissed the question. "I'll find you."

* * *

"Anyone seen Zeke?"

Sue's question greeted Pepper as she entered the kitchen.

"I haven't."

"He'll come when he gets a chance." Harold answered.

"I guess he hasn't starved yet." Sue returned a sandwich to the fridge.

Pepper reached for Sue's arm. "Could you put this half back for me? My time's up." She addressed Harold. "Is there something special I should be doing before one o'clock when I take Buster back out?"

"Just make sure he's all set." He looked up from the newspaper he'd been reading. "You did a good job this morning, little lady. I'm glad you put the idea into Zeke's head and he put it into mine."

"I am, too." Sue confirmed her husband's words.

Pepper shrugged her shoulders and grinned. "I am, too. What a great job I have." She hugged Sue quickly. "Thanks for the outfit. It's perfect."

"My pleasure."

* * *

Pepper located her newest tall friend at the mule's outdoor pen. Tayzia held out her phone, snapped a picture, moved to a different spot, and took another.

"How's the photography going?"

Without answering, Tayzia pivoted toward Pepper and pushed the button yet again. "Really well." She lowered the phone. "I could stay here all day shooting and writing. This place is—"

The rumble of an engine interrupted them. Toby and the Gator rounded the corner of the barn and came into view. He waved at Pepper and swung the utility vehicle toward her, stopping a few inches in front of her feet.

"You trying to hit me?"

"Did I scare you?"

His words addressed Pepper, but his eyes wandered toward Tayzia.

"Toby, meet Tayzia Santiago, world traveler, helper of children, and my newest friend." Pepper gestured from Tayzia to Toby. "Tayzia, this is Toby Davies, youngest member of the Davies Orchard clan, lover of all cars, especially my Mustang, and world-class picker of delicious strawberries."

Tayzia extended her right hand.

127

Toby stared openly at her but held both his hands out, palms upward. Red splotches, mingled with dirt smudges, covered his skin. "I'm a mess. Occupational hazard." He gestured toward the strawberry-filled bed of the vehicle.

Tayzia leaned toward the Gator. "They're worth the trouble." She smiled at him before pulling her phone from her bag and taking a close up of the fruit-lined Gator. "Mind if I get you in the next one? Newspapers like pictures of people."

"Newspapers?"

Pepper smiled at the "duh" expression on Toby's face. "Tayzia's going to write an article about her trip to PA once she returns on California. You might be famous."

"You're from California?"

"Yes." She lowered her phone.

"And you write for a newspaper?"

A gust of wind whipped hair across her face. She brushed it away. "I sometimes submit articles. Usually they're accepted." She stepped to the back of Toby's vehicle.

Toby angled his body, draping one arm over the front edge of the bed and turning toward the back."

"On three." She positioned her phone.

Toby settled himself and flashed a toothy grin.

"One. Two." The click of the phone sounded. "Three."

"You didn't wait until three." He scowled at her.

"I never do." She pulled the phone away from her face. "The pictures are better if I snap them after "two.""

"Not fair."

Stepping toward Pepper she held out the phone. "I'd say I caught him at the right time."

Pepper studied the picture on the screen. She bobbled her head toward Tayzia.

"Let me see." Toby scooted across the seat, narrowing the distance between them. Tayzia extended her phone. Toby's eyes squinted. "That's one good-looking dude."

Tayzia and Pepper looked at each other and rolled their eyes. "And so humble," Pepper said. She swatted Toby's ball cap from his head.

Tayzia tucked her phone away. "The rest of the Son-Light crew will be here soon. I'll walk down to the parking lot to meet them."

"Will I see you later with some other little admirers?" Pepper asked.

Another of Tayzia's infectious laughs filled the afternoon air. "Probably several. Buster's really popular with them." She took a few steps toward the parking area and then turned back. "Thanks, Pepper. I had fun." Looking toward the Gator she added, "Nice to meet you, Toby."

With long strides Tayzia headed off. Pepper watched for a moment.

Then she remembered Buster. "I need to get to the barn." Whirling around, she started in that direction.

Toby hadn't moved. His gaze still followed the willowy young woman. Pepper cuffed his arm. "What's the matter? Did she 'tase-ya'?"

He blinked, shook his head, and blinked again. "Yeah. I think so."

"Good thing you don't have to think to pick strawberries."

"Ugh." Toby flung his arms around the steering wheel column and slumped forward.

Pepper laughed and slapped him on the back. "I'll tell her you said goodbye."

CHAPTER 14

On weekdays, the orchard closed at 5:30. By 5:40 on Tuesday afternoon, Fred Hanna had left for home. Pepper helped Sue and Anna with kitchen clean up.

"Whew." Anna returned a stack of large baking sheets to their storage places. "How many pies did you sell today, Mom?"

"Over fifty."

"Fifty pies?" Pepper gaped at Sue.

She smiled and nodded. "We bake eight at a time. I know we did seven batches." Sue dried her hands on a towel. "Are there any left in the pie safe next to you, Pepper?"

"You know what a pie safe is?" Zeke had stepped inside in time to hear his mother's question.

Aside from the encounter when he'd delivered Pepper's new outfit, their paths had crossed very little throughout the day. No doubt he was busy. Was he also avoiding her? Probably.

"I'm guessing it's this thing." Pepper opened the doors of a large cupboard having glass panels in the double doors and air vents in the three sides. Three pies, along with one from which some pieces had been removed, remained in storage.

"Good guess." Stepping behind Pepper, Zeke reached his long arm around her, and snagged one of the pieces. "Three wholes and two slices, Mom. Minus the piece I'm eating. I missed lunch."

"We wondered." Sue gathered dish cloths and towels into a laundry bag. Walking by the door, she hung the bag on the doorknob. "Supper at 6:30." Coming over to Pepper, she said, "We'd like you to eat with the family tonight. Since Dad has gone home, and you and Mom did therapy this afternoon, you don't need to rush off. We always like to compare notes at the end of the first day. We're eager to hear about Buster."

Pepper leaned against the counter. "Are you sure?"

"Absolutely." Sue reached into the pie safe and pulled out two pies. "Grab the other one, will you?"

Within two minutes, Sue had wrapped each pie and the remaining slice in its own plastic bag and placed all four in the cooler. "We'll sell these 'day olds' tomorrow at a reduced price." She crossed to the door and reclaimed the laundry. "See you at supper."

* * *

"You have to up your game, Zeke." Toby voiced his opinion as the Davies brothers stored the day's produce and supplies before going to supper.

Ike set two quarts of strawberries in the cooler and then stared at his youngest brother. "To compete with a doctor who earns a six-digit salary and drives a Porsche? Right."

Apparently Ike shared Zeke's confidence level.

"Pepper likes Zeke. Everybody knows that." More input from Toby.

At least he hadn't said "Zeke likes Pepper." Could Toby be right about her?

"Should Zeke be 'in the game' with a girl who doesn't love God?" Joe's question was the clincher.

"Enough already." Zeke made eye contact with each brother. "Stay out of this. I'll handle it."

* * *

How was he going to handle it? The idea was easy. The plan wasn't. Cleaning up before going to supper at Mom and Dad's, Zeke tossed one idea after another around in his brain.

Avoid her. He'd managed to for most of the day. But when she had two donkeys to drive and more riders to carry, he would need to be near her more often.

Give her the cold shoulder. And forfeit any opportunity to live out God's kindness to her and help her see her need.

Be a friend. And brace himself for being no more than a friend who watched while she dated, and maybe fell in love with, someone else.

As usual, the hardest choice was the best. Closing the door to his house, he started for supper. "Help me, God."

* * *

131

"Pepper made fifteen trips each hour." Zeke sprawled in a recliner next to his dad. "You must have had multiple riders. The can had twenty dollars each time."

"She made forty dollars all day?" Toby elbowed Pepper who sat next to him on the couch. "Move her to the strawberry field. As fast as she picks, she can make a lot more there."

Sitting on Pepper's other side, Anna asked. "But how many people came today because of the donkey rides? And bought strawberries, black raspberries, pie, or something from the gift shop while they were here?"

Joe entered both the room and the conversation. He held a single sheet of paper in his hands. "Whatever the reason, this was our best opening day ever. Sales were nearly twelve percent higher than last year."

Shouts, cheers, and high fives filled the room.

"Good job, everyone." Harold made eye contact around the circle. "I feel like I should be giving awards to each of you. Thanks for working hard."

"I do have one presentation to make." Sue lifted a gift bag from the floor at the end of the couch. "Pepper, this is for you."

"Another present?"

"*Another* present?" Four masculine voices echoed Pepper's.

"I didn't get a present today," Ike protested. "Did you, Zeke? Toby? What about you, Joe?"

During the hubbub, Pepper had looked inside to find exact copies of the clothes she had opened earlier. With misty eyes, she turned to Anna.

"So that you have a spare. Wear your own clothes home tonight. Leave these here. We'll wash yours along with everyone else's."

"I can do my own laundry." She leaned toward Anna. "And Fred's, too."

"Mom prefers to do it all. That way everyone's clothes wear and fade the same."

"It's more work for her."

Sue disagreed. "Adding one more to the load is no work at all. Go and change out of those." She gestured at Pepper's clothes.

"I left mine in the office."

Zeke rose. "I'll get them."

"I'll go with you." Pepper jumped from her seat. "I think my head band is there, too."

* * *

Zeke should say something. But what? Nothing came. Reaching the barn, he slid the door open, stepped inside, and turned on the light. "I'll grab your clothes. You look for the—"

Her snicker cut off the rest. She covered laughter with her hand.

What had he blurted? "I didn't mean it that way."

Her eyes gleamed. "I know." She laughed again. "Freudian slip."

"Yeah."

Her giggles stopped. She stared up at him. "You're one of the few guys I know who wouldn't mean it that way."

She'd paid him a compliment. Her words shouldn't sting. But they did.

Friends. That's all he and Pepper could be.

* * *

The bustle of Wednesday, Thursday, and Friday of week one kept Pepper hopping. The Saturday pace left her breathless. When she wasn't driving the cart, she was picking strawberries, selling them, or running back and forth to the Hannas'. Each one-hour slot for donkey rides had been expanded to an hour and a half, and small passengers were encouraged to double up. Still, some children and their parents left with frowns. Having Axle would help, but he wasn't ready, and Pepper had had little time this week to devote to his training.

Zeke caught her as she hurried toward the Mustang just after 4:00 on Saturday afternoon. "I hate to ask this." He averted his gaze momentarily. "Can you come an hour early or stay an hour late each day? We need Axle."

How could she argue? "We do." Where would she find the extra time? She changed position so that Zeke blocked the afternoon sun she was gazing into. "I'm not a morning person." She looked askance at him when his eyes rolled upward. "Evenings would be better for me."

"I thought so." His words were serious, but his eyes glimmered slightly.

She added, "But they might be harder for Maggie."

"I talked with Gramps. He can take supper home when he leaves at night."

Zeke raised his hand to squelch her interruption. "You'll eat here." He shifted his weight. "After closing, we'll work with Axle until Mom's ready for supper."

"What about the end-of-day responsibilities?"

"The others can handle them."

"I'll be skipping out on Maggie."

"But working more here."

"Your family is already doing so much for me."

Looking toward his shoes, he shook his head. "You're helping us."

"I don't see how."

"Sales are up."

"The strawberry crop is really good." Picking sessions with Toby had yielded more information than simply learning how to gather baskets of berries quickly. "Great berries. More people."

"It doesn't always work that way."

She slanted her head and stared at him.

"Everyone's crop is good this year. People can buy strawberries anywhere."

His logic was sound.

"The trick is to bring people in." He gestured broadly with his hand. "You and Buster have helped to do that."

"I'm having so much fun."

"People can tell." His gaze met hers and held briefly. "Is tonight too soon to start?"

Even with Saturday's earlier closing, Pepper would be pushed for time. "I can't tonight."

* * *

She was going out with Marco. Zeke read the truth in her eyes. He pulled the bill of his ball cap lower on his forehead. "We'll plan for Tuesday."

"I could work on Monday."

The one weekday that the orchard was closed. "I'll be gone all morning. Maybe in the afternoon." He started toward his house. "Someone will let you know when I get back."

"You'll call me then?"

Was there enough distance between them that she'd believe he hadn't heard her last words? Distance was crucial.

* * *

At 6:00, Pepper heard the doorbell.

"I'll get it," Fred called.

"I'll be out in a minute."

Fred's voice carried down the hallway. "Good evening, doctor."

134

"Hello, sir." Marco's reply drifted her way. "How are you? And how is Maggie?"

"Maggie's good. She does more each day. Right now she's on the phone with our son in Maine." Pepper heard the door close. "I'm tired out. Busy, but good, week at the orchard."

"I was surprised to learn that your apple orchard was opening this week. Hadn't heard about the strawberries."

"We're a lot more than orchard these days."

"Diversification probably helps."

"Ezekiel's been saying so for years. We're all glad we listened."

Pepper entered the living room. Marco's eyes smiled at her. "I am, too. Diversification gave Pepper a job and a reason to be here."

"Actually," Pepper said, stepping closer, "Maggie's knee replacement is the real cause of my being here."

Marco smiled. "Guess I'll have to thank myself for your arrival."

"Not so fast, you two. It was all in the good Lord's plan." Fred's frank assessment left little room for argument.

"See you in the morning," Pepper said, hurrying herself and Marco toward the door."

* * *

"Did Fred mean that about God's part in Maggie's surgery?" Marco had escorted Pepper to his Porsche and opened the door.

"I'm sure he did." Pepper settled in before addressing Marco. "Fred thinks that God controls everything in our lives. He prays to God like you and I talk to people." She waited for Marco to go around and get in. "He reads the Bible every day. That's how God talks to him."

"He never struck me as one of those."

"Those what?"

"Faith-over-science people."

Pepper pursed her lips and wrinkled her forehead. "He had you do his wife's surgery, didn't he?"

"Yeah. So—"

"So he trusts science to some degree." Pepper pondered a moment and then said, "Fred doesn't think faith and science are mutually exclusive." Memories of Maggie's husband reading the Bible and praying prompted her to add. "But I'm pretty sure he trusts God more."

* * *

135

Pulling into a nearly-filled lot a few minutes after seven, Marco parked, left the car running and said, "Be right back." He slid from the Porsche, and, before closing the door, bent to glance at Pepper. "My favorite pizza, coming right up. Wine? Water? Infused Tea?"

"Not wine." Her debacle of a few weeks ago still haunted her. "Tea or water will be fine."

Next, Marco treated Pepper to a showing of "Shakespeare in the Park," one of the annual presentations of the bard's plays that were held each summer in Harrisburg. This evening's event was *Antony and Cleopatra*. Never one to sit and read, Pepper had experienced few classics and had never seen a live performance of one of Shakespeare's works. Had she known Marco's plans, she might have tried to dissuade him, especially since the trip from Lewisburg to Harrisburg took slightly more than an hour.

During the performance, they enjoyed the artisan pizza topped with asparagus, mozzarella, ricotta, pesto, and olives. The combination was as foreign to Pepper as was live Shakespearean theater, but she enjoyed both.

By evening's end she had gained a level of admiration for the long-deceased playwright. The acting level, the costumes, and the outdoor stage combined to enliven the characters and engulf the audience in envy, treachery, disgrace, reconciliation, and love.

Returning to the car shortly after ten, they began the trip home. Soothing jazz floated through the surround-sound speakers.

"Thanks for a great evening."

Even the dim dashboard lights caught the glow of Marco's eyes. "You're welcome."

"How did you know about this?"

"I grew up here." He negotiated the on-ramp to the interstate. "I've seen several 'Shakespeare in the Park' programs."

"Ever seen this one?"

"Twice before. It's a favorite."

"I can see why."

The conversation navigated from Pepper's childhood in Philadelphia, to Marco's family still in Italy, to her days with Maggie and Fred, to his busy practice. Somewhere in the middle of his recitation of first-year struggles, Pepper's early start, her long day, and her protracted evening caught up with her. Silky tones of a saxophone lulled her into contemplation.

Would Maggie and Fred choose faith over science? How did a person reconcile those two concepts? How long would it be before Axle was ready? Would Zeke still be talking to her after tonight?

"Pepper? Are you asleep?"

She jerked to attention. "No, just thinking. Sorry."

"Thinking is generally considered a good thing."

"Not when it's more like daydreaming. You'll think I didn't enjoy myself." Leaning toward him, she added, "I had a really great time."

"So did I."

He turned the car into the Hannas' driveway.

Finally focused again, she ran her fingers through the somewhat squashed curls at the back of her head. "I'm a sight."

"One I've enjoyed watching all evening." His warm hand caressed her lower arm. "One I'd like to see again."

Warm fuzzies invaded Pepper's heart and head. "I'd like that, too—no—not to see me again—but for me to see you again—for us to see each other."

Marco laughed and squeezed her arm. "I agree." He held her gaze. "Next week?"

She nodded.

He got out, went around, and helped Pepper from the car. "I'll call."

* * *

Eleven thirty. Zeke rubbed the sleep from his eyes and reread the numbers. Definitely time for bed. He could stay here on the couch. His bed was more comfortable. The couch was already warm. The bed was roomier. He shoved himself up, crossed to the kitchen and flipped off the light above the sink. Car headlights and the roar of a souped-up engine jogged Zeke's memory of Marco Girardi's white Porsche.

Marco and Pepper. If Zeke slept, he wouldn't have to think about them—together.

CHAPTER 15

Early Tuesday morning, Pepper entered the kitchen and found Maggie standing in front of the stove. Maggie's walker abutted the range. Pepper's jaw dropped. "Did Dr. Girardi say you're ready for this?"

Maggie smiled at Pepper. "He's a nice young man and an excellent surgeon, but he doesn't know how I feel."

"He knows those knees. He understands how they work in someone's body."

"I'm much stronger these last few days. You said so yourself."

Pepper recalled her own words. "You'll be running around in no time." She hadn't been serious. "Does Fred know you're out here?"

"He went to the orchard early."

"So he doesn't know."

"He would worry." Maggie's eyes misted over. "I feel so useless."

Pepper erased the distance between them. "It's been only a little over two months since your surgery." She placed her hand on Maggie's shoulder. "Please sit down."

"Two months is a long time," Maggie sighed. She stared at Pepper before turning the walker and maneuvering herself to the table.

"It seems that way." Again Pepper patted the older woman's shoulder. "But full recovery from bilateral replacement usually takes four to six months. And that's without infection."

"I want to do the things I usually do: plant flowers, make meals, ride along with Fred on orchard business."

"And you will, eventually." Pepper wrinkled her forehead. "You might have to wait until next spring for the flowers."

A smile rose to Maggie's lips and then glimmered in her eyes. "Probably best."

Pepper checked the stove to be sure everything was turned off. "So, what can I get for you?"

"Nothing. I'm not really hungry. I just wanted to feel useful."

"Keep me company while I eat." Pepper grabbed the milk from the fridge and a bowl from the cupboard. "A more suspicious person might think you were trying to get rid of her." She reached for a spoon and snagged her favorite cereal.

Maggie's laugh erased her earlier gloom. "A more suspicious person would be wrong."

"Good. Because I'm not ready to leave here, but I wouldn't want to wear out my welcome."

"I can't see that happening."

Mentally, Pepper added two items to her growing "to do" list. 1. Talk more with Maggie. 2. Ask others to visit her.

Loneliness and impulsiveness were often a patient's worst enemies.

* * *

"Whoa, Axle." Pepper steadied her charge while Zeke eased the arms of the cart nearer the donkey. No matter how carefully Zeke approached, Axle sidled and shifted away. Pepper had stopped counting after six attempts.

This effort ended abruptly. Axle kicked at the bar, knocking it from Zeke's hand. The clatter echoed throughout the barn.

Zeke huffed. He threw his cap onto the floor and slammed his fist onto the top rail.

"I have an idea," Pepper said. It might be ridiculous, but since they'd made almost no progress since closing time, how much could it hurt? "Let's bring Buster out here, hook him to the cart, and stand him next to Axle." She stepped around the donkey and picked up Zeke's hat. "These two seem to communicate. Maybe Buster can send some donkey sense to Axle. Or at least some courage."

Zeke released the railing and turned toward her. "I can't think it will work." He accepted the cap from her. "But let's give it a try."

Five minutes later, Buster once again wore the harness. But another complication had arisen.

Anna stuck her head into the barn. "Supper's ready."

"I can't come for a few minutes," Zeke said. "Pepper can explain. Tell Mom I'll be in as soon as possible."

To Anna's questioning look, Pepper replied, "I'll tell you on the way."

* * *

Zeke shut the door after Pepper and Anna. He led Axle, who had been eating while they harnessed Buster, from the pen. Zeke untied the younger donkey, allowing him free access to his friend. Axle sniffed the harness. Buster glanced over.

Zeke watched for several minutes without moving. The two did seem to be sharing secrets. Had Buster shared enough?

Moving deliberately and allowing Axle to watch every step, Zeke unharnessed Buster, easing the leather reins, the girth, and the traces onto Axle. So far, so good. Buster stood as though still restrained. Positioned between the two donkeys, Zeke lifted the shafts above Buster and over Zeke's own head. Repositioning his hands on the bars, he lowered them slowly onto Axle. The donkey's hide shivered slightly as if he were repelling an insect. Buster whinnied. Axle stood still. Without being kicked at or backed away from, Zeke slid the red shafts into the loops on the harness.

"Thanks, Pepper."

* * *

"The meal was great." Pepper smiled at Sue. "I know everyone usually stays and talks, but would you excuse me? I want to see if Zeke was able to get Axle hooked up to the cart."

"Is he having trouble?" Harold asked.

"Axle won't cooperate." Pepper slid her chair backward. "He can't give cart rides without a cart."

Chuckles emanated from around the table.

"Go ahead, then."

Pepper turned the corner into the kitchen and scurried out the door and down the driveway. She heard the creaky slide of the massive barn door. A few seconds later, a donkey, complete with cart and rider, emerged.

Pepper squealed and ran toward them. "Axle, you did it." She patted his neck and rubbed his shoulder. "You look dashing in all of your finery."

Grinning, she approached Zeke. "You look a little crunched in that cart."

"I fit but not comfortably." He eased from the tight quarters and handed Pepper the reins. "It worked. Thanks for the idea."

"A thought born out of desperation."

"Or sent from God just when I needed it." He looked away. A moment later he said, "Sorry I gave in to my temper."

Was throwing his ball cap and pounding a rail a display of temper? "I wanted to do more than that, and he wasn't kicking at me."

A half-hearted smile crossed his lips. "Still, I shouldn't have done it." He gazed at her.

Pepper's heart thumped. Whatever was between Zeke and her, it hadn't gone away.

"Can you spare a few more minutes."

Pepper's head bobbled excited.

"Climb aboard. I'll walk beside him until we're sure that Axle knows what he's doing."

If only Pepper had a clue what she was doing.

* * *

What are you doing? The question reverberated through Zeke's brain. *Being a friend.* That was the plan he'd adopted. They had to work together. He couldn't stay mad at her. Even though he sometimes wished he could.

She was fun. She was quick. She was cute. She made him want to laugh.

She ignores God.

The two-edged sword of reality cut Zeke's heart. After Saturday's date, she hadn't gone to church with his grandparents on Sunday. No more opportunity for her to hear God's truth. No discussion about what the sermon had meant. No apparent reason for him to hope for a change.

But he could still pray. And when he did, he'd also ask God for willpower. He would need lots of it.

* * *

After her 11:30 lunch break on Wednesday, Pepper spent about thirty minutes selling strawberries before getting ready for the next donkey cart times. She had pulled a small wagon load of berries to the display area and was lifting quart containers into the empty spaces when someone tapped her on the shoulder.

She turned and stood facing her friend and former employer. "Emma!" Amid squeals and laughter, the two hugged, stepped apart, and then hugged again. "You look great."

Emma's brown eyes sparkled. Her short, straight brown hair framed her pretty face. She didn't seem any different even after a nearly fatal bout with bacterial meningitis.

"So you traded chocolate for strawberries." Emma appraised the fruit in front of her. "I think I'll take some of these with me and dip them."

"Oh, yummy."

"Remember me?" A voice drifted from behind Emma.

Pepper looked up. "Landon." She stretched to hug the tall, well-built man whose arm had rested on Emma's shoulder. "I'm so excited to see both of you." She clasped Emma's arm and dragged her forward. Toby stood at the Gator, unloading berries onto a wagon like the one Pepper had been using. "Emma Porter, this is Toby Davies. He's the one to see about strawberries."

"Hi." He nodded his greeting.

"Toby, this is Emma Porter."

"The candy lady you talk about all the time while we pick?" Toby grinned and elbowed Pepper.

"The very one." To Emma, she added, "It's all good."

"How many strawberries do you want?"

"Three quarts. But—"

"But?"

"I need three quarts of large berries, fairly equally sized so that I can dip them and sell them individually." She raised both hands, palms up and shrugged. "Can you do that?"

"We can do that." Zeke had joined the group and answered Emma's question. "I'll sort a few quarts and bring you the selects. Mom can use the smalls in jam."

"Emma, this is Zeke Davies. The oldest brother." She didn't divulge the circumstances of their meeting. "Zeke, this is Emma Porter, and this is—"

"Landon Steele. I know." He extended his hand toward Landon. "We graduated from Penn State the same year."

Pepper checked to see if she needed to scrape her jaw from the concrete. Zeke and Landon had been classmates?

"You didn't drive over an hour just to buy strawberries, did you?" she asked.

Emma answered, "We came to see you." A blush crept up her cheeks.

Landon clasped Emma's left wrist and raised it to Pepper. "And to show you this."

"You're engaged!" People gaped in their direction. Pepper clapped a hand over her mouth. She lowered her voice. "When is the wedding?"

"September fifth." The gushing couple spoke in tandem.

Pepper's brows furrowed.

"The first Penn State game this year." Emma giggled. "PSU football brought us together."

Pepper studied Emma's ring. "I would have guessed New Year's Day, the day Emma made up her mind."

"Too long to wait—both then and now." Landon's warm gaze spoke volumes.

"You were one love-sick puppy at Christmas." Pepper tilted her head to glance sideways at Landon.

"And you didn't make my life any easier. Not telling me what I wanted to know."

"Just doing what the boss had asked."

Landon squeezed Emma to his side. "It all worked out in God's time."

Zeke went to gather the specialty berries for Emma. Pepper, Emma, and Landon talked until Pepper was needed for cart rides.

"We also came to see you in action. We're going to wave at you each time you pass." Emma hugged Pepper once again. "It's so good to see you. This looks like a great place to work."

"It is. The Davies family is wonderful."

When Zeke re-appeared bearing strawberries, Landon stepped with him to the register and paid for them.

"Any of them especially wonderful?" Emma's eyes gleamed. Her brows wiggled.

"Well—"

"Zeke?"

Pepper looked down.

Emma grabbed Pepper's arm. "I thought I sensed some chemistry. Come visit soon." She released Pepper and turned to find Landon. Looking back, she called over her shoulder, "Bring more berries. And Zeke."

* * *

"It all worked out in God's time." Landon's words repeated in continuous play in Zeke's brain. Was Landon a Christian? Zeke thought hard, trying to retrieve all the information he knew about Landon Steele. He recalled the *Sports Illustrated* article. He'd read the entire thing, pleasantly surprised at the humility of the guy and how often he spoke of God.

What had been necessary to "work out" between the two of them? How had God done it? How long had it taken? If only Zeke had had the time and the courage to ask.

The conversation offered hope. By autumn, Emma and Landon would be married.

Pepper's joy had bubbled over. Zeke smiled at the mental picture of her bobbing up and down. *Happy endings still occur.*

Those words displaced Landon's as Zeke returned to the fruit stand. Was one of them headed in his direction?

* * *

"What's on your schedule for Monday?" Pepper asked at the end of the day Wednesday.

Zeke paused in his motion of tossing hay into the mule's pen. He studied her. "Nothing firm that I remember. Why?"

Unexpected butterflies swirled in Pepper's stomach. "What would you say to making a small delivery in Bellefonte?"

He threw the hay over the railing. "A few quarts of select strawberries to a chocolate shop?"

Zeke had paid attention. "I'll buy the gas, and you can drive my car," she said.

He adjusted his ball cap. "That's hard to refuse."

She bounded toward him. "Really?"

"I'll have to check my calendar." He picked up another handful of hay.

Pepper blocked his path. "Go. Check." She pointed toward the office.

"I'm feeding animals." He glanced over the hay. "It can wait."

"But I can't. C'mon, Zeke." She grasped the hay.

He didn't relinquish his hold. "The sheep are hungry."

Pepper growled but let go. "Stupid sheep."

Zeke leaned away. "Did you just call my sheep stupid?" A glint lit his eye. "Thought you loved animals."

"Except when they interfere with my plans." She extended her arms again.

He held the hay out of her reach and bent toward her. "That's not love."

"We're talking sheep, not people." She settled her fists at her waist. "Hurry."

"If you'd move . . ."

She complied.

A few seconds later, Zeke traipsed toward the office, Pepper hurrying him along.

He surveyed the calendar on the wall before turning back to her. "All clear."

"Yea!" She grabbed his forearms. "We're going to the candy shop."

"You don't need sugar."

144

"But wait till you taste Emma's work." She rubbed her tummy and allowed her head to loll backward. "Blissful."

"What time?"

Jerking her head forward, she quipped, "The shop opens at eight a.m. Let's be there by then."

"Sure about that?" He picked up a marker and reached toward the calendar. "We'll need to leave a few minutes before seven. It's your day off." His hand poised above Monday's square, he looked back at her.

She cast him an oblique glance. "I'm getting used to being up early."

* * *

After prayer service on Wednesday evening, Zeke returned to his office. They'd been open less than two full weeks, and already the paper work was piling up. Checking the clock on the wall, Zeke glanced past his calendar. On Monday's date he'd written "Bellefonte, 6:45-??" He'd wanted to write "Pepper." He'd even considered adding a heart or two. What a sentimental dolt he'd become.

He reached into the bottom right-hand drawer of his desk. Lifting a paper from the rest of the stack, he uncovered the photo of Pepper and her mom. How many times had he studied it?

If Pepper knew how strongly she resembled her mother— Better not think about it. He focused on their faces. Both sets of eyes conveyed wariness and longing. Not for the first time Zeke wondered that those emotions co-existed. Did Pepper realize she yearned for her mom? Would she slap him if he suggested it?

Approaching footsteps startled him into action. He hurried the picture into its spot and covered it up, sliding the drawer shut at the same time that Joe entered.

"Dad wanted me to give this to you."

Zeke accepted the paper his brother held. The feed bill. One more check to write.

"Thanks, Joe."

"Troubles?"

"No, why?"

"You're up late." Joe turned a bucket upside down and sat on it. "A lot, recently."

"Everything's fine with the orchard." Zeke shuffled some papers on the desk.

"I know. I help with the books." Joe stared at his older brother. "It's not the orchard, is it?"

145

Zeke released the papers in his hands but didn't look at Joe. "Nope."

"She might not change."

Finally, Zeke turned to Joe. "I'm praying you're wrong."

"I am, too."

* * *

Marco called on Thursday evening. "Monday is your day off, right?"

"Right." Tightness crept into the area around Pepper's heart.

"I'll see if I can reschedule my afternoon. We'll spend the rest of the day together."

"Not this—"

"What sounds good?" He paused. "Did you say something?"

Trying to catch him up, Pepper answered, "Lots of things sound good. But not for Monday."

"Why not?"

"I'll be out of town."

"Where you going?"

"To Bellefonte. To visit my friend Emma. I worked for her for a while."

"Need an escort?"

He was persistent. "I know the way. Besides, I'm leaving early."

"Maybe we can do something that night."

"Not sure what time I'll get back."

After a couple minutes of polite banter, she ended the call. Why hadn't she mentioned Zeke? He wasn't a secret to Marco. She hadn't lied. She simply hadn't volunteered information.

Zeke didn't drive a Porsche. He wasn't a doctor. Was she ashamed of him? Absolutely not. But their tenuous relationship was a treasure. Something to guard. Putting it on display would be like leaving a newborn rabbit outside in a thunderstorm. It would survive, but it wouldn't be strengthened. Until they had sorted out where they were with each other, Pepper would ponder things in her heart—not broadcast them to the world. Especially not to Marco.

* * *

"She's expecting us at the store at eight?" Zeke set a box holding four quarts of select strawberries on the floor behind the driver's seat.

"She's expecting us early. I hated to say eight o'clock for sure." Pepper looked at her watch. "Wasn't sure what time we'd be on the road."

146

"You all set?"

"I think so." Pepper rehearsed things, keeping track on her fingers. "Maggie's therapy is finished. Anna's coming later to help with her bath. Fred shooed me out with, 'Just go and have fun.'" She opened her door. "Guess that's it."

During her list, Zeke had stepped around the Mustang. He waited for her to settle. "Ready?"

She nodded, and Zeke shut the door. They were off.

* * *

Zeke stepped out of the way as Pepper scurried behind the counter and reached for a pair of plastic gloves.

"What can I do?" she asked.

The phone rang. "Answer the phone."

Zeke and Pepper had entered the shop at 8:05. Already people were lined up. The display case was well-stocked, but Emma couldn't keep up. Pepper had taken action.

"A friend of Betty Steele about some candies for an art show tonight." Pepper covered the mouthpiece while she spoke.

"I'd better talk to her." Emma stripped off her plastic gloves and cradled the phone. "Yes, Mrs. Abernathy."

Pepper slipped her hands into the gloves she'd picked up. "Oh, hello, Mr. Carter." A middle-aged man was next in line. "So good to see you again."

Finding a favorite coffee flavor and the most out-of-the-way chair, Zeke watched the pair in action.

Emma was the master of her product. She elaborated on the name and willingly offered small samples. On the display case glass, she had placed precise labels explaining the candy and listing ingredients. Pepper deferred all questions about the product to Emma.

In dealing with the customers themselves, Pepper was Emma's match. Her pleasant smile met everyone equally and made each happy to be purchasing chocolates. Zeke had grown up around customers, but he would never be as much at ease in a crowd as Pepper was naturally.

Nearly forty-five minutes later, the rush had finally subsided. Emma and Pepper turned to each other and began giggling.

"What's so funny?"

"Oh, Zeke, I'm sorry." Emma hurried from behind the counter. "I haven't had a Monday like this in weeks." She placed her hand on his

147

shoulder. "Thank you for coming today. I don't know what I'd have done without her."

"I just viewed a model of customer relations." He stood. "I know, in part, why your shop is busy, but I'll have to taste something besides this great coffee to see why people flock in at eight in the morning."

"Anything you want. On the house."

Still standing behind the counter, Pepper asked, "Are you all set with the chocolates for tonight? And what about the smaller orders for this afternoon?"

"Yikes. I'm not. I wasn't expecting to be so busy." Emma surveyed the items in the case. "Thought I'd have time to create between waiting on customers."

Zeke looked at Pepper. She gazed at him. His slight nod brought a huge smile to her face and a nearly breath-stopping obstruction to his throat.

"Zeke and I will help. He can run the cash register and handle some smaller orders." She rushed toward Emma. "Put on your creative genius cap and go create."

Emma started toward the kitchen. Her quick steps halted. "Landon's leaving work early. We wanted to take you for a picnic in the park." Her sigh was heavy and protracted. "Why can't I say 'no' to customers?"

"Customers mean business," Zeke said. As a boy, he'd heard Gramps repeat the words *ad nauseam.*

Emma looked around Zeke and at Pepper. "I knew I liked this guy."

Pepper winked at Zeke. "He kinda grows on you." She winked again.

Smiling, Emma bolted into the kitchen. The clatter of metal ensued. Zeke studied the cash register while his heart calmed. He tried to recall the last time a girl had winked twice at him. Girls often winked at Joe and sometimes at Ike. But Zeke—not so much. Once again Pepper had affirmed his conviction. She was unlike any girl he'd ever known.

A huge gasp from the kitchen reached his ears. "There are four quarts of beautiful strawberries in my fridge."

Zeke chuckled.

Pepper yelled, "I walked right by you when I carried them in."

"They're gorgeous." Mere moments passed. She appeared in the doorway. "And there are over fifty of them. One of the confections for tonight's shindig is going to be chocolate covered strawberries." She beamed at Zeke. "You truly are an answer to prayer—even before I asked."

No wonder people frequented Heavenly Chocolates. This woman was as sweet as her candies. Landon Steele was a blessed man.

"I bet this wasn't the way you thought the day would play out."

Zeke sat in the passenger seat of Landon's silver Camry. The trunk was loaded with sweet treats. He looked across at Landon. "Not really." It was actually better in some ways than he had hoped. "I did want to talk to you. Wondered whether I'd have the chance."

"About what?"

"You said about Emma and you that God had worked things out in His time." Zeke stared ahead. "Mind telling me what you meant?"

"What do you believe about God?"

The straight-forward approach reminded Zeke of the interview Landon had given.

"He's the Creator, the Sustainer, and, if we ask Him to be, our Savior."

"I assume, from your words, that you have asked Him to be." Landon scrutinized his passenger. At Zeke's nod, he continued, "Both Emma and I had, too, when we met. But she was living much closer to God than I was." He slowed to negotiate a curve. "If I spill these chocolates, Emma will have my hide." He raised one eyebrow. "She can be feisty."

"So can Pepper."

"That's for sure. That one's a spitfire." Landon glanced at Zeke. "Are you two dating?"

Zeke had expected to ask, not answer, the questions. "That's the part God has to work out." Zeke clutched the seat. "She hasn't accepted Him yet."

"And you won't be a part of an unequal yoke." Landon stopped at a light. "That's tough." The light changed. Landon eased into traffic. "Want some advice?"

"Definitely."

"Focus on your relationship to God. Not only on hers." Landon shook his head. "It sounds crazy, I know."

It really did.

"Read the Bible to hear God's voice. Pray. For you. For her." Landon pulled into a parking space near the back door of a large motel. "We're here." He popped the trunk open. "Most of all, don't rush her. But don't give in to what's not right."

* * *

149

"This was a wonderful day." Pepper rested her head against the back of the passenger seat. "Thank you for being so helpful. And for letting us change your plans."

"I didn't have any plans." Well, maybe one. But the Lord had worked it out. "Except to take you and some strawberries to Bellefonte."

"The strawberries. What made you bring four quarts when I'd only asked for three?"

"Wanted to be generous." Zeke couldn't explain it in any other way.

"And you were. More than you knew." Pepper grasped his arm. "If you'd brought only three, she wouldn't have had enough."

"God knew what Emma needed." Zeke blinked at how easily the door had opened. "He used us to provide for her." He glanced sideways. "The same way He used you in her shop."

"You really think God cares about things like that?"

Zeke detected curiosity but not skepticism. "I know He does."

"Besides what happened today, give me three examples."

Did she think he couldn't do it? "Anna and I finding you that Friday night before someone else did."

Her head slumped. Moments later, she looked up, pushing the curls from her eyes. "I'm really grateful." She turned toward him in her seat.

"Your being a pre-med major who knows about knee replacements and polio survivors." This was easy.

"It could be just a coincidence."

Zeke shot her his best I-can't-believe-you-said-that look. "Your liking animals and being the 'perfect fit' for a donkey cart."

She drew in a breath. "Everything you've said is about me."

"God uses people to help people." He momentarily looked away from the bare stretch of road. "I've got two more." And probably others if he had time to think. "Your people skills and your prior retail experience."

Her walls rose. "Other people have those abilities."

"In combination? Near enough to help? Willing to do so?" Would she see the Lord had put her into his family's lives?

Silence engulfed them. She was thinking. He was praying.

He'd never seen such stillness about her. Occasionally she glanced toward him. When he noticed, he looked back and smiled.

They reached his grandparents' home shortly after ten. A dim light shone from the living room. Zeke's Jeep waited in the driveway. He walked her to the door.

"Thanks, again." Facing him, Pepper placed her hand lightly on his arm. "For everything."

Covering her hand with his, Zeke whispered. "See you in the morning."

He turned toward his car. It had been a wonderful day.

CHAPTER 16

After the breakthrough moment with the harness, Axle caught on quickly. He made his debut on the following Friday, the kickoff of an event called the Ex-Straw-Vaganza, two days of drawing extra attention to in-season strawberries. In addition to the fresh berries and strawberry jam that were always available, visitors to the orchard could purchase strawberry shortcake, glazed strawberry pies, and strawberry smoothies. Sue hired more help to handle the additional baking and the extra responsibilities.

In honor of the occasion, Pepper cut out large paper strawberries and placed one on each side of the cart. She also attached paper strawberries to the harness medallions that hung on either side of the donkey's head. With the inclusion of Axle, Pepper was slated to give four hours of cart rides. Buster would begin at 10:00. Axle would make his entrance at 11:15. Each donkey would also pull for an hour in the afternoon, Buster at 2:00 and Axle at 3:15.

By 12:15, Pepper's head was awhirl from alternately chatting with children and encouraging her four-footed friends. Passengers had piled in two-by-two on every ride.

She expected to see Zeke or Joe in the barn to help her remove the harness from Axle. When neither appeared, she tackled the job herself, silently thanking Zeke for requiring her to learn how to do it. Success came, but slowly. Pepper left the barn shortly before 12:45.

"There won't be rides at one o'clock," Zeke had said earlier in the week. "If all goes well, this place will be so busy that we'll need some catch-up time by lunch." How right he was.

She muttered her thanks. Heading past the fruit stand, she saw a long line of customers waiting at the smoothie canopy. Anna was manning that station. "Need some help?"

"Do I ever," she gasped as Pepper approached. "My helper never showed. Mom has someone else coming, but she hasn't arrived yet."

"Let me wash up. I'll be right back."

"Hurry." Anna hit the "on" button on the blender. "Don't forget an apron."

Pepper ran to the bake shop, washed her hands at the designated sink, snagged a long white apron, and scurried back. Anna chopped, measured, and blended. Pepper took and delivered orders and collected money.

"Is Buster ready to go?"

Where had Zeke come from?

Removing his hat and rubbing his sleeve across his forehead, he added, "It's twenty minutes 'til the next cart rides."

Pepper gasped and seized the apron strings tied behind her. "He isn't." She slipped the cloth loop from around her head, and tossed the apron onto a chair.

"I can manage now. Heidi just arrived." Anna wiped the table top. "Thanks, Pepper."

Glancing toward the crowded fruit stand, Zeke asked. "Can you handle the harnessing?"

"Yes." She would have to hurry.

"Good." He started off. A few steps later, he called behind him, "And thanks."

* * *

"That was fun, Miss Pepper." Four-year-old Brady patted the donkey's shoulder and grinned once again. "Bye, Buster."

Brady's mom closed her phone and smiled at Pepper. "He'll talk about this for weeks. The picture makes it even better." Her eyes misted over.

"My pleasure." Pepper choked on her words.

Holding his dad's hand, Brady waved before the two ventured toward the shortcake canopy. The pre-schooler could walk, but his gait resembled a waddle, and he stumbled easily.

Looking closely at Brady's mom, Pepper asked, "Muscular dystrophy?"

Tears welled in the young woman's eyes. "Diagnosed a year ago." She pulled a tissue from her pocket. "He started falling a lot."

The words "I'll pray for him" flew to Pepper's mind. Fred would have uttered them easily, and he would have followed through. "I'm sorry." She truly was. In more ways than one. "Bring him again any time."

"We're from New Jersey." The boy's mom wiped her eyes. "Traveling back today from visiting family. We saw the ad in the newspaper. Brady loves animals."

"So glad you came."

"Me, too." She gulped, smiled sadly, and hurried to reach the others.

Pepper watched them go. Would her prayers for Brady have helped him? Could she have prayed if she thought they would?

* * *

Only two more trips after this one. Pepper's backside begged for relief. The seat seemed to be padded with gravel rather than foam. Clouds had rolled in. Small children needed naps more than cart rides. Pepper longed to join them in sleep.

She edged alongside the hitching post Zeke had erected as a starting and stopping point for all of the routes. Axle eased to a halt. Pepper slid from the cart and wrapped the reins around the post. Stepping in front of Axle, she headed toward the passengers still buckled in the cart.

A jet of water pelted the side of her face. Another zipped by her, blasting Axle's head. He brayed and jolted backward, straining at the reins. Pepper lost her balance and stumbled sideways.

Before she righted herself completely, several blips flashed through her mind, seemingly in slow motion but simultaneously. An unknown man grasping Axle's halter. Zeke snatching a water blaster from a teenager. Ranie calming two startled riders. Ranie. What was Pepper's mom doing here?

* * *

"If I ever see that kid here again, I'll—I'll." Zeke slammed his hand onto the hitching post. "Shooting a defenseless animal with water. Scaring little kids." He balled his hands into fists. "Startling Pepper. Nearly getting her hurt."

All of the Davies men, along with Pepper and her mom clustered at the hitching post when the work day had ended.

"Never seen you so mad, Zeke." Toby's eyes bulged. "Thought you might punch that kid."

"I wanted to."

"Good thing you didn't." Joe's quiet voice matched the calming hand he laid on Zeke's shoulder.

"Yeah." Zeke looked at his dad. "The word *lawsuit* blared through my brain. I eased up."

Harold nodded before addressing Pepper. "Good thing you left the kids buckled."

Pepper redirected the praise. "Good thing Zeke included the safety belt." Scenes of kids falling out and being run over and of bloody noses

154

and broken bones had flashed repeatedly through her mind in the minutes following the calamity. Her gaze met his.

"It's also a good thing you were here." Harold spoke again, this time to Ranie. "I know you're Pepper's mom, but I can't remember your name."

"It's Ranie. Short for Laurane."

"Ranie." Harold chuckled. "Sort of like cloudy and overcast?"

Ranie returned his laugh. "Sort of."

"We're glad you were here, no matter what the weather."

Pepper didn't echo Harold's sentiment. Maybe this one time she should make an exception. For the sake of two small, frightened boys. Maybe. But probably not.

* * *

The Davies crew was enjoying supper. Ranie had declined their invitation to stay. Pepper had changed out of her orchard clothes and had scurried to her car. Ranie was there waiting. The two stood alone between Pepper's Mustang and Ranie's Volvo. "Why are you still here?"

"I want to see you. You're not making it easy."

"You know all about making life difficult." *Get in your car and go.*

Ranie studied the stones. She sighed heavily. She scrutinized Pepper. "I'm sorry. I shouldn't have left all those years ago." She looked toward the house and then back at Pepper. "I should have found a way to cope."

"Yes, you should have."

Ranie wrung her hands repeatedly. "I was terrified. Of not being a good wife. Of not knowing how to care for a newborn."

"Lots of women are." Pepper stared relentlessly. "Not many desert their families."

"Do they repeatedly have visions of taking their own lives?"

Hopefully not.

If Ranie was acting, she could have won an Oscar. Her eyes pleaded for Pepper to understand. Her voice dripped with pathos. Her tears fell intermittently. Pepper leaned against her closed car door.

"The night before we were released from the hospital, the vision was of me wandering along a deserted highway in the dark. I saw headlights. I started running toward the vehicle. A few steps away from it, I dashed into the street, into the path of a fast-moving car. Brakes squealed. A horn blasted. Headlights glared at me—and at the baby in my arms."

Pepper's heart thumped. She whisked away the wetness in her eyes. When had tears formed? "You could have gotten help."

155

"Where?" Ranie flung both hands in front of herself. "My parents wanted nothing to do with me as soon as I told them I was pregnant."

Pops' parents couldn't have helped. Both had died before Pepper was born. "Your doctor. A free clinic."

Ranie slapped the back of one hand into the palm of the other. "Great options today. Especially for someone under age." She sighed in a huff. "But over twenty years ago, the options weren't the same."

Pepper had read evidence that supported Ranie's claim. She tried diversion. "Pops wanted to help."

The tears had returned. Ranie delved into the pocket of her capris and retrieved a tissue. "He tried." She mopped her eyes and blew her nose. "He couldn't. He didn't know any more about it than I did. And I couldn't explain."

"So you ran."

"But not like you think." Ranie's backbone stiffened. "Not like a freed prisoner heading home."

The vision flitted through Pepper's mind.

"I ran like a hunted animal searching for shelter."

"Shelter from an infant child and a loving husband?" Who ran from that?

"From myself. From my troubled mind."

Mental illness was real. Pepper couldn't deny that. It was also immensely powerful. But it could be treated. "You ran for help?"

"I tried." Ranie turned away from Pepper.

Pepper stepped closer. "Where?" What was she hiding?

"Old friends." Ranie covered her face with hers hands, massaging her forehead with her fingertips. "Who'd known me before."

The words were muffled but incendiary. "Before you had a husband and child?"

Pepper nearly spat the words.

Ranie's head jerked up. Her hands plummeted to her side. "Before I'd become suicidal."

This time, Pepper was the one to look away.

"I needed someone to say I'd be okay. To assure me that I had once been normal and could be again."

"Normal? You call it normal to run away from people who love you and need you?" Pepper turned and reached for the door handle. No more time for excuses and sad stories. "If you wanted normal you should have come back. Maybe Pops and I could have had some kind of normal, too."

Pepper swung the door wide, climbed in, and started the engine. She backed from her space before shifting into drive. Her heavy foot sent gravel flying. Using the rearview mirror, she glared back.

Ranie hadn't seen any of the soaring debris. She was sobbing into her hands.

* * *

Zeke alternated between staring into the parking lot and closing his eyes to pray for the women there. Body stances and gestures told a tale of explanations and frustration coming from both sides. A tissue and dabbed eyes testified of tears.

Was Pepper listening? Had Ranie come with reasons or with excuses?

His heart soared when Pepper stepped toward her mother. It plunged to his feet when she slammed the door and screamed away in a whirl of dust and stones.

Ranie Phelps cried until she exhausted her tissue. She wiped her eyes on her sleeve. Placing her raised arms on the roof of the car, she sobbed into the door frame. Anguish. Ranie personified it.

Zeke turned toward the dining room. The rattle of plates and silverware told him he'd nearly missed his meal. He glanced back.

Ranie lowered her arms from the car. She wiped both eyes with her fingertips. She tugged the hem of her shirt down and drew herself up to her fullest height. Before going to the driver's side of the car, she looked toward the house.

Zeke hurried to the door. Either the sound of the door's opening or the clomp of his steps caught Ranie's attention.

She called to him. "I'm not giving up."

A few seconds later, her car made a less dramatic exit from the orchard.

Zeke knew very little about Ranie Phelps. And most of what he did know wasn't flattering. But she had grit, the same kind he'd often witnessed in her daughter. Even under better circumstances, the two probably would have butted heads. Given their situation, conflicts were inevitable. She, however, had vented her emotions more appropriately than Pepper had.

Pepper. The name fit her. Spicy. Sharp. Capable of bringing tears to your eyes. Today's encounter with her mother showed yet another glimpse of her. Not a pleasing one.

Zeke leaned his back against the closed kitchen door. Should he and Anna have helped her that night? Yes. No doubts there. Should he have

157

called? What about his asking Anna to befriend her? The same questions he'd been asking for months bombarded his brain. New ones added ammunition. Was her curiosity about God only a front? Zeke had already told her that a relationship hinged on her decision. What about her fiery temper? It controlled her more than she realized.

Shoving away from the door, Zeke walked to the dining room and stood beside his mom's chair. "Sorry about supper." He clutched her shoulder and squeezed gently. "I'll get something later. Have to drive into town anyway."

She turned to look up at him. "Can I help?" Her gaze probed his face.

He recalled childhood days when she'd seemed able to read his troubled mind. Focusing on the wall on front of them, he said, "Don't think so." He squeezed her shoulder again. Avoiding eye contact with everyone else in the room, he hurried outside. His stomach growled. Better head to town now.

* * *

Not even the satisfaction of shunning her mom, coupled with the speed of acceleration could calm Pepper. Anger buzzed through her thoughts. When an occasional qualm appeared, her ire chopped it to bits. The engine hummed, Pepper fumed, and the miles sped away. Her first glance at the fuel gauge brought two stark realizations. Her Mustang needed gas, and she had no idea where to find it. She had no clue where she was. What road was she on? What direction had she headed? Philadelphia was east of Lewisburg. State College slightly west. Where was the sun? Where was her phone?

Pulling to the side of the road, she located the sun and determined she was driving north. Did she know anyone who lived north of Lewisburg? She grabbed the phone from her purse. "Siri, where is the nearest gas station to me?" *Please don't say you can't answer that.* Siri and she didn't always communicate well. A few seconds later, the phone lit, and Siri gave directions.

Ten minutes from here. Heading north. Not what she wanted to hear. "Siri, what is the closest gas station between here and Lewisburg?"

Siri cooperated again. Fifteen miles.

One of Priscilla's few faults was the old-fashioned fuel gauge, with no digital readout and only a peg that rested somewhere between Empty and Full. As a result of her dad's relentless hounding, Pepper rarely let the tank go lower than one-quarter full. She had never seen the needle leaning so far to the left. Could she make it fifteen miles? Should she try the closer station even though it was out of her way?

She tapped her fingers on the steering wheel. "Come on, baby." She patted the dashboard. Turning around in the deserted street, she headed toward Lewisburg.

Lurch. Chug. Sputter. Lurch. "Priscilla!" Pepper slapped the steering wheel with one hand. They had navigated thirteen miles of the fifteen-mile trip. Thirteen. Why hadn't she chosen the closer gas station. Chug. Sputter. Wheeze. Silence. Priscilla was empty.

"Noooooo!" Pepper pounded her feet on the floor. Whom should she call? She scanned her mental list. Anna. She wouldn't mind coming to rescue her friend, and Pepper would swear her to secrecy as to why being rescued was necessary. Pepper called. After only two rings, Anna's phone went to voice mail.

Pepper growled. She returned to her list. The only other nearby options all had the last name of Davies. And none of them would be willing to keep things quiet. Pepper dug for her wallet and removed the AAA membership card. Once again she returned to her phone.

* * *

Knowing that Saturday promised to be busier than Friday, Pepper arrived at the orchard early. Anna met her in the parking lot.

"Sorry I missed your call. Charging the battery."

Pepper often forgot to charge hers. Good thing she hadn't yesterday. "Everything okay?"

"Yeah. Had an issue with my car."

Anna placed her hand on the hood. "Not Priscilla."

Pepper hadn't recovered from being betrayed by her beloved vehicle. "You can't trust anybody these days."

Anna's eyebrows drew together. Her mouth opened.

Pepper forestalled any questions. "I'm fine. C'mon."

Anna joined her. "I'm setting up the smoothie booth. How about you?"

"Going to find Zeke and get my marching orders."

Anna handed some papers toward Pepper. "Save me a trip and give these to him, will you?"

"Sure."

"Probably in the barn. I think he slept there last night."

"In the barn?"

159

"Falls asleep doing paper work. If we don't see light coming from his kitchen window by five thirty, we know something's up." Anna paused as Pepper turned toward the barn. "See you later."

Given the heads up a moment earlier, Pepper didn't yell her entrance. Instead, she slowed her pace and lightened her tread. The office door was wide open. Somehow, Zeke had coaxed his rickety chair into a somewhat reclining position. His feet, still wearing the heavy work shoes, rested on the desk, and his long legs stretched out on an incline. His hands lay on his thighs. How could he sleep with his head cocked at such an angle?

Evidently, paper work had exhausted him. Zeke still held something in his hand. She stepped over to set the pages from Anna onto his desk.

His eyes blinked. Dragging his feet from the desk, he groaned and sat up. "Morning."

Disheveled would have been a kind word for his appearance. "I notice that you didn't put *good* in front of it."

"Not awake enough for that."

She redirected the papers toward him. "These are from Anna."

Stretching his right hand out to take them, he noticed the item he still held. Pepper saw it, too. She gasped. "What are you doing with that picture?"

He stared up at her but made no response.

"Did she give it to you?" Pepper snapped the words at him.

"If by 'she,' you mean your mom, no, she didn't." He hadn't raised his voice or lifted his body from the chair.

"Give it to me." She snatched at it.

"No." He pulled it away from her and stood up.

"I don't want her around. I don't want to be in photographs with her."

"That's your choice." He perched on his desk, one leg on the floor, one dangling in the air.

"Apparently not, since you have a picture of us." She stepped directly in front of him and held out her hand. "I want that picture."

"So do I."

Her hands on both her hips, she tapped her foot repeatedly. "But I don't want you to have it." Her volume had risen with each word. She grabbed for the photo once again. Snagging it, she tugged hard, but Zeke didn't let go.

A second later, Pepper gaped at the jagged photograph in her hand. Ranie stared up at her. "Give me the other half."

He stared at Pepper's likeness and then at her. "Guess I'll call your dad."

She hung her head to one side and rolled her eyes. Did he think she was a kid he could intimidate by tattling?

Handing her the tattered picture, Zeke said, "He gave me that one." He crossed to the door before looking back. "I'm glad you stopped in. I was going to find you." His gaze hardened, but his voice remained calm. "If you ever again tear out of this parking lot like you did last Friday, you're fired."

Blood rising to her face, Pepper blurted, "Might as well fire me . . ." The bray of a donkey and the sudden drooping of Zeke's shoulders suspended her outburst. She stared hard at him. Then, shuffling the pieces of the torn picture from hand to hand as she went, she strode past Zeke toward the stall where Axle and Buster waited.

* * *

Pops had given Zeke the picture. Pepper paced round and round the donkey pen.

Axle and Buster were outside in the petting zoo enclosure. Even with their constant exposure to children during the cart rides, they still liked being near people during their off times. Usually Pepper would have shared their enjoyment of others.

Today she was hiding out.

If only Ranie hadn't dropped back into her life. Her mother had upset everything—again. Sad stories and lame excuses, that's all she offered. Pepper completed one circuit of her hide-away lair.

And new beginnings.

She slapped her hand onto the railing and the words from her mind. She didn't want any more new beginnings. She'd already started fresh with new friends, new summer responsibilities, and two new dating opportunities.

Maybe only one now.

Pops was partially to blame. He should have told her about the photo. It had been taken on graduation day. The minutes immediately following commencement were mostly a blur. So many people sharing congratulations. So many calling, "Look over here. Smile." She remembered Zeke taking several pictures. Must be some of those had been for Pops. Why had he offered one to Zeke? Why hadn't he given one to her?

He's not stupid.

Midway through another circle, Pepper plopped onto the straw bedding on the floor. Pops wasn't stupid. He knew Pepper's answer without asking the question. But why Zeke?

She tucked her legs up close to herself and rested her chin on her knees. Pops didn't know about Zeke and Anna's rescuing her from a drunken stupor, and she hadn't told him about Zeke's protective instincts.

What had she told him? Anna's oldest brother. Twenty-seven years old. Tall. The basics paraded through her memory. What else? Loves animals. Finds ways to modernize the orchard. Works hard. Loves God. Loves his family.

He's not stupid. Pops knew Pepper was interested in Zeke.

But what about the picture? Was it to thank Zeke for capturing an image that Pops undoubtedly treasured? Why not deliver a hearty handshake and a slap on the back?

Why had Zeke taken that particular photo on graduation day? He had barely heard of Ranie until then. What made him think that Pops would accept a picture of the woman who had caused him so much pain?

Pepper turned her head to one side. She scrutinized the wood grain of the railings. After counting twelve distinct knotholes, she raised her head. *He's not stupid.* Maybe Pops had calculated the evidence and deduced that the chemistry between Pepper and Zeke went full circle.

"Pepper." Zeke's voice. She pulled her legs tightly toward herself. She tucked her head and stilled her movements. Maybe he wouldn't see her.

His footsteps halted. She could feel his stare. Placing her chin on her knees, she lifted her gaze toward him.

He glanced to the side before making eye contact again. "What are you doing?"

She placed her forehead on her knees and addressed the floor. "Avoiding you."

"I thought so."

She looked up. His lower arms rested on the top rail. "I'm sorry," she said.

Zeke leaned back, clutching the board with his hands.

Pepper rushed on. "For the picture. For peeling out the other day. For—for whatever else I've done to offend you."

He placed one foot on the lowest rail. His gaze met hers.

Before she could speak again, he looked away at something above her head.

"Will you forgive me?"

"Yes." His eyes remained focused above her.

Why wouldn't he look at her? "I really am sorry."

162

"I think you are." His gaze skittered past her.

"But . . ."

"Are you sorry you peeled out? Or simply sorry that I called you on it?"

Pepper stood and dusted off her pants. "What's the difference?" She leaned against the back wall of the pen.

"Would you be sorry about your recklessness if I hadn't said anything?"

She opened her mouth, but Zeke's words stopped her.

"What if a customer had seen your actions?"

Pepper's thoughts raced. How many children wandered the parking lot each day? Would their parents dismiss her actions as lightly as she had?

"What if flying gravel had hit someone or broken something?" He looked at the concrete floor. When he raised his gaze to Pepper, a steely glint lit his eyes. "And what about my photo?"

Pepper's spine stiffened. "You shouldn't have taken it."

"Your dad gave me his camera. Asked me to snap some pictures."

"Pictures of me."

"You and others." Zeke removed his foot from the railing. Standing to his full height, he continued, "I also took one of you and your dad and one of the three of you."

Pepper had copies of the other two. "Did my dad give you those, too?"

"No." He shuffled some hay around on the floor with his work boot. "Just the one."

"Why?" She hurried forward and clutched the railing in front of him. "Why that picture?"

"Your dad is the one with the answers."

CHAPTER 17

When had Pepper suffered through a more miserable Saturday? Crowds swarmed during the morning, keeping everyone scurrying. Around one o'clock, a persistent drizzle settled in. Donkey cart rides were canceled for the rest of the day. Children whined and cried. Parents grumbled and went home. By three o'clock, the drizzle had become a downpour.

The final hour of the day consisted of hurrying the equipment and food supplies from the makeshift booths to more adequate shelter. Being pelted by rain made the whole process slower and more dismal.

Five o'clock was fast approaching when Pepper sloshed to the house in wet clothes and soggy shoes. Removing her waterlogged shoes and her squishy socks on the porch, she hurried to the downstairs bathroom and changed. Her off-hours clothes warmed and soothed her. She draped the sodden ones over the sink and padded back outside.

Disdaining the thought of mushy socks and shoes, she rolled up the legs of her pants and dashed to the car. She could turn up the heater in Priscilla and blast hot air onto her feet. Visions of a warm soak danced more sweetly than sugarplums through her head.

* * *

Half an hour later, hot water calmed her muscles but had done little to quell her turmoil. How was she going to replace that photo? If she called Pops, he would send her another, but not without exacting an explanation, which would inevitably prompt his asking more questions. But as far as Pepper knew, Pops was the only one who had the picture.

Why did she have to replace it anyway? If Zeke had let go, the picture wouldn't have torn. *Then you'd have it.* Pepper held her breath and sank under the water. Seconds later, she resurfaced, spewing air and wiping her eyes. Underwater contemplation had cleared her head. She needed a diversion. She was taking herself to the movies.

164

She dressed quickly, towel-dried her hair, and fluffed her curls. Then she put Maggie through her physical therapy routine and oversaw her bath.

Returning to her room, she applied minimal makeup. Then she found the theater schedule. She had plenty of time to make the eight o'clock show. Before grabbing her purse and keys, she checked her phone for any new messages. No one had tried to reach her. It had been that kind of day.

She grabbed a hoodie and started down the hall. Maggie and Fred were in the living room playing checkers.

"Are you going out?" Maggie turned to Pepper but looked back at her husband. "Don't cheat while I'm talking."

"I never cheat." Fred's wink belied his shocked tone.

"Unless I'm winning." She wagged her forefinger at him. "Which I am."

"So Fred cheats, does he?" Pepper gaped in his direction. "No wonder I never win."

"Hmmph." Fred leaned back in his chair and looked up at her. "I don't have to cheat when I play you."

Her mouth gaped. "Well, I know when I'm not needed." She smiled at the two of them. "I'm taking myself to the movies." Sliding the fallen purse strap back onto her shoulder, she headed toward the door. "I'll see you in the morning."

"Need an umbrella?" Fred started to rise from his chair.

"Umbrellas are for old people and sissies." Synchronized chuckles met her ears. "I have my hood." She waved and dashed outside.

* * *

Pepper located the theater without any trouble. Even if she hadn't seen it on a previous trip to town, the line in front would have given her a clue. Must be she wasn't the only one who had free time tonight. Thankfully, the rain had relented, and ticket buyers weren't being soaked.

Finding a parking place was a little trickier. Good thing she wasn't running late. She pulled into a curb-side space on a nearby street, got out, locked her door, and started up the sidewalk. A feminine laugh drifted up from behind her. A woman's voice followed.

"It was so funny. You should have seen him."

Her rich laughter was joined by a masculine tone.

"My nephew is a character. I miss living close to him."

Pepper's gasp nearly sucked in an unsuspecting bug. The voice and the laugh sounded like Marco Girardi's. He was walking behind her. In

165

the company of a woman. Pepper lengthened her step, and the voices faded slightly. Turning the corner a few seconds later, she glanced back to see them heading toward her.

Of all the luck. She'd never been to Lewisburg by herself, except in driving through. Now, here she stood, alone on date night while Marco and his companion approached.

Across the street were a drug store, a bar, and a restaurant. She would duck into one of them. The movie could wait. Stepping to the curb, she watched for traffic.

"Pepper." Marco's familiar voice met her ears. "Pepper, wait."

Why were so many cars passing by right now? She exhaled loudly and then pasted a smile on her face before turning around and acknowledging him. "Hi, Marco."

"Good to see you." His friend joined him. "Allison, I'd like you to meet Pepper Staley." He motioned from the magazine cover beauty to Pepper. "Pepper, this is a friend from back home, Allison Levy."

Allison extended her hand. Her clasp was as firm as her smile was warm. "Marco has been raving about how much you've done to help with the recovery of one of his patients."

With each word Allison spoke, the emerald-eyed monster that had claimed Pepper's heart a few minutes earlier, began to retreat. "I don't do that much."

"Are you alone?" Captain Obvious had nothing on Marco.

"Yeah. I needed a diversion." Pepper wagged her head toward the theater. "Thought a movie might do it."

"But you were headed across the street?"

Now you've done it. "Hoped I could hit the drug store first." A lie to save face. She glanced at her watch. "But there isn't time now."

"We'll get your ticket for you." Allison was too kind. Really. "What did you plan to see?"

Pepper gave the name of the action drama.

"That's what we're watching." Allison's eyes glimmered. "You can sit with us."

"No, you go ahead." Being the third person on someone else's date. No way.

"You're welcome, really." Marco repeated Allison's invitation.

"I do need some things at the drugstore." She seldom took time to shop. "If I hurry, I won't miss much." She backed toward the street. "Nice to meet you, Allison. Bye, Marco." When she reached the curb, the light had just changed. She scurried across. Looking toward the theater, she saw

Marco and Allison hand-in-hand as they took their place in line. The miserable day had slid into a depressing evening.

* * *

By the time Pepper found and paid for her items, half an hour had passed. Too late to watch the eight o'clock show. She'd catch the one at ten. What to do until then? Walking back outside, she surveyed her options. The bar was on her left, the restaurant, on her right. Alcohol or coffee? She hadn't touched anything alcoholic since that April night. She'd learned a lesson in moderation. She shifted her package and settled her purse. A few steps later she reached for the heavy door and entered the dimly lit tavern.

She'd taken three steps toward the bar when a heavy-set, middle-aged man swaggered up to her.

"Hello there, little lady." He wrapped his sweaty, beefy fingers around her upper arm. "Let me buy you a drink."

Zeke's words flashed through her brain. "Nothing happened . . . really." If she lost control tonight, that wouldn't be the case. Her heart pounded heavily. She yanked her arm from the predator's hand and dashed for the door.

* * *

Eating alone made some people nervous, but Zeke enjoyed it, especially at his favorite Lewisburg haunt. He knew some of the staff by name and occasionally was waited on by a young waitress who flirted with him. He hadn't been seated at one of her tables tonight, but she did refill his coffee on her way by. "Hi, Zeke. What're you doing here on a Saturday night?"

"Having coffee before I go home." He looked from her to the sugar packets in front of him.

"Why aren't you on a date?"

Zeke rattled the packet he'd picked up. He cleared his throat. "Too busy. Too tired." When he looked up, she was shaking her head.

"You need some fun in your life." She patted the table and grinned at him. "See you around."

He paid his bill a few minutes later and walked down the street to his Jeep. Pulling his seat belt around him, he noticed a familiar, petite, dark-haired woman. Pepper had just left the drug store. A plastic shopping bag in one hand and her purse draped over the opposite shoulder, she stood on the sidewalk, looking around.

Prior to today and their conflicts, he would have opened the door and yelled to her. Instead he watched mutely.

She stared across the street, then at the restaurant he'd just left, and finally at the tavern. She glanced at her watch, scanned the three choices, shifted her package, and started toward the bar.

"Don't do it." Despite Zeke's urgent plea, she disappeared into the pub. He gripped the steering wheel and yelled. Why was she so rash? She did first and thought later. How many scrapes would she experience before she wised up?

Ignoring his guilt at leaving her to her own devices, he started the engine and waited for traffic. His foot was on the accelerator when she exited the tavern. She bolted down the street.

Zeke hit the gas and followed her. She had dashed nearly a block by the time his Jeep was next to her and he could pull over. He lowered the window. "Where you going?"

Her pace quickened. "To my . . ." She halted mid-stride. Finally she looked toward the Jeep. "Zeke!" Clutching the plastic bag and her purse closer to her, she rushed to his car. He flung the door open. She climbed in and hunched forward over her knees. Tears overtook her.

Zeke turned off the engine and handed her some napkins from his collection in the console.

"Why did I . . ." Shudders seized her. "A bad idea. I knew it." She wiped her eyes. "Horrible man."

"What man?" Zeke hadn't seen anyone.

"In the bar." She stifled a quiver. "Met me as soon as I walked in." She sniffled. "Put his slimy hand on my arm." For the first time since she'd gotten in, Pepper looked at Zeke. "I ran."

"Good." He nodded firmly. "I saw you."

"Saw me come out?"

"And go in."

"Where were you?"

She'd gone from fear to curiosity. "In my car a few spaces down from the drugstore."

"Going to the movie?"

"Just leaving the restaurant."

She wiped her nose. "You didn't eat at home?"

"I did." How had this become about him? "Went in for a cup of coffee."

Her head sagged, and she wrung her hands and studied her fingers. "You saw me go in?" She looked askance at him. "But you didn't come after me?"

Her sideways stare was no less intimidating than a full-on one would have been.

"Thought you cared about me."

"I do." No use to deny it.

"But you didn't stop me."

Was she really blaming him? "You're an adult."

She inhaled, gathering steam.

Zeke cut her off. "You don't take advice well."

"I do, too."

He angled his head toward her and stared. "Since when?" Surely she wasn't that blind to her own faults.

"Thanks for your help." She opened the door.

What was happening? "Wait."

"Are you going to give me advice?"

His accusation had provided her the perfect escape. She stepped to the concrete and turned back the way she had come. Zeke stared ahead, not even glancing in his rearview mirror to see which way she had gone.

* * *

Gramps sidled into the pew next to his grandson. "Morning, Ezekiel."

"Hi, Gramps. How are you?"

"Better than you, I'd say."

Zeke nodded. "Probably."

"Don't know if this will help or hurt." He handed an envelope in Zeke's direction. "She asked me to make sure you got it." Gramps hadn't needed to explain who "she" was. "Maybe I should have given it to you after the service, but it seemed important."

Zeke took the envelope and began running his finger along the top. Pausing, he stood up. "Guess I'll read this in the foyer." He stepped to the other end of the row in order not to disturb Gram. Opting for more privacy, he found his Jeep and climbed in. He pulled out the single sheet of notebook paper.

You make me crazy.

No greeting. Nothing. Just an accusation.

Maybe it's because you're one of the nicest men I've ever met.

Zeke blinked and then smiled.

169

Maybe it's because I have such a strong attraction for you, and I wonder if it's mutual.

It definitely was.

Maybe it's because I'm amazed that you seldom lose your temper at me, even when I deserve it.

Remembering his thoughts and reactions the previous night, Zeke shuddered.

Maybe it's because I think that all of the other reasons are tied up in the fact of your being "religious" (I know you don't like that word).

He didn't. But right now it wasn't important.

Maybe it's mostly because I've forbidden you from explaining.

We need to talk—before they admit me to the sanitarium.

Pepper.

This time God had opened the door. Now seemed like the best opportunity. Zeke prayed for the right words.

* * *

Garbed in her Hello Kitty pajamas and armed with a banana and a glass of milk, Pepper strolled through the living room. She laughed again when she reread the note Maggie had left on the checker board. "I won."

In the rocker, Pepper found Fred's Bible still open. He had been reading it when she handed him the letter for Zeke. Had he delivered it?

Both pages of the book had the word *Philippians* written across the top. Several portions of the pages were underlined. The margins had numerous hand-written notes in them. Setting her glass and her banana on the end table, Pepper picked up the Bible and sat in the rocker.

The doorbell sent her momentarily off the seat and clutching at her heart. Who would be here on a Sunday? Everyone should know that the Hannas would be in church. She placed the Bible back in the chair and hurried to the window. Zeke stood at the door. He held what looked like a Bible in his left hand.

Pepper opened the door. Zeke didn't say anything. He simply held up the envelope. Fred had completed his mission. She stepped back, and Zeke let himself in. He stood for a moment, studying the floor. Then he looked up and smiled. "I take no responsibility for your being crazy."

Smiling, she shook her head and motioned toward the living room.

* * *

170

He sat on one end of the couch and looked at her. She plopped near the other end and stared back. She inhaled as if it might be her last breath. "I couldn't sleep last night."

"Me either." He'd been awake searching for and writing down verses. He'd had no idea how soon he would need them.

"The nasty things I've said and done played over and over." She jumped up and began pacing back and forth on the other side of the coffee table. "And they were things from only the last few days."

Zeke watched her movements.

"I owe you an apology for last night." She paused in front of him. "Several, really." The pacing resumed. "I left that bar so scared I had no idea where I was headed." She stopped. "And out of nowhere, you drove up and rescued me." She walked around the table and parked herself next to him. "How did you know?"

"I didn't." He turned toward her. "I had no idea you were in town."

"If I didn't know you better, I'd think you were stalking me."

"I wasn't."

She raised both hands before letting them drop back into her lap. "Don't you see how crazy that sounds? At the exact moment I needed you, you showed up."

"God knew—"

"That's another thing that makes me crazy." Her face was close enough for him to feel the heat radiating from it. "How does God know?" She leaned back against the couch. Springing forward again, she asked, "And if He does know, why doesn't He do something about evil?"

"Whoa." He raised both hands, palms toward her. "I'll do my best to answer you. But let's lay some ground work."

"Fine."

He turned to face her more directly. "The cats are distracting."

She surveyed her outfit. "Too juvenile?"

"That, too." Grinning kittens tended to lessen the serious nature of things.

"Too?" She rested her hands on her knees. "How else?"

He cleared his throat. Did he really have to explain this to her? "Too—pajama."

She pondered. He recognized the light bulb moment.

She said, "Too intimate."

He nodded and looked away.

"That's sweet, Zeke." She waited until his gaze met hers. "You might not be as crazy as I thought." She bounded down the hall.

171

Zeke exhaled. Loudly. Then he opened his Bible and the paper on which he'd written several references. He turned to Hebrews chapter 11. Closing his eyes, he prayed, "Open the eyes of Pepper's heart, Lord. Help her to see You." By the time Zeke had finished his prayer, Pepper was returning. She wore blue jeans and a Penn State sweatshirt. At least her clothes wouldn't be a distraction.

"Sit."

She obliged by positioning herself next to him.

"What is faith?"

Her forehead creased. "Faith is trusting something you've never tested."

"Good answer." He moved the Bible closer to her and pointed at verse 1 of Hebrews 11. He read aloud, "'Now faith is the assurance of things hoped for, the conviction of things not seen.' Knowing God requires faith."

She nodded.

He continued. "People trust God to be as He says He is and to act as He says He will."

"But how do we know about God?"

"Through the Bible." He kept his finger in the page, but closed the book and looked at Pepper. "God has many attributes. Three of them are omnipotence—"

"All power."

"Right." This might be easier than he had anticipated.

"Omnipresence."

"A presence everywhere."

"And omniscience."

"All knowledge."

Zeke looked hard at her. "How do you know all this?"

"'Omni' is a Latin prefix meaning 'all.' Many medical terms come from the Latin. We learned the word parts."

Now she needed to apply all those terms to God. "God knows all, is everywhere, and can do anything." He watched her eyes as they narrowed and then dilated. "That's how He knew you needed help last night."

"But if God can do anything, why doesn't He stop some things?"

"That's a harder question." He opened the Bible. "We need to look at two more of God's qualities. One is goodness." He turned to the New Testament book of James.

"Look at chapter 1 and verse 17. 'Every good gift and every perfect gift is from above, coming down from the Father of lights with whom there is no variation or shadow due to change.' God is the definition of good. He is goodness."

"But all the bad things?"

"Hold that question." He prayed for the right words to explain. "One of the hardest attributes for me to grasp is transcendence."

"Meaning to 'go beyond.'"

"Exactly." Perhaps she would grasp this concept quickly, too. "But here's the thing. Because God goes beyond any other being we can experience, no analogy can completely describe Him." Zeke searched for something that would relate. "It would be like trying to explain the color blue to someone who has always been blind."

"Impossible."

"Trying to sum up God in terms that people can understand is impossible, too. His thoughts and ways transcend ours. He isn't bound by our thinking."

"I'm getting a headache."

He noticed the banana and the milk. "Are those your breakfast?"

"They were going to be."

He handed both to her. "The milk is warm," he said.

"Yuk." She set it aside and began peeling the banana.

"I agree." Zeke flipped his paper over and scanned down the page. "One more thing."

"More fuel for my headache?"

"Man's free will." A free spirit like Pepper should certainly understand this concept. "God wants everyone to love Him and do what's right—right as He defines it."

"Like telling the truth and not stealing."

"Exactly." Once again she grasped the idea. "But men can and do steal if they want to. And lie. And cheat. And do lots more."

"God could stop it."

"He could." Zeke paused. "But He allows man to choose."

Zeke needed a way to apply all these ideas to Pepper. He hoped his idea would solidify the concepts without hardening her heart. *Please, God.*

He plunged ahead. "You were turned down by six medical schools."

"Ugh." She buried her face in her hands. "Don't remind me."

"God knew your plans. He could have made sure you were accepted. But He didn't. You thought that was terrible."

"It was."

"Was it?" Would she follow his train of thought. "If you'd been accepted by those other schools, you wouldn't have been on the lawn that night."

She sat back and pulled her bare feet onto the couch. Her toenails were bright pink. He blinked.

Focus.

She remained silent for longer than he would have thought possible.

"No Anna. No orchard," she said. "No summer job here." She peered at him with a gaze that nearly paralyzed his heart. "No you."

Once his heart restarted, he gulped. "Bad turned into good."

* * *

Why couldn't she sit here and stare at him for, say, an hour or two? Because he had asked her a question.

"What?"

"I have one more thing I need to say." He reached for her hand. "Hear me out."

His method of persuasion was rock solid. She squeezed his fingers. "Okay."

"Apply this same idea to Ranie."

She clenched her free hand and pursed her lips.

"You said you'd listen." He covered their clasped hands with his other one.

Do it for Zeke. She took a deep breath and then rested her free hand on her knee.

"What she did was wrong."

"Absolutely." Pepper shook her head emphatically.

"What you went through was bad."

Again she agreed.

"And God could have prevented it."

"But He didn't." She couldn't keep the edge from her voice. "Pops and I really hurt."

Zeke's brown eyes lit with a tenderness she hadn't seen before.

"But we don't know what God may have protected you from."

Had he been listening in on Pepper's conversation with Ranie? Would God say that He had protected her by having Ranie leave? Possibilities she had never before considered, now paraded through her mind like picketing workers, each one eliciting a new protest.

"Pepper?" Zeke squeezed her hand.

She shook the murkiness from her brain and smiled. "Long way off."

"But you're back?" He bit one side of his lip. "And you're not angry?"

She bumped into him with her shoulder. "At you? Never."

"Right." He ran his hand through his wavy hair. "But I still make you crazy?"

"Maybe not so much."

* * *

Grasping a tall, cold glass of milk, Pepper smiled and waved as Zeke looked back. He waved to her when he reached the Jeep.

She looked at her watch. One o'clock. Maggie and Fred were usually back before this. Hopefully nothing was wrong. But their late return had allowed more time for Zeke and Pepper.

She smiled to herself. He did crazy things to her heart, but her mind trusted him and wanted to trust his God.

She chugged the milk, took the glass to the sink, and hurried to her room. Digging into her purse, she found her phone and hit a familiar button.

"Hey, Pops."

"Hey, to you, too. Good to hear your voice."

"Yours, too." In a minute, he might not be so sure about that. "I need a favor."

CHAPTER 18

"You're cheery this Monday evening."

Zeke looked away from the blueberry bush he was standing in front of. Anna walked toward him. A plastic pail hung from a belt at her waist. "You think?"

"You're whistling a happy tune." She patted his shoulder as she passed. "And you're smiling at a plant."

Had he been?

Anna began picking from the bush next to Zeke's. The soft plunk of the berries into the pail marked her progress.

"I talked with Pepper." Anna wagged her eyebrows and grinned.

"I'm not surprised."

"Guess what we talked about." Again she looked his direction.

"Axle?"

She tipped her head to one side. "Yes—eventually." A handful of berries landed in her bucket. "What else?"

"Buster?" He could prolong his sister's agony a bit more.

"Him, too." She swatted at Zeke. "And who else?"

"Me?" He smiled at the bush.

She stopped picking and faced him. "A lot." Her deft fingers once again clambered across the leaves. "And Who else?"

Zeke's hands slowed. His sister's words had turned from teasing to thoughtful.

"God?"

"Exactly." Anna stepped over and hugged him. "She asked so many questions. Good questions." A glint entered Anna's eyes. "How long were you there, Zeke?"

Too long. His heart was completely snagged. "Not long enough."

"Hmmm." Her raised eyebrows spoke more than her words.

Zeke rushed ahead. "To explain everything."

"Okay." She reached for his arm. "You did well. She's really thinking."

Zeke sighed. "I hope so."

"Me, too." She squeezed his arm. "For her sake. And yours."

* * *

The seasons were changing. Strawberries were heading out. Cherries and raspberries were in full tilt. Blueberries were coming on. Pepper chuckled at the irony of the Davies' family business. The orchard had been started as an apple farm. These days, however, the family had harvested and sold several other crops by the time apples arrived. Even the earliest apple didn't ripen until late July.

Tuesday morning Pepper helped Anna in the gift shop.

"Zeke wants the orchard to be our livelihood like it has been for Dad and Gramps."

"What about marriage? Having your own family." Change was bound to come.

"We all talk of marriage." Anna was unpacking a box of handmade soaps, pricing them, and setting them on a shelf in the gift shop. "Even Toby." She laughed. "His words on the subject usually are, 'If I get married, I won't have money for cars.'"

Pepper could imagine the conversation.

"No one has to stay." Anna handed the circular pricing tags and the marker to Pepper. "But Zeke wants us to have that option." She grabbed the empty box and headed to the storeroom at the end of the gift shop area.

Pepper followed.

"With five of us, we needed to sell more than apples."

"Would Zeke ever leave?"

"Can't see it hap—" Anna gulped. She pursed her lips. She draped one arm over Pepper's shoulder. "Thankfully, there's a hospital within ten minutes."

Was Pepper that obvious or was Anna very observant? Or both?

* * *

On Wednesday afternoon at closing time, Pepper went looking for Zeke. She found him in the orchard mowing between the rows of trees. He was far down the row, headed away from her. She moved to the next row. On his return trip, he smiled when he saw her.

Her heart thudded in response. She met him halfway.

"Want a ride?"

"Okay."

177

"Come around." She crossed to Zeke's left, and he extended his hand. "I look over my right shoulder." Unsure of what he meant, she climbed the two steps anyway, until she stood next to him. For once, she had the height advantage.

"You want to sit or stand?" He raised his voice to be heard above the engine noise.

She crinkled her face and shrugged her shoulders. "Which is better?"

He leaned away from her. "You've never been on a tractor?"

"Nope." She giggled at the dazed look on his face.

"You're past due, city girl." He grinned and patted the fender. "Riding shotgun, sort of."

"You want me to sit up there?" Her eyes widened. "You sure it will hold me?"

"It holds me." His eyes dared her to climb up.

Shrugging, Pepper slid up onto the green fender. The flat surface seemed almost designed for the purpose of passengers.

Zeke pointed to the fender. "Hold on."

She did. Tightly. Especially at first. After the initial adjustment, she began to relax. And smile.

The ride wasn't smooth, but the view was great, open air coupled with a height advantage. The apple trees sported little green fruit. An adjoining field held the rows and rows of strawberry plants from which she and Toby had gathered berries. And Zeke was right in front of her.

He glanced over occasionally, but generally, he divided his attention between the row in front of him and the mower behind him. It cut a wide swath, but didn't clip the grass as short as a lawn mower would.

"How often do you do this?" Pepper shouted toward him.

Navigating a dip in the terrain, Zeke never took his eyes off the cutting machine. "Depends on the weather. Usually every couple weeks or so."

When they had mowed several rows, Zeke stopped and turned off the machine. "You had enough?" He squinted into the sun as he spoke.

"Have you?"

"Of mowing? Too much." He adjusted the bill of his hat. "Of having you as a passenger? No way."

Definitely the nicest guy she'd ever known.

"It's been great. But . . ." She looked at her watch. "I should get going. It's time for Maggie's therapy." She slipped down from her perch. "I only meant to . . ." She slapped the fender. "I almost forgot why I came looking for you." She pulled an envelope from her back pocket and handed it to him. "I hope it's not rumpled."

Opening the envelope, he pulled out its contents. Long seconds passed before he looked up. "Thank you."

"I'm not sure why you're so fond of it, but—"

His gaze cut her off. "Someday I'll tell you."

"Maybe someday I'll know."

He looked at the photo before turning back to Pepper. "You will."

"Thanks, Zeke." She set one foot on the first step. "It was fun."

"It was." He lifted the picture from his lap. "Thanks again."

Pepper jumped to the ground.

"See you tomorrow." He waved and started the engine.

She waited until he looked back at the mower. After a quick wave, she bolted toward the house. Late. Late. Late. But so worth it.

* * *

Zeke opened his desk drawer and set the envelope on top of the papers there. The photo was his again. Pepper had obviously gone through her dad in order to get another copy. Mr. Staley was now aware that Pepper had seen the picture. If only Zeke could have heard that conversation.

She had sought Zeke out in order to deliver the photograph. He smiled to himself. Reaching for the envelope, he reclaimed it and removed the slightly bent picture. It still retained the rounded form of her back pocket. Better not dwell on that.

He focused his thoughts on the ride and his being the one to introduce her to a tractor. She'd hesitated at first—a rarity for her. Then her smile had broadened. Eyes wide, she had scanned the horizon. Occasionally she had asked Zeke a question. If only he hadn't had to focus on the mower, he could have given her more attention. His disappointment was tempered by the fact that she had watched him. He had felt her gaze. A few times, he had caught her staring.

Her heart was once again soft toward Zeke. Was it more tender toward God?

* * *

The arrival of Friday, although it wasn't the end of the work week, lightened Pepper's step. Saturday brought an early closing and two days off. If she went to church with the Hannas, she could spend time with Zeke and maybe ask a few more questions. After their discussion last Sunday, she had Googled the attributes of God, printed off a list and some

179

verses, and gone looking for Fred. He'd been sitting on the porch, reading the paper.

"Mind if I borrow your Bible for a few minutes?"

He'd lowered the paper and raised an eyebrow. "Not at all. It's in my bedroom on the dresser." Before she could leave the porch, he'd set the paper aside and said, "I'll get it for you. Maggie's lying down."

"I can read it later."

"No, I'll get it." He handed her the newspaper on his way past. "News will be the same in two minutes."

Pepper watched him leave.

Returning a short time later with a smaller Bible than the one she often saw in the living room, Fred offered it to her. "Here's a copy I don't use much anymore. The print's too small." He reclaimed the paper and resumed his seat.

Smiling at his frank assessment, she took it from him. "Thanks. Are you sure?" She rubbed her palm over the leather cover.

"You're welcome. I am. It needs to be used." He leaned toward her chair. "Do you have a particular verse you're looking for?"

"Yes, a list of them."

"Do you know how to find them?"

Pepper shrugged and raised her eyebrows. "Not really."

"Well, let me show you how it works." Leafing through the pages, he explained chapter and verse divisions and then took her to the table of contents. "If you know the order of the books, you don't need this, but until you learn them, you'll find it very handy."

Pepper glanced at the list of names, many she'd never heard of. "How many are there?"

"Sixty-six. Thirty-nine in the Old Testament and twenty-seven in the New."

"And you know them in order?"

"Since I was in elementary school." His expression softened. "Earned my first Bible by memorizing them."

She looked up from the list of names. "I'm impressed."

"Don't be. Kids memorize fast." He looked back at the Bible. "Let's say you wanted to look up John 3:16. How would you do it?"

Pepper studied the page. She found four listings for John. "Which one do I want?"

"If it doesn't have a number in front of it, you want the Gospel of John, labeled only 'John.'"

She located the page number for John. When she found the page, she asked, "Chapter 3?"

Fred nodded. "Verse 16. One of the best-known verses in the Bible."

After a few seconds, Pepper located it.

"Read it aloud."

"For God so loved the world, that He gave his only Son, that whoever believes in Him should not perish but have eternal life."

Fred had recited it along with her.

"What's it mean?"

"That every person has done wrong and is sinful, but because God loves all of us, He provided a way for us to be forgiven of our sins. Jesus paid the penalty for us."

"What was the penalty?"

"Separation from God forever."

Fred's expression was as serious as she'd ever seen it. "I'm looking up verses about God." She'd sprung from her chair. "Thanks again."

She'd spent time each night this week doing research. Anna and she had talked some and texted, but Zeke was her first choice for answering questions. And for most other things. She wasn't fooling herself. Sunday might soon become her favorite day of the week.

* * *

Just before nine on Friday morning, Pepper was replenishing the fruit stand.

"Beautiful day in Pennsylvania." Zeke stopped next to her.

His assessment brought a grin to her lips. "Fred says that all the time. Says he's quoting some guy named Pete with an odd name like 'Wombat.'"

"I think it's Wambach." A smile lit his face.

"That sounds more reasonable." Setting a quart of blueberries on a table in front of her, Pepper added, "Fred's expecting a high in the low 80s with lots of sunshine."

"That's what I heard, too."

"I hope you're both right. That's my kind—"

A loud but distant squeal met their ears. Followed by another. Crashing metal punctuated the screeches. A revving engine roared.

Zeke had started down the driveway. Pepper followed him. "What was that?"

"Accident. Probably at the end of the road."

He was running to his Jeep.

"I'm coming with you."

181

Zeke put the Jeep into reverse almost before Pepper shut her door. He yelled to the family members who had also come to investigate. "We'll check it out."

A few seconds out of the driveway, Pepper gasped. Bright sunshine illuminated the scene. A car stood on its left side in the deep ditch along the far side of the main highway. Its dirty, gray underbelly faced them. A short distance past the intersection sat a brown SUV. The front end had taken the brunt.

Zeke called 911. "There's been an accident." He gave the names of the roads at the intersection.

"Tell them there's a trained EMT at the scene."

Zeke relayed the message. He pulled up a short way from the stop sign, put on his emergency flashers, and jumped out. He was on the phone again. "Dad, bring the tractor and the guys."

Pepper ran toward the intersection. Traffic had stopped. She dashed to the driver's side of an SUV. Zeke raced past her, going toward the upturned vehicle. The air bag of the SUV had deployed. Gases from the bag hadn't quite dissipated even though the window had shattered. Without touching anything, she called, "Are you okay?"

No answer. The male victim either hadn't heard her or couldn't respond. She called again. "Sir. Sir, can you hear me?"

It was then that a whimper from the back seat caught her attention. Two men stepped up, one on either side of her. "Keep calling him," Pepper instructed. "I'll be right with you." She lifted the door handle. The door didn't open.

"Unlock the back," she barked to the man nearest her. A click indicated his success. Pepper yanked the door open.

There, in a rear-facing car seat sat a young child, her face splattered with part of the contents of a spilled cup and her lap wearing the rest of the liquid. The moment she saw Pepper, tears formed and she wailed. Her cries roused the driver.

"My baby," he muttered. "Is she okay?"

"She looks fine." Pepper reached for the seat belt to unhook her. A hand on Pepper's arm restrained her. She turned.

* * *

Fear had gripped Zeke's heart as he approached the white Volvo. The immediate necessity was to set the vehicle on its wheels. With the car in its present position, no one could help the person inside.

Zeke pounded on the exposed roof of the car. "Can you hear me?" Silence. Again he pounded and called. Still no one replied. Dad, Ike, and Toby arrived in the pickup shortly after Zeke's first attempt to rouse someone.

Joe was bringing the tractor. If it was needed, he would do the driving.

Zeke redialed 911. He repeated the same information, but this time he added, "One vehicle is on its side. We have equipment to right the car. Should we do so?"

"Is the driver in immediate danger by staying in the car?"

"You mean like fire?"

"Yes."

"No, not now."

"Wait. An officer has been dispatched. ETA is two minutes."

Zeke hung up. He approached the vehicle. Getting down on his hands and knees, he looked inside through the windshield. The driver's dark curls chilled his blood. The item he saw next nearly catapulted his heart through his chest. A program from the most recent Penn State commencement exercises lay lodged between the dashboard and the windshield. A tag bearing the name Ranie Phelps had been clipped to it.

His head drooped. His stomach clenched. Pepper had to be told.

* * *

"We need you at the other car." Zeke's blanched face was right in front of her.

It must be bad. Where was that ambulance?

"Come on." He clasped her elbow and propelled her across the main road.

Sirens pierced the air.

"The paramedics are here." Her feet tried to slow, but Zeke dragged her along. "What are you doing?"

Nearing the other car, Pepper cringed at the damage of the still-sideways vehicle. At least it wasn't one of those tiny subcompact cars. Passing the trunk of the car, Pepper glimpsed the auto maker's logo. Volvo. A sturdy line, acclaimed for safety features. Volvo. A white Volvo. Her feet halted. Her heart pounded. Her breathing increased.

She clutched Zeke's hand and stared up at him. "Ranie?"

He nodded.

She raced forward. Shoving through the small assembly of onlookers, she jumped into the ditch a few feet away from the car. "Ranie. Ranie. Can you hear me?"

She lay on the dew-soaked ground and inched herself closer. "God, don't let me lose her again."

"Do you know the driver?" A firm male voice addressed Pepper.

She turned her face from the car and looked into the knees of a squatting policeman. "I think this is my mom's car."

"There's a tractor and operator here to move it. Do you want—"

"Yes."

"Move away from the vehicle."

He stood.

Coming to her hands and knees, Pepper whispered, "Don't die."

Zeke reached out and helped her to her feet.

"Your tractor? The one I rode?"

Zeke nodded. "Joe will drive." He clutched her arm and squeezed. "He's the best."

Pepper looked around. A fire truck, an ambulance, a police cruiser, and a large green tractor. Could this scene be real? She glanced back. The white Volvo certainly was.

Rescue workers halted traffic. The green tractor roared into action. Moving perpendicular to both the road and the Volvo, Joe drove the front end of the tractor up to the car. Toby hooked a heavy chain between the Volvo and the bucket on the front of the tractor. Joe raised the bucket.

Pepper faced Zeke. "Why the bucket?"

"So the car lands gently."

She pressed her face into Zeke's chest and clutched his shirt with both fists.

* * *

Warm tears seeped into Zeke's shirt. "Joe can do this."

Pepper lifted her face toward him.

Fear. Like the fear he'd seen in her eyes a few nights ago. Only deeper. Her fingers still clung to his shirt.

"Want to watch?"

"No." She spoke into his chest. "Yes." Her eyes again faced him.

He raised his hands and clasped both of hers, drawing her fingers away from his shirt. He squeezed both of her hands and then turned her toward the tractor.

The engine revved. Keeping the chain taut, Joe inched the machine backward. Metal creaked. The onlookers held their breath. As Joe gently tugged, the angle of the car slowly decreased from ninety degrees. About halfway through the car's descent, gravity took over, and the chain went from pulling the car down to suspending it above the concrete.

Pepper gasped.

Zeke squeezed her fingers. "It's okay."

Halting the tractor, Joe turned his attention to lowering the bucket. A few seconds later, a collective sigh rose from the onlookers. The Volvo's four tires rested on the pavement.

Emergency workers rushed toward the bent metal that encased the injured driver.

Pepper dashed forward. The policeman stepped in front of her.

"I'm an EMT. That's my mom." She didn't give him time to respond.

* * *

During the harrowing experience of righting the Volvo, the driver of the SUV and his daughter had been transported to the hospital. Rescuing Ranie from her car and transferring her to a second ambulance looked to be a more complicated procedure.

Zeke paced at the back of the car. Pepper and others attended to Ranie. Did Pepper realize that while she worked alongside the other EMTs, she intermittently wiped away tears? How could she remain detached enough to perform the proper tasks while experiencing the human emotion clearly displayed on her cheeks?

Seeing the mangled metal, the shattered glass, and the splattered blood, Zeke struggled to keep his breakfast down. Walking helped both his mind and his stomach.

His dad approached him.

"Guess we'll head back now." He clapped his hand around Zeke's upper arm. "Stay as long as you need to."

Zeke gulped. "Thanks, Dad." He looked away. "And thank Joe. He did great."

Dad nodded. He pointed toward Pepper. "How's she doing?"

"Not sure."

"Has she called her dad?"

The moments since just before nine replayed in his mind. "Don't know how she could have."

"Seems like he'd want to know."

Zeke remembered Ken Staley's appreciation of the photo Zeke had taken of Pepper and Ranie.

"Yeah. He would." Zeke removed his hat and twisted the bill round and round between his hands. "Gramps has his number. I could call." He put the cap back on. "But it would be best from her."

"It would be. But it would be better sooner than later. This is serious." Waiting until Zeke looked at him, he added, "It won't be easy."

Dad was stating the obvious, on both counts. But Ken Staley's trip here would take a few hours. He needed to know soon. "I'll call."

"We'll be praying."

Zeke removed a small notepad and pen from the pocket of his shirt. He hit the keypad on his phone.

His grandmother answered shortly. "Hello."

"Gram, this is Zeke." He waited through her greeting. "Can you find the card with Pepper's dad's number on it?"

"Is something wrong with Pepper?" Worry seeped through each word.

"Her mom's been in a bad accident. At the end of our road." Zeke cleared the lump from his throat. "Pepper's an EMT. She's busy."

"I have the card now." She dictated the numbers.

"Thanks. Gramps can let you know more at lunch."

Zeke ended the call. He swallowed hard and moved toward the front of the car. Ranie remained in the wreckage. Why hadn't they taken her out?

"I need another dressing." A middle-aged man called to Pepper. "She's still bleeding."

Pepper tore a large bandage from its package and handed it to him.

Without acknowledging her help, he barked. "Hold this." He waited until she had placed her hands where his had been. Then he pulled a small flashlight from his pocket and checked Ranie's eyes. He took her pulse. "Her skin's clammy, her eyes dilated. She's going into shock. We've got to get her out."

Another worker called, "The foot is almost free."

"Hurry."

The EMTs words were meant for his co-worker, but they spurred Zeke into action. Once again he opened his phone. Four rings into the call, he almost hung up.

Then Pepper's dad answered. "Hello, Zeke Davies."

Was the tone suspicion? Caution? Or something else?

"Hi, Mr. Staley. I'm calling to—"

"Is Pepper okay?"

This inflection carried worry. "She's fine." Zeke heard the older man's release of breath. "But Ranie's been in an accident."

186

"No."

Zeke hurried on. "They're almost ready to put her into an ambulance." He'd spare the gruesome details but include a warning, "She's not answering anyone."

"I'm coming. What's the name of the hospital?"

After giving the necessary information, Zeke ended the call. He looked around. Emergency workers still buzzed around the car. Metal and plastic debris still littered the area. Onlookers still hung around the scene.

The officer approached him. "You were one of the first ones here?"

"Yes."

"How many vehicles were here when you arrived?"

"Two." Why was he asking?

"Are they where they were when you arrived?"

"Yes, except that the Volvo was on its side."

"Tell me everything you saw and heard when you got here." His pen was poised to write.

"I heard the accident before I came."

"How's that?" The officer looked away from his paper.

"Our orchard's a quarter mile up there." He motioned toward it. "We were outside getting ready to open when we heard the crash."

"Who is 'we'?"

"Pepper and I." Again Zeke waved his arm.

"The one whose mom is the driver?"

Zeke nodded.

"She's your wife?"

Zeke shook his head. "She works for my family."

"So the two of you were outside. You heard the crash."

"Yes."

"One crash? Two crashes? More than that?"

Zeke closed his eyes and replayed the sounds. "Squealing tires. A crash. A much louder crash. A thudding crash. A revving engine."

The officer finished writing. "Say it one more time."

Zeke thought and then reiterated. "Squealing tires. A crash. A much louder crash. A thudding crash. A revving engine."

"You're sure the engine was last?"

"Yes. Why?"

"Neither of these revved up after the crashes."

Zeke's eyes widened. "A third car?"

"We're checking into it." He scribbled something else on the page. "I'll need your name and address, and hers, too." He flipped to another page in his book. "She'll need to come to the station and make a statement."

Zeke gave the information the officer asked for, but he couldn't stop thinking about the possibility of a third vehicle. No matter how often he retraced his thoughts, the engine roar always came last.

CHAPTER 19

Pepper slumped into a chair in the emergency room waiting area. She had already bitten every fingernail. She was too tired to pace. Adrenalin was seeping away.

Ranie's left foot had been wedged between crunched exterior metal and the floor of the car. Although the foot injury wasn't life-threatening, it had created other problems. The most crucial had been the prolonged time in extracting her from the car.

She had also lost blood due to a gash on her head and had gone into shock. The external wounds weren't serious, but the larger issue would be traumatic brain injury which occurred internally when the brain was jostled around in the skull. A brain scan would be needed to determine if any internal injury had occurred.

The air bags, which had probably saved her life, had also cracked two ribs. She was a mass of bruises, scrapes, and abrasions; her recovery wouldn't be quick or easy. But she was alive.

You helped her survive. Pepper's EMT skills had, indeed, been invaluable. Knowing what to do and how to do it had curbed the blood loss, treated the shock, and bought Ranie the necessary time to free her foot.

Pepper rested her elbow on the chair arm and laid her head on her hand. She shut her eyes.

You wouldn't listen. Pepper's eyes popped open. *She came back to see you.* The condemnations had dogged Pepper all morning. Was she to blame? She buried her face in her hands.

"Hi, honey."

Could it be?

She flung her hands away from her face. "Pops." She dashed from her chair and threw herself into his arms.

He clutched her and held on.

Drawing away eventually, she looked up. "How'd you know?"

Her dad nodded toward the door. Zeke stood in the doorway.

She released herself from her dad's arms and joined Zeke. "How? When?"

"After Joe left." His gaze met and held hers briefly. Then he focused on the floor. "You were busy. Your dad left his number with Gramps."

She squeezed his hand and stepped into his gaze. "Thanks."

Darting back toward Pops, she asked, "Did they tell you?"

"About her foot?" He nodded and led her back to the chair she'd been sitting in. He sat down next to her.

"She won't be out of surgery for a while yet."

"That's what they said."

Zeke cleared his throat. "I'll be going now."

Pepper hopped up again. "I'll walk you out." She looked over her shoulder at her dad. "Be right back."

"I'll go track down a Sprite." He rose from his chair, too. "Thanks, Zeke."

* * *

"Will you spend the night here?" Zeke voiced his first clear thought since they'd started toward the car.

"I don't know." She paused and hit the button for the down elevator. "Guess I'll wait and see what happens this afternoon."

They stepped inside the empty car. "Ground floor," Zeke said.

She touched the G on the key pad. The door closed. They leaned against the rail on the back wall.

She began, "Pops can drive me out to your grandparents' home later for Maggie's therapy."

Simultaneously, he said, "Don't worry about this afternoon's therapy with Gram. Anna can do it."

They both chuckled. He spoke first. "Anna will want to do this for you."

The chime sounded, and the elevator stopped. Before the door opened, she whispered, "I don't deserve all of you." Her hand encircled his arm just above his wrist.

In one motion, Zeke pulled his arm through her hand, turning his wrist so that his palm faced upward and her fingers rested in his. "Yes, you do."

When the door opened, Pepper moved first. Her forward progress would have drawn her fingers from his, but he held on, hurrying to catch up with her and to grasp her hand more fully.

190

They exchanged glances on their way down the hall, but neither spoke until they emerged from the hospital. Zeke pointed to his right. "I'm parked over here." He led her toward his Jeep.

Nearing the driver's door, he stopped. "I was proud of you today," he said. His gaze darted from side to side before resting on Pepper. "I couldn't have done what you did."

"It's the training." She rocked back and forth in her sneakers. "I couldn't have done what Joe did, either."

"He wasn't rescuing our mom."

Her tears gushed.

Zeke blinked. What had he said? Didn't she see it was a compliment?

"Don't cry." He patted her arm. "I'm sorry." He clutched her hand. Opening the car door, he snatched a napkin from his console and held it toward her. "Here."

Her whimpers slowed. A smile crept over her face. "I flustered you. I'm sorry."

"It was a compliment."

"I know." She stuffed the napkin into the pocket of her jeans. "I can't believe I did it, either." She turned her teary face toward him. "I prayed to God." Her gaze moved skyward. "To help me remember what to do. To let Ranie live."

Zeke cleared his throat. He swallowed hard. He looked away from Pepper's emerald eyes. Still, no words formed.

She stepped forward. Placing both hands on his shoulders, she stretched up and kissed his cheek. Her lips lingered against his skin. "Thanks for everything," she whispered near his ear.

A slight twist of his head brought his lips to hers. Their softness exceeded his expectations. He placed his hands on her waist, drawing her toward him, pulling her against his chest.

Agonizingly soon, she backed away, settling herself a few inches from him. Time elapsed as she breathed deliberately before readjusting her shirt.

"I'll stop by the orchard later. Or call." She turned to leave.

"Stop by."

She looked over her shoulder. "When we know more."

* * *

What a mess. He'd overstepped the bounds he'd set for himself with Pepper. Even worse, he'd done so at a most inappropriate time. Judging by her reaction, he'd gone beyond her limitations, too. He'd compromised his resolve to avoid an unequal yoke. He'd attached *guilt* to his list of complications in their relationship. And he'd added one more temptation to avoid.

How was he going to be near Pepper and not remember that kiss and the sensation of her in his arms? He wasn't. Even now, as he tried to rein in his thoughts, the memories assaulted him.

He stared at the quart of blueberries on his desk. He'd been so distracted, he'd walked right past the cooler and brought it with him to his office. Distraction had become a way of life with him, and he'd made it worse.

What relationship did she want between them? She'd stormed out of the barn the night he hadn't kissed her. She'd ridden with him the other day and seemed disappointed when she had to leave. Today she'd kissed him first, even though it was on the cheek.

Pacing around his office wasn't helping. The tennis ball was at his house. He didn't jog. What could he do to regain his equilibrium?

Pray. An obvious answer. Why hadn't he thought of it before?

He crossed to his desk chair, sat carefully, and propped his elbows on the desk. Cupping his chin in the base of his palms, he spoke aloud. "Lord, I messed up. Please forgive me." He opened his eyes and stared at the photo of Pepper and her mom. Pressing his lids closed again, he continued. "I'm confused about what to do next. How do You want this to go? I need answers." The sound of the Gator going past the barn door interrupted his thoughts. He pushed it aside. "I'm sure of some things. You love Pepper. You want her to love You. Don't let me get in the way."

Had he already become a barrier? Eyes open again, he stared ahead while pictures of recent events projected in his mind.

With a loud sigh, he shut his eyes and summoned his courage. "I know I want to love her, too." He exhaled. "Can't believe I'm saying the words. Never thought I'd meet someone like her."

He shifted his palms from under his chin to the middle of his forehead. "Don't let my longing for her be more important to me than my love for You. Or Your love for her." Opening his eyes, he stared at the desk top. "Help me to know what's right. And to do it."

Rising from his seat, he turned toward the door.

* * *

Pepper recognized Zeke's voice and halted a step outside his office. Hearing her name, she inched forward, peering around the corner. Seeing him deep in concentration, she backed away. His voice still reached her ears.

192

"I want to love her, too."

She gulped. Tears welled in her eyes. She sat down on the cold floor, pulling her knees up to her chest. She shouldn't listen. She couldn't stop.

The creak of the chair spurred her into action. She stood, brushing lingering tears away. She wiped her hands on her jeans and looked up. Straight into Zeke's chest.

"Pepper." He back stepped quickly. "I didn't hear—"

"I should go."

She spun on one heel.

He grabbed her arm and turned her back around. "Why are you here?"

The truth rolled off her lips. "Stopping by with an update."

"How long have you—"

"Not very." She couldn't look at him.

"Long enough?" He released her arm but caught her chin in his hand. She couldn't look away. "Did you mean it?"

He studied the concrete. His gaze returned to hers. "Yes."

"Were you going to tell me?"

"Hadn't thought that far."

You weren't supposed to hear. But she had. "Now what?"

* * *

Excellent question. Too bad he had no answer. How could God have let her come right then? He'd prayed for direction, not another problem.

"I don't know." He clasped her elbow and drew her into the office. "Have a seat."

"In that rickety thing? I'd rather stand."

"That's *my* job." He spun the chair so that it faced her. "You'll be fine."

She sat.

He crossed the office twice before speaking again. "Do you see the problem?"

"It's God."

"Yes— No—" What was he saying? "It has to do with God, but He's not the problem."

"The unequal yoke business."

Was she being sarcastic? He couldn't tell. Maybe something more specific would help.

"How could we build a life together?" Moving the stranded blueberries, he sat on the edge of his desk. "I'm in church every week,

193

usually two or three times." He extended his right hand. "You," he raised his left, "have been to one service since you came."

She could have gone each week with Gramps and Gram.

He gestured to himself. "I've never been inside a bar."

She spoke before he had the opportunity. "I went in last Saturday."

He'd pressed a point she couldn't argue.

"But I didn't stay. And I didn't drink."

"I'm glad." The understatement of the week. He cleared his throat. "I read the Bible—often." He picked up the blueberries and stared at them.

"I've read every day this week."

His head snapped upward. "What?" Had she really?

She stared at him. "The attributes of God: Love, Mercy, Goodness."

A dagger of guilt stabbed his heart. He'd been praying she would search for answers, but he'd assumed she hadn't. "I'm sorry."

"It's all new, Zeke." She stood and stepped near. "And it's not the only part that is." She removed the quart basket from his hand, and put her hand in its place. "I never expected to meet anyone like you, either."

Why couldn't he blink or look at the ceiling or go take care of those blueberries? Anything to escape her captivating eyes and give him the grit to pull his hand away.

"Do you want to know how I feel about you?"

His head moved up and down without his permission.

"Don't you already know?"

He reached for her other hand. "I thought I did, before . . ."

"Before what?"

"Before I kissed you." He looked down. Sensing her stare, he lifted his gaze to her green eyes. "You pulled away."

"You were fighting yourself." She glanced at their entwined hands. "I didn't like being the cause." Lifting her eyes toward his, she said, "I don't want you to kiss me again unless you can do it and be at peace."

Everything she said made sense. It solved problems. It helped Zeke honor God. It gave both of them space to think. And it cut at his heart like a pair of pruning shears on an overgrown branch.

* * *

"She came through surgery. Her vital signs are stable," Pepper said. The CT scan on her brain didn't show anything. She's conscious but not really alert." Pepper and Zeke stood in the Davies' kitchen. Sue, Anna, and Harold were seated at the table.

"What about her foot?" Anna's face personified pain.

194

"It's too soon to know for sure. But it's badly broken."

Harold spoke next. "Anything more about what happened?"

"Nothing." Pepper snapped her fingers. "I didn't go to the police station." She glanced at her watch. "Will anyone be available to take my statement after six o'clock?"

"I'd hope there's someone there around the clock." Zeke set his ever-present ball cap on a chair. "Do you know where the station is?"

"No." She rolled her eyes.

"I could drive you there." He reached toward his hat.

"No, that's all right. I want to get back to the hospital as soon as I can." She handed her phone toward him. "Could you put the address in for me?" When he had finished, she said, "I'd better get going. I'll see you in the morning."

"We'll be praying for you and your mom." Sue's eyes were wet when she stood and hugged Pepper. "We love you, honey."

Pepper tightened her grip on Zeke's sweet mom. She tried to echo the sentiment, but her voice wouldn't come.

"I'll walk you out." Zeke snatched the cap—the one he'd recently set down—and adjusted it onto his head. "Be right back, Dad." He opened the door and followed Pepper.

"Will you stay at the hospital?" Zeke asked as they strode toward her Mustang.

"No, Pops will stay tonight." She quickened her step to keep up with Zeke. "After the police station, I'm going to your grandparents', taking a quick shower, and scooting to the hospital to give Dad a break."

She halted abruptly. "What about the donkey rides today?"

"Had to cancel this morning's rides." He scuffed his shoe across the stones. "And use a substitute driver this afternoon."

"Who?"

"Me." He scrunched down, his forearms resting on his knees. "Kind of tight quarters."

Pepper laughed.

"I called Mr. Milton to make sure the donkeys could handle my weight. He assured me that either one could. They didn't like it much." He resumed his full height. "The kids weren't too thrilled, either. Wasn't much room for doubling up."

She giggled again. "I wish I'd seen it."

"I'm glad you didn't."

They had reached her car. He grabbed the handle but didn't open the door. "I'd like to pray for your mom before you leave. Okay?"

She leaned on the car. "Sure."

Yet again he removed his hat. Setting it on the roof of the car, he gently took Pepper's hand, closed his eyes, and bowed his head.

"Dear God, it's been a rough day for Pepper, her dad, and especially her mom. Thanks for sparing Ranie's life. Thanks for those who are caring for her. Give them all wisdom. Thanks for enabling Pepper this morning." The pressure from Zeke's hand increased. "Thanks for bringing her here. Help her as she endeavors to learn more about You."

"And thank you for the Davies family, especially Zeke." She squeezed his hand.

He paused and then added, "Amen."

Opening her door, he waited for her to climb in. "Be careful."

She wagged her eyebrows. "I'm the soul of caution."

He rolled his head in a circle. "Right."

"I will be tonight." She smiled. "Be sure to thank Joe for me. See you tomorrow." She drove slowly down the long drive, honking the horn as she pulled onto the road.

* * *

Ranie's room was dimly lit when Pepper entered. Pops dozed in a chair next to the bed. Pepper set her bag on the floor next to one wall and stepped around an IV pole and a vital signs' monitor. She approached her mom.

Bandages, bruises, and tubes covered most of Ranie's face and arms. Her left leg, sticking out of the bed covers, was elevated and wrapped. Pepper's heart clenched. She recalled the impeccably dressed, very stylish Ranie of graduation day. It would be a long time before that foot fit into the trendy shoes her mom had worn. Maybe it never would. Overall, the woman in the bed in front of her didn't bear much resemblance to that other person.

An old memory surfaced, and Pepper gloated over her mom's misery. Now she was suffering like Pops and Pepper had done.

A knife-like stab pierced her psyche and gouged her heart.

You want to be a doctor?

Pepper would encounter all kinds of people in her profession, some pleasant, some not; some who had caused or contributed to the problems she would be trying to treat; some who had loved ones around them; some who faced their trials alone.

Where is your compassion?

Why could she muster little sympathy for the woman who gave life to her? If Pops knew her thoughts, he would be mortified. But how could she love someone who should have been near but wasn't?

She navigated through the equipment and found another chair. Picking it up, she moved it closer to Pops, dragged her duffle to her, and settled in. The arm chair was large enough for her to turn sideways in, pulling up her knees and resting them against the opposite arm.

She pulled out Fred's Bible. Five sticky notes protruded from the top. Three held references for verses on Love, Mercy, and Goodness. One of the others pointed to John 3:16, the verse that Fred and she had looked up. The remaining note was in the same book a few chapters later. Pepper had stumbled upon it while looking up a verse about God.

She flipped to that note, shaking her head as she scanned the column. The first verses of Chapter 15 spoke of vines, branches, vinedressers, and fruit bearing, not at all what she was looking for. But by verse 9, the context had changed.

"'As the Father has loved me, so have I loved you. Abide in my love. If you keep My commandments, you will abide in My love, just as I have kept my Father's commandments and abide in His love. These things I have spoken to you, that My joy may be in you, and that your joy may be full. This is My commandment, that you love one another as I have loved you. Greater love has no one than this, that someone lay down his life for his friends.'"

Pepper reread the words. She let her head hang backwards over the arm of the chair. Staring at the ceiling, she pondered.

Were these verses an answer to a question she'd been asking? For weeks she'd wondered how the Davies family could be such nice people. They were kind to each other and caring toward others. They spoke love and displayed it.

Zeke and Anna had helped Pepper when she was not very lovable. Sue and Harold had welcomed her into their home from her first arrival. Harold and his sons had shown love to strangers during an accident. Joe had used his tractor-driving skills to rescue Ranie. Not two hours earlier, Sue had spoken the words, "We love you, honey," into Pepper's ear.

She looked back at the book in her lap. Verses 12 and 13 hit her. "'This is My commandment, that you love one another as I have loved you. Greater love has no one than this, that someone lay down his life for his friends.'"

According to those verses, the love that the Davies possessed was not only tied up in their religious beliefs, it was expected of them.

Glancing back at the page, she noticed verse 11. "'These things I have spoken to you, that My joy may be in you, and that your joy may be full.'" Pepper had never known a more joyful family. They enjoyed each other. They shared their joy with others. They were even joyful in work.

Pepper hadn't polled the visitors to Davies Orchard, but she would bet that those who came would give the Davies family the highest marks in friendliness and helpfulness.

She closed her eyes. Images danced before her. Toby joking while he picked berries. A smiling Anna handing a smoothie to the first one in a long line of customers. A weary Zeke, grinning as he gathered a huge bundle of pruned limbs and carried them off.

There was a connection between their beliefs in God and the way they lived. What was it?

* * *

"Pepper." A hand touched her arm. "Wake up, honey."

She blinked and widened her eyes, staring up at her dad. "What's up, Pops?" She groaned as she turned. Pops rescued the Bible that slid from her lap and set it on top of her bag. She stretched her legs in front of the chair and her arms above her head.

"It's getting late. I thought your neck needed a break."

It did. Pepper stretched it from side to side.

"And your phone has been making noises."

"Ringing?"

"More like chirping or chiming."

"Texts coming in." She reached into her bag. Scanning the screen, she asked, "How's Ranie?"

"In pain." He glanced toward the bed. "She moans a lot, especially when it's time for medication."

Looking up from her phone, Pepper once again studied her mother. "She looks like she lost a fight."

"She did." His voice cracked. "At least she's still in the battle." He settled back into the chair he'd been sitting in. He gestured at Pepper's phone. "Anything important?"

"One from Anna. One from Zeke. Both asking about Ranie." She tucked the phone back into her purse. "I'll get back to them later."

Pepper watched Ranie a few seconds longer. "Pops, does she have anyone else?" What had stirred Pepper's concern?

"Not that I know of." He rested both elbows on his knees and studied the floor tile. "Both parents are dead. They didn't have anything to do with her anyway."

"After she got pregnant?"

"Yeah."

Ranie had been telling the truth about that. Pepper squirmed in her chair. "She's pretty. Wonder why she never . . ."

Dad's upturned face and raised eyebrows halted Pepper.

"She is, Pops."

"I've always known that." He reached one hand toward Pepper. "Just surprised to hear you say it."

"It's hard for me to find anything good in her."

"If only you had known her before. She was kind, funny, responsible."

"Responsible?" Pepper raised herself in her chair and stared at him.

He clutched the arms of his chair. "This is what has always happened when we talk about your mom." He stood up. Setting the Bible in his seat, he said, "You would wonder something about her, and when I tried to explain, you wouldn't listen."

He crossed the room and entered the hallway. Pepper followed him out the door and down the hall. He kept walking until he found a deserted stairwell. He faced the wall and placed his hands above his head on the tiles. Then he took up where he had left off. "If I blamed Ranie, you labeled her a criminal. If I defended her, you thought I was a traitor." He paused long enough to breathe. "Finally, I quit trying."

For once, Pepper bit back the retort on her lips. Pops was willing to talk. If she wanted the truth, she had to listen.

"I really thought she would come back," he said.

"But she didn't, Pops."

"She didn't." He turned from the wall, lowered his arms, and leaned back, crossing one ankle over the other. He crossed his arms. "About two years later, I started digging. Hired a private investigator."

"Aaahh!" Pepper's intake of breath surprised her.

"He found her in a mental health clinic. Living under her maiden name." Tears pooled in Dad's eyes. "She'd tried to take her life."

Ranie hadn't been lying about that either.

Pops leveled a hard gaze on Pepper. "What if you had been nearby when she tried?"

Pepper flung herself at her dad. He wrapped his arms around her and clung tightly. "Sorry, Pops." She lifted her head and wiped the tears from her eyes. "I should have listened."

"There's more." He crossed to the stairs and sat on the first step. He patted the floor next to him.

Pepper took her place.

"After that, I kept track of her." He rested his forearms on his knees and folded his hands in front of him. "She would do well under treatment. Get out. Find a job."

Pepper reached for her dad's hands.

"Then something would happen." His head drooped.

She looked sideways at him. "Like what?"

"Not taking her medication. Being fired because she didn't have transportation to work since she'd forgotten to renew her license or register her car." He sighed. "One time she got mixed up with co-workers doing marijuana. It really messed up her mind. But, thankfully, no one pressed charges."

Pepper's eyes widened. "And then?"

"Then she'd lapse into depression, end up in an institution, and start the sequence again." He unclasped his hands and brought them to his sides, resting them on the step he was sitting on. "The longest cycle lasted just over three years." Pops angled his head toward Pepper. "Until five years ago."

"What happened five years ago?" She inched closer and lifted her dad's hand into her lap.

"She was released the last time just after you finished your junior year of high school. The first year went well."

He addressed the wall opposite them.

"The first letter I'd received from her since the one early on, came two weeks before you were to graduate from high school. She wanted to attend."

"Was she there?" Surely Pepper would have seen her.

"No, I told her not to come."

The pain of that decision still emanated from his voice. Pepper shivered at her memory of the night Pops had told her about Ranie's coming to share the PSU commencement. No wonder he had turned Ranie down.

"The last four years have been her best ones as an adult." He shifted to lean against the slats of the stairs and face Pepper more directly.

"How so?"

"She has a good job in communications. She rents an apartment she likes. She hasn't had to be hospitalized for a little over five years." He smiled at her success. "About a year ago, she contacted me, asking if I she could try to reconnect with you."

"And that's when you gave her my phone number?"

"That's when she asked for it." He laid a hand on Pepper's shoulder. "I didn't give it to her until a few months later."

Pepper massaged her forehead with the base of her palms. How could she take all of this in, especially while dealing with the accident and its aftermath? She'd have to sort through most of it later. Right now she desired one answer above all the others.

"What made the difference these last five years? How has she gotten better?"

"She gives most of the credit to her friend Lucy, a widow whose husband died when they were both in their early thirties."

What did being a widow have to do with being a great friend? She didn't ask.

"Lucy has encouraged Ranie, helped her set up a medication schedule, made sure she writes down appointments and meetings. Basically, she's taken Ranie under her wing."

As the words sank in, a fire lit in Pepper's heart and glowed in her eyes. "You mean like being the mother to her that she never was to me?" She leaned away and glared at her dad.

"And here it comes."

"What?"

"Your tantrum. 'Life's so unfair. I don't have anyone.'"

Pepper stood and glared down at him.

"Go ahead and stomp off."

"Have you lost your mind?"

"No. Just my patience."

It was time to leave. Pepper tromped to the door. Her hand was poised to pull it open when Dad said, "I won't beg you to stay, and I'm not coming after you."

Her backward stare met his equally adamant gaze.

"But I'll be here when you're ready." He sent her a sad half-smile. "Like I always have been."

His words stung. Pepper faced the door. She let go of the handle. Leaning forward, she rested her head on the wood. How many children had no parent to care for them? How many were abused by parents who were supposedly nurturing them? Had Pepper ever been without something she needed? With feet that felt like they were encased in fifty-pound shoes, she trudged toward Dad. She sank onto the step and wrapped her arms around her dear, sweet Pops.

"Why do you put up with me?"

"Because I love you."

CHAPTER 20

Hearing an incoming text, Zeke pushed the power button on the television remote. The meteorologist vanished.

"R U up? Call me?"

"Call you at 11:30? Where are you?" he mumbled. Was there trouble? He hit the keypad.

"Hi. Thanks for calling."

"Sure." He'd call her at 3:00 a.m. if she needed him. "What's up?"

"Why do you like me?" She sighed, inhaled, and was off again. "Because right now, I don't feel very likable."

A sign in his brain flashed, "Possible landmines ahead." Zeke took a deep breath. "You are likable. Why don't you feel that way?"

"To myself, briefly, I gloated over Ranie's injuries because of all the emotional hurt she's caused me."

He heard a thud in the background. A shoe? A book? Was she throwing something?

"What kind of aspiring doctor does that?" she asked.

Another thud.

"Don't answer that."

He wouldn't have known where to start.

"Pops and I had an argument about Ranie."

He might have guessed that.

"Pops said he puts up with me because he loves me." The sound of running water muffled some of her words. "You say I'm likable. Why?"

He'd say she was lovable, but now was not the time to quibble.

"Zeke?"

"Are you finished?"

"See what I mean? Likable people let other people talk, especially when they want an answer."

He smiled into the phone. "Some people would rather hear likable people talk than talk themselves." He cleared his throat. "But, since you asked, I'll tell you something that I like about you."

"Only one?"

"Only one tonight."

"I can live with that."

"You're not afraid to be spontaneous."

"Hmmm." Silence ensued. "Are you afraid to be spontaneous?"

"Most of the time."

"When was I spontaneous?"

"When you crawled under the railing of Axle's pen to show me that the spaces were too wide. And when you told me you would be perfect to drive a mini donkey cart that we didn't even have."

She had begun to laugh.

"I could go on."

"I get the picture." Her laughter stopped. "See you tomorrow."

* * *

By Saturday morning, news of the crash near Davies Orchard had been reported by two newspapers and three local television stations. The child passenger in the SUV had been treated at the local hospital and released. The father would remain hospitalized for a bit longer. He had sustained a concussion and a cracked rib. Ranie continued to be stable. She still showed no sign of brain injury, but her foot would require more surgery.

Ranie had been interviewed by a police officer. Her story corroborated the investigating officer's suspicion. A third vehicle had caused the accident but had fled the scene. According to Pops, the officer hadn't seemed confident that the third vehicle and its driver would be located.

Axle and Buster hurried to the gate of the pen when Pepper approached. She petted each of them enthusiastically. "I missed you two." Grabbing a currying brush, she asked, "Did you make new friends yesterday?" She brushed Axle first. "We're supposed to have another beautiful day. You guys will love that. So will all those kids." She lowered her face to their level. "I hope you have your running shoes on, because we'll be busy today."

"Are you talking to the donkeys?"

She hadn't heard Zeke enter the barn. "Yes. What's your point?"

"My point?" He handed her two small slips of paper. "I don't have a point." Looking over the railing, he said, "See you later, guys."

Pepper opened the first folded paper. "Spontaneity #3 Deciding before even meeting Gram that you were the answer for her care this

203

summer (you were right)." She giggled, read the words again, and laughed once more.

After tucking that piece into her pocket, she opened the other. "Likability #2 Love of animals. Axle and Buster are really glad you came."

These were treasures. Tears threatened her vision, but she couldn't have said whether she was laughing or crying.

* * *

By Saturday evening, Ranie's condition had been upgraded, but she still slept the majority of the time. The pain medications made much of her communication incoherent.

To fill the evening visiting hours, Pepper borrowed a checkerboard from Fred, and she and her dad set it up between the arms of two adjacent chairs. Both of them would be looking at the board sideways, but the handicap would be equal. "Tell me about Zeke Davies."

"I already have." Dad was fishing for information, and he was good at it. If she wasn't careful, she'd be divulging all sorts of things. Not that there was anything scandalous to tell.

"I'll rephrase." He moved his checker into a safe square. "Tell me about what's between you and Zeke."

"We share a love of animals." She slid her checker into an adjacent square. He jumped it.

"I already knew that. What else?"

"He says I'm spontaneous."

"All day. Every day."

"No one is spontaneous all day, every day." She rolled her eyes.

He shrugged and moved his checker. "You come close."

"He threatened to fire me."

Pops leaned sideways in his chair. His eyes grew large. "What did you do?"

"Why do you think I did something?" She raised both hands to her chest, but she couldn't suppress her smile. "Maybe he was being unreasonable and simply tossing out threats because he's the owner's oldest son."

Pops laughed out loud before quickly stifling the noise and looking at Ranie. "I could ask him."

The tilt of his head and the glint in his eye declared the truth of the moment. Once again her dad had tugged something out of her without her even realizing that the rope was in place.

"How do you do that?"

"Do what?"

Pops was also a pretty fair actor. Was his question for real, or was he putting her on? "How do you make me divulge information that I'd rather you didn't know?"

"Practice." He looked at the neglected checker board. "Whose turn is it?"

"Yours, I think."

He deliberated a moment before sliding his checker. "So, tell me. What did you do?"

She raised her hand above a red checker. Glancing out of the corner of her eye, she said, "Peeled out of the driveway."

"At the Hannas'?" His eyes bulged.

"At the orchard." She covered her face with one hand. Then, lowering her defense, she added. "After hours. No one saw me do it."

"Obviously someone did." He looked askance at her.

"Zeke the ubiquitous."

"Ubiquitous."

"It means—"

"I know what it means." He rolled his eyes at her. "Zeke always seems to know what's going on, does he?"

"I can't get away with anything."

Pops pulled his hands away from the checkers and leaned back. "I like this guy more every day."

"You would." Turning her attention back to the board, she moved a black checker.

"That's my piece."

Lifting her hand, she stared at the board. "You've made me lose my concentration." The game had ended.

"Or maybe focus it somewhere else." He leaned sideways toward her. "Why did I send you a copy of the picture of you and your mom so that you could give it to Zeke? He has one."

"He needed another one." She began gathering all the checkers into a pile.

"Why?"

"His tore." Opening a small bag, she dropped the checkers into it.

"Look at me."

She plopped her hands into her lap and turned her head. "I saw the photo in his hand. I hadn't known about it. I got mad."

"And?"

"And I tried to take it from him, but it tore." She squished the bag, making the checkers rattle. "He wanted another one."

"Is this relationship a matter of the heart for you?"

Dad's eyes no longer hinted of laughter. Pepper nodded.

"For him, too?"

"Yes." Since overhearing his prayer, she could answer definitely.

"You've been dating?"

"No."

He pinched his lips together. "Why not?"

"He loves God." She studied her fingers. "He knows I don't."

After setting the checker board on the floor, Pops moved his chair close to Pepper's. He draped his arm over her shoulder and drew her to himself.

A few minutes later he spoke. "This is why you asked about prayer and church."

"Uh-huh." Gazing at her dad, she said. "I've always hated God for letting Ranie go away. But Zeke . . ."

Dad clenched his arm, pulling her closer.

"Zeke says that people have a free will. Ranie left because she chose to."

Pepper hadn't seen Pops reach for the tissue box, but somehow he produced a tissue and handed it to her.

"He also says that God uses bad things to bring about good."

"How's that work?"

Pepper cringed. More damaging information to divulge. "Do you know how I met Anna and Zeke?"

After telling the story, she added, "God used my bad judgment to bring Zeke, Anna, their family, and me together." She squeezed Pops' hand that hung around her shoulder. "He's one of the best things in my life. I want to agree with him about God."

"Because of God? Or because of Zeke?"

"Both, I hope." Turning her body sideways, she scrunched herself into the chair and faced Pops. "Why the worried look? You like Zeke."

"I do. And so far I trust him. But I'm skeptical of religious types." He scanned the ceiling before refocusing on Pepper. "Too many hypocrites."

"He isn't one. Neither are the others in his family." She nodded slightly to solidify her words. A second later, she bobbed up and down in her chair. "Tomorrow's Sunday." She grinned like a kid on Christmas Day. "Come with me to their church. We'll surprise them."

* * *

206

"Park right here, Pops. That's Fred and Maggie's car over there." Her dad complied.

"Parking lot is nearly full. Are we late?"

"The service starts at eleven o'clock, but it's the second one. Bible classes are at ten."

Pepper hopped out. Pops joined her. He pocketed his keys and adjusted his tie.

"You nervous?"

"A little." He offered Pepper his arm. "I haven't entered a church since I was a kid."

Pepper tilted her head in his direction. "Not even to get married?"

"We went to the district magistrate."

Before they'd reached the door, someone held it open for them. Pepper recognized the man as the pastor.

"Good morning, young lady. Aren't you the one who's helping Maggie Hanna?"

Pepper smiled. "I am."

"They arrived a few moments ago."

He offered his hand to Pepper's dad. "I'm Pastor White."

"This is Ken Staley, my dad."

"Glad you could come today." His brow furrowed, and he addressed Pepper. "Wasn't it your mom who was in the accident on Friday?"

"Y—y—yes." How had he known?

"Sue called and added her to our prayer list that night. How is she doing?"

"Improving each day."

"We'll keep praying."

Others had come in behind them. Pepper thanked the pastor and headed toward the chapel.

"Hey, Pepper." Toby's voice met her from down the hall. She turned.

"Hi, Toby." She watched him gulp back surprise at her being there. "Say hello to my dad."

"Dad, this is Zeke's youngest, and tallest, brother Toby."

Dad shook Toby's hand. "What does your mom feed you? You're all tall."

"Everything, and lots of it."

"I'd say so. Nice to meet you."

"And this . . ." She reached around Toby to catch Joe's shirt sleeve. "This is Joe."

Pops gulped. In a raspy voice he said, "You drove the tractor."

Joe blushed. "Yes, sir."

Pops shook Joe's hand and clasped his elbow. "Thank you."

"The tractor did the work." Joe nodded and back away. "Nice to meet you."

Pepper watched a pretty young woman step up beside Joe and take his elbow as he entered the chapel. She must be Bethany. Once again Pepper had missed the opportunity to meet her.

"Good morning, Mr. Staley."

Pepper turned to see Zeke and Pops shaking hands.

"Morning, Zeke."

"Glad to see you." Zeke looked at Pepper. "And you, too."

Pepper's heart fluttered.

Deciding where everyone should sit involved the same shuffle that it had when Pepper attended before. By the time the service started, she was sitting between her favorite men, Pops and Zeke.

With Zeke's help, Pepper found the passages in her Bible and shared them with Pops. She also shared a song book with him and showed him how to follow the words along.

But her attention wandered to Zeke whenever it could. His wavy hair was tamer than usual, but his eyes, serious as always. The rolled-up sleeves of his dress shirt showed tanned arms that looked, and were, strong. He'd chosen purple with a striped tie. Black slacks and shiny black shoes completed his transformation from work day jeans and pullover. Zeke was a fine-looking man. Definitely fine.

Was his concentration on the service as sporadic as hers was? Probably not. But if the glances he sent her way were any indication, his thoughts were roaming sometimes, too.

* * *

"What did you think, Pops?"

"Zeke's family seems very nice. His grandfather is funny."

They were on their way back to the hospital. "Fred has quite a story, some of it hard, but he's one of the most joyful people ever." She put the window down a crack. "What did you think of the service?"

"The Parable of the Prodigal. Probably one of only a few things from the Bible with which I am familiar."

"You'd heard that story?" Her life was full of surprises lately.

"Parts of it. The son takes his inheritance, wastes it, gets in trouble, and decides to go back."

"And the father? The character who represents God?"

208

"That part was new." Pops wasn't wasting any time. The speedometer read ten miles over the limit.

"Do you think God loves us like that father loved his son?"

"It's a nice thought." Pops slowed as he neared town.

"I wish Zeke were here."

"I'm not surprised." He turned and grinned at her.

She swatted at his arm. "So he could explain things."

"Oh. That's the story, is it?" He turned down the street to the hospital. "Then I'm going to be your favorite dad, because I asked him to come into town this afternoon. Thought we'd take a break. Maybe sit outside and chat."

She leaned across the center console and planted a kiss on his cheek. "You're the best Pops ever."

* * *

"Look who has been awake for almost five minutes." Linda, one of Ranie's nurses, greeted them as they walked in.

Pops crossed directly to the bed going to the far side. "Hi. It's good to see your eyes."

Her lips turned up slightly. "Hi, Ken."

Her voice was breathy and hard to hear.

He bent closer. "You scared us."

"Scared me, too." She took a labored breath. "Pepper?"

"She's here." He motioned for Pepper to come forward.

The accident had been only two days earlier. How was Ranie coherent already? Pepper wanted more time to prepare. Her feet moved. Her heart lagged behind.

From the other side of Ranie's bed, Pops motioned to her with his head. His eyes begged her to comply. She approached the bed, coming only close enough that she could reach the rail. "Hi."

"You prayed for me."

Pepper's face blanched.

"I heard you." Ranie's hand lifted infinitesimally toward her daughter. "I didn't want to die." A single tear slid down the side of her face.

Pepper's stomach catapulted to her knees. Words from the Bible echoed in her mind. "'This is My commandment, that you love one another as I have loved you.'"

Her thoughts flew to the father of the prodigal, loving the son who had denied him, exploited his generosity, and left him. The father hadn't

209

deserved his son's scorn, but he took the abuse, continued to love his son, and constantly watched for his return.

Ranie was the prodigal. Could Pepper emulate the father? Did she want to?

She lifted her gaze from her mom's face and stared into her father's eyes. How often had she seen that look? The one that not only understood her pain but also urged her to rise above it.

Her gaze never leaving Pops, she whispered, "I didn't want you to, either." She looked down. Ranie sighed and shut her eyes.

Pops rounded the end of the bed and engulfed Pepper in his arms. "The pride I felt for you on graduation day doesn't come close to what I feel now." He held her a bit longer. "I'll be back in a minute."

He left the room, pulling a handkerchief from his pocket as he went.

Pepper stood watching her mother's still form. Zeke had commented weeks earlier that Pepper looked a lot like Ranie. She had slugged him. "I don't look like that woman." He had shrugged his shoulders and retreated, citing how much work he had to do.

Even the bandages and the tubes couldn't disguise the resemblance the two shared. Pepper waited for the anger she had vented on Zeke to rise from the pit of her stomach. It didn't come.

What did make their way to her mind were the words she'd remembered a few minutes ago. "'This is My commandment, that you love one another as I have loved you.'" Pops had been preaching for years that forgiveness was a part of loving someone. Maybe he was right.

Stepping closer to the bed, she reached forward and laid her fingers on the back of Ranie's hand.

CHAPTER 21

Waiting for the elevator to reach his floor, Zeke carefully lifted his arm and looked at his watch. Only 1:45. He hadn't given them much time. But Mr. Staley hadn't specified when to come. The elevator stopped. His hands full of flowers, he stepped from the car—and directly into Pepper's dad.

The older man's reflexes were quick. He grabbed both of Zeke's upper arms, halting him before the two collided.

"Wasn't expecting you quite as soon, or with so many flowers." He lifted one vase from Zeke's arms. The Get Well balloon bobbed around above Mr. Staley's head.

"My family sent those." Raising a potted plant, Zeke added, "This one's from Gram and Gramps."

"And those?" Ken Staley pointed to the cut bouquet of assorted wildflowers.

Zeke cleared his throat. "They're for Pepper."

He didn't ask who had sent them.

"Let's talk."

Without further comment, he strode down the hall, stopping at the nurses' station. "These are for room 320. May we leave them here for a few minutes?" He held up the arrangement in his hand and pointed to the ones Zeke held.

"I'd be glad to take them down for you," said a young woman wearing a tag which said *Volunteer*.

"Thanks, but we'd like to take them ourselves. We need a few minutes, though."

"We'll keep them for you."

Once they had handed over all of the flowers, Ken Staley headed back to the elevator.

* * *

211

"Both you and Pepper are adults. You don't have to answer to me." The two had found a bench outside the hospital. "But I have something to say. I hope you'll listen." He angled his torso toward Zeke. "You have turned Pepper's world upside down—not that parts of it didn't need upsetting."

It was easy to see where Pepper got at least part of her directness. Zeke faced the man next to him. "What do you mean?"

"She's always been impulsive. I've learned to deal with that." He addressed Zeke with a slanted nod. "With you she's become more reflective than I've ever seen her. That worries me." He drew one ankle onto his other knee. "She wonders what you're thinking or how you would explain something."

Zeke's heart smiled, but he squelched any outward sign of a grin.

"I should be happy to see this in her. But I can't help wondering how you've done it."

Zeke's jaw dropped. "What do you think I've done?"

"I don't know. Anything she's told me has made me think you're a good person and a positive influence."

"Then why—"

"Religion makes me nervous and cynical."

At last the enemy had shown itself.

"I conjure pictures of communes, multiple wives, stores of weapons, Mayan calendars. You name it."

The comment might have been funny if Ken Staley hadn't looked as though he'd been told he had a brain tumor. Zeke addressed each issued, counting it off on his fingers. "The orchard is not a commune. People visit every day. We don't ask them to live there, and we don't divide our profits with them." He looked away from Pepper's dad before turning back and continuing. "Dad and Gramps have one wife each. If and when I marry, it will be a commitment to one woman for a lifetime." Zeke had daydreamed about Pepper's being that woman. He didn't divulge that information. "We do have three guns on the property, a hand gun that's registered, and two hunting rifles that we use with licenses. I have no idea about the Mayan calendar."

"But you are religious."

"I don't like that term." Zeke leaned forward, placing his elbows on his knees. He turned his head toward Pepper's dad. "*Religious* refers to someone who places faith in any religion. I follow God and His word. I have a personal commitment to Christ. I am a Christian."

Had Zeke ever before spoken so clearly to defend his faith? He wasn't finished.

"About my influencing her." He lifted a hand to shield his eyes from the afternoon sun. "She has, of her own free will, attended one other Sunday service. She and Gramps have talked two or three times about God. She and I have discussed a few things. Gramps gave her a Bible to use. She read it this week. That sums up any religious influence."

"I don't think so."

Zeke waited.

"Your religion—faith—influenced her before she entered a church or began reading the Bible."

Zeke swallowed. Apparently he hadn't compromised his testimony. "I try to live by two principles," he continued. "Loving God with my heart, soul, and mind. Loving others as I love myself."

Zeke's voice had long ago faded when Mr. Staley spoke. "Thank you for being frank and forthcoming. Especially when you could do whatever you want and I could do nothing about it." He lowered his head. "By the time I was Pepper's age, she was four, my wife had left me, both of my parents had died, and I was a young entrepreneur struggling to pay the bills."

"I'm sorry."

"I want better for her." He looked back at Zeke. "Your influence has made her life better. She knows that." He smiled for the first time since sitting down. "I think I did, too." He stood and headed in the direction of the hospital door.

* * *

"These are from Mom, Dad, and the family."

With Ranie sleeping, Pepper accepted the flowers and set them on the window ledge. "Love the balloon."

Why wasn't he surprised? "These are from Gram and Gramps. Gram says potted plants give more lasting memories."

"They're both beautiful."

He handed her the wildflowers. "These are from me."

"Aren't you a part of your family?"

A few feet away, Ken Staley guffawed. He grinned up at Zeke.

"Yes, but . . ." Zeke studied the brightly-colored blooms. "These are for you."

She encircled the stems with her hand, touching his fingers as she did. "Thanks." Looking away from Zeke, she inhaled the scent of the blossoms. "I love wildflowers."

"I thought you might."

"Are you hinting that I might be a bit wild?"

"If he's not, I am," Mr. Staley said.

Pepper's dad had obviously not lost interest in the wildflowers.

Zeke grinned. "Maybe." He reached into his pocket and pulled out two slips of paper like the ones he had handed her yesterday.

She reached for them and addressed her dad. "Pops, are you ready for that conversation with Zeke?"

He's already had it.

"You go ahead."

Without hesitating, Pepper said, "See you later." She scooted toward the door.

Zeke nodded in her father's direction and hurried after her. He found her just around the first corner. She was reading one of the pieces of paper. Her lips moved as she silently read the words he'd written. "Spontaneity #4 Flirting with me (in front of my mother) the first time you came to my house."

She looked up and giggled. "You noticed, did you?" Placing her hand on his wrist, she said, "I thought you might be too shy to see."

"No one's that shy."

"Oh, come on, I wasn't that bad."

She rolled her eyes and unfolded the other paper. He said the words aloud as she read them to herself. "Likability #3 Being interested enough in me to flirt with me (in front of my mother) the first time you came to my house."

She wagged her eyebrows at him. "Flirting made quite an impression. I might have to try it again."

He coughed. "I think you already have."

"You're quicker than you used to be."

The banter continued as they left the hospital. Zeke drove them to a coffee shop and then to a park. They sat in adjacent swings, facing in opposite directions. "I think Ranie's the prodigal."

"In what way?" He hadn't seen that coming.

"She went away, stayed away, and suddenly came back. Now she wants us to forgive her."

"In some ways it fits." He set his empty Styrofoam cup near him on the grass. "Were you watching for her, waiting for her to come back? Did you welcome her with open arms?"

"I didn't say I was the father. I said she was the prodigal."

"She might be a prodigal. But she isn't the only one." Zeke prayed for the Lord's strength to explain it.

When she was a child, the swings had been Pepper's playground favorite. She would beg Pops to push her until he pleaded for her to let him stop. She and Zeke weren't soaring through the air, but being on a swing again was enjoyable, especially with Zeke next to her.

She didn't wait long before once again broaching the subject of the pastor's sermon. "Are you saying that I'm the prodigal?"

"Promise to let me explain?"

She cocked her head to one side. "You afraid I might do something spontaneous?"

"The thought had crossed my mind." He pushed his swing sideways, moving his body closer to hers.

"I'll listen."

"The prodigal is all of us at one point in our lives. Some of us never move from that stage. At this point in your life, you are the prodigal."

What was he saying? Using her feet, she swung sideways away from him and then back toward him.

Zeke grabbed the chain and held it. "God is the father in the story."

That much she understood from the preacher's earlier words.

"He loves each of us. He wants a close relationship with us—like the one you and your dad have."

If she ever deserted him, Pops would wait for her and watch for her to come back, just like he had for Ranie all these years. She could see how God would do the same if he really loved people.

"Like the prodigal, all people are separated from the Father."

"That's the part that puzzles me." She made small circles in the dirt with her foot.

"Have you ever done anything wrong? Told a lie, envied someone, stolen something?"

It was a serious question, but she smiled anyway. "Sure."

"Then you're a sinner. You've offended God."

She looked away.

"We're all sinners." Taking the chain with his opposite hand, he covered Pepper's hand with his nearer one.

She turned back toward him.

"Like the prodigal, we take all the good things that God gives us and squander them selfishly."

Pepper heard the crack in his voice. She made more circles in the dust.

"But He waits and watches. Wanting us to come to Him, but not making us."

She looked up. Compassion glimmered in his eyes. Compassion and hope.

"How would someone do that?"

* * *

Don't mess this up.

Zeke released his hold on the swing chain and wiped his sweaty palm on his jeans. No doubt his other palm was moist, too, but he didn't let go of Pepper's hand. "Let's sit over there." He motioned to a nearby picnic table.

During the short walk, myriads of thoughts bombarded his brain. None of them centered on the small hand enclosed in his. Instead, he searched for ways to influence her mind and soften her heart toward God. When Pepper sat on one side of the table, he took a seat across from her.

He bowed his head. "Lord, Pepper wants to hear more about coming to you by faith in Christ. Please give me the words she needs. Amen."

"Since all people have sinned, and God can't tolerate sin, anyone who wants to have fellowship with God has a problem."

Pepper remained uncharacteristically quiet. Her green eyes watched him intently.

Another wave of sweat swept over him.

"God solved man's problem."

While he explained Christ's coming to earth, His sacrificial death on the cross, and His miraculous resurrection, her gaze remained fixed on Zeke. After he'd explained the need to repent, he asked, "Do you understand what I'm saying?"

"I understand."

Then Zeke recited two verses he had learned long ago. "If you confess with your mouth that Jesus is Lord and believe in your heart that God raised Him from the dead, you will be saved. For with the heart one believes and is justified, and with the mouth one confesses and is saved."

Her fingers tapped the table, but her attention stayed on Zeke.

"Accepting Christ isn't difficult." He saw the struggle in her gaze. "Deciding to might not be easy."

Finally, she broke her near-silence. "I understand what you've said. I know you believe it's the truth." She squeezed his hand. "And I thank you for caring enough to tell me."

He heard the "but" that she hadn't said. His gaze dropped to the table and stayed there until he heard her get up. She made her way slowly to his Jeep.

216

He waited, giving her time alone. Then he gathered up the empty cup and prepared himself for a gloomy ride to the hospital and an even more dismal Sunday night.

* * *

Pepper stayed late at the hospital. It was well after one in the morning when she unlocked the Hanna's door and crept softly to her room. Not even the ticking of several clocks was enough to drown out the roaring thoughts in her mind. She lay awake.

What was this feeling? Guilt? Frustration? Confusion? Maybe a combination? Over and over she debated the justifications for feeling each. Finally, in the near-morning hours, her exhausted brain could formulate no more arguments. She slept.

* * *

"Dear, are you all right?"

Pepper rolled over, rubbing her eyes and shaking her head. Was she hearing things?

"Pepper?" A soft knock sounded. "Are you ill?"

She blinked and dangled her feet over the edge of the bed. "Maggie? Is that you?"

"Yes."

"Come in."

Maggie's face, framed by her silver-white hair, peeked in. "Is everything all right?"

Rubbing her eyes again and brushing miscellaneous curls from her face, Pepper said, "I think so. Why?"

Maggie entered the room. "It's almost noon. I was getting worried."

"Almost noon!" She jumped from the bed. "I'm so late for the orchard." She started past the older woman. "And I missed your therapy." She raised both hands into the air.

Maggie's arm stopped her progress. "It's Monday. The orchard's closed. Fred does therapy with me."

With a sigh, Pepper turned and performed a face flop onto her bed. In a muffled voice she said, "I love Monday." She lifted her head from the comforter. "I don't think I've ever said that."

Maggie laughed. "Most people don't."

Pepper rolled over and then sat up. "I'm sorry you had to come check on me."

217

"I'm sorry I woke you." She motioned to the bed. "May I sit with you?"

Pepper scooted over. "Of course."

"You're sure nothing's wrong?"

Pepper couldn't go as far as that. "I got in late. Then I couldn't fall asleep."

"You're too young for not being able to sleep." She grinned and placed a hand on Pepper's shoulder. "Is it your mom?"

This time, the problem wasn't her mom. Would she be struggling less if Ranie were the issue? "No, she's doing okay. She was awake for a little bit yesterday."

"I won't pry." She rose to her feet cautiously. "I guess I was being a worry wart."

Pepper giggled and then sobered. "Do you have a minute?"

"Yes." She inched closer to lower herself gently.

"Wait. I'll get you a chair that will be easier for you to get out of."

"Or we could both sit on the porch. It's a lovely day."

Pepper glanced out the window. "It does look beautiful."

"I'll go and settle myself." She started out. "You do whatever you need to and join me when you're ready."

After Maggie left, Pepper stood in front of the mirror. She should shower, dress, and have some coffee. The dark circles under her eyes screamed for a pick-me-up. But being picked up emotionally was more important. She pushed her feet into her slippers, grabbed a raggedy but comfortable robe, and took herself and Hello Kitty to the sunshine of the porch.

When Pepper stepped outside, Maggie was culling some dead petunia blossoms from the flower box on the porch railing.

"These petunias are such a beautiful color."

Pepper nodded her head. "Would you say it's pinkish purple or purplish pink?"

Maggie pulled one last dead blossom from the petunias. "I'd say it's a lovely cross between the two." She made her way to the wooden bench and sat, leaning onto the back rest.

Being careful not to bump either of Maggie's knees, Pepper pulled an Adirondack chair up in front of her elderly friend.

"So, what has extinguished the light in those green eyes of yours?"

Where should Pepper begin? "Did you grow up here, Maggie?"

She drew one hand to her chest and laughed. "Goodness, no." Pointing out a hummingbird as it sampled nectar from a petunia, she added, "I grew up in New York City. My dad had a prosperous law office in Brooklyn." She studied the flowers intently. "He gave up his practice when he was fifty because of heart problems."

Pepper swallowed hard. "What happened then?"

"Dad, Mom, my sister Milly, and I moved into a rambling farm house about ten miles from here."

Pepper abandoned her slippers and pulled her feet up beside her legs. "I bet that was a change." Why couldn't parents see how their actions affected their children?

"One that I never let my father forget." Her eyes clouded over. "Every day I nagged at him to take us back to the city."

"He never listened?"

Tears had sprung to Maggie's eyes. "He died ten months later. Had a massive heart attack."

Pepper reached for Maggie's hand.

"He was gone before I could apologize."

Smacked by the onslaught of grief, Pepper slumped forward. How had Maggie overcome the sadness and guilt?

Zeke's grandmother cried a moment longer. Then, using the hem of her shirt, she dried her eyes.

"Mom and Milly went back to New York two months after Dad's death."

"And you?"

She shook her head. A slight smile curved her lips. "The week after we'd moved here, Dad went to the barber for a haircut. One of the other men in the shop was the local pastor, a man by the name of Roy Hanna."

Pepper's intake of breath was met by Maggie's chuckle.

"Despite Dad's agnostic views, Pastor Hanna and he became friends. Our families shared meals on a number of occasions."

Pepper thumped the chair arms with both hands. "And you met Fred Hanna and fell in love."

"Yes—and no."

Pepper leaned forward.

Fred's voice drifted toward them. "Crazy girl didn't know what was good for her."

Both women looked toward the open living room window. His face could be seen through the screen. He had pulled the rocking chair near the wall and was obviously listening in.

"Fred Hanna, you're the boldest eavesdropper I've ever met." She waved one hand toward him. "Move that chair back where it belongs and go about your business instead of butting in on ours."

"Just waiting for the part where you came to your senses."

"You make me wonder if I ever had any sense." She shooed him with both hands. "Now go away." Putting her face close to the screen, she watched until he had left the room.

She looked at Pepper and laughed. They both laughed. The weight on Pepper's heart lessened by half.

"What's the part where you 'came to your senses'?"

"In many ways, Fred hasn't changed. He was funny and quick-witted then, too." She shook her head. "Each day for a month he asked me out."

Pepper's eyes widened. Good thing Fred wasn't easily discouraged.

"Every day I turned him down." Her smile faded. "It hurts me now when I think that he could have given up."

Would Zeke give up Pepper?

"On the thirty-second try, he said, 'This could be your last chance.'" She folded her hands in her lap and watched them momentarily. "By then, I knew I didn't want to pass him up."

"So you went out with him, realized you loved him, and lived happily ever after." Pepper sighed an "aaaahhhh."

"Not quite."

"You still weren't convinced?"

Maggie wagged her head in the air. "I went with him on a hayride with the young people from his church."

"A hayride?" What in the world?

"It's really a wagon ride—a wagon that has some hay bales in it to sit on."

That made some sense.

"He asked me to attend a service with him. My family went to church only on Christmas and Easter. Since this was in August, I said no." She lowered her voice.

Was Fred listening again?

"That was the beginning of the hardest six months of my life."

Pepper could relate. "What happened?"

"Not knowing whether God was important to me, Fred's father had given him permission to ask me out on the condition that he also invite me to church. If I accepted the date but turned down the invitation, he wasn't permitted to go out with me again."

"Fred agreed to that?" Why would he?

"Yes. You're surprised?"

"Shocked."

"So was I." Maggie spotted another hummingbird and pointed it out. "The situation put a huge strain on our families' friendship and made the two of us miserable."

220

Once again Maggie's story coincided with Pepper's.

"Then Dad died, and Mom nearly fell apart."

Maggie's tears resurfaced.

Why hadn't Pepper retrieved a box of tissues earlier? She started to rise from her chair, when the front door opened slightly, and a thin, wrinkled-skinned arm extended through a crack. At the end of the arm was a hand holding a tissue box.

Hurrying to the box, Pepper snatched it from Fred. She would excuse him this time even though he hadn't heeded his wife's warning to mind his own business. Handing a tissue to Maggie, Pepper sat back down and waited.

"We survived Dad's death with the help of the people in that church. Fred's family most of all." She dabbed at her eyes before continuing. "They loved us through it, doing everything from handling Dad's funeral service, to helping Mom with the family finances, to making arrangements to sell the house when she decided to move back to New York City."

"She sold your home?" Maggie's story became more incredible with each sentence. "Where did you live?"

Right on cue, Fred stepped onto the porch. "In a one-bedroom home. With me." He hobbled to his sweetheart and draped an arm across her shoulder.

In a matter-of-fact tone, she addressed Pepper. "I married him first." She turned to Fred with a warm, watery glance.

Pepper gulped and reached for the box in her lap.

"We'd known each other not quite eleven months. But I'd committed my life to Christ only a few weeks before our engagement."

Fred took up the story. "Lots of people doubted." He nodded, first at Pepper, and then at Maggie. "Said we'd never last."

"Many thought my decision about Christ was a sham. Just a way to mollify Fred's parents and solidify his feelings."

Fred's gaze focused on Pepper. "I knew better. I knew my Maggie had taken the time to make up her heart and mind about God."

Teary-eyed and stunned, Pepper asked, "How long ago was this?"

"Celebrated our fifty-second anniversary last October." He withdrew his arm from around Maggie. "I've interfered enough." He grinned at the two women.

"You certainly have." She swatted his arm.

"It's a story I never tire of hearing."

The choke in Fred's voice sent a tremor into Pepper's heart.

"Or interrupting—so it seems."

"I'm going." He raised his arms in a semblance of surrender. "Guess I'll have to beat myself at a game of checkers."

"Are you up for a bit of a stroll?" Maggie asked when Fred had disappeared.

"Sounds heavenly, but you shouldn't be walking on uneven surfaces."

"How about the porch?"

Pepper smiled. "Around the porch would be fine."

Coming slowly to her feet, Maggie steadied herself and then slipped her hand through the arm Pepper extended to her.

"You've heard my love story." Her soft blue eyes looked directly into Pepper's green ones. "Now I'd like to hear yours." Maggie squeezed Pepper's arm just above her wrist. "And I don't think it includes a certain young doctor, does it?"

Surprisingly unable to drag the words from her throat, Pepper shook her head.

"Zeke?"

Pepper's head switched from shaking to nodding. Still no words came.

"He feels the same." Maggie wasn't asking a question. "First time I've ever seen him smitten."

Pepper stopped. She grinned. The grin gave way to laughter.

"That's the look and sound of love."

Pepper hugged Maggie Hanna. "I'm so jealous. I wish you were my grandmother."

Maggie chuckled. "Maybe someday I will be."

Would God let something so wonderful happen in Pepper's life?

Completing a stint around both sides of the porch, the two returned to where they had begun.

"Are you up for one more jaunt?"

The smooth, dry surface was perfect exercise for Maggie. "I'm ready if you are."

They started again, and Maggie spoke. "Are your uncertainties about God keeping this love story from becoming a 'happily ever after'?"

Not only did Maggie Hanna know Pepper's thoughts about Zeke, but she also understood Pepper's questions about God. Once again Pepper stopped short.

"What's wrong?" Maggie asked.

"I was so cocky." She leaned away from Maggie and faced her squarely. "I told Anna I was your answer for this summer. You needed my help."

"We did." Maggie patted Pepper's arm.

Pepper shook her head. "No, I needed your help."

Looking back to where they had been sitting, Maggie altered her course. "Think of it this way. The Lord knew that we needed each other. He brought us together."

"I didn't think that God cared about me."

"He does. More than you can imagine." Maggie resumed her earlier position on the bench. Pepper joined her.

Now for the ultimate question. "Do you think I can come back? Like the prodigal?"

"Absolutely." A tear rolled down Maggie's cheek. "Do you know how?"

Pepper nodded. "Zeke told me yesterday."

"Are you ready now?"

The up and down movement of Pepper's head brought a huge smile to Maggie's face. "Do I just talk to God?"

"Like you are to me."

"Should I stand? Or maybe kneel?"

"God will hear and understand whatever posture you choose." Maggie clasped her helper's hand.

Pepper closed her eyes and began. "God, I didn't know that You cared. I don't really understand why You do." Her mind envisioned the prodigal's father with arms outstretched toward his son. "I know I've done wrong, and I know I need You. I'm asking You to forgive my sins." Inhaling deeply, she continued, "I accept what Christ has done for me. I want to trust Him and come to You."

A few minutes later, both women stood and hugged. Pepper still wore a ragged robe and cartoon character pajamas. She hadn't grown any taller, nor were her green eyes a different shade. On the outside, she was completely the same. But her heart had been changed.

Maggie spoke. "Fred says that the first thing a person should do after coming to Christ is tell someone of that decision." Her eyes grew large.

In unison the two said to each other, "Zeke."

CHAPTER 22

Pepper hurried to her room. Reaching it, she swung the door closed, and flung the slippers from her feet. Why hadn't she dressed earlier? Which was the better choice, a shower, followed by a half-hour get-ready ritual or a sponge bath, some clean clothes, and being on her way in fewer than ten minutes? Expediency trumped vanity.

She flung her pajamas onto the bed and scurried to the bathroom. She exited a bit later, her toothbrush in one hand. She continued brushing while she rooted through her closet for a shirt and some shorts. Where were her favorites?

Five minutes later she snagged her phone while she combed her brunette curls into order.

"Hi, Anna." She ignored the fluttering sensation in her stomach. "Where's Zeke?"

"I'm not sure. He was here for lunch but . . ." She interrupted herself. "Call his phone."

"No." More desperate than she'd wanted to sound. "It's a surprise."

"What's up?"

Great. Now she'd alerted Anna's suspicions. "I'll tell you later. Any idea where I should look?" She spotted a pair of cute sandals, snatched them from the closet, and put the first one on.

"He might have gone to town."

Could Pepper search Lewisburg and track him down?

"Wait. His Jeep's in the driveway. So is the orchard pickup. He's here somewhere."

Pepper sighed and reached for the second sandal.

"Joe, have you seen Zeke?" Anna evidently had company.

Joe's response was unintelligible to Pepper.

Anna understood it. "He's behind the barn working on the tractor."

"Thanks. Don't tell him I called." Not waiting for her friend's reply, Pepper hit *end* and dropped the phone into her purse. She ran through the house and out the door.

Zeke heaved the mammoth back tire off the bolts that held it to the tractor. Setting it on the ground, he rolled the tire until he located the cause of the flat. Something had definitely sliced the tire. Hopefully, Denny, the local tire repair guy, could patch it today, and Zeke would be able to get back to mowing.

Allowing it to fall to the grass, Zeke picked up the metal nuts he'd removed in order to free the tire. Kneeling down on one knee, he began screwing each nut onto a bolt. Losing one of them wouldn't be smart.

He felt a tap on his shoulder. Shifting his weight and lifting his knee from the ground, he spun to his left.

Pepper. "Hi," he said. He set the remaining nuts on the ground. Brushing off his hands as he stood, he faced her.

"Hi." She grinned.

*Cute as a butto*n. It was an expression he'd often heard his Gram use. What did it mean? How cute was a button? Somehow, the expression fit her. His heart flip-flopped. Did she know that her shirt matched her eyes?

Her eyes. Something was different about them. They'd always mesmerized him, but today they held more power over him than ever.

"Do you know that your grandparents have an amazing love story?"

He blinked and shook his head. How long had he been staring? "Love story?" Finally he could think again. "Yeah." He smiled as he remembered it. "They do."

"Maggie struggled with Fred's devotion to God in the same way I struggled with yours." The glint in her eyes seared a trail to his heart.

"She thought he was as crazy as I thought you were." She crossed her arms and arched her back slightly to look up at him. She waited.

For what? "The same way I struggled." "I thought you were." Her words repeated in his mind. Why were they on rewind? What was he missing? Clutching the bill of his cap, he shifted the hat around on his head before readjusting it and looking back at her.

She still stared. Her grin grew larger.

"The same way I struggled." "I thought you were." *Struggled. Thought.* Past tense. He erased the short distance between them and, bending to reach her, wrapped his arms around her small frame. "You're not struggling anymore?"

"No." She leaned back. Her eyes turned upward. "Through Christ, I've found peace with God." She rested both hands on his upper arms. "Maggie's story gave me courage."

"Courage?"

"Maggie took the time to make up her heart and mind about God. Her decision wasn't about Fred. It was about God and His love for her. Once she decided, that was it." Pepper slid her hands down to his. "Fifty-two years later, she still knows she made the right choice. Fifty-two years from now, I know I'll say the same thing."

Zeke's heart lurched, raced, and thudded. She'd done it. She'd asked Christ to save her.

He drew his hands behind his back, pulling hers with them. Then he withdrew his hands and put them at her waist. "I'm glad you're not struggling anymore. I'm not either."

He bent and kissed her. Weeks of waiting and wondering vanished. Wrapping his arms around her, he lifted her from the ground. He felt her lips curve into a smile. A moment later he raised his head.

Her eyes were as big as he'd ever seen them. Laughing, he set her down.

"Wow!" Her mouth gaped.

He laughed again. "Should I be insulted?"

"No." She snickered. "I just wasn't expecting a kiss like that."

"You didn't think I knew how to kiss?"

"Not like that."

The rare moment. He'd surprised her. Could he do it again?

"Hmmph. I'm going back to my tractor." He lowered his arms and squatted in front of the wheel.

Out of the corner of his eye, he saw her blink and shake her head. She knelt beside him. "Did I hurt your feelings?"

He continued to screw a nut onto a bolt.

"You're so quiet and serious that I . . ." She leaned in closer. "You surprised me, that's all. I—"

Standing up suddenly, he grabbed her arms and pulled her along with him. "I love you."

She blinked. Once. Twice. A third time. Then she gulped. "Double wow!"

Surprise accomplished. What was her reaction?

He cradled her elbows in his palms and stared down at her. "Anything other than 'double wow'?"

"I love you, too."

He kissed her again.

* * *

After he'd secured all the nuts onto the bolts, Zeke stood the tire upright.

"Do you want to stand here with this thing while I go get the truck? Or do you want to drive the truck here while I hold the tire?"

"You'd let me drive the Davies Orchard truck?"

"From the other side of the barn to here." He pointed next to the tire. "If you're tall enough to see over the dashboard."

Her jaw dropped, and she slapped his arm. "I'll be right back."

"Call me if you need me." He pulled his cell phone from his shirt pocket.

She turned around and quipped. "I won't."

His laughter followed her around the end of the building. Once on the other side of the barn, she climbed into the tall truck. The keys weren't in the ignition. Under the mat? No. Above the visor? No. In the ash tray? No. Where else should she look? She felt between the seats and looked under them.

She sighed and pulled out her phone. Zeke answered. "Where are the keys?" she asked.

He laughed. "In my pocket."

"You rat."

In spite of being the brunt of his joke, Pepper smiled to herself. Zeke Davies loved her. How could she be miffed over a practical joke? Would she, however, let him see how sentimental she'd become? Absolutely not. There would be practical joke payback.

She climbed from the truck and headed back to get the keys.

Coming out of the house, Anna waved to her. "Did you find him?"

"Yes. He's around back." Pepper picked up her pace.

At the end of the barn, she turned—and gasped.

His back pressed tightly against the side of the barn, Zeke had flung out his arm, snagged her at the waist, and pulled her to him. With her back against his chest, he leaned over and kissed her neck. She squirmed and giggled. Again he pressed his lips to her nape. She sighed.

"Pepper, why did you need Zeke?" Anna stood inches from them.

* * *

Of all the times for his sister to come looking for Pepper. Zeke let go of Pepper and stood his tallest. "It's not what you think."

"It's not?" Both Anna and Pepper refuted him. One added a shocked stare, the other a knowing grin.

"Pepper has great news." He turned to her. Would she bail him out?

"I accepted Christ today."

Anna squealed and hugged her friend. "I've been praying since the night we helped you."

"I owe all of you so much." Pepper reached for Anna's hand. "Maggie prayed with me. When we finished, she said that I should tell someone. That's when I called."

Pepper's gaze turned to Zeke. Her green eyes reminded him of leaves shimmering in the sunlight.

"He had news for me, too."

"I don't even have to guess what it was. I'm so happy for both of you." She stepped back. Her gaze hardened but her eyes twinkled. "And this?" She waved her hand toward the two of them. "This display that I saw a moment ago?"

"Was me getting carried away," Zeke confessed.

"And carrying me with him." Pepper wagged her eyebrows.

"Be careful." Anna's voice held admonition. "And I'm not saying, 'Just don't get caught.'" She hugged Pepper one more time and squeezed Zeke's arm. Then she disappeared around the end of the barn.

Pepper faced Zeke. "Will she tell your family about us?"

"No." He took her hand and started toward the other side of the barn. "She won't spoil your surprise." He squeezed her hand.

"And the other?" She stopped, halting him with her.

He shook his head. "She said what needed saying."

"Was what we were doing wrong?"

A seemingly simple but quite complex question. "Let's get this tire loaded." He resumed walking. "Ride with me to the mechanic's? We'll talk on the way."

"I'd love to." She bumped him with her hip. "I guess I missed my chance to drive the pickup?"

"I guess so." He chuckled softly.

"You really are a rat sometimes." Her smile belied her uncomplimentary words.

"But you love me anyway?" He stopped and tugged on her hand to make her face him.

"I do," she said.

"That's good." It was an understatement accentuated by the monstrous thudding of his heart.

* * *

"Is it wrong for us to kiss?" Pepper needed an answer.

"The Bible doesn't say, 'Thou shall not kiss before marriage,' but it's very plain that other things are wrong."

"Such as?"

Zeke stared out the windshield. Long seconds elapsed.

Pepper stretched her seat belt far enough to reach across the gear shift and touch his arm. "Zeke?"

"Such as sex." He continued to stare ahead.

"You mean with a man and a woman who aren't seriously in love." Like she and Zeke were.

"With a man and a woman who aren't married."

"Does the Bible really say that?" It wasn't something dreamed up by old-fashioned prudes?

"Not in the Ten Commandments. Nor as a part of other 'Thou shall not's,' but, yes, it does."

"What does it say?"

"I might miss a word or two, but just after God created Adam and Eve and brought them together, He said that a man should leave his father and mother and hold fast to his wife, and that those two would become one flesh."

"One flesh?"

He cleared his throat. "Through sexual contact."

"The Bible says that?"

"In the second chapter of the first book." Removing his right hand from the wheel, he clasped her hand. "It uses the word *wife*, not *girlfriend* or *fiance*, or anything else."

Pepper mulled the words. "The research would also concur," she said, "that keeping sex inside marriage is a good idea. Too many children growing up without both parents." She looked toward him. "I was one of them. Maybe if Pops and Ranie had waited—"

"Maybe." Zeke's hand clutched hers.

"But kissing?" Their conversation had moved to a topic far beyond a kiss on the neck.

Zeke sighed. "That's trickier. Let's think about your parents."

Did they have to?

"How'd they meet?"

"They went to school together."

"Do you think your dad walked up to your mom one day and asked her to go to bed with him?"

Pepper blinked. "I seriously doubt it."

"What do you think he did?"

Pepper's "aha" moment arrived. She watched the right side of Zeke's face as she spoke. "He held her hand. He kissed her."

Zeke faced her. "And it went on from there." He looked back at the road and put both hands on the wheel while he negotiated a sharp curve. "Physical contact is exciting but dangerous."

"It is exciting." Simply replaying Zeke's kisses made Pepper's heart pound.

"That's what makes it dangerous." He made a right-hand turn and pulled into a driveway. After turning off the truck and unbuckling his seatbelt, he angled his body in her direction. "I'm going to kiss you, get out of the truck, unload the tire, and take it in to Denny. You're going to stay here."

She giggled. "Safer?"

"Much."

Zeke was a man of his word. Watching him roll the unwieldy tire up to the door, Pepper licked the lips he'd just kissed. When he turned back and grinned, her heart hammered. Yes, the man was hot, fine—and dangerous.

* * *

"Have you seen either of your parents today?" Zeke asked as he climbed back into the truck.

"What about the tire?" He hadn't returned with it.

"Denny's backed up. He'll call when it's ready." He buckled his seat belt. "What about your mom and dad?"

"I'm surprised Pops hasn't called."

"I'll go to the hospital with you—"

"That would be great."

"You didn't let me finish." He tilted his head and held up one finger. "I'll go if you let me hold your hand. Even with your dad watching." Raising his eyebrows, he gave three quick head nods.

Pepper laughed and averted her eyes.

When she looked back, he nodded again.

"What has gotten into you? What happened—"

"You have. You're what happened." He nodded once more, slowly and deliberately. Then he kissed her forehead and started the truck.

Was this what people called being "head over heels?" She'd suffer through a sleepless night for it anytime.

* * *

230

"Good evening, Ezekiel." Gramps opened the front door and flung it wide. "How are you?"

"I'm fine."

"Maybe even better than fine?" Gramps winked.

"A lot better."

"Kinda thought you might be." He thumped Zeke's shoulder. "Where are you two headed?"

"The hospital." Zeke looked around. "Where's Gram?"

"In Pepper's room. Those two are thick as thieves these days." Gramps waved toward the hallway. "Speaking of which, here they come."

Zeke turned. Pepper entered the room first. She had pulled some of her curls back from her face and clipped them into small barrettes. Her printed shirt was a mixture of dark shades of brown, green and purple. A denim skirt touched her knees.

Flimsy but attractive flat sandals covered the bottoms of her feet but left most of the tops bare. He stared, blinked, and stared again.

"Maggie and Fred bought me a birthday present while I was gone." She hugged Gram, who followed her.

Zeke gulped. "It's your birthday?"

"My second birthday."

"Born again," Fred chirped. "I wheeled Maggie through those stores in turbo." He stopped long enough to breathe and to grin at Gram. "Had to hurry, since we didn't know how long she'd be gone." He nudged Zeke's elbow. "How'd we do?"

Feminine. Alluring. Desirable. Every description fit. "You did great." His words were for his grandparents. His gaze only for Pepper.

Her return smile sent shock waves to his heart.

"I'm all set." She scowled at Gramps. "Don't stay up too late." Reaching the door, she added, "Tomorrow's a work day."

"Be sure you follow your own advice." He gestured to Zeke. "You, too."

"We will." Their tandem response made them both laugh.

"Your grandparents are the best." Pepper linked her hand through Zeke's arm as they walked to Zeke's Jeep.

"Can't argue with you on that."

"Their gift overwhelmed me."

"Gram picked out everything?" He definitely would have needed help.

"Even the barrettes and the sandals." She glanced down. "I wasn't sure about the skirt when I saw it. I don't wear skirts much."

Zeke didn't remember ever seeing her in one.

231

"But I like it," she said.

He opened the passenger door and helped her in. His eyes scanned her shapely legs. "I do, too."

"I'm glad. I think I'll . . ." Her eyes noticed what his were watching. Shoving him with her palm, she grinned and said. "Get into the car." She pulled her door shut.

* * *

"You're sure you're ready to face Pops like this?" Pepper lifted their entwined hands up in front of them. "He's not keen on religion."

"I know."

"How do you know?"

"We talked yesterday."

"You did?" Why hadn't she known? "When?"

"Before I came to your mom's room with the flowers."

"But you'd just gotten to the hospital."

They had stepped off the elevator at the third floor.

"No." Zeke pointed to the nurses' station. "Your dad asked the nurses to keep the flowers for us while we went outside."

He drew her close to the wall so that people could pass.

"What happened?'

"Interrogation about what I had done to make you change."

Her jaw dropped. "You're kidding."

Zeke smiled and shook his head. "He also asked about communes, multiple wives, guns and Mayans."

"Huh?"

"My thought exactly."

"What did you tell him?'

"No commune, one wife, three guns, no Mayans."

She smiled. "You have one wife?"

His smile reached his eyes. "I want one wife." Interlocking his fingers with hers, he said, "Come on."

As they approached, Pepper squeezed Zeke's hand and looked up at him. They both stopped and breathed deeply. Time for the big moment. Zeke moved first.

* * *

Three steps later, he halted. His eyes bulged.

Pepper shoved him aside and ran to the bed. "What's going on?"

232

Rhetorical question. Pepper's dad was leaning over the bed. He and Ranie had been kissing.

"Why are you kissing that woman?" Pepper's hands flailed as she leaned across the bed rail. She glared at Ranie.

"Because I want to . . ." His voice trailed off. He glanced tenderly at Pepper's mom. "It's been a long time since I've been able to kiss my wife."

"Your wife!" Pepper clutched the rail in front of her.

"We never got divorced." He cast a slight smile toward Ranie.

"You're still married?" Pepper leaned over the bed, her face as close to her dad's as it could be. "You never bothered to tell me? You omitted the small detail . . ." Sarcasm dripped from her voice. "That you're still husband and wife?" She turned her back to both of them and stomped her foot.

Zeke flinched, gulped, and looked for a place to hide or a way to disappear. He found neither.

Pepper's dad stared at her from his side of the bed. "Perfect example of why I didn't." He gestured toward her. "Any time I told you anything about Ranie, you flew off the handle. You wouldn't listen."

She spun back toward the bed. "I deserved to know."

"You're right." Her dad pointed at her. "But I got tired of seeing you blow up. Of always having to defend myself and Ranie."

"She broke your heart once. Don't let her do it again."

Ranie opened her mouth, but Mr. Staley spoke first. "I guess that's between the two of us."

"Is it? I thought I was part of the equation."

"You are. If you want to be." He looked from his daughter to Ranie.

"Not if it includes her." Pepper hurried around the bed to her dad's side.

A few steps from the bed, Zeke stood, his mouth slack-jawed, his thoughts muddled. Ken Staley had been kissing—his wife.

Pepper's voice interrupted Zeke's amazement. "Who will be there for you when she leaves again?" She clutched her dad's arms and stared pleadingly into his eyes.

Mr. Staley cleared his throat. "You're assuming that she will?"

"She did last time." Pepper's eyes turned from her dad to her mom. A steely glint hardened her glare. "You may want to stay and listen to what she has to say, but I don't. I've heard enough already." Letting go of her father's arms, Pepper retraced her steps and headed from the room.

Zeke watched her storm past him. He saw tears stream down Ranie's face. He observed the conflict in Ken Staley's eyes. How did a man choose between the daughter he'd loved for all of her life and the woman he'd loved for most of his?

"I'm sorry." He hurried to find Pepper.

She wasn't in the hall. Or the elevator. She hadn't waited for him at the entrance. He rushed through the door, and ran down the sidewalk toward the parking lot. His Jeep was locked. She couldn't have gotten into it. She wasn't waiting by either of the front doors. Where was she?

Zeke walked between the Jeep and the car parked on the right of it. He'd drive through the lot and find her somehow. He dashed toward the driver's side and nearly ran into her. At the back of the car Pepper stood pounding her fists on the tail gate.

"Why did I help her? Why did she come back? Why do I care?"

"Pepper, it's me."

Her fist hit the metal again. "Why did I help her?"

"Stop." He reached in and clutched her wrists.

"Why did she come back?"

Was she expecting an answer?

"Why do I care?"

This one he could answer. "Because she's your mom. You're connected by blood."

"I don't want to be."

He didn't believe it. Didn't think she did, either. "But you are."

"I'm never going to forgive him for this."

Zeke cringed. "What did you say?"

"I'm never going to forgive my dad for this."

"You don't mean that."

She yanked one hand free and pointed her finger in Zeke's face. "Yes, I do."

He inhaled deeply. He searched her eyes for signs of compromise. "Get in the Jeep." He pulled the keys from his pocket and hit the unlock button on the remote. Turning for the driver's side, he barked, "Get in."

He climbed in and started the car. She was in and buckled up. He left the parking lot and headed for his grandparents'. Silence prevailed for most of the trip.

"I'm so angry," she sputtered.

"Me, too."

"I can't say who I'm madder at, Ranie or Pops. She's stirring things up again, and he's falling for it." Pepper emitted a noise that was somewhere between a scream and a growl. "Who gets your vote?" She turned toward him.

"Neither of them." He stared hard at Pepper.

"They're the only two involved . . ." She stopped short. She flinched. "You're mad at me?" Her hands clutched the printed shirt at her chest. "What did I do? This isn't my fault. I'm caught in the mid—"

"Do you really want to know?" Zeke raised his voice to be heard above her.

Her tirade ceased. She breathed a heavy sigh. "Do I want to know what?"

"Do you want to know what you did?"

A calm settled over her. Was it the eye of the storm? The lapse between an earthquake and an aftershock?

"You lost your temper."

Pepper didn't move or make a sound.

"You showed disrespect to both your dad and your mom."

"She's not my mom."

"She is, no matter how many times you say otherwise." Zeke draped his arms over the steering wheel and laid his head on them. Speaking to the steering column, he explained, "You also ruined a perfect opportunity to be a witness for God."

"What?"

"You have a new relationship with Christ. You are a new creation in Him." He lifted his head and looked at her. "Remember the attributes of God: Love, Mercy, Goodness? Once we accept Christ, we can and should live those out."

Why couldn't she apply that truth to her dad and Ranie?

"Did you show love? Did you display any mercy? Did your dad or Ranie see goodness in you?"

Could she see the ache in his heart?

"One thing hurt more than anything else," he added.

For the first time since he'd stopped the Jeep, she faced him directly.

"You said, 'I'm never going to forgive my dad for this.'"

She lowered her head. She sat on her hands.

"Do you love your dad?"

"Yes."

"But you're not going to forgive him?"

Her body remained stationary.

"Do you love me?"

The head bob was quick and obvious.

"What happens when I do something you can't forgive?"

"You won't." She extended her hand and touched his arm.

"Why should I believe that?"

Why should Zeke believe her? Because she'd said so? How many thousands of times had she confirmed her love for Pops? Yet a short time earlier she had vowed not to forgive him. Zeke had heard her outburst. Why should he trust her?

She stared at her knees. "Does God still love me?"

She heard his movement and looked sideways. He'd slid as close as the floor console would allow.

"Absolutely."

"Even though I'm not loving or merciful or good?"

"Even then."

"Even when I hurt Pops—and you—the two people I love the most in this world?"

Zeke clutched her arm. "Then, too."

A glimmer of hope crept into her heart. "What should I do now?"

"What do you think you should do?"

The right answer leaped to her head but lodged in her throat. She swallowed and inhaled deeply. "I should apologize to Pops and you."

"And Ranie."

"I can't."

"You can't on your own."

"You'll help me?" Zeke could say the words and mean them.

"I'll go with you." His face nearly touched hers as he spoke. "God will help you."

"He can't tell her, can He?"

"He could." Again Zeke squeezed her arm. "But I don't think He will."

She heard the smile in Zeke's words.

"He'll give you the courage you need and the words to say." He lifted his hands to cradle her face. "It won't be easy. It's never easy to forgive someone who has caused us pain. But with His help, you can do it."

Could she do it? Could God help her to apologize to a woman that Pepper often felt she hated? Memories of pain and loss resurfaced, fortifying her refusal to ask forgiveness.

Chasing them through her brain were images of Anna and Zeke who'd offered their love and forgiveness before she knew them well. And visions of Pops, who understood her best of all and had always absolved her and welcomed her back.

"If God will help me, I'll try."

Zeke laid his head against hers. "That's my girl."

Courage surged through her veins. She looked at the digital clock. Nearly 8:30.

"Will the hospital let us in now?"

"If it's not too late."

"Will you be ashamed to be seen with me?"

"Never."

She reached for him. He wrapped his arms around her. For several moments, she basked in his strength. "I guess I'm ready," she said, releasing herself from his embrace.

"I'm sorry, Zeke." She couldn't stop the tears from forming or falling. "Please forgive me."

"Any time." He hugged her. Reaching for the key in the ignition, he paused.

"You do need to make one other apology. It really should have come first."

Whom else had she offended?

"Asking for God's forgiveness is most important."

She bowed her head. "God, I'm new at all of this, but I know I messed up. Please don't stop loving me. And don't let Pops or Zeke stop, either." Now for the hardest part. "And help me to forgive Ranie and to ask for her forgiveness."

* * *

Pepper's prayer wasn't eloquent or polished, but Zeke's heart swelled with pride. When she raised her head, he asked, "To the hospital?" At her nod, he started the Jeep, made a U turn, and headed back.

During the short time, Pepper prayed silently. Through his peripheral vision, Zeke saw her lips move. Her foot tapped incessantly. She wrung her hands.

He prayed, too. That the hospital, her dad, and Ranie all cooperated.

The parking lot had emptied substantially by the time they arrived. Pepper pointed as soon as they turned in.

"There's my dad's car."

Zeke headed toward it.

"Looks like he's in it."

He was. The space to the right of his car was vacant.

Stepping out after parking, Zeke crossed in front of the Jeep. He opened Pepper's door. "Don't worry. It'll be okay."

Pepper looked in her dad's direction. Ken Staley hadn't moved from his car. Taking her hand, Zeke led Pepper to the far side of her dad's vehicle.

She tapped on his window.

A dull stare met them. Pepper pointed down with her index finger. The window lowered.

"I'm sorry, Pops. So sorry." She reached in and touched his shoulder. "Please forgive me."

Seconds after she stopped speaking, the haze lifted from his eyes. Moisture replaced it. He unlatched the door and stepped out. "Oh, honey, you've come back."

"I have, unless—"

Zeke's throat tightened.

"Unless you can't forgive how terrible I've been."

Blood returned to Zeke's face.

"Of course I can."

The bear hug he gave his daughter added confirmation to his words.

Pepper backed up. "Do you think Ranie can, too?"

Her words staggered him. He reeled backward. She reached to steady him. Each stared at the other. He wrapped an arm around her shoulder, and headed for the door.

Zeke prayed while he walked behind them. Into the hospital. To the elevator. Down the hall.

At Ranie's door, Pepper stopped. Was she losing courage?

She faced Zeke and her dad. "I need to do this on my own." She reached a hand out to each of them. To Zeke she added, "Pray hard."

* * *

As Pepper neared the bed, Ranie turned. She scanned Pepper's face and looked away.

You deserve that. Pepper moved closer.

"I'm sorry, Ranie."

No reaction.

"I mean it." Pepper continued to address the back of her mom's head. "You tried to explain. I didn't listen." The standoff persisted. "You asked for forgiveness, which I wouldn't grant. Now I'm asking, and you are the one who can refuse. I guess that's fair."

Pepper quelled the temptation to growl and run out of the room. Instead, she inched closer to the bed. "Can you forgive me?"

238

The squeak of nurses' shoes in the hallway accentuated the silence of several moments. "Yes." The soft answer reached Pepper's ears before Ranie turned.

Pepper grinned back at Pops and Zeke. In a moment, the family stood together. When Zeke hung back, Pepper motioned him to join them.

The reunion lasted only a few minutes longer. The events of the evening had taken a toll on Ranie. Before Pepper left, she said, "I'll see you tomorrow."

Ranie's green eyes sparkled.

* * *

While the three stood between the two cars, Pepper said, "Pops, you and I talked the other day about Zeke's faith." She cast a stern look in his direction. "And I hear that you grilled him about it yesterday."

Her dad smiled before looking at the pavement.

"I know you're distrustful of religion. And, earlier tonight, I gave you more reason to doubt it." She looked straight into Pops' brown eyes. "But this afternoon I confessed my sins to God and asked Christ to be my Savior." Did he understand what she was saying?

"Did that decision have anything to do with your coming back tonight?"

Pops knew more than she had expected. "Yes."

He looked first at Pepper and then at Zeke. "I think of religion as a crutch that I don't need."

A sting like an electric shock zapped Pepper's heart.

Pops wasn't finished. "But you have changed for the better." His gaze rested momentarily on Zeke before settling again on Pepper. "If faith makes you a better person, I'm happy for you. And for the rest of us."

Pepper hugged him. "Sorry I make your life hard sometimes, Pops."

"You make it better all the time."

Zeke spoke then. "There's one more thing."

Dad glanced at their entwined hands. "I thought there might be."

Pepper waited for him to look up. "Since God has a place in my heart and life now—"

"Zeke does, too."

Pops had guessed correctly. He clapped Zeke on the shoulder.

"I think you're a good man. You'd better be good to her."

"I will be."

Pepper glanced from one to the other. God did love her.

239

CHAPTER 23

"I can't believe the summer is almost over."

On the mid-August Wednesday over a month after Ranie's accident, Pepper and Anna added some more jellies to the shelves in the gift shop. "I'm going to miss the busiest part of your season."

"We'll wish you were here, especially to give cart rides."

"I bet Joe won't."

Anna giggled. "Not as much as the rest of us."

Joe's girlfriend Bethany had been asked to take Pepper's place as chief driver of the donkey cart. She had trained with Pepper for two weeks. She'd learned quickly and was now a favorite of Axle and Buster. "I'm leaving them in good hands."

"But when you have a weekend that's not jammed, come back. Bethany said she'll turn the reins over to you while you're here."

"I'll do my best to." She handed a jar to Anna.

"Gram told us last week how quiet the house will be without you."

"They'll probably be glad about that."

"You know they won't."

"They have been a highlight of my summer."

Having finished in the gift shop, the friends moved to the fruit stand. Early fall apples had begun to ripen. Available today were Yellow Delicious, Gala, Jonamac, and Honey Crisp.

"I was thinking last night about how eventful this summer has been for you."

Pepper nodded her head while she sorted apples and filled baskets. "To think that it all began on a night that I made a terrible decision."

The two hugged across a display rack. "God turned bad into good."

"In so many ways." Pepper dabbed at her wet eyes with the hem of her shirt.

"How is your mom?" Anna asked.

"Good." Pepper stared a moment at the blue sky. "Her foot is still healing, but it's doing better than the surgeon had hoped it would. Ranie's staying with her friend Lucy who is caring for her while she's on crutches."

Holding a large apple in front of her, she continued, "The police still haven't caught the driver of the third vehicle."

"That's too bad." Anna shook her head. "How's your father?"

"Dad's business is slow. He and Ranie talk often. They're trying to decide whether they should get back together."

"After all these years. Incredible."

"Yeah. I don't know whether I'm more amazed that they want to be together or that I'm okay with it if they are."

"The second is more surprising to me."

"They both still need Christ, but Mom's more receptive."

Anna started. "What did you say?"

"Mom's more receptive to my talking about God."

"Mom?" Anna gaped.

Pepper blushed and rolled her eyes. "Another miracle. When Ranie asked me last week to call her 'mom,' I agreed." Pepper reached for another bushel basket to fill. "I nearly dropped the phone when I heard myself say yes."

"I almost lost my teeth just now."

"Sometimes I call her one name, sometimes the other. It's a hard habit it break."

The two worked in silence for a while. Zeke passed the stand on his way to somewhere. He waved.

Pepper waved back. "He's the best event of my summer."

"Aaww." Anna shoved Pepper with her hand. "Don't get all mushy and cry on the apples."

Pepper giggled. "Just wait 'til it happens to you."

"Not for a while, I hope."

"That's what I said before Zeke."

"Glad you came along. We'd almost given up on him." Anna wiggled her eyebrows and set the pricing signs in place. "Twenty-seven years old with no prospects in sight." She gathered up some empty boxes. "I'm off to bake pies."

Pepper chuckled to herself. God had saved Zeke for her. She turned the top apple in each basket to its prettiest side.

Two long arms reached around her from behind. "Guess who."

"I don't have to."

"Guess anyway."

"My favorite Davies."

"Great answer. You win."

His breath on her neck made her shiver. "Win what?"

"A date with me on Friday night."

She turned and faced him. "Thought I already had one."

"Didn't want you to forget."

Not likely. He stared long enough to make her toes curl.

Backing away, he said, "See you at lunch."

Her heart lurched—and ached—as she watched him hurry across the stones.

* * *

Thursday was wonderfully excruciating. After three days of intermittent rain, the sun glistened all day. People flocked in, buying apples, purchasing gifts, and sampling pies and turnovers. Every Davies family member scurried to replenish produce and satisfy customers. No one could keep up.

At closing time, Pepper was filling quart baskets with apples in preparation for tomorrow's influx. She dropped one apple onto the ground. Scurrying to retrieve the rolling escapee, she bumped a filled basket. Five other Honey Crisps joined the fray.

"Oooohhh!" She scrambled to reclaim the runaways.

"Having trouble?" Approaching from a few feet away, Zeke gathered a fugitive apple and bent to recover another.

"I'm not going."

He blinked. Creases formed between his brows. "Going where?"

"To Pitt. To med school."

He gulped. "What?" Setting the apples in a "seconds" crate, he grasped Pepper's elbow and guided her outside to the Gator parked nearby.

"I've made up my mind." She sat sideways in the passenger's seat.

Zeke squatted in front of her.

"I'm not going."

"Of course, you are." His eyes stared into hers. "It's been your dream since you were a kid."

"It's not anymore." She clasped his hand resting on the fender. Couldn't he see her dilemma? She stared at the stones beneath her. "I'm not leaving you."

* * *

Zeke's spirit soared—and then plummeted. "You have to."

Her head jerked upward. "You want me to go?"

242

Grasping both her shoulders, he gazed at her. "As much as I want a bud-killing frost in May." He reached to hug her. Whispering in her ear, he said, "But you have to."

"Why?" She withdrew from his arms. "I've changed my mind."

Zeke stood. Taking her hand in his, he searched for a quiet place. For the previous few seconds, he and Pepper had been the center of attention for several last-minute customers still straggling in the fruit stand. Joe would be in the barn. Ike had gone to Mom and Dad's. Who knew where Toby would show up at any moment? Zeke led her toward his house.

Pulling his phone from his pocket, he punched buttons with one hand. "I'll be a few minutes." He and his dad had been about to start a two-man project in the barn. "Something's come up."

"Trouble?"

"I hope not." Zeke looked down at Pepper who was staring up at him. He pocketed the phone and opened the front door.

When both were inside, Pepper pivoted in his direction. Clasping her hands around his neck, she kissed him. He gasped. But pleasure quickly displaced surprise.

Her soft lips presented a compelling argument.

What about her dad?

Pulling her hands away from his neck, Zeke backed up. "Whoa." He swallowed and inhaled deeply.

"Don't make me go." Her eyes begged him to listen. "Please." Placing her hands on his biceps, she stretched up toward him.

He kissed her cheek and clutched one hand. Crossing to the sofa, he sat down and pulled her to the space next to him.

"Let's think about this." The desire in her eyes as she looked up at him fuddled his brain. One more kiss before conversation. He leaned over.

What about her dad?

Zeke halted. Sitting up straight, he asked, "What about your dad?"

She wilted, slightly.

"He's not going to med school."

He cast a wry smile at her. "He's expecting you to go."

"After I explain, he'll understand."

Had she lost her mind? "He'll understand the thousands of dollars in tuition for pre-med?"

Pepper opened her mouth. Zeke spoke.

"He'll understand forsaking a life-long plan?" Rattling through Zeke's mind was Mr. Staley's admonition that he wanted a better start for his daughter than he himself had had. "He'll understand if you give up that dream for someone who may have brainwashed you?"

She looked down at her hands.

Zeke pressed whatever advantage he had. "You really think he'll understand that your decision isn't somehow God's fault?"

Her shoulders slumped. She lowered her head into her hands. Maybe she had come to her senses.

Zeke gently pulled her hands away from her face. "I dread Sunday. And Monday. And every day until you come back." He squeezed her fingers. "But you have to go."

"I don't want eight or nine more years of school, Zeke. Not now." Her eyes sparkled. "I've spent a summer with your family. I've seen the love between your mom and dad and between Maggie and Fred." Her gaze trapped his. "And I feel it between you and me."

How could he disagree?

"You said I'm a new creation in Christ. More has changed than simply my thoughts about God." She grabbed a quick breath. "My ideas about family and friends and career have all been turned upside down—in a good way."

Zeke's prayers had been answered. For Pepper's acceptance of Christ. For her reconciliation with her mom. Now he had to deal with the results.

She rushed ahead with her plans. "I bet your grandparents would let me stay with them. I could pay room and board."

His heart yearned for this plan to work. His head saw the foibles in it. "What about your dad?" She had to face the daunting obstacle that was her father.

"What if I could convince Pops?" She grasped Zeke's arm between her hands. "If he gave his consent, would you be okay with my staying?"

Zeke leaned forward, laying his elbows on his knees. He rested his eyes on the heels of his hands and pondered.

A few seconds later, Pepper edged closer to him and leaned down so that her face nearly touched his. "What do you think?"

Zeke rubbed his hands in circles around his eye sockets before he looked sideways ever so slightly and directly into her eyes.

"I think your dad will yield to whatever you want."

"I do, too." Slapping her hands on her knees and starting to rise, she said, "I'll call him." She dug into her pocket for her phone.

Zeke's hand snatched her wrist. He huffed, "Were you listening earlier? You could be opening the door for your dad to accuse God or me or 'religion' of ruining your life."

She eased back onto the couch. "My life won't be ruined." Turning her arm, she released her wrist from his hand and touched the side of his face. "Even if Pops thinks it will be."

In a twinkling, her eyes beamed the conviction of her words straight to his heart. "Are you sure?"

"More sure than I've ever been about being a doctor. And I've spent years working toward it."

"But your dad." Zeke couldn't quell the unrest he experienced when he thought about Mr. Staley. "Will he ever trust any of us? Or listen to anything about God?"

"I did." She gestured to herself. "Pops is no more hardened toward God than I was. He's already seen changes in me. Positive ones." Leaning forward again, she positioned her face next to Zeke's. "It may take a while for Pops to agree completely about medicine or God, but I think he will."

Was there a possible compromise that would keep Pepper at the orchard and still appease her father? If so, where was it?

Sitting up, he turned toward her. "I wasn't planning a road trip for tomorrow night, but if your dad can meet us halfway, maybe we can get together and talk about your plans."

Pepper whooped and hollered. He halted her festivities by adding, "You have to promise me that you'll play fair when we talk to him."

"Play fair?"

"No guilt trips, no threats, no tears, no tantrums."

She pooched her lower lip outward.

"And no pouting, either."

"I promise." A bright smile lit her face. "I'll save those methods to try on you."

* * *

Pops was agreeable. Suspicious but agreeable. Pepper had said nothing more than that she would like to see him on Friday night. She hadn't mentioned that Zeke would be joining them. If she had, her dad would have guessed what was up.

She called Zeke after ten on Thursday night. "Pops will meet us at Allentown. His distance is shorter, but he'll deal with afternoon traffic."

"Dad was okay with our leaving early. You told your father we'd be there at seven?"

"I said seven." She swallowed. "I didn't say 'we.'"

"What?" His volume had risen. "What happened to playing fair?"

"You didn't say it included arming the opponent."

He chuckled. "It's a good thing we both love you."

"Yes." She sent an "air kiss" into the phone. "That is a very good thing."

* * *

Shortly after 4:00 on Friday, Anna entered the gift shop where Pepper was running the cash register. She waved her hands and said, "I'll take over for you. Get going."

"What about the bake shop?"

"The three thirty batch of pies is in the oven, and the ones to go in at four thirty are ready." Anna looked at her watch. "Now go."

"Where's Zeke?" Pepper stepped from behind the counter.

"Finishing a few things in the fruit stand before he heads to his house." She shooed Pepper one more time. "Get to Mom and Dad's. Zeke will be ready before you know it."

Pepper hurried out the door and ran to the house where her change of clothes waited for her in the upstairs bedroom that she'd stayed in when she first visited Anna's home. Half an hour later she'd showered and changed. She gathered her things and hurried outside.

Zeke waited by his Jeep.

"Could we take Priscilla? Dad will be expecting her."

"Since he doesn't know I'm coming." He tightened his lips and cast her a sideways glance.

"Something like that." She grinned. "You want to drive?"

"Sure."

She handed him the keys, and he unlocked the doors. Pepper opened the passenger door, pulled the seat back forward, and deposited her things. By the time she'd reset the seat back, Zeke was waiting beside her door. She turned past him and sat down.

"You smell good." She inhaled once more.

"Thanks." A self-conscious grin crept over his face. "You, too." He shut the door and came around.

* * *

"Have you thought about what you're going to say to your dad?"

"I couldn't sleep last night because of thinking."

"Should've called me." He glanced at her.

"You were awake, too?"

Nodding, he said, "Let's pray about it."

"You're driving. How are you going to pray?"

"With my eyes open."

"Does that work?"

246

He laughed. Her naive questions reminded him of how new she was in knowing Christ. "God can hear us however and wherever we are."

* * *

Pulling into the appointed restaurant a few minutes before seven, Zeke turned off the engine. How would this meeting go in so public a place? Too bad there hadn't been a better choice. Silently, he asked for God's wisdom.

Pepper opened her door before Zeke's mind had registered "Amen." "Pops."

Mr. Staley had evidently seen them pull in. With a cross between a puzzled stare and a loving smile, he walked toward his daughter. His gaze darted between Pepper and Zeke.

"You made it, even a few minutes early." He hugged her. Turning to Zeke, he added, "What do you think of Priscilla?"

"I know why she's a classic." Zeke extended his arm, and the two shook hands.

"Let's go in. I have a table already." He offered his arm to Pepper. She glanced at Zeke before placing her hand in the crook of Mr. Staley's elbow. Zeke tagged along behind them to a rectangular table near the back of the restaurant. At one place setting, a half empty cup of coffee was getting cold. Pepper took the seat across from her dad. Zeke settled beside her. Mr. Staley's briefcase occupied the fourth chair beside him.

"I didn't know you were coming, Zeke. But I'm glad you did." He looked to his right and raised his voice slightly. "I brought a guest, too."

From a table a few feet away, Ranie stood up. Her back had been facing them. Mr. Staley crossed to her, helped her position her crutches, and moved slowly with her while she made her way to where Pepper and Zeke waited.

Zeke's pulse increased. Pepper and Ranie hadn't seen each other in almost two weeks since Ranie's discharge from the hospital. Were things really better between mother and daughter? The importance of the meeting intensified.

Ranie stepped to Pepper's side. Zeke gulped. Pepper and Zeke stood. When Ranie placed one arm around her daughter, Pepper hesitated slightly. Then she enclosed her mom in a light hug.

After Zeke carefully shook Ranie's hand, Pepper and he sat back down. He reached for her hand underneath the table and squeezed it gently. Her smile assured him. She knew how proud he was of her regarding Ranie.

Mr. Staley removed his briefcase so that Ranie could sit next to him and facing Zeke. He helped her into the chair and then set her crutches out of the way. The waiter was leaving the table after taking their order when Mr. Staley set his napkin in his lap. "So, why are we all here?" He directed his question and his gaze to Pepper.

Pepper clutched his hand so hard that Zeke started. "I leave for med school on Sunday," she said, looking at both parents. "At least I'm supposed to." Her focus narrowed to only her dad. "I don't want to go."

He cleared his throat. "I see." Looking to Ranie he said, "We suspected as much."

"Look, Pops, I know . . ." Zeke's hard pressure on her fingers suspended her words. She inhaled deeply. "What do you think?"

"I think you're crazy not to go." He drummed the table with his fingers and avoided Pepper's gaze. Then his fingers stilled and he stared hard at her. "It's something you've always dreamed about and worked for. Volunteering at the hospital, summer jobs at the free clinic, an internship at Geisinger." He raked his hand through his hair. "You're throwing it all away. For what?"

A sharp kick hit the side of Zeke's foot. He flinched. Pepper looked at him and then at her dad.

Ranie's voice interrupted the prolonged silence. "What will you do if you're not in school?"

"I'll work at the orchard. I can stay with the Hannas. Maggie says they'd be glad to have me."

Zeke swallowed the smile that threatened to emerge. He'd asked Gramps the same question and received an identical answer.

"I'll pay them room and board."

"And when the orchard closes after Christmas?" Ken Staley knew the seasonal nature of the orchard.

"I'll find another job."

"Lewisburg is teeming with college students during the term. How do you expect to find something then?"

"I have my EMT certification. Maybe I can use that, at least part-time."

"How will you pay your bills?" Mr. Staley's raised eyebrows framed more of a challenge than a question. "I'm not going to do that for you. I've paid for an education you won't be using. If you step out on your own, you'll be responsible for yourself."

Pepper gulped. Zeke glanced at her, and she turned his direction. Her shell-shocked expression seized his heart.

248

Mr. Staley swigged quickly from his coffee cup and began again. "You don't need something part-time for a few months. You need a career, like medicine, that will be there for a lifetime."

Zeke cleared his throat. "Maybe I can help." He drew Pepper's and his entwined hands to the table top and focused only on her. "I've been looking for someone to share my life with me." He felt the moisture in his own eyes and saw it in Pepper's. "In April the Lord led me to her."

Pepper lifted her free hand to her lips but her eyes never strayed in their focus.

"What I'm offering you is a full-time, life-time position. As my wife."

Pepper's dad slapped the table. "Wait a minute."

Zeke heard Pepper inhale. He gripped her hand quickly and dashed ahead, addressing Mr. Staley. "I know you wanted more for her than what you started out with."

"I was beginning to think you hadn't heard a thing I said."

"She already has more than that—a college degree, an EMT certification that has proved invaluable . . ."

Zeke turned to Ranie. She smiled.

"And a position at Davies Orchard, where people love and respect her."

"What if something terrible happens?" Mr. Staley now clutched the table rather than tapped on it. "You could stop loving her just like that." He snapped his fingers.

"Did you stop loving Ranie?"

* * *

Pepper barely breathed. What was happening? A marriage proposal? A heated debate?

Pops looked at Ranie. Clearly he hadn't stopped loving her. Pepper now recognized the hints she should have seen years earlier.

"Why can't you wait until she becomes a doctor?"

Pepper's argument was preempted by Zeke's. "I turned twenty-eight last month. Pepper still has eight or nine years of schooling, internship and residency. And then she would need time to start her practice. I'll be nearly forty by then."

Pepper couldn't stay silent any longer. "And I'll be in my early thirties."

Pops employed another tactic. "No one's saying you can't get married while Pepper's in medical school. Lots of people do."

Pepper sighed. "But when could we start a family? While I was in school? During my residency? After I set up my practice?"

Her dad cleared his throat. "Women start families later in life all the time these days."

"I don't want to." She looked at Zeke. "And I want to be there for my family. Not at the office or making rounds or on call." She reached across the table and grasped her dad's hand. "I want to take my kids to school, be there when they get home, and read to them at night—not have someone else do it."

Without speaking, Ranie extended her arm and covered both Pepper's and Pops' hands with her own. Then she turned to him. "She wants the kind of family that I thought we would have."

Pops exhaled audibly and looked at Zeke. "What does your family think about this?"

"Mom and Dad—"

Pepper interrupted. "You've talked to your parents?"

"Early this morning."

Pepper gulped and then smiled.

Once again Pops asked, "What did they say?"

"They said that Pepper helps me enjoy life." He turned to her before looking back at her dad. "That her decision for Christ seems genuine. And that she already seems like family."

Part of the Davies clan. The thud of her heart almost scared her.

"I still think—"

Pepper snatched her fork and tapped her plate with it. When everyone looked her direction, she spoke to Zeke. "I know I promised not to threaten or cry or throw a tantrum or make Pops feel guilty." She saw her dad's eyes dilate. "I've kept my promise."

Zeke smiled.

"But I didn't promise to let everyone talk around me as if I'm not here." Her gaze scanned from Pops, to Ranie, to Zeke. "Was there a question that went along with that job offer?"

Pops raised both hands in the air and sighed. Ranie laid a hand on his shoulder. Zeke got down on one knee.

"Pepper Alicia Staley, I love you." His brown eyes sparked. Her pulse quickened. "Will you marry me?"

She held his face in her hands. "Do I get to stay at your house rather than at your grandparents'?"

"Wouldn't have it any other way."

"Do I have to pay room and board?"

"We'll negotiate terms." The glint in his eye held enough electricity to light all of Lerisburg.

She giggled and threw her arms around his neck. "Yes, I'll marry you."

Could a person's heart explode from joy? Pepper's was in real danger. She clung to Zeke until he leaned away from her. Jamming his hand into his pocket, he removed a small velvet-covered box.

"Aaahhh."

Pepper's gasp brought a huge smile to Zeke's face.

"You bought a ring?"

Opening the box, he reached for her left hand. The small silver band containing a diamond solitaire slid onto her ring finger. "I love you," he whispered.

"I love you, too." She hugged him as hard as her arms would allow. Lifting her hand so that she could see the sparkle, she gushed, "It's beautiful. And it fits perfectly."

"One of the advantages of having your things at my grandparents'." He pulled another ring out of his pocket and held it up. "Gram borrowed this from your dresser this morning."

"You bought this engagement ring today?"

"As soon as the jeweler opened."

Voices in the background finally permeated Pepper and Zeke's euphoria. An elderly couple leaving the restaurant passed by. The woman spoke. "Congratulations to you, young man, on finding such a sweet girl. Best wishes to you, honey. He looks like a keeper."

When they had gone, Pepper reached across the table and again took her dad's hand. "Can you be happy for me, Pops? Even if I never become a doctor?"

His words formed slowly. "Can you be happy if you're not one?"

She lifted one hand to touch the side of Zeke's face and feel the dark waves of his hair. "I can be. And I will be."

She looked next at her mom. "What do you think?"

Ranie pondered Pepper with a sad, thoughtful gaze. "My hope for you is to be a better wife than I was." A soft smile displaced her sadness. "And to give me an another opportunity to be your mom."

* * *

"Pinch me and tell me that this night really happened." Pepper looked up at Zeke as he drove.

"Tempting idea." He laughed and clutched her hand. "Look at your ring finger."

She did. She had been. Often.

"In less than twenty-four hours you talked to Fred about my staying, got your mom's and dad's opinions, found a ring, and had it sized?"

"Toby picked it up this afternoon about half an hour before we left. You should have heard the ruckus he made when I told him what I needed him to do."

Pepper heard the smile in Zeke's voice.

"He's going to tell everyone all about it."

"Who else knows?"

"All the family knows I was prepared to ask. I wasn't going to unless I believed that your dad was at least open to the idea. Everyone was praying."

"Have you told anyone my answer?"

"Not yet."

She squealed and then rummaged through her purse. "Who should we call or text first?"

"Call my parents."

"Do you want to talk? Or should I?"

"You dial. I'll relay the good news."

The phone rang three times. Sue answered. "Mom, you're going to have a daughter-in-law."

Laughter. Tears. Congratulations. Both shared their joy. Next Pepper sent a text from Zeke's phone to each of his brothers. Toby's response was classic. "The Mustang will be part of the family."

Then she called Anna, and the two jabbered until Zeke said, "Don't forget Gramps and Gram." Pepper hung up in a hurry.

"I'll call." She tapped her fingers on the dashboard while the phone rang. Maggie's voice said hello.

"My wish came true."

"You're going to be my granddaughter?"

"I sure am. And Fred will have to put up with me for a lot longer than a few months. Maybe even long enough to make a champion checkers player out of me." After everyone had been notified, and they were nearly home, Pepper sat back in her seat and replayed the evening. One picture resurfaced constantly. Zeke, on one knee, his brown eyes gazing unto hers, asking her, "Will you marry me." Shivers and goose bumps assailed her each time.

"How about if I drop you off at Gram and Gramps' house tonight? You can ride with him in the morning and drive your car home tomorrow."

"Great idea." She squeezed his arm.

Within five minutes they were parked in the Hannas' driveway. The house was dark except for the small table lamp that Fred and Maggie used as a nightlight when Pepper was still up, but they had gone to bed.

Zeke came around and opened Pepper's door. She offered her hand, and he clasped it and drew her into his embrace. His kiss, gentle at first, increased in its intensity. Putting her hands on his chest, Pepper reluctantly distanced herself.

He bent and breathed the words, "When are you moving?"

"Moving where?"

"In with me."

"But you said—" Didn't he remember his own beliefs?

"When are we getting married?" He sprinkled kisses on her neck.

She sighed and then giggled. "Soon."

"Not soon enough."

"I need some time."

"Time for what?" He scrutinized her face.

"Time to make everything perfect."

"You already are."

EPILOGUE

"Why did you tell Anna you would do this?" Pepper interrogated herself aloud once again on a sunny autumn morning. Bending over, she reached for another bushel of apples to divide.

"Don't even think about picking that up." Zeke's scolding voice arrived a few seconds before he did. "Ask someone to help you." He wagged his finger at her and then hefted the bushel onto the counter where she was working.

"I feel like an invalid."

"Pregnant women aren't invalids. They're—pregnant."

"You have an astute grasp of the obvious." She rubbed her protruding baby bump.

"And you have an aversion to being careful." He turned her toward himself and hugged her. "I don't want anything to happen to either of you."

Pepper sniffled and wiped her eyes on his shirt.

"What's wrong? Did I do something?"

How could she say "nothing's wrong"? Again. "It's the wedding." She blubbered into his chest.

He rested his chin on her head. "You're thrilled for Anna. You really like Luke." Gently pushing her away, he asked, "What's the problem?"

She placed her hands on either side of her belly. "This is the problem. This and that tailored dress it's supposed to fit into on Saturday."

"Your dress doesn't fit?"

"It did a week ago." She turned back to the apples. "It's just that—all the other bridesmaids are so—so thin. And I'm—"

"Thin, too." He stepped beside her and wrapped his arms around her, his hands resting on her opposite hip. "But this baby needs room."

"All the wedding pictures," she whined. "My dress will look like a tent compared to the gowns of those toothpick girls."

"You will be the most beautiful woman there." Zeke cast a conspiratorial look around. "Don't tell my sister."

"Why don't I tell her that I can't be in the wedding?" She whisked away a stray tear. "I don't know why she asked me to be her matron of honor when she knew I would be seven months pregnant."

"Because you're her best friend and her sister-in-law. She wants you to have a special part in the day, just like you wanted her in our wedding a year and a half ago." He clenched his arms slightly. "She wouldn't mind if you wore a burlap bag as long as you stood up next to her."

"I'd feel a lot better if everyone else was wearing burlap. Burlap stuffed with a pillow."

He chuckled. Wagging his eyebrows, he said, "The best man's a handsome guy."

Anna was marrying one of Zeke's closest friends, a young man who had known her all her life and had waited for her to see him as more than the buddy of her oldest brother. Zeke would be standing next to him.

"He is." She smiled up at him. "He won't care if my belly leads the way?"

"He'll be honored to escort you." Zeke laid his hands on the home of their growing child. "Both of you."

AFTERWORD

Cindy Bingham's works

Lion's Awakening
Perfect Timing

can be purchased at
www.cindybinghamwrites.com,
at www.amazon.com,
or through other booksellers

Made in the USA
Middletown, DE
19 February 2015